The Halsey Brothers Series

Marshal in Petticoats
Outlaw in Petticoats
Miner in Petticoats
Doctor in Petticoats
Logger in Petticoats

MINER IN PETTICOATS

The Halsey Brothers Series

by

Paty Jager

Windtree Press
Beaverton, Oregon

MINER IN PETTICOATS

COPYRIGHT © 2022 by Patricia Jager
All rights reserved. No part of this book may be used or reproduced in any manner whatsoever without written permission of the author or Name of Press except in the case of brief quotations embodied in critical articles or reviews.
Contact Information: info@windtreepress.com
Cover Art by Karen Ronan
Windtree Press
Visit us at http://windtreepress.com

Publishing History
First Edition
Miner in Petticoats 2009 (Print and ebook)

Second Edition
Miner in Petticoats 2011 (Ebook only)

Third Edition
Miner in Petticoats 2022 (Print and ebook)

Published in the United States of America
ISBN 978-1-957638-28-7

Acknowledgements

While there is a Cracker Creek outside of Sumpter, Oregon and there was mining up and down the creek, there was not a Cracker Creek Stamp Mill.

Chapter 1

Sumpter, Oregon
1889

"Have you lost what little sense you had?"

Ethan Halsey focused his gaze from the map spread across the table to his younger brother. "I've had more sense than you for a long time, Clay."

"Not if you think you can just walk up to that husband-killer and kindly ask to purchase her land!" Clay shot out of the chair, knocking it over, pacing two steps and back again.

"Why are you calling the Widow Miller a husband killer? That's not too neighborly of you, especially when we want to purchase some of her land." His grown brother acting like a boy who saw a ghost was too good not to tease. Ethan let loose a rib-shattering, belly laugh. He hadn't seen Clay so worked up in a long time.

"Knock it off. This ain't something to laugh about. I heard Judd Loudeman tell how they found

Mr. Miller with his head bashed in layin' in front of his mine. And how the wife and boy weren't seen for weeks after."

"All that tells me is they were scared and hiding." Ethan rolled up the map. "I traipsed over the ridges and canyons in a five mile section. The slope with Cracker Creek running at a good clip in that corner of their property is where we're going to build a stamp mill." He stood, placed the map on the front window ledge, and faced his brother. "I made a promise when Ma and Pa died to make sure you and the others are taken care of." And Lord, he would never take on the responsibility of another family again. "I also promised the miners around here we could provide a way for them to squeeze more gold out of their claims." He crossed his arms and stared at Clay. "Have you known me to ever squelch on my word?"

"No, but I'm telling you, that widow ain't none too friendly." Clay filled a cup for himself and clanked the coffee pot down on the potbellied stove.

Ethan raised an eyebrow at his brother's unnatural selfishness. He strode across the small cabin and poured himself a cup. "You seem to know a lot about this woman. Maybe you should be the one to make her the offer?"

Clay spewed coffee across the room, missing Ethan by all but two drops. "I'm not setting foot on her land. Miles said she's marked by the devil."

"Since when have you given a dime about anything that no-account Miles Osborne had to say?" Ethan was fed up with all the bad-mouthing of a woman neither one of them had met. Miles had been making up stories to get attention since they were boys.

"He said her bonnet blew off one time when she was in town, and her face has dark markings. He said it was the devil's mark."

"I say again, since when was anything Miles had to say worth listening to? And how would he know the devil's markings? He been keeping time with the fellow?" Ethan sat at the table and pointed to the chair across from him.

"Clay, you're four years younger than me. I would say that makes you a mite old to be going around believing everything you hear. You're also old enough to know better than to badmouth someone you haven't met." Ethan took a sip of coffee, never taking his eyes off his brother. It was something he learned twelve years ago, when the sudden death of his parents left him in charge of four younger brothers. Always look them in the eyes and never back down. Of course being the tallest at six-five and the broadest helped too, but eye contact always made them buckle under to his way of thinking.

His brother bowed his head and stared into his coffee cup. "Yeah, I guess I shouldn't let what other people think influence me." He looked up. "Kind of like Maeve. From all the mush Zeke always spouted, I expected some soft, doe-eyed schoolmarm. Instead, she's a prickly, sharpshooter with more spit than polish." He laughed at the picture he painted of his new sister-in-law. Ethan joined the laughter.

"Zeke definitely met his match in that one." Ethan cocked his head listening to the approaching horses. "That should be Hank with the miners who'll profit from our stamp mill."

Clay smiled. "This is one time, big brother, when I think you finally found a way for Pa's claim to make a handsome profit."

"That's the plan. Come on, let's talk to them outside where there's more room." It would be impossible to discuss the stamp mill in the one room cabin. Clay, Hank, and himself barely had room to turn around when all three were inside.

Clay headed out the door. Ethan took one more sip of coffee, grabbed the map off the window sill, and headed out to see how many of their neighbors were willing to pitch in some money and labor to make the Cracker Creek Stamp Mill a reality.

Aileen Miller plucked the oversized straw hat from her head and wiped the sleeve of her shirt across her brow. She'd dug at the side of the mine since breakfast. All she had to show for it was a couple buckets of rubble. Fresh air and the gurgle of the stream beckoned. She leaned the pick against the side of the cave and reached down to catch the rope handles of the buckets in her hands.

"Momma! Momma! Colin won't he'p me!"

"Stay put, lassie. Ah'm comin' out." Aileen called to her four-year-old daughter and gem of her heart. "Nae need for yetocome in this bloody tunnel."

She ducked and stepped out of the cave opening. The sunshine warmed her face as she took a deep breath of the clean air. Small arms wrapped around her legs. She looked down, taking in the angelic face of her darlin' Shayla.

"Where be the laddie?" she asked, scanning the area for her twelve-year-old son. Where Shayla was her gem, Colin was her soul. He came from the seed of a man she loved with her whole being. She nearly died the evening her father came and told her he'd been killed. There were times when she and the laddie communicated without speaking. The morning had begun that way, with Colin quietly taking the pick and heading for the mine without her so much as saying: "Today, we'll work in the mine." When the area became too small for the two to work, he'd just as quietly left the confines.

"He's pannin'." Shayla tugged on the bucket Aileen had yet to set down. As the child spoke, she spotted her red-haired son.

"Aye, so he is. And why are ye pesterin' him?" She packed the buckets down to the sluice box and dumped the contents into the top level of the wooden boxes. Shayla followed alongside, dragging her feet.

"I'm hungry. I asked him to he'p make a sammich." The dark-haired angel extended her lower lip and placed her hands behind her back.

Aileen laughed and patted Shayla's dark curls. "Let's find a bite for yer wee tummy." She held out her hand and clasped the small fingers in hers. "Colin! Come laddie, a body cannae work on an empty stomach!"

He nodded, and stopped sloshing water over the side of the pan. He placed the pan on the ground careful to not lose any of the trailings. When he stood, her heart lurched. Each day he became more and more like his da— a man who voiced his concerns and worked to better his and his neighbor's plight. Aye, Patrick, if only ye could see yer bonnie laddie.

Tears burned the back of her eyes. Aileen tugged on Shayla and headed to the cabin. Colin had a way of knowing when she felt lonely or sad. She didn't want to spoil his day with her longing for something that would never be again.

"'Tis a good thing we baked bread yesterday or yer belly would be whinin' as much as ye," Aileen tweaked her daughter's nose and patted her backside. "Wash yer hands and fetch a jar o' preserves from the lean-to."

When Shayla finished washing, Aileen leaned down, submersing her hands and arms into the bucket. She scrubbed the sweat and dirt from her skin. It had been a month since she'd had a good soaking. Her body carried the stench of her labors. If they planned to get supplies at the store tomorrow, today would be a good day to take a bar of soap down to the creek and clean up.

Colin stopped beside her, waiting for his turn to wash. "There's my laddie." She kissed the top of his head and wrinkled her nose. "We'll all hike down the creek this evenin' and give us a wash."

His green eyes narrowed slightly. "This mean we're going to town tomorrow?" The disinterest in his voice didn't fool Aileen. Colin disliked going to town, yet refused to let she and Shayla go alone.

"We need supplies. I know ye didnae like to go, but we need to eat, and there's gold that needs to be exchanged."

"I know. I just don't like what the people say

about us." He shoved his fists into the water, sloshing the contents down his legs and over his boots.

She ruffled his hair and gave his shoulder a squeeze. "Ye are so much like yer da. Ye go against what ye feel to do what is right. If only that day he wouldn't have gone with his feelings and not been goaded..." Tears burned her eyes, and she ducked into the cabin. If only Patrick hadn't felt the need to stand up to the English, he'd be beside her today.

The one window allowed only a small amount of light through. She left the door open for more light and air. No matter how much she cleaned the house, she couldn't get rid of the stench of her second husband. He'd lived in the cabin before the marriage and peed in a corner when he drank, which happened to be every day.

They fought over the drinking and the habit. She eventually won, but the house reeked, and the reminder of him made it hard to sleep most nights. She preferred the outdoors and did only the necessary indoor living. Even in the bitter cold of winter, they all preferred to work in the mine to being shut in the house with all its reminders.

She grabbed the bread, knife, a board to cut on, and carried the lot out to the small, covered porch. They spent most meals gazing at the babbling creek and staring up the other side of the tree-covered canyon.

Colin took the board and knife, placing them on a log they used as a table. Since they spent this time of year on the porch, their chairs already waited for them. Shayla returned with the preserves and her usual smile.

Aileen sliced the bread and spread the preserves, handing a slice to each child.

"Ma, ain't you gonna eat?" Colin asked his eyes rebuking her even if his words didn't.

"In a minute, someone's coming down the hill." She tugged the floppy straw hat down to her ears to hide her face, and stood. The slow approach of the horse and rider felt like a bomb ticking. They had few visitors and never anyone alone. Not since the death of Mr. Miller.

Chapter 2

Ethan kept the horse at a leisurely pace. He didn't believe the trio under the porch roof would shoot him, but the things Clay and the other men said when they found out who he was headed to talk to, niggled in the back of his mind. There was nothing cowardly about being cautious. Even if all he saw was a child, a young boy, and a tall, sturdy woman dressed in men's clothing.

The clothing didn't bother him. The other men had made mention of how the widow woman wore the dead husband's clothes. Both his sisters-in-law wore britches as much as they did dresses. They allowed it made riding and working outside easier. If the widow worked the claim, she needed to wear practical clothes. And her dead husband's would be handy and free.

He stopped his horse near a tree and dismounted, wrapping the reins around a limb.

"Afternoon," he called, sauntering toward a cabin smaller than the one he shared with his brothers. The only difference between the two structures was the state of disrepair and the lean-to in the back.

The woman nodded, but didn't say anything. None of them appeared hostile. The boy stared blankly. The little girl's grin was infectious, and he found himself grinning back at her. He pulled his attention from the curly-haired imp to study the woman. She was tall. Not near his height, but she had to be gaining on six foot. The men's clothing she wore did nothing to hide her attributes. The pants clung to her wide, round hips, and her full breasts gave the buttons on her shirt a working.

"Mrs. Miller?" he asked, extending his hand. She kept her head tipped forward just enough her face was shadowed and hidden behind the brim of the hat.

"Who be askin'?" Her voice caught his attention with its deep, lyrical tone.

"I'm Ethan Halsey. My brothers and I have a claim just over the ridge." It aggravated him he couldn't see her face and register how she took his words.

"Are ye lost?" The voice vibrated under his skin, causing his body to warm.

He cleared his throat. "No, I'm not lost. I'm looking for Mrs. Miller. I'm assuming that is you, since you're the only grown woman I see here."

"Ah m Aileen. Ah don't fancy bein' called Mrs. Miller."

This disclosure piqued his curiosity. "Mrs—Aileen. I've come with an offer." Her head tilted, tipping the wide-brimmed hat to the side and revealing a slip of her face.

"And what may this grand offer be?" He saw the slightest curve on one side of her lips.

"Ma'am, not to sound bossy, but I'd like to see your face as we discuss this proposition." Her shoulders dipped slightly before she squared them, stretched her neck to its full length, and whipped the hat from her head. Copper sparks reflected off her hair as the sun lit her dark locks.

Ethan hadn't believed the words of a cowardly man like Miles, and he was happy to see there wasn't any kind of mark on the woman's face, at least none put there by the devil. Her skin was abundantly sprinkled with angel kisses. That was what his mother had called the freckles on her face. Angel kisses. He'd always had a fondness for freckle-faced women and children.

"Thank you, I appreciate seeing people's eyes when talking business." Ethan took a step closer to the porch, waiting to be invited to the shade.

"And what be yer business?" The woman didn't seem inclined to invite him any closer.

"I've scouted the land all around our claim. The five acres of your land down where Cracker Creek drops in elevation is the perfect spot to set up a stamp mill. The side of the canyon has the right slope and the water is moving fast enough to power the mill."

"So yer business is askin' me to sell my land?" She clamped work-reddened hands onto those ample hips and glared at him.

"We'd give you a fair price for the five acres, and you could use the stamp mill to claim more gold from your mine." The information didn't seem to change her opinion. She still glared at him.

"We're allowing the nearby claims to build rails to bring their ore to the mill. They can use the stamp mill, giving us a small cut of their profits." He smiled at his family's generosity.

"So ye're doin' this out o' the goodness o' yer heart? Takin' yer neighbor's land and their gold." Her light green eyes flashed with indignation.

Was she mocking him? "No, we're not doing this out of the goodness of our hearts. We're doing it to find more gold in the bedrock and to allow our neighbors the opportunity to find more gold in their claims. And yes, we do feel if we put the money into building the stamp mill, others should pay a fee to use it. At the same time, they'll be extracting more gold from their claims using the stamp mill than they would by not using it." Ethan threw his hands in the air. What did it matter if this woman found fault with the stamp mill. All she had to do was sell him the five acres.

"I'm here to offer you five dollars an acre for your land."

The crazy woman burst out laughing. If she hadn't been finding fault with him, he would have relished the deep richness of the tone.

"That's more than fair!"

"Nae for the land o' my bairn." She stood with her hands on her hips in a stance as unmoving as a full grown pine tree.

"I can't go any higher than seven dollars an acre," he growled, not really wanting to spend that much, but he'd set his family's future on the stamp mill.

"Ye dinnae be needin' to. Ah no' be takin' yer offer." She raised a long arm and extended it, point-

ing down the small valley. "This be the only thin'
Mr. Miller left us o' value and ah'll no' be sellin'
the land. It belongs to my bairn and ye'll no' claim
one foot o' it."

"Mrs—" She lanced him with a dagger of a
look. "Aileen, what if I come back tomorrow with a
map and the figures all drawn up?"

"Ye can come, but ah'll no' be changing ma
mind. Geroot, Mr. Halsey."

Aileen tipped her head toward the man's
horse, hoping he'd get the idea and leave. He was a
fine figure of a man. Broad across the chest, taller
than most, and his face was no hardship to stare at
as they badgered over her land. Nae, she'd never
sell a portion of the land. Her family had been
pushed out of Scotland and then after marrying an
Irishman, an Englishman had killed her husband
and taken over their land. She wasn't about to lose
this land. There was no place else for them to go.
Not yet anyway.

However, she wouldn't mind butting heads
with the man again.

When she removed her hat and he smiled
rather than frowned, she nearly smiled herself.
A man that didn't find fault with her discolored,
freckled face was a rarity indeed.

The man acknowledged her farewell, walking
to his horse and mounting. "I'll be back tomorrow
with the map."

"Ye'll be talkin' to yerself then. We've a need
to visit town tomorrow." She smiled at his irritation.

"I'll be here the following day."

She waved her hand and called back, "We'll

be here." She glanced down at Colin. "But he'll be talkin' to deaf ears." Aileen winked at her son and was rewarded with a smile.

"Ah'll be after that sandwich now." She sat down in her chair and watched the broad back of Mr. Halsey slowly disappear through the trees. She'd not sell any of the three hundred and sixty acres. Not till she had enough money to head back to Ireland and reclaim her son's legacy. Twenty five dollars and the loss of five acres wouldn't help her fulfill her commitment to reinstate her son to his da's lost land.

When her father pulled her and Colin onto the ship bound for America, she made a vow to bring her son back to the land of his da and fight for the O'Lear land the Englishman took. If they could continue to bring out the same amount of gold each year from the land, they'd have enough to buy that bleeding Englishman, Roderick's, estate and reclaim it for the O'Lears by the time Colin was of an age to carry on as the master. That was her goal— to have the funds when Colin came of age and return to Ireland, giving her son his father's legacy.

"Momma, he had friendly eyes," Shayla said, breaking into her thoughts.

"Aye, ye be noticin' too." She smiled at her daughter. The lassie had a knack for seeing the good in everyone. And they in return showed her they were worthy of her trust.

"He was a big man." The warning in her son's voice sent shivers down her spine.

"Aye, he was." Mr. Miller had been nearer her size and had beat her unconscious more than once. She'd never let a man do that to her again. And to think what kind of damage a man with the hands the size of Mr. Halsey... she shuddered. "We wouldn't have to worry, Colin. Ah dinnae plan to let any man hurt our family again."

Chapter 3

Ethan couldn't believe the woman turned his offer down. He saw the small, dilapidated cabin and the crude furniture they sat on. How could she refuse easy money? It didn't make sense.

He dismounted and led his horse to the barn.

"Well, did you get the land?" Clay asked as both he and Hank followed Ethan to the barn. They were both dark haired like all the brothers and built for hard labor.

"No." It still rankled the woman dismissed him like he'd asked to take one of her children.

"I told ya, she was trouble." Clay stuck his hands in the back pockets of his britches and nodded his head.

"She really turned down our offer?" Hank shook his head. "I'd a thought she'd jump for the extra money."

"Looking at how they live, I was sure she would take the money. But she's one stubborn woman." Ethan unfastened the saddle cinch and set the saddle on the stall railing.

"Did she look like a killer?"

Ethan glared at Clay. "What does a killer look like?"

Clay ducked his head, and Hank laughed, smacking Clay on the back with his hand.

"She looks like a woman with her hands full. Think I'll go into town tomorrow and see what Myrle knows about Aileen." Ethan led the horse to the corral.

"Aileen? One trip and you're calling her by her given name?" Hank's back straightened from his lax stance against a pole and he stared at Ethan.

"She refused to talk to me if I called her Mrs. Miller."

"I told you she killed her husband, and now she don't want anything to remind her of the deed." Clay rubbed his hands together, looking like a man about to eat a delicious pie.

"I didn't ask her why she prefers to be called by her given name, but I'll do just about anything to get that land." It rankled that the woman didn't realize a good thing and had the power to hold up his plans. Ethan stared at his brothers. "We'll be building that stamp mill, and it will be running by winter, I guarantee."

Ethan walked up the steps of the only place in Sumpter a person could purchase a meal. It wasn't a restaurant, only a house in the middle of town with a woman—old enough to be his mother—who cooked for a living. When her husband left her a widow two years after gold was found in the area, she did what she did best—cooked meals for the miners when they brought their ore in to be assayed. That was over twenty years ago. She still did all the cooking, but the last few years she'd recruited other widows to help her out. Giving them a place to stay and a few coins to spend.

"Ethan, what brings you to Myrle's? Finally couldn't stomach any more of Hank's cooking?"

Ethan hugged the gray-haired woman, whose head rested against his belly, and chuckled. "That, and I'm in need of information."

She pulled out of the embrace and tipped her head back to look at him. "Well, plant yourself in that chair. I'll bring you some grub, and we can talk."

"Sounds good." Ethan sat at the table Myrle indicated near the kitchen door and smiled at the Widow James, who walked out the door Myrle disappeared through. A bashful smile trembled on the widow's lips as she poured him a cup of coffee.

He nodded his thanks to the woman. She tittered and stood staring at him. Ethan shook his head. For some odd reason he addle-patted Mrs. James. She was a good fifteen years his senior, but she acted like she'd jump into his arms if he gave her any indication. Which he never would. He planned to live out the rest of his days single. He didn't need a wife and kids. He had his brothers and their families to watch over. That was more than enough for any man.

Myrle returned carrying a plate heaped with eggs, biscuits, and a steak on the side.

Ethan's mouth watered as the aroma's wafted to his nose. "Who else you planning to feed?"

"You're a big man with a big appetite. I've run this place long enough to know how much fills up a man your size." Myrle winked at him and sat down. She picked up an empty cup and waved it in the air. Mrs. James rushed over to fill her cup and then hovered.

Ethan rolled his eyes, and Myrle laughed.

"Edith, I think Charlotte needs help in the kitchen." When the woman reluctantly headed to the kitchen, Myrle leaned forward and patted his arm. "The poor dear has her sights on you. But I tell her you're too much man for her."

Ethan spat the coffee he'd just slurped across the table. "That's mean, even for you Myrle."

"What, you don't think I know what kind of woman you need?"

"Don't start that again. I didn't come here looking for a woman. I've told you, I don't need nor want a wife."

"But you do need one, Ethan. You can't be a bachelor your whole life. It would be a waste. There is so much you're missing out on not being a husband and a father." Tears glistened in her eyes. "Didn't you boys come to me when your ma and pa were taken from you? And didn't I promise to feed you when times were poor?"

Ethan nodded. If not for this woman, he and his brothers would have had some pretty slim winters. "I appreciate all you've done for the boys and me. Two are married, and I'm sure the other two will find a good woman soon. Don't worry about me."

"And you'll be all alone in that cabin. What are you going to do then?"

"Enjoy the peace and quiet. Maybe finally get to the books in Ma's trunk I've wanted to reread." He thought of the only thing he treasured more than his brothers—the trunk full of his mother's books. He'd started reading them as a young man, but after he took on the responsibilities of his brothers he hadn't picked up a book.

"You could read them to your children." Myrle patted his hand and stared at him with her rheumy, faded eyes.

Her words sifted in and swirled around. He liked the idea of sharing the stories with a child curled up in his lap. He shook his head. No. His wants came after Clay and Hank were married and happy, not before. He could read to nieces and nephews.

"What did you come here to ask me?" Myrle took a sip of her coffee and watched him.

"What do you know about the Widow Miller?" He chuckled at the way the old woman's gray eyebrow arched.

"I thought you weren't looking for a wife?" Her accusation, sliced through him.

"I'm not. I have business dealings with the woman, but she's none too hospitable."

Myrle snorted. "No, that one isn't. What kind of dealings?"

Ethan told her of the stamp mill. How they could employ up to four men around the clock to keep it running and help the miners around them produce more from their claims. "But I need to purchase five acres of the widow's land. She informed me yesterday there is no way she'd sell anything to me or anyone else.

"Seeing how she and her children live, I'd think she could use the extra money. I don't think her and that scrawny boy are pulling enough gold out of their claim to live proper."

Myrle's expression softened, and she shook her head sadly. "That's a woman with more grit than ten, I swear. That animal she was married to used to beat her something terrible. When I questioned her, she clammed up and tucked the boy to her side. I wouldn't doubt the bastard threatened to harm the boy if she said anything." The woman's face reddened, and her eyes sparked with outrage. "That oldest is from her first husband. Before Miller started beating her on a regular schedule, she came to town, and we had a couple cups of coffee together.

"She loved her first husband. You can see it when she talks about him and that boy. She never told me how he ended up dead. Only said her father made her and the boy come to America, but her father died on the trip over. She answered an ad for a wife and ended up married to Miller."

"Why does Miles say she killed Miller? Is there truth to that do you think?" Ethan could see the woman swinging a board to protect her children if the man had been beating on them.

"Miles is an idiot! He tried to spark her a year after Miller was dead. When she laughed in his face, the little rooster started spreading that lie."

"Thanks Myrle that gives me a little better idea how to go about getting her to sell."

Aileen held tight to Shayla's hand. She hated

coming to town as much as Colin. The people always stared. The only person to ever give her a smile and a greeting was the widow who fed people out of her home. They passed Myrle's house as Mr. Halsey and Myrle stepped out onto the porch.

"Morning, Aileen!" Myrle called and waved. "How about a cup of coffee?"

Longing to sit with Myrle and chat pulled at her. She missed female conversation or any kind of adult conversation. Aileen glanced down at Shayla grinning like she'd found a new toy. She followed her daughter's gaze and found Mr. Halsey smiling back at the child. His gaze shifted from Shayla to her. The humor left his eyes. In its place a darker interest gleamed.

Colin tugged on her sleeve. "Let's get the supplies and head home."

Aileen sighed. "No' today, Myrle." Colin moved down the street, and she followed, afraid to leave him alone. Whenever she did, he seemed to find a fight. She looked back at the woman and man standing on the porch and sighed. Aye, maybe next time she could visit.

"Ma, I know you like to visit with the widow, but I don't like the way Shayla cottons to Mr. Halsey." Colin's words stopped her feet.

She grasped Colin's sleeve and turned him. "What do ye mean?"

"That's all she jabbered about yesterday after he left. Big man. Happy man." He rolled his eyes.

Shayla stood between them. She grinned. "I like Happy Man. He makes me smile."

Aileen shook her head. "Lassie, he's no' a man to be friendin'."

"Why?" Shayla stuck out her bottom lip, and tears glistened in her eyes.

Pulling Shayla against her skirts, Aileen gave her a hug. " 'Cause he wants to take away some o' our land."

"He's not a bad man." Shayla pushed out of the embrace and stomped her small foot.

"Stop blubberin' and pitchin' a fit." Colin grabbed his sister's arm roughly.

Aileen pried his hand from Shayla's arm and stepped between them. "Ye'll no' touch a female roughly." She bent down, making herself eye level. "Ah dinnae care if she has embarrassed ye or made ye mad. Yer da wouldn't have harmed a female, and ye'll be like yer da no' that monster."

Colin's eyes widened before he shuttered his emotions. He jerked from her grasp and ran down the street.

"Colin! Come back! Colin!" Aileen took a step to follow when a large hand grasped her elbow. She jumped, sucking in air.

"Don't worry, I'll get him." Mr. Halsey ruffled Shayla's hair before he headed between the two buildings where Colin disappeared.

Aileen jammed her fists on her hips and watched the man's long-legged stride carry him away. If he only knew how Colin felt about him, he would think twice afore chasing the boy down.

They couldn't stand in the street all day. It brought more attention than she liked.

"Come on, let's get our supplies and be ready to head home when Colin returns." She grasped her skirt in one hand, Shayla's hand in her other, and headed to the only general store in Sumpter.

"Don't worry, Momma, Happy Man will find Colin." Shayla's young optimism made her smile.

"Aye, Lassie, ah'm sure he will." But what will he find when Colin turns all that anger on him.

Ethan followed the boy down an alley. He arrived behind the saloon as Colin charged a young man.

"Hey!" Ethan grabbed Colin by the collar, hauling him off the larger boy. "What's this all about?"

The larger boy scrambled away not even looking back. Colin glared up at him and visibly slumped. His eyelids lowered, shielding his thoughts.

Ethan set the boy down on his feet and brushed the dust from Colin's shirt. "You don't have to tell me what it was about, but it isn't very smart to get into a fight when your ma needs you."

Colin's head snapped up, and his chin stuck out. "Did you do something to her?" The accusation and hatred burning in the boy's eyes, nearly caused Ethan to take a step back. It had been a long time since he'd witnessed such distrust in anyone, let alone a child.

"No, I haven't done anything to your ma. She needs a man to help her. One that isn't useless from getting beat on." Ethan picked up Colin's hat and offered it to the boy. He snatched it and dashed down the alley.

"That's a heap of hatred he's got stored up." Ethan rolled his shoulders. The boy's distrust and angry eyes tightened every muscle in his body.

He'd glimpsed more than anger in those light green eyes like his mother's. There was something eating away at the boy. Something he didn't think his ma even knew.

Today wasn't a good day to approach the Widow Miller about her land. He'd seen enough of the family argument in the street to know she wouldn't be in a favorable mood. But he didn't believe in missing an opportunity when it arose, and he planned to make the most out of the little girl's acceptance.

Chapter 4

Colin stalked through the mercantile door as Aileen made the decision to hunt for him. "Where have ye been, laddie? Ah need yer help with these supplies."

He winced and moved forward to gather the packages in her arms.

"Did ye hurt yerself?" she asked, patting him down, testing for soreness. He shook his head but kept his gaze averted. Something happened. Something that had to do with Mr. Halsey. She didn't know whether to thank the man or tell him to leave her family alone.

She handed Shayla the basket containing eggs and butter before loading her arms with parcels as well. "Let's be gone." The door opened right before she reached out to give it a tug. Her parcels spilled to the floor covering her feet.

"Let me help."

The deep voice set off quivers in her belly. She knew who stood in the doorway without even looking up.

"We can get it," Colin's young voice growled as he dropped to his knees to round up the parcels in his already full arms. She stared into the dark brown eyes of a man she shouldn't befriend.

"Here, you can't get them all by yourself." Mr. Halsey crouched down next to Colin and loaded his arms with packages. "There, you have a good load, and so do I." He stood. "Where are you headed?"

"Mr. Halsey, ah'll take those." She reached out to grab her supplies. He turned, and she caught hold of his arm instead of the packages she sought. The limb was hard and warm. She jerked her hand away from the heat.

The playful grin on his face did little to settle her fluttering stomach. She needed distance between them. She stepped backwards, bumping into Shayla and the basket. They both tottered a moment before she caught them.

"Ah'll take the basket, Lassie. Ye get the door for Mr. Halsey and yer brother." Shayla jumped at the opportunity to be trusted with an important job. It gave Aileen a moment to collect her thoughts before confronting the man set on helping.

On the street, she looked neither left nor right as she led the group out of town. At the head of the dirt path leading to their claim, she stopped and turned to Mr. Halsey.

"Thank ye, but we'll manage fine from here." She handed Shayla the basket and reached for the packages in the man's arms.

He turned, holding them out of her grasp. "I'll

haul them to your place, no sense dropping them again trying to shuffle from me to you." Without so much as an apologetic smile, he headed up the trail.

She exchanged glances with her son and hurried after her daughter, who swung the basket recklessly as she followed Mr. Halsey.

What was the man after? Did he think by carrying their supplies, she'd give in to his offer? She tossed about all the reasons she couldn't sell the property and wondered why this man, who should be her enemy, made her feel—feminine. Something she hadn't in a very long time. Her gaze didn't stray to the man, though she wanted to take stock of him. She watched the determined steps of her son as he kept up with the man's longer stride. Shayla trotted alongside, smiling up at him, never once complaining she was tired.

Aileen fisted her hands at her side. Why had Mr. Halsey intruded on their family? Her stomach knotted from all the thoughts whirling in her head. She placed a hand over her belly as the group broke through the trees and stood between the creek and the cabin.

She hurried forward, stopping Mr. Halsey just short of the rickety porch. "Ah'll take them now." She nodded to Colin to hurry into the house and empty his arms. When he returned, she loaded him with packages from Mr. Halsey's arms. She gathered the rest to her chest and hurried into the cabin. Shayla chattered like the annoying magpies that sometimes interrupted their meals as she entertained Mr. Halsey.

Aileen dumped the packages on the table and

hurried back outside. Sometimes things came out of Shayla's mouth she'd rather the man sitting on an upturned stick of firewood didn't hear.

"Thank ye." She scanned the area. "We've got work to attend." She didn't let her gaze settle on the man's face. He'd already shifted her thoughts in directions they hadn't been in a long while.

"You're welcome." She felt him stand, and it drew her gaze back to him. He patted Shayla on the head, nodded to Colin, and settled a beguiling smile on her. "What time tomorrow may I come and talk about my offer?"

Aileen dashed a glance at Colin. His expression said he didn't like the idea of the man returning. Nothing, short of a fortune, would make her give up even a parcel of the land, but to have a conversation with an adult—even one she didn't wish to encourage and who made her body react in ways it hadn't in years—seemed like a glorious thing. She squared her shoulders and looked the man in the face. Her stomach quivered again at the upturned lips and dark brown eyes that goaded her.

"Any time after the noon meal, we'll be waitin' to talk." She grasped Shayla's hand and turned on her heel. She didn't want the man to think she'd be counting the minutes. Even though she would.

Ethan smiled as he climbed the ridge separating their claim from the Miller's. The little girl, though at times hard to understand, was a charming child without any bad feelings toward him. The boy remained a mystery. He defended his mother and sister with the fierceness of a warrior, but what he'd glimpsed in the boy's eyes—he shuddered. Those emotions shouldn't exist in a boy his age.

Now, the mother—he couldn't help but admire the spunk of the woman. And from Myrle's conversation, Aileen had to be tough to live through multiple beatings by a man.

He remembered Miller. The man wasn't an overly large man, but he'd been about the same height and more weight than his wife. Ethan stopped at the top of the ridge and glanced back down toward Cracker Creek. He followed the silver thread of the stream through the trees and up to the Miller claim. Why did she refuse to be called Mrs. Miller and insist on calling her husband Mr. Miller? Because of his treatment? This woman was an intriguing puzzle. One he had to unravel to get the stamp mill built and make his family a profit.

"You stand around like that a lot?" Hank stepped out of the trees to his right.

"Just thinking." Ethan started down the other side of the ridge. "What are you doing sneaking around? I thought you were going to head to Baker City and get the papers drawn up."

"Clay and I discussed it and figured it would be best to wait until you actually had the widow's word she would sign." Hank fell into step beside him.

Ethan stopped. "You two think she isn't going to sign?"

"Yeah, and there's no sense spending money on a paper that's no good."

"Why do you think that?" This should be good

since as far as he knew his brother had never met the woman.

"She flat turned you down with the first offer. She lives in a shack, and she doesn't invite anyone to be friendly." Hank put a hand on his shoulder. "That tells me she's a woman who doesn't want nothing or no one close, and she won't take kindly to you setting up a stamp mill with six to eight men traipsing so close to her home several times a day."

"That why you're up here? Watching the woman?" Ethan didn't like his brother or anyone else watching the Widow Miller. He'd sensed she liked her privacy. In fact, he'd butted into her family circle this morning and witnessed her hackles go up.

"That, and Miles came racing to the house to say someone seen you leaving town with the Widow Miller. He was afraid you'd end up dead. Rather than him running up here and causing trouble, I offered to have a look."

Ethan watched his brother to see if he took the idiot Miles words to heart.

Hank grinned like a man who'd told a whopper. Ethan slapped him on the back. "You didn't believe I'd get hit over the head did you?"

"Nope, but I wondered why you'd follow the widow home." His brother turned concerned eyes on Ethan. "You're the oldest, and we want you to be happy. You know, with a wife and family-"

"I'm not saddling myself with a woman or kids. I've got my hands full with all of you." Ethan stopped and crossed his arms. "You think I'm following this woman because I'm randy?" He snorted. "I'm getting into her good graces so she'll sell me the land I want."

Hank started walking. "I just want you to know, if you do find someone and want to marry, we all want you to. Don't let us keep you from having a family."

Ethan stared at his brother's back. He didn't need any more family than he had. Sure he had an urge now and then that a trip to the Baker City whore house took care of, but he could live without a woman. They created more complications than he needed. A woman was out of the question.

Chapter 5

Aileen ran a hand over her hair, making sure any loose curls were tucked away. She wrinkled her nose, the shack reeked of urine. She'd spilled a bucket of water while filling the kettle to make the morning's porridge. How could a visit from Mr. Halsey make her so distracted? He meant nothing other than a diversion from her long day.

Worried the stench would cling to her clothes, she put a pan of water on the hook over the fireplace and tossed in some herbs to dilute the offensive smell.

She didn't plan to talk to Mr. Halsey in the house, but the smell might be noticeable on her clothing, and she'd rather he didn't know their living conditions.

"He's coming," Colin called in a less than enthusiastic voice. The two had talked about this visit last evening. Colin believed she should just tell the man no and to get off their property. But the boy didn't understand her need to visit with an adult.

Even one who wanted something she wasn't will-ing to give.

The water boiled, and Aileen wafted the steam toward her clothing. She wouldn't smell like an outhouse when she greeted Mr. Halsey.

Shayla skidded to a stop at the door. "He's here!" Even at four, she understood the condition of the house and beckoned her mother to hurry.

Aileen's stomach fluttered as she stepped out into the sunshine. She raised a hand to shield the sun and watched the confident stride of the man approaching the house. Colin shoved her straw hat in her hand before walking toward the sluice box at the edge of the creek. They'd picked and dug a pile of rock and dirt from the mine this morning. He placed a shovel full of the material into the box and slowly poured a bucket of water over the mound, washing away the dirt and smaller par-ticles, hopefully catching the gold on the wooden slats called riffles in the graduated boxes.

"Is he always this industrious?" a deep voice asked, drawing her attention from her son. The question wasn't offered as a slight. The warmth of his tone and the admiration in his voice was genuine.

"Aye. My laddie is a hard worker." Colin had helped her place the chairs under a tree where he could keep an eye on her from the creek. She ges-tured for Mr. Halsey to move in that direction.

He waited until she sat before he removed his hat and sat on the chair angled toward hers. A long time had passed since she'd been around a man who treated her with respect. She wasn't sure whether it was out of respect or because he wanted something.

Not one to ever back down from her thoughts, she asked, "So, ye helpin' us with the supplies yesterday and showin' me respect, would this all be a ploy to make me thinkin' ye have our best interests in mind?" She smiled inwardly as his eyes sparked briefly before he looked down at the hat he held in his hands.

"No ma'am, I'm not treating you any different than I would any other female I came across." He raised his gaze to settle on her face.

Lord help her. Her stomach quivered at the honesty she saw in the dark depths of his eyes. She tamped the happiness starting to burgeon in her heart with a thought of Mr. Miller.

"What will ye be tryin' to deal with me today?" she asked, rearranging her skirt so she could focus her gaze somewhere other than his intriguingly handsome face.

"There's no dealing, ma'am. I need that corner of your land for my family, and I plan to get it." The conviction in his voice brought her gaze back to his.

"Just how are ye plannin' to take our land, Mr. Halsey?" She put more steel in her question than she felt. This play of wits was the most exciting bit of conversation she'd had in nearly seven years. Not since Patrick was alive. The thought of her darlin' Patrick brought stinging tears to her eyes. She looked away quickly and brushed at them. "Rubble," she offered, when he watched her with a raised brow.

"I'm not in the habit of taking your land or anyone else's, Mrs—" She sent a scathing glance his way. "Aileen."

"Then how be ye proposin' to use my land when I dinnae plan on sellin'?" She glanced at Colin. He listened intently as he worked. Shayla had taken a spot on the ground next to Mr. Halsey's leg. Her daughter watched the man with wide, innocent eyes and a large, dopey grin.

"I've been thinking about that." He smiled at Shayla and reached in his pocket, pulling out two long, red and white sticks of peppermint. "This is for you." He handed her one of the sticks. "And take this one to your brother." The girl snatched both sticks and giggled, running toward her frowning brother.

Aileen glared at him. "Ye cannae buy me land by givin' my children treats."

"I'm giving your children treats because I feel like it." He held her gaze. "I don't think they've had many frivolous things in their lives. I wanted to give them something."

"How dare ye say I cannae provide for my bairn!" She shot to her feet and clenched her fisted hands to her side. The urge to haul off and hit him rose and withered just as quickly, knowing what her temper had gotten her in the past.

Colin ran to her side. "I think it's time you left mister," his voice purred a low threat.

Ethan wasn't sure what nerves he'd hit. Both the mother and son looked ready to take a swing at him. When he arrived, the woman had glowed; her eyes twinkling with invitation, yet, she made it clear there would be no sale of her land. That's when the idea hit him.

"I'm not bad mouthing your mothering. It's

got to be hard just you and the boy digging in the mine and panning the creek. I'm sure you scrape up enough to eat and buy some clothes, but wouldn't you like to make more?"

Her eyes glimmered with interest. She wanted money, like every other miner out there. Greed motivated most of them. Greed was wanting something for yourself. He wasn't greedy. He meant to make a good living for his brothers and their families with the stamp mill.

"Ah'm listenin'," she moved the boy aside and took a couple steps toward Ethan.

"Ma..."

"Shhh, Colin. We can get home faster. Tell me Mr. Halsey, how ye plan to make us more money?"

So it wasn't greed, but something else that motivated her. Another mystery about the woman. Ethan smiled and motioned for her to return to her chair.

"Since you aren't interested in selling how about we build the stamp mill on your property and you can use it one day a week. We won't take any percentage for you using the mill." He could tell by the wrinkles marring her forehead and the way she tapped a finger against her pursed lips, he'd have to explain more.

"How are ye planning 'to get our bing to the stamp mill?" She stared past him down the creek.

"Bing?" He'd never heard such a word.

"The rubble we pull from the mine."

"Oh, your diggings. It's all downhill from here to where the mill will sit." He glanced at the boy. Colin shook his head, not willing to commit.

"An how ye think the laddie and me could get

the likes of dirt and rock to there even downhill?" She narrowed her gaze, crinkling the freckled skin around her eyes.

"My brothers and I will build tracks. You can put your diggings in ore carts and run them down to the mill." He didn't know if his brothers would go for the idea, however, they wanted the mill as much as he did.

"And where are ye thinkin' we'd get an ore cart or two." She swept her arms around. "If we could afford the carts we'd no' be haulin' buckets to the sluice."

Dang, she was a tough one. He sighed. "You can use our ore carts. We'll leave some empty for you during the week to fill." He'd have to talk a good talk to make his brothers agree to all these things he found himself saying. The woman's eyes gleamed with triumph. She knew she had him.

"Sounds like a better deal than twenty-five dollars." She extended a hand.

"We'll shake today, but I'll bring back papers in a couple of days for you to sign." The frown returned, and she started to pull her arm back. He grasped her hand. The calloused palm could have been that of another man, yet the slender fingers and hesitant grip told him otherwise.

"The papers won't say anything different than what I've offered." He held onto her hand, waiting for her to argue. She stared into his eyes, his heart rammed into his ribs. Surprise and confusion widened her eyes before she glanced away and jerked her fingers from his.

He cleared his throat and rubbed his tingling hand across the thigh of his pants.

"I'll ride to Baker City tomorrow and get the papers written up by a lawyer and bring them back day after tomorrow." He stood.

"When will ye start buildin' the mill?" The hesitation in her eyes made him wonder if she'd change her mind once they started to build.

"As soon as you sign the papers we'll start stacking the rock foundation."

Her eyes widened before she glanced at the boy. "That soon."

"I want this up and running before winter sets in. Miners can stockpile their diggings, and on their day, haul it to the mill through the winter, making less down time." He glanced around. "I'm sure you don't pull near the ore out of your mine during the winter as the other months. With the mill you can work less and get more."

This time the boy took an interest in what he said.

"You saying by using the mill, Ma wouldn't have to work so much?"

He'd found the boy's weakness. "Yes, you and your ma will get more return from your work. If you can keep several ore carts filled a week, she won't have to do as much." Ethan glanced at Aileen then back to the boy. "I could even hire you on to help at the stamp mill." The boy shot a glance at his mother and then lowered his gaze.

"We'll give yer say some thought, Mr. Halsey." Aileen rose.

He knew this was his cue to leave. Ethan stood, extended his hand to Colin and ruffled Shayla's hair. The little girl wrapped her arms around his legs. His heart thumped up into his throat, and his eyes burned. She smiled up at him as though he'd given her a beloved treasure. He'd never experienced anything as fulfilling.

He couldn't speak. He plopped his hat on his head and gently pried the arms loose. Clearing his throat a couple times, he touched her nose with the tip of his finger. "See you day after tomorrow." He walked over to his horse.

Ethan didn't look back as he rode out of the clearing and into the trees. The desire in Aileen's eyes when they shook hands and the tingle her touch left in his palm, made his heart race and a certain body part enlarge. He'd never been the desire of any woman. He thought of the Widow James. Well, not one that made his heart race and his body react at the thought of her.

The business transaction gave him power. The thought of Aileen wanting him shook his confidence.

Chapter 6

"That's asinine!" Clay shot out of the chair. "You can't put a stamp mill on her property and give her the use of the thing." He slapped one hand into the upturned palm of the other. "If we don't own the land it's sitting on, she can boot us off at any time! It's her land!"

"I have to agree with Clay on this." Hank nodded.

"She isn't going to sell." Ethan ran a hand through his hair and stared at his brothers. How did he make them realize it was the only way to make their dream come true? "We'll have the lawyer write it up as us renting the land."

"And she can revoke the lease at any time!" Clay paced to the stove and back.

"Not if we put in writing we are renting it indefinitely." He had to make them agree.

"Then how is she going to sell when she's ready if we have an indefinite rent on that part of her land?" Hank took a sip of his coffee and leveled curious eyes on him.

"I'll buy the land." He'd thought about it on the way home. Asked himself all these same questions and the answer was simple. When she was ready to move on, he'd buy the land. By then the mill would be making money, and he'd have the funds to do it. "We could even put in the contract that we'd purchase all the land when she gets ready to sell."

"What if she likes that idea and says she wants to sell before we can afford it all?" Clay turned the chair and sat with his arms folded across the back.

"From what she said today, I think she needs more money than the sale of her property will get her. I'd say she isn't looking to sell for at least five years." He smiled. "We'll be solvent by then, boys."

"I still don't like it, but if it's the only way we can get the mill started and be done by winter, I guess we don't have much choice." Hank patted Clay on the shoulder. "What do you think? Are you okay with this?"

"I'm in, but I'm not okay." Clay narrowed his eyes and stared at Ethan. "I just hope your thinkin' with your head and not another part of your body."

"What is that supposed to mean?" Ethan surged off his chair and leaned across the table toward his mouthy brother.

"Every time you come back from seeing that woman, your eyes are glowing and you smile a whole lot."

"That's ridiculous! I may be smiling but that's because I know we're getting the stamp mill." Ethan didn't like his attraction to the woman was so easily detected.

"Yeah, so you say." Clay took a sip of coffee, but his gaze never left Ethan.

"Let's write all this down. I'll take a ride into Baker City and bring the contract back in the morning." Hank grabbed a pencil and a piece of paper from the middle of the table.

Ethan crossed his arms and began reciting the promises he'd made the Widow Miller.

Aileen slammed the pick into the side of the mine. Rubble rained down around her. They'd hit a good pocket of quartz this morning. She ran a hand over her face to clear away the dirt. This vein should have meant extra work for her and Colin. She smiled. Instead, they'd stock pile the rubble and send it to the stamp mill when it was up and running. The only toil would be getting it there and walking away with a bag of gold.

She still couldn't believe Mr. Halsey had given them track, ore carts, and free use of the stamp mill just to build on their land. He planned to make a grand pot of money from the venture. Which made it easier for her to stomach the deal.

One thing she was was fair. If the Halsey's padded their pockets from her land, there was no reason they couldn't pad theirs as well.

"Ma, he's comin'" Colin's voice echoed through the tunnel.

She dropped the pick. "Cach!" The heavy tool landed on her foot. She bit back the tears, grabbed the lantern sitting on a stone, and hobbled to the entrance.

Colin stood in the opening. She couldn't see

his expression for the sunlight behind him shining brightly.

He rushed forward. "What's wrong?" He slipped a strong arm around her waist helping her along.

"Ah dropped the bloody pick on ma foot." She cast a glance at the tree where Mr. Halsey fancied to tie his horse. There he was, bent down, conversing with Shayla. "Ask Mr. Halsey to show ye exactly where he plans to build this stamp mill."

Colin started to shake his head.

"Do it. While ye have him gone, ah'll hobble on out o' here, clean up a bit, and be sittin' in the chair under the tree when ye get back." She squeezed her son's shoulders. "Ah dinnae want any man to see me weak. Not again."

His eyes flashed with recognition.

"Be sending Shayla my way."

He nodded and walked out of the mine, his slender back held tall. His gait grew more and more like a man's every day.

Aileen watched from the shadow of the entrance as Colin stopped in front of Mr. Halsey. The man glanced toward the mine, put some papers in the saddlebag on his horse, and headed down the creek. Shayla shifted back and forth. Her gaze followed the two as her feet finally carried her toward the mine. Aileen smiled. The child was smitten with the man.

"I want to go." Shayla looked over her shoulder to where the man and boy disappeared.

"Ah be needin' yer help, lassie." Aileen found a stick not too far from the mouth of the mine and leaned on it as she hobbled to the shack.

"Momma, are you 'k'?" Shayla grasped her free hand, holding it up as though she could help take weight off the throbbing foot.

"Dropped the pick on ma toe. Help me clean up and sit in the chair under the tree." For the first time since setting eyes on the rickety shack, she was happy there weren't any steps to climb. She stopped in front of the bucket of water and scrubbed the dirt from her face. "Is the filth gone from my face?" she asked the child hovering by her side.

Shayla motioned for her to lean down. The darlin' child clutched the hem of her own shift and dabbed at a spot on Aileen's cheek.

"Now yer bonnie, Momma." The sweet thing kissed her cheek and smiled.

"Thank ye, lassie." Her heart melted all over again for the sweet bairn who made all her beatings a faded memory. She scrubbed her hands and arms and brushed at the dirt and debris on her clothing.

"Help me to the shade." Aileen used the stick to keep pressure off her foot and hobbled to the chair beneath the tree. Shayla followed along beside her. The child remained near, helping prop her foot up and offering to bring her a glass of water.

"That's a dear. My throat is parched." Aileen glanced toward the stream. Mr. Halsey and Colin walked toward her. She breathed a sigh they hadn't come any sooner and caught her hobbling around. She would not show this man or any man weakness. No one would use fear to humiliate her again.

"Aileen." Mr. Halsey removed his wide-brimmed hat and took the seat adjacent to hers.

"Mr. Halsey." She turned to Colin. "And was Mr. Halsey showin' ye the area he wishes to build the stamp mill?"

"Yes, Ma. It's a section not far beyond where we bathe."

Where they bathed? She turned to Mr. Halsey. "Is there no' another spot ye could go?"

"The water falls quickly just beyond that pool creating the force we need to make the mill run." Ethan didn't miss the near panic in the woman's eyes, nor the tremble in her voice. "Have you searched upstream for a bathing spot?"

"Tis too rocky and shallow."

He glanced at the boy. He'd get no help from him.

"We cannae be bathing so close to the mill." She glared at him. "Ye'll have to move the mill."

"I told you there is no other spot to put it." Her eyes challenged him. His mother held a lot of stock in bathing. It seemed Aileen did as well. He wasn't about to have her back out over a small thing he could easily provide. Hell, if he was giving her track, ore carts, and free use of the stamp mill, a bathtub was nothing. "I'll bring you a tub. One you can put either down by the creek or up here in your lean-to."

Her eyes narrowed, and her head tilted to the right as she watched him. Filtered snips of sunlight highlighted her dark brown hair, illuminating streaks of copper. The scattering of freckles across her pale face gave her a delicate lacy appearance. Her light green eyes peering at him, slowly lost their hardness, and as they softened, the color deepened and wrinkles at the corners of her eyes formed.

"Do yer family know the things you offer?"

"Up until the bathtub, yes."

Her soft laughter bubbled forth, mingling with the twitter of the birds in the tree above them. He couldn't help but smile at the sound and the sparkling eyes that mocked him.

"Yer sure to get a lick for promisin' the loony widow a bathtub."

He grinned, thinking of how Clay would take this latest news. "Yes, I'm sure Clay will have a good time with this." He leaned forward, ignoring the glare he received from the boy. "I've already had to fight for your requests. Let's keep the bathtub between us."

She nodded and leaned in toward him. " 'Tis our secret. But ah dinnae want a small one. It best be a sittin' tub, not one ye stand in."

Now how would he explain the purchase of a full tub over a wash tub? He cleared his throat. This woman was going to make him appear weak to his brothers. Yet, after hearing her sparkling laughter, he'd do just about anything to be treated to that warm sound again.

"One full-sized tub it will be."

"And it be showin' up here afore ye start buildin'." She shook a finger at him. "We'll no' walk around in filth waitin' for the tub while yer busy puttin' up yer mill."

He bit back his retort and stood. "I'll get the contract." Ethan walked over to his horse. She had him by the balls, and she knew it. He saw it in the little quiver at the corners of her mouth as she made her demands and in the mirth dancing in her light green eyes. He hated the fact he'd do just about anything to get her signature on the contract. He'd sell himself if it would consummate this deal.

The thought sent heat straight to his loins. He nearly moaned at the vision of lowering his body upon hers and taking away her loneliness if only for a brief time. She tried to hide it, but he'd witnessed the flashes of longing in her eyes. Could he ease her longing? From his few trips to prostitutes, he'd learned a brief coupling did little to relieve loneliness.

"Are ye findin' the papers?" Her musical voice called out.

"Yes, just trying to find a pencil." And wait for my pants to loosen. He dug around in the saddlebag until he could move without looking like he had a stick in his britches.

He returned to the seat under the tree.

"Colin, be fetchin' Mr. Halsey a glass o' water." Aileen waved her hand toward the shack. The boy glanced at him then his mother before he headed at a brisk clip toward the building.

As soon as the boy was gone, she said in almost a whisper. "Mr. Halsey, I know enough to read a newspaper but my abilities to read a contract are failin'." She glanced at the house where Colin hurried back to them. "My laddie also has limited learnin'. I'd be forgivin' ye the takin' o' our land, if ye could offer to read the contract out loud." She leaned closer. "T' save my Colin's feelin's."

Ethan nodded. Having a mother who taught her children everything she knew about reading, writing, and ciphering numbers, he could understand why Aileen felt she let her children down with her limited knowledge.

When the boy handed him the chipped glass of cool water, Ethan took a swallow and licked his lips. His gaze strayed to Aileen's face. The smile curving her lips just about sprung the front of his britches.

Clearing his throat, he turned to the boy. "I thought I'd read the contract out loud so both you and your ma could see that I didn't put anything in here we didn't agree on the other day."

The boy nodded, and Ethan began to read aloud. Shayla curled up at his feet with her head resting against his leg. He reached down to pat her curly head. Glancing up, he caught Aileen listening intently her eyes closed as she nodded her head. Colin stood with his long, skinny legs apart, his arms crossed in an unyielding stance.

When Ethan finished, he handed the paper and pencil to Aileen. She set it on the upturned hunk of wood between them and scratched her name across the paper. Then she handed the pencil to Colin.

Ethan raised an eyebrow.

"Where we come from, the laddie is the man of the family since his da be gone. But I know ye'd no' like it if he be the only one signin' the paper."

"It doesn't matter to me as long as you both understand this contract allows us to build the stamp mill on your land that we are renting by you using the stamp mill at no cost. And that we have the right to purchase the land when you are ready to sell."

"Aye. We understand."

"Fine. I'll be here tomorrow morning to start laying the foundation."

"Aye, but what o' my bathtub?" Her green eyes flickered with distrust. "Ye'll no' be goin' back on yer word. Ye said ah'd be havin' it afore ye started the buildin'."

"I'll go to town right now and get it and deliver it in the morning when I arrive." The woman was cagey. She hadn't appeared that taken with the idea of a bathtub, yet here she fought for it. Ethan grinned. "I have a feeling we'll be sparring quite a bit before this stamp mill is finished."

"Only if ye be failin' to stick to yer word."

He saw the twitch at the corner of her lips and grinned. Damn, if it wasn't going to be stimulating butting heads with her.

"I'll stick to my word."

"We'll be seein' that ye do."

He slapped his hat on his head and stood. Holding out his hand to Colin, he smiled. "If you want a job, come by the site. I'm sure we can find something for you to do." He turned to Aileen. "I'll be by with that tub in the morning." He extended his hand. She tentatively touched her fingers to his palm before clasping his hand.

His palm registered every curve and callous of hers. What made him so sensitive to her touch?

"Be sure and ye do that. Or ye will be doin' no' buildin'." She pulled from his grasp and nodded toward his horse. A sign she wanted him to leave.

Ethan dropped his arm and studied her face. She lowered her lashes, hiding her emotions from him. He leaned down and captured Shayla, holding

her up in the air as she giggled. "See you tomorrow."

"Yes!" She placed her small hands on either
side of his face and dropped a feather-light kiss on
his forehead.

His heart squeezed at the ease with which
this child bestowed her feelings. He didn't know
what to do. Surely giving her a kiss back would be
frowned on by the mother. He glanced sideways.
Aileen appeared just as perplexed with the situation as he.

"Thank you, Shayla." He set her back on the
ground and hurried to his horse. Placing the contract in the saddlebag, he mounted.

He rode out of the valley stunned by the intimacy he felt with the widow and the happiness
the child swelled in his heart. The innocent kiss of
the child, the loneliness and desire in the woman's
eyes that set his body on fire, and the censure in
the boy all pulled at different emotions. Emotions
that would only get him in trouble.

Chapter 7

"What do you mean you have to order a bathtub?" Ethan slapped his hand down on the counter in the mercantile and stared daggers at the merchant cowering behind the long, wood structure.

"I don't have any bathtubs only wash tubs. I could sell—"

"I need a bathtub. By tomorrow morning." Ethan ran a hand over his face. It was already getting near dark. He could get to Baker City tonight, but by the time he waited for the mercantile to open, loaded his purchase and headed back, he wouldn't get to the Miller's until mid afternoon and would have lost a whole day of work.

"Who was the last person to buy a tub from you?" If he couldn't get a new one, he'd purchase the next best thing and replace the one he bought.

"It was months ago. Don't have much call for the fancy sitting tubs."

"Who was it?" He wished they had one at the cabin. Then he could haul it over to Aileen and not stand in the middle of the damn mercantile feeling like his world had spun out of control over a damn bathtub.

"Widow James over at Myrle's."

Ethan groaned. Could it get any worse? Myrle wasn't a problem, she'd understand. But how the hell was he to explain to the besotted Widow James why he needed her bathtub?

He stomped out of the mercantile and stared at Myrle's house. The chill in the late afternoon air did little to dispel the ripples of apprehension tickling his neck hairs. He had men coming tomorrow to start work on the foundation. If Aileen didn't get a bathtub, they couldn't work.

Growling, he set his teeth and headed to Myrle's. The door swung easily in his hand as the Widow James opened it for him and tittered. He didn't want to lead her on, but he needed her bathtub.

"Afternoon, Mrs. James." He doffed his hat and smiled even as he ground his teeth.

"Mr. Halsey." Her eyelashes fluttered, and she placed a bony, wrinkled hand to her loose-skinned throat like a coy young woman.

"Myrle here?" He knew he couldn't avoid the woman when she was the one he had to speak to, but he hoped maybe Myrle would be his go-between. Ask the woman for the tub and all. That way he could avoid saying anything that would give the woman thoughts of a marriage proposal.

"She went to the doc's."

"Anything wrong with her?" He didn't like the idea of Myrle being sick.

The widow giggled. "No, she just likes to visit

with the doc. She should be back in a while." Mrs. James slid her hand around his arm, drawing him to a table. "I could sit with you while you wait." Again the graying eyelashes fluttered.

The sight made his skin crawl with wariness. "I could use a cup of coffee." With something stronger added. He sat in a chair with his back to the wall. He didn't want this woman sneaking up on him.

She returned with two cups and a coffee pot. She filled the cups, set a colorful pad down, and placed the pot on top.

"What did you need to see Myrle about? Maybe I can help." She lifted the cup and took a dainty sip never taking her gaze off him.

Ethan squirmed and took a gulp of the coffee. He set the cup down and eyed her. She gave off all the signals of a woman out looking for a man. Damn. He rubbed his hands on his thighs and didn't miss the wayward glance she sent to his crotch.

"Mrs. James..." he swallowed, "I have a favor to ask." Her eyes lit up like he'd handed her bag of gold. Or a wedding ring.

"I'd do anything for you Mr. Halsey." Her breathy statement tipped him back in the chair.

He cleared his throat, not sure if he really wanted to be beholden to this woman. "Ma'am, I was wondering if you could give me your bathtub. I'd replace it with a new one."

Her head jerked, and she stared at him. "Why ever do you want my tub?"

"It's a long story ma'am. But I need a bathtub by tomorrow morning. The mercantile doesn't have any. I'll have Mr. Holcomb order you one, and I'll pay for it."

Her glance darted to his lips and then back up to his eyes. He groaned inside. What kind of a deal would he have to make to get that damn tub?

"So you need this tub—pretty bad?" She leaned closer. The lines on her face and the sag in her skin did little to stave off the fear quivering in his gut.

"Yes, ma'am it will save me a lot of money to get your tub."

Her thinning eyebrow shot up, and she tipped her head. "How could my bathtub save you money?"

"I told you it was a long story."

"If you want my tub, I think you need to tell me this long story." She leaned closer, her hand reaching out to his.

Where the hell was Myrle? This woman was making like a whore, brushing up against him and practically purring.

"If you don't tell me, no tub." She eased her chair closer to his.

He took a large swallow of coffee and stared into the cup as he began his tale of building a stamp mill and how he got the rights to build it on Cracker Creek.

"You want my tub for that husband killer!" The Widow James shot to her feet. "You think I'll give you my tub so you can make another woman happy? Especially that woman!" She shook her head. "And to think, I thought you were a respectable man." She huffed out of the room as Myrle came through the front door.

"Now you show up!" He ran a hand over his

face in frustration.

"What did you do to Edith?" Myrle crossed the room, staring at the slammed door.

"I asked if I could take her bathtub and replace it with a new one." Women, every one he'd come in contact with lately did nothing but aggravate. And they all wondered why he didn't want to marry.

"That doesn't sound like Edith. Especially the way she feels about you." Myrle sat down. "But why do you need her bathtub? You can order one from Mr. Holcomb at the mercantile."

"I need one tomorrow morning." He really didn't want to repeat everything he told the Widow James.

Myrle cocked her head. "Why would you need one by tomorrow morning? You have company coming?"

"No. It seems the site where we're building the stamp mill is in plain view of where the Miller's usually bathe." The woman's eyes lit up and she smiled. "And Aileen said we couldn't start building until she had a tub since there isn't any other spot along Cracker Creek suitable for bathing. At least by her dictates." He scowled. She'd swindled him out of one more thing. "I have a crew headed up there tomorrow morning to start on the foundation. She said unless she has a bathtub, they can't start." He stared at the woman in the chair across from him.

"That woman has me over a barrel by not selling me the land, but letting us build. At first, I figured she was just being greedy, but then she mentioned something that showed me she had a good reason for not wanting to part with the land.

But now, I think she planned this just to get every-thing she can out of me and aggravate my life."

Myrle laughed. Her whole body shook and tears streamed down her face. When the belly laughs subsided, she wiped at tears in her eyes. "Good for Aileen. She may have been used once, but that woman is not going to be used again."

"You think it's funny she's causing me trou-ble?" Ethan stared at the woman. He didn't need trouble. That mill would be running by winter or he'd die making it happen.

"We've got more than one tub in this house." Myrle patted his arm. "You can take the one out of the downstairs closet."

Ethan shook his head. "Why the hell couldn't you have been here when I arrived? The Widow James nearly crawled in my lap. I'm going to have nightmares here on out."

"That's spiteful." Myrle smacked him upside the head. "I never thought you'd grow up to be so mean spirited."

He rubbed his head and glared at Myrle. "I never thought I'd be seduced by a woman nearly old enough to be my mother."

Myrle's laugh boomed through the empty room. "Finish your coffee, and we'll get that tub."

"What's the bathtub for? You all of a sudden don't like cleaning up in the wash tub?"

Ethan glared at Hank. All the way from town he fretted about what to tell his brothers about the tub in the back of his wagon. "I'm doing a favor for Myrle." His skin heated at the lie.

"What kind of favor?" Clay grabbed the metal side and started to pull on the tub.

"Leave it there. I have to deliver it in the morning." Ethan jumped down from the wagon and started to unhitch the horses.

"I thought we were starting on the stamp mill in the morning." Clay shoved the tub back into the wagon. The wood bottom scraped on the wagon bed.

"And where's the supplies to get started?" Hank moved to the other side of the horses, grasping the headstall on the far horse.

"A couple of the men I hired from town are bringing the supplies in the morning." He led his horse to the barn and started taking the harness off, hoping Clay and Hank would let the conversation drop.

"So how are you going to deliver a tub and be at the mill to start the work?" Clay took the leather straps from Ethan and carried them into the small building they used to store tools and tack.

"It's on the way." Ethan led his horse to the corral, putting distance between himself and his over-curious brother. He let the horse loose and stood at the fence, watching the animal meander over to the feed trough. "Grab some oats while you're in there," he hollered over his shoulder.

Hank put the other horse in the corral and leaned on the fence next to him. "You taking that tub to the widow?" His accusing tone riled.

"I might be. But I figure that's my business and not yours." Ethan swung away from the fence and stomped to the cabin. All he wanted was for this day to be over with and the crew to start work on the stamp mill. He didn't need his meddling brothers telling him what he already knew. He'd sunk lower than he'd ever thought he'd go to get what he wanted. And he wanted that stamp mill up and running. He cringed. He also wanted to make the Widow Miller happy.

Aileen couldn't remember the last time she woke this happy. She sang as she prepared the morning meal of porridge.

"Come alang, come alang, wi' your boatie and your song. Tae my hey! Bonnie maidens, my twa bonnie maids! The nicht, it is dark, and the redcoat is gaun. And you're dearly welcome tae Skye again."

Shayla clapped her hands and tried to sing. Colin entered the cabin with a scowl on his face.

"Why are you two so happy?" The glare he shot his sister as he snatched the tin plate of porridge from his mother's hands whisked away her happiness.

"Ah'm feelin' like things may be turnin' for the better for us, that's all." Aileen motioned for them to go outside. She carried her plate and Shayla's to the cool, fresh air. Colin took his usual spot, while Shayla knelt by the upturned log. Aileen set the hot plate on the log and took her seat.

"With the stamp mill and all the Halsey's are givin' to help us get our gold to the mill, ah feel like we won't kill ourselves to get what we need to return to yer land." She took a bite of the hot oats and watched her son. He'd nearly cleaned his plate of the porridge. He was a growing boy, one who would soon eat twice as much as she and Shayla.

"You sure you aren't happy Mr. Halsey is coming back?" The accusation in his changing voice stung like a slap.

"Ah'll admit, ah enjoy workin' that man and gettin' our family more than he'd set out to give. But dinnae ye go thinkin' ye know in my head. Ah may be a woman, but yer da told me more than once, ah've the mind of a businessman." She shook her finger at her son. "Ah'm only takin' from this man what we deserve."

"We'll see." Colin stood, gave her a long, unflinching appraisal, and headed to the creek to wash his plate.

Aileen shook her head. Why did her happiness make him uneasy? Yes, she enjoyed being in Mr. Halsey's company, but she would never subject her family to a man again. She shivered thinking of her last husband. She would never again be a man's property.

The sound of horses and the rumble of wagon wheels shook her from the wretched memories.

"Happy Man!" Shayla jumped up and ran to the wagon as fast as her chubby legs would take her.

Aileen couldn't help but smile at her daughter's enthusiasm. If only Colin were that accepting of the man who could make their dream of returning to Ireland happen sooner.

Ethan stopped the horses and wagon in front of the house. "Where do you want your bathtub?" For the first time since meeting the sharp-witted woman, her eyes sparkled, and her rose-colored lips curved in an enticing smile. The change started his heart thumping in his chest, his body heating.

She hurried to the back of the wagon and ran her hand over the metal contraption. The awe and delight in her eyes, made him wish he'd been able to give her a new tub instead of a used one.

"Beside the cabin will be fine."

He jumped down from the seat, jolting his body in hopes the enlarged member in his britches would shrink.

Aileen looked his way as he moved his jarred knees to make sure they still worked. "Ye don't have to hurry and hurt yerself."

He moved by her keeping air between them. "I've got men waiting for me at the mill site."

"Oh." The breathy sound pulled his gaze to her. The crestfallen look and slight slump of her shoulders tugged at his conscience.

"They know what to do. Where exactly do you want this?" He grasped the wooden handle on the end of the tub and pulled it out of the wagon. He held the tub like a large cooking pot, waiting for her direction.

"This way." He watched her trouser-clad hips sway back and forth as she walked to the side of the cabin. Shaking his head, he yanked his gaze from her backside the moment she turned to see if he followed.

He placed the tub on the ground and looked at the openness of the area. "You aren't planning to use it here are you?"

She frowned. "Nae! No' with the men ye have runnin' on my land."

"I can put it in the lean-to."

"There's nae room. Ah'll think on where the

best place will be."

Shayla crawled in the tub and stomped, making thumping noises on the wooden bottom while clinging to the metal side.

"Lassie, ye'll break it afore we can use it."

Ethan grasped the child under the arms, lifting her out. Her arms and legs wrapped around him like string on a top. Her soft hair tickled his chin. The scent of raspberry and soap filled his nostrils.

"Thank you," she said, before small, pursed lips buzzed his cheek.

Stunned, he stood like a boulder as she clambered down and headed off in the direction of her brother.

"She's never had a man around. Ah'm afraid she's a bit cheeky." The lyrical words pulled him back to the present.

"What about her father?" He studied the woman. She stared straight in his eyes.

"The man was dead afore she arrived. Ah'm thankful every day she'll never know the meanness of her father." Her eyes lost their sparkle, becoming dull and distant.

He wanted to reach out and show her not all men inflicted pain. She wouldn't believe his sincerity. Not yet.

"I want to bring two of my brothers over this afternoon to meet you."

"Two? Ye have more?"

"Yes. I have four all together. Gil and his wife live in Galena, and Zeke and Maeve travel with their work."

"And why do ye think ah should meet them?" She put her hands on her hips and watched him.

"I want you to feel comfortable going to them if I'm not around." He took a step toward her. She stood her ground, but her eyes widened. Scanning her angel-kissed face, his gaze moved down her long, slender neck to the opening of the man's shirt she wore.

She swallowed. "And where might ye be?"

"Off buying more equipment. Hiring men." He returned his gaze to her face. Did disappointment flicker in her eyes?

"How many men will be traipsing across my land?" Her voice wavered.

"I've given orders no one is to come past the curve in the creek. If they do, I want you to tell me who, and I'll send them away." He didn't want her to fear for herself or her children.

"Why?"

"Why what?" He liked that she barely had to tip her head to look up at him. When a woman had to step back to look him in the eye it felt like he talked to a child. This woman didn't remind him of a child. Her full breasts and round hips were those of a woman. Her intelligent, sad eyes told him of her sorrows. This woman had lived a hard life.

"Why would ye send a man away just because he passed the curve?"

"You are doing me a favor by allowing us to build the stamp mill. To show you my gratitude, I will make sure no one bothers you or the children."

Her lips slowly curved into the devastating smile she flashed earlier. "Ye are an interestin' man, Mr. Halsey."

"Ethan."

She tipped her head to the side. "Ethan."

"Mr. Halsey, you better get back to your men." Words laced with anger, Colin stepped between them, his expression as unyielding as stone.

Having handled his brothers in many situations, Ethan placed a hand on the boy's shoulder. The young man flinched and swung his arm up, slapping the hand off and backing into his mother.

"I wasn't going to hurt you, son." Ethan knew enough to not push the issue, but he'd done nothing to make the boy think he would cause him or his mother and sister harm.

"He knows that, Mr. Halsey." Aileen grasped the boy by the shoulders, pulling him into a hug as her arms slid across his chest. The boy's eyes flared with indignation, but he didn't fight to leave his mother's embrace.

"I'll be back this afternoon with my brothers." Ethan touched the brim of his hat, ruffled Shayla's curly hair, and climbed into his wagon.

He'd bring Clay and Hank over this afternoon. Maybe between the three of them, they could figure out how to break through Colin's hostility. If he couldn't break through, Aileen would stay distant and make his life harder with her demands.

Chapter 8

"I still don't see why we have to go see this woman." Clay followed behind Ethan, mumbling.

"I want Aileen to feel comfortable with you two in case I'm not around." Ethan slanted a look at his brother. Why was he so against meeting the woman? "She isn't going to try anything with three of us there." Even as he said the words, Ethan realized he was playing into Clay's fears about the woman.

"Clay keep an open mind. Ethan has been dealing with her and look..." Hank grinned and slapped a hand on Ethan's shoulder, "he's still raring to go back."

Ethan flung out his hand, stopping both brothers just as they rounded the bend in the creek. He turned, putting his back to the cabin and confronted the two imbeciles. "I don't want either of you to say anything other than polite conversation. One of you fools could spout out about your fears..." he glared at Clay, "or your presumed thoughts I'm having about this woman..." he narrowed his gaze on Hank, "and ruin the whole deal."

"If she signed the contract, why the hell are you making us pussyfoot around her?" Clay crossed his arms and glared back.

"Because, she—hell, her husband beat her—a lot, according to Myrle. If she gets scared, thinking one of us or the men working at the mill are going to go after her, she could very well cause trouble." He hadn't wanted to spill Aileen's vulnerability to them, but he had to get them to behave.

"Happy Man!" The excited squeal from Shayla shifted his thoughts from vileness to innocence.

He turned and she ran to him, clutching his legs. The snickers behind him didn't take away from the giddy bubble expanding his chest. He picked her up, presenting her to the surprised men. "Shayla, these are my brothers. Hank and Clay."

"Hi." She giggled and buried her head against his chest. Peeking at the two, she giggled again.

"Hi, Shayla," Hank reached a hand out, and she grasped his finger.

"You're not as big," she said in a slightly disapproving tone. Ethan laughed when Hank frowned.

"What about me?" Clay stepped forward and flashed his devilish grin.

"What happened to your nose?" She reached out giving it a tweak.

"Hey!" Clay stepped back, giving Ethan and Hank a good laugh.

"Where's your ma?" Ethan asked, setting the child on the ground. He knew her squeal had to have been heard by the mother or at least the brother.

"She's in the mine with Colin." She pointed to the opening in the earth and wrinkled her nose.

"Can you take my brothers to the tree over where your ma and I talked the other day? I'll go get her and your brother out of the mine." Ethan motioned to the large tree with the chairs still placed underneath. Shayla grasped a hand from each of his brothers and started chattering and walking toward the spot.

He hurried across the ground to the mine. Ducking, he entered the narrow passage. It was definitely a one man or one boy and one woman operation. The shaft was only wide enough for one person to walk. Every fifteen feet, he'd find a larger area where pockets of ore had been dug out. Fifty feet in, his hat scraped the ceiling. He ducked before smacking into the low ceiling.

The passage wound back in the mountainside farther than he'd anticipated. The air grew thick and hard to breathe. He used his hands to navigate the dark passage. Scraping noises and the chink of steel on rock rang through the darkness. Light began to filter along the passage.

He stepped into the ring of light and watched the boy and woman as they took turns swinging the pick and knocking trailings from the sides of the shaft. How could they work in the thick air? He could hardly breathe and he wasn't working.

"You really need to add some vent holes."

Aileen jumped and Colin swung around with his pick, ready to defend.

"I didn't mean to scare either of you."

"What are you doing sneaking up on us?" Colin squeaked.

"I'm not sneaking. I brought my brothers just like I said I would." He didn't miss both their gazes darting past him to the dark depths behind. "Shayla is keeping them company. She told me you were in here."

Aileen leaned her pick against the side wall and stilled her thrumming heart. "Colin, take the light and head out." There was no way this man could know how many times Mr. Miller had attacked them in this very shaft. He'd be out drinking and come home to find them slaving away and beat her senseless because she didn't have a meal ready. A person lost track of time while deep in the bowels of the earth.

Colin glared at Mr. Halsey and edged by him. She didn't miss the way he made sure he didn't touch the man.

"I'm sorry if we appeared startled, Mr. Halsey."

"Please, call me Ethan." He motioned for her to follow Colin. She glanced from his large hand extending down the tunnel toward the dimming light, to his face. The concern in his eyes told her he knew why they'd been hostile to his unexpected appearance.

She twisted sideways to move past him. He turned as well. Her breasts skimmed his chest. Heat rippled through her, and a nearly inaudible groan escaped his lips. She stopped, her body pressing against his. The light of the lantern no longer lit the tunnel. She couldn't see him, but his warm breath swept across her face, and his hands clasped her upper arms.

"We need to move on." His voice sounded pained. And she knew why when she squeezed along his body and felt his growing desire. The tunnel was dark and empty. She fumbled along the dirt walls, headed in the direction of the mine entrance.

"Ma! Ma!" Colin's concerned voice echoed through the shaft. The light before her grew as she hurried forward, and he rushed back toward her.

"Ah'm comin'," she called and checked over her shoulder to make sure Ethan followed. Making her way to the opening, she trembled not from cold but from the heat the man's body had instilled. Many years had elapsed since she'd succumbed to the heat and sparks of desire. She had to keep her distance from this man. She wasn't going down that road again. Not with anyone. Especially not with a man the size of Ethan.

She stepped into the daylight and shaded her eyes. Shayla stood under the trees, swinging her arms, and no doubt telling a whopper of a story to two men, who definitely resembled Ethan. They had the same coloring and the same build, though not as large as Ethan. She heard him exit the opening and walk up behind her.

"I didn't mean to scare you back there." The soft, husky words referred to more than his appearance in the mine.

"Ah'm fine. Just don't do it again." She continued forward afraid he might see how flushed her face had become. Aileen marched over to the tree. Both men stood and offered her a chair. Manners ran in the Halsey family.

She took her usual seat. Ethan moved to a spot between her and his brothers.

"Aileen, this is my brother Hank and my

brother Clay." He motioned them each forward as he spoke their names. Clay appeared nervous. Fidgeting and not quite meeting her gaze. He had the crooked nose of a man who got in brawls. She would have expected him to hold his nerves better.

"Ah'm sorry yer brother saw fit to bring ye here to meet the crazy widow." She said it with humor, but saw the apprehension flash across Clay's face.

"You aren't a crazy woman." Ethan jumped to her defense and both the brothers' eyebrows arched.

She laughed and motioned to Colin. "Take yer sister with ye and bring these men a glass o' water."

The glare Colin snapped her direction wasn't missed by the visitors. "He's a good laddie, just a bit overprotective of his sister and ah." When the boy shuffled out of sight, she narrowed her eyes and speared each brother with her gaze.

"Ethan said ye two were to be our 'protectors' if he's away." She glanced at Ethan. He watched her with the same protective gaze Colin did. It both warmed her and irritated her. She resumed her grilling of the brothers.

"Can ye tell me right now that ye dinnae have a problem with watching out fur us?" She glanced from one to the other. "Because if ye do, ye might as well crawl back to work and no' bother pretending."

Hank cleared his throat. "Ma'am, I don't have a problem with you or the younguns as long as you all stay away from the work site. I don't see any of the men wandering this way unless provoked."

"Provoked!" She rose out of the chair and poked a finger at the smart-mouthed man. "How are we to provoke them? Answer me that. What do ye take me for? Ah'm no' a whore and any man that lays a hand on me or ma bairn will find his balls layin' at his feet."

Ethan snickered at the white faces of his brothers. Obviously they had both underestimated the wrath and ugliness this woman had been dealt. She stated it plain as day. She wasn't going to be taken by any man and damn if that didn't make him want her more than he did when she squeezed past him in the mine.

Colin charged from the house at her outburst. The water sloshed over the pitcher he carried. Shayla hurried behind him, juggling stacked glasses.

He stopped beside his mother. His gaze darted between the men, his mouth twisted in anger. "Get off our land!"

"Colin, don't get lit up, your ma was just testing my brothers, to see how much they could stomach." Ethan inched closer to the woman. "Right, you were just fooling with them to see how much backbone they really had. I mean, if they don't have any backbone, they really aren't worth a dang to you or me."

Aileen glanced at him. He winked and she burst into laughter. Her lilting amusement washed over him like a ray of sunshine on a winter day.

Clay stepped forward. "Now see here, when did you start calling us cowards?" His voice shook with uncertainty and anger.

"I'll only call you a coward if you don't step

up and do your part to make sure Aileen and her family aren't harassed by our men." Ethan reached down and picked up Shayla. She smiled and held her arms out to Clay. He looked at Aileen. When she nodded, he reached out to the child, taking her in his arms.

"My momma won't hurt you," she said and patted him on the cheek. Clay's eyes lost their anger. Shayla reached over and patted Hank's shoulder. "You either."

Ethan burst out laughing. One small child had diffused his brothers and had them clamoring for her attention.

"Come on, boys, we better get back and make sure things are getting done." Ethan took Shayla from Clay. He set her on the ground next to her mother. "I'll come by every couple of days and see if you have any concerns."

"That ain't necessary." Colin placed himself between his mother and Ethan.

"Any time you want to come to work at the mill, come on over," Ethan said, ignoring the boy's hostile words. He wasn't sure how to break through the boy's anger, but he'd give it a try.

"Thank ye," Aileen said, putting a hand on Colin's shoulder.

"I'll be by in a couple of days." Ethan stared into her green eyes. He wanted to touch her, but knew that wouldn't set well with his brothers or the boy bracing himself in front of his mother.

He turned and motioned for Hank and Clay to follow. He'd spend the rest of the day hefting beams to work off the energy pumping through him. A dip in the creek outside their cabin would be needed before he fell into bed tonight. His body still fevered from his contact with the woman in the mine and her feisty comeback to his brothers.

When they were out of earshot of the cabin, Clay whistled softly. "That's one angry woman! I could see her killing her old man."

Ethan grabbed him by the shirt front. "If you say something like that again, you'll answer to me."

Clay raised his hands in submission. "I didn't say she did it, but I could see her doing it." He squirmed as Ethan shook him.

"Shut up. You're just digging yourself deeper." Hank put a hand on Ethan's arm. "Put him down. And cool off."

Ethan took a deep breath and slowly released the idiot's shirt. What was happening? He'd never attacked a brother before.

"You turned just as white as I did when she said she'd cut off our balls." Clay sidestepped the hand that came up to cuff him.

"I never realized you had such a problem keeping your mouth shut before." Hank smacked him when he dropped his guard.

"Knock it off, both of you." Ethan pulled his hat off his head and glanced back at the cabin. The small group still stood under the tree watching them. "Come on." He headed around the curve in the creek and ducked behind the arm of earth reaching out from the mountainside.

"Damn it. We have to show we work together not against one another. How will they feel safe, if we argue about them?" He stopped, pivoting to face his brothers.

"Why do we have to make them feel safe?"

Hank searched his face.

"Because I want them to feel safe. Do you need more reason than that?" Ethan sat on a boulder.

"I think you're getting soft." Clay plopped on one side of him and Hank on the other. "Not that it's a bad thing."

"But it is a bad thing. I can't run a business and try to cater to that woman's wishes." Ethan wanted to make every day a happy day for the family in the rickety shack. But, he had more people to think about than those three.

"You haven't catered to her any more than was necessary to get this mill going." Hank waved to the men moving boulders to create the foundation for the stamp mill.

Ethan stared at the beginning of his family's future. The mill would provide for his brothers and their children and perhaps, if the mountains continued to produce gold and silver, for their grandchildren as well. Bringing the closest miners in on the deal had not only garnered his family more working capital, it had also shown the miners their faith in the mountain and the bounty it would produce.

"Boys, let's go see if we can't move this process on a little faster." He stood and headed to the group of men pushing and levering a boulder. He'd spend the next few days immersed in getting this project off the ground. When the building started to take shape, he'd bring Aileen over to see what they'd accomplished.

He stopped. Why would he want to show it to Aileen? Because, you care what she thinks about you and this project.

"What's wrong?" Hank placed a hand on his shoulder.

"Nothing. I just had a thought that…" He shook his head. "Never mind. Let's get busy."

<h1 style="text-align:center">Chapter 9</h1>

Aileen woke each morning wondering when Ethan would come by. She didn't understand why her body responded to the man. He was larger than either of her husbands, yet, he had a calmness about him neither had possessed.

Shayla, too, watched the bend in the creek each day. Aileen patted her daughter's curly head.

"He's busy puttin' up his mill. He'll come around when he's the time." She picked up a faded shirt from the basket of washed laundry and hung it over a rope stretched from the tree to the corner of the lean-to. The best part of laundry day was working outdoors. She breathed in the clean scent of lye soap and the tang of the pine trees around the shack.

Shayla let out a squeal of delight.

Aileen shaded her eyes and peered at the creek. Flutters in her stomach tickled, and she smiled at the sight of Ethan's strong stride carrying him toward them. He waved to Shayla, and a broad grin thinned his full lips.

Colin rose from his crouched position by the sluice box and walked briskly toward her. The boy was too protective. In his younger years she found it endearing. Now it had become too much like her second husband. A man who wouldn't even let her use the outhouse without permission.

"What brings ye here?" she asked as Ethan walked straight to her.

"There'll be three wagons loaded down with the mill equipment coming through in the next few days. I wanted to make sure you knew they were supposed to be here." His gaze didn't stray from her face. The intensity in his eyes curled heat in her belly and spread upwards, flushing her face.

She cleared her throat, continuing to stare into his eyes. "W-we appreciate the information."

He took the wet breeches from her hands and placed them over the rope.

"We could use Colin's help as well." Ethan turned to Colin, giving her a chance to run her cold, damp hand over her heated face. Mercy. The man was a walking torch.

"What kind of help?" It would do the laddie good to work with men and see not all were as mean spirited at Mr. Miller, but she wasn't gonna let him go without a bit of sparring with Ethan. She had to keep their relationship at odds. It was the only way to keep from thinking he would be good in her bed.

"As the men build higher, we need more bodies to scramble up and down the structure with materials..."

"Ah'll no' have my child hangin' from a skeleton o' a buildin'!" The nerve of the man putting her only son in danger.

"You didn't let me finish." Ethan crossed his arms and stood toe to toe with her. The twinkle in his eye didn't escape her. He relished their squabbles as much as she.

"What's to finish? Ye said as much he'd be crawling up and down an unstable buildin'." She placed her hands on her hips and leaned forward just enough to get a whiff of his clean shaven face.

"Colin won't be climbing. He'll do the cleanup work on the ground." He didn't back up as she'd anticipated. Rather, the cheeky man leaned in as well.

"How much does it pay," Colin asked, stepping in and forcing them to take steps backwards.

Aileen pushed a stray strand of hair behind her ear as she scrutinized her son's bold behavior. Could he finally be comin' around to see Ethan wasn't a threat?

"Fifty cents a day. And that's for a day's work."

Colin's eyes grew round as he stared at Ethan then over to her. "Ma, I could help you in the mine after I come home from working at the mill."

"If we can haul the same buckets o' bing out o' the mine every day, ah'll no' stop yer from makin' a man's wage." She turned her gaze on Ethan. "But if my laddie is hurt, may the cat eat you and the devil eat the cat."

Ethan raised his hands in a show of surrender. "I promise, he'll only do cleanup. There isn't any way he could get hurt. And I'll keep an eye on him."

"When do ye want him to start?" They'd yet

to start in the mine today. She had hopes of getting enough dug to work the sluice the following day. If there were going to be wagons with more men coming through the area, she wanted to keep an eye on Shayla.

"Tomorrow." He tilted his head and listened. Muffled voices and the dull ring of hammers on rock could barely be heard. "When you hear the clank of the hammers on the rock in the morning, come on over."

The glow in Colin's eyes made her heart swell. It was time he moved about the adult world. She glanced up at Ethan. He was a good man to offer the job. He wouldn't let anything happen to the boy.

"Thank ye," she said, putting her gratitude into the words.

"He's helping me. It's hard to get help. The miners want to keep working their claims while the weather is good, and the farmers need to take care of their crops. Good labor is hard to come by."

She didn't miss his inflection of 'good'. He'd witnessed her son's work ethic.

"Laddie, go get started on the section in the mine we opened yesterday. We'll have to pull out more bing today to keep me busy while yer wor-kin'." Aileen smiled and nodded her head in the direction of the mine. Colin frowned. He knew she wanted him to leave. Even though he accepted the job, he still didn't like her to be alone with Ethan. She puzzled over this as he headed to the mine.

"He's a good boy." Ethan said, edging closer to Aileen. He didn't want her to think he gave her son a job to get in her good graces.

"That he is." Her light green eyes became misty. "He'll no' be a boy for much longer, though."

"No. That's why I offered him the job. My brothers and I discussed it after we left here the other day." He didn't miss the haughty way her head snapped around, and she peered at him down the length of her petite nose.

"And why be ye discussin' my laddie with yer brothers?" The fire in her eyes and the flush of her cheeks excited him. She was a lioness when it came to her children.

"We were discussing the fact Colin needs to be around men folk."

"And what is wrong with a mother raising a boy?" Her indignation expanded her chest, pushing the buttons on her shirt to their limit. Her ample breasts thrust toward him. He stifled a groan.

"There's nothing wrong with you raising him. But he's getting to the age where he needs to work with men and see anger doesn't make you a man." He knew that wasn't the real reason behind Colin's anger, but it was a start. Whether it stemmed from the abuse he'd received from his stepfather or something else, he and his brothers talked it over and decided they were all going to take on the job of teaching him how to handle the anger and put it to good use. They were not only doing the boy a favor but the community too. They didn't need a hothead growing up and causing trouble.

The color drained from her face. Ethan took two quick steps and placed a hand on her arm. She flinched, but he didn't drop his hand.

"I will never hurt you," he said softly, moving his hand up and down her arm in a caress.

She glanced at his hand, then up into his eyes. The desire he saw nearly had him pulling her into his arms. He ached to hold her. The pain she must have received from her last husband still lingered in her eyes, but shining through the dullness was the heat of a woman wanting a man's arms around her.

Clearing his throat, Ethan dropped his hand and backed up. He couldn't afford a woman and her children right now. Hell, he didn't know how to treat a woman other than at a distance as a friend.

"Remember to let me know if you have any troubles. I'll see Colin first thing in the morning." He spun on his heel and ran into Shayla.

"Bye," she said, handing him a disfigured wild-flower with pink petals. Her infectious grin and offering melted the resolve he'd made to stay away from her family.

"Bye, take care of your ma." He ruffled her hair and headed back to the mill site. Before he turned the bend, he looked back. Aileen stood where he'd left her. A smile slowly formed on her lips, the color of the flower Shayla handed him.

He smiled back and waved slightly before ducking around the bend. He'd spent the past three days working from daylight to dusk alongside the men he'd hired. He fell into bed exhausted, but Aileen's angel-kissed face, sparkling, light green eyes, and teasing smile haunted him until he'd fall into a fitful sleep and wake wringing wet with sweat, wanting her.

In all his adult life, he'd never craved a woman and now was not the time to start. Especially with this one.

Colin arrived every morning as the first hammers rang up the valley. The first day, Ethan introduced him to the men and set him to work cleaning up the pieces of lumber littering the work area. By the third day the boy proved he wasn't a slacker having cleaned up the area and learned how to whittle the pegs used to put the frame together.

Ethan bent over a post, boring a hole, when he spotted Shayla enter the structure. He sprinted to stop her advance, but she stood in the middle of the framed building— a look of amazement on her face.

A shout rang out as a board fell. It landed on end and flipped, cracking her in the head. Her small body crumpled to the ground.

"Shayla!" Ethan yelled her name and knelt on the ground beside her. The blood staining her dark hair curdled his stomach.

Colin dropped beside him, tears shining in his eyes. "Why did she come here?" he wailed.

"I don't know. Let's get her to your ma." Ethan gently cradled the child in his arms. When he stood, he noticed all the concerned faces gathered around.

"Want me to get the doc?" Hank asked at his shoulder.

"There's no guarantee he'll even be in Baker City when you get there." Ethan looked down at the limp child in his arms. "Her ma should know what to do." He started at a brisk pace toward the curve in the stream.

"S-she isn't going to die, is she?" The fear in the boy's voice made Ethan hug the child closer.

"No. She just has a bad hit on the head. She'll be fine." *I hope.* The child in his arms had become as important to him as his own kin. The warm, loving girl couldn't die. He wouldn't let her.

"Shayla!" Aileen screeched when she spotted her darlin' lassie dangling from Ethan's arms like a rag doll. She ran toward them. "What happened?" Her hand smoothed the dark curls and became wet. She spied the blood and nearly crumpled. Colin put his arms around her. She forced her legs to straighten and follow Ethan. He carried her precious daughter into the shack, placing her on the small bed in the corner near the fireplace. Opposite the disgusting, smelly corner.

Ethan's nose wrinkled, and he scanned the tidy room.

She didn't want to answer his question and started in with her own.

"What happened?" She sat on the bed next to Shayla and began parting the hair where she bled.

"She walked into the structure before I could stop her. A board fell and hit her on the head." The agony in Ethan's voice drew her gaze to him. He blamed himself. Lordy, but this man took on more than most.

"Colin fetch me fresh clean water from the creek." When he hurried out the door, she glanced at Ethan. "Fetch me the white drawers hanging on the line outside." He obeyed as quick as Colin.

Alone with her daughter, Aileen leaned down to gently hug her darlin'. Why had she scampered off when her mother's back was turned? She'd been askin' since Colin started to work to go see him. Why hadn't she kept a better eye on the child?

Ethan entered with her newest pair of drawers. They weren't anything fancy, but they'd make the best dressing for the wound.

"Over there," she pointed to her mending basket sitting by the door, "in the basket are my trimmers." Ethan retrieved the item and handed them to her. She cut a square to use as a wash cloth and another to fold to put over the wound. Colin returned with the bucket of water.

"Cut strips long enough to tie around the lassie's head." She handed the trimmers and what was left of the drawers to Ethan. She immersed the square in water and worked at washing the blood away from the wound. At the sight of the small gash, she breathed a sigh of relief.

"Tis a wee cut." Her stomach stopped churning now that she knew the gash would not require stitches. Aileen folded the other square, placed it on the wound, and wrapped another around the child's head and tied it snug.

She leaned down. Her daughter's breath puffed against her cheek. Her color was pale, but her breathing strong.

"All we can do now is wait." She grasped Shayla's hand, held it in her lap, and peered up at the man and boy staring at the unconscious child.

Colin touched Ethan's arm. "Do I have to go back to work?"

"No. We'll stay here and take turns sitting with Shayla." Ethan took his hat off and placed it on the peg by the door.

"There's no need for ye to miss work."

His gaze lingered on Shayla before it moved to her face. The regret in his eyes told her she'd not get rid of him very easy.

"I'll stay here and wait. You'll need a break." He went out the door and returned with two chairs. He handed one to Colin and placed the other one by the table.

His presence gave her strength. Even Colin didn't stare at him with daggers in his eyes. She nodded and smoothed a wayward curl from Shayla's eyes.

Once she'd waited for a cousin to awake from a blow. She glanced at Colin. His brow furrowed in worry and concern etched his face. How many times had he waited for her to wake after Mr. Miller beat her? Three? Four? His face was always the first thing she saw when she woke.

Ethan cleared his throat. "Colin bring in some more wood. We'll see about making tea for your ma and some broth for Shayla when she wakes up." He nodded to the door. The stiffness and keen attention the boy paid to his sister proved this wasn't the first time he'd waited for someone to come around. He had a strong hunch the other times had been Aileen.

The boy glanced at his mother, she nodded, and he left the shack.

"Thank you," she whispered. Her light green eyes were dull with sorrow. He wanted to draw her into his arms and soothe away her worries.

"He's waited for you to wake hasn't he?" He didn't believe she'd talk about it, but he had to know.

"Colin was the first face I saw each time that monster beat me." The hatred in her voice should have offended, but it merely made him hate a dead man even more.

Colin entered with an armload of wood. Ethan started a fire in the fireplace with the glowing coals from the morning meal. He handed the boy the bucket of bloody water. "Dump this out and bring in fresh so we can start water for tea and the broth."

He found a small pot to boil water for tea and a larger one to use for the broth. "What do you have to make broth?"

"Are ye a cook as well as a miner?" The wobble in her voice did nothing to soothe the change of subject.

"After our parents died, we had to learn to cook to survive. I can make coffee, tea, and stew. Hank does the baking, Clay can make a hot cake that melts in your mouth, and Zeke can eat." He laughed at the memory of Myrle teaching them to cook.

"That's only four. What about the fifth brother?" She sat on the bed next to Shayla, but he'd drawn her out of her worry for a minute.

"Gil took off shortly after our parents were killed. He had the foolish notion it was all his fault. He was about Colin's age when the Indians killed Ma, Pa, and our youngest brother. Gil had been out goofing around. When he returned and found them dead, he blamed himself." Ethan shrugged. He and his brothers tried to find him, without any luck. When he rode back into their lives it healed the grief none of them had realized still lurked.

"He came home two years ago along with a wife. He's the marshal of Galena." He smiled. Gil had found his match in Darcy, his independent wife.

"It sounds like you have a nice family." He caught the wistfulness in her voice.

"Do you have any family? Other than Colin and Shayla?" He hoped to find out more about the woman.

"Ah believe cousins and the like still live in the Highlands and some in Ireland." The wistfulness disappeared, replaced by anger.

"Highlands?"

"Of Scotland. My family was o' the clan Mac-Corrie in some o' the finest Highland country. When the lords brought in sheep, they forced us off our land. My father took us to Ireland to live with a cousin." Her eyes became misty. "Twas there ah met Colin's da, Patrick O'Lear."

Jealousy hit him in the chest. The woman still loved her first husband. It was evident in the breathy way she said his name and the softening of her eyes.

"What happened to Patrick?" His suspicious nature started to rear.

"Tis no' for yer concern." She swiped at the tears on her cheek and turned her attention to putting more covers over Shayla.

Colin entered the shack with the water. Ethan set about filling the pots. "What meat do you have hanging in the lean-to?" he asked.

The boy looked toward his mother. "Ma and I aren't much good at bringing down game."

"Do you have a rifle?" Ethan had noticed no

weapon hung above the door.

"Just an old thing we keep at the entrance to the mine."

No wonder they were so protective of their privacy, they didn't have a way to protect themselves.

"I'm going to get a rifle from Clay. Then you and I are going to get this family some meat." Ethan reached out to pluck his hat from the peg by the door.

"That isn't necessary." Aileen stood. Her back stiffened, and her shoulders squared.

"Shayla needs proper food if she's going to get stronger." He wasn't going to argue with the woman. This time she would have to eat her pride.

Chapter 10

"How's the girl?" Hank asked when Ethan walked up to him.

"Still unconscious. I'm going to borrow your rifle," Ethan said to Clay as he walked up beside them.

"You're not back here to work?" The censure in Clay's voice rankled. The Miller family needed him more than the men working on the mill.

"Not until Shayla wakes up."

"Then what are you doing here? Shouldn't you be holding that woman's hand?" Clay's derogatory remark and Hank's silence made Ethan grit his teeth.

"She doesn't need her hand held, but they need meat. Shayla should have proper food to eat." Ethan crossed his arms waiting for the accusations.

"Since when did some widow and her family take priority over your family?" Clay stepped closer, poking him in the chest.

Hank pulled Clay out of his reach. "You're the

top man on this job. You can't just leave and expect things to keep going." Hank crossed his arms, taking a stance similar to Ethan's.

"I can leave whenever I want. You two are capable of getting this mill built. Besides it will only be for a day, no different than if I went off buying supplies. And you know where to find me if you have questions." He strode to Clay's horse. The brunt of their glares burned into his back. His brothers could share more of the responsibility on this project. After all, they would profit just as much from the mill as anyone else.

He pulled the rifle from the scabbard, gave Hank a nod, and headed back toward the Miller shack.

His first glance of the rundown building when he rounded the arm of the mountain made him shiver. How could the three live like they did? No meat, poor cooking and heating conditions, and the stench. He'd have to ask Aileen—no he'd ask Colin about the odor while they hunted.

He set the rifle against the side of the doorway and knocked. The door shook like woven cloth rather than wood.

"Aye."

He entered the building. The whole thing needed shore up, new roof, and more room. The narrow path between the beds, table, and fireplace were fine for the occupants, but he had to place his large feet creatively to not kick something.

Aileen measured tea into a small, clay pot. She glanced up, her eyebrow raised at his empty hands.

"I left the gun outside. Is she any better?"

The woman shook her head.

He turned to Colin. "You ready?"

"I'm not leaving Ma and Shayla." A stubborn glower darkened his face.

"I'm going to show you how to get meat. They'll be fine. Shayla isn't going to wake up any sooner with you here."

"Go, Mr. Halsey is tryin' to help ye become a man." Aileen squeezed her son's shoulders and mouthed the word thank you over his head.

The boy shook off her hands and stomped to the door. The anxiety darkening her face as she watched the boy was unwarranted. Shayla needed all of her strength right now. Ethan shrugged and winked at Aileen.

The woman blushed and turned back to the steeping tea.

"Put some water to boiling. We'll have venison to toss in when we come back." Ethan wanted to cross the room and give her a comforting hug, but he still wasn't sure she wouldn't follow through on her threat to castrate him. Instead, he opened the door and motioned for Colin to exit in front of him.

"Will ye be back afore dark?" The worry lines furrowing her brow started his feet toward her. He squeezed past the table before she took a step back. Slow. He had to move slow and easy around her.

"I know where a small herd hangs out just over the top of the ridge. We'll be back before dark." He had to touch her. His fingers tingled with the urge. He cupped his hand and gradually raised it until he cradled her cheek in his palm. His fingers entwined in the wayward strands of her soft hair.

"Shayla's going to be fine." The words came

out on a released breath. Aileen didn't back away. His heart hammered in his chest as she nuzzled her cheek against his palm.

"I thought we were goin' hunting?" Colin's angry retort sucked the small moment of joy out of the room.

Aileen stepped back, and Ethan spun on his heels. The touch had fulfilled him more than any of the times he'd held a prostitute. He didn't look back, just ducked out the door and captured the rifle without stopping.

He trudged up the slope, ignoring the branch snapping behind him as Colin huffed to keep up. When they topped the ridge, he held a finger to his lips and moved along the ridgeline toward the ravine where he'd observed a small herd of deer the past week.

Ethan caught sight of the herd and raised his rifle. A tug on his shirt drew his attention from the animals to the young man still seething behind him.

"I don't want you touching my ma." Colin's hands fisted at his hips. His chest heaved from the climb and his agitated state.

"I would never hurt your ma, or Shayla, or you" Ethan whispered and walked back the way they'd come. He didn't want this discussion to scare the deer. He'd promised Aileen they'd be back before dark and didn't plan to waste time hunting for another herd.

"Mr. Miller was all nice at first. But it didn't last." Colin scanned the length of him. "And you're a lot bigger."

"Son—"

"I'm not your son!" The boy spit the words out as if they soured his tongue. "He'd call me that—son, like he couldn't remember my name. Then he'd…" The boy's face turned crimson and contorted.

Ethan's heart lurched.

"Colin, I don't know how I can make it any plainer. I won't hurt any of your family. I don't believe in hitting women and children." He sat on a fallen tree. The act put him a couple inches shorter than the standing boy. "You can ask my brothers and anyone in Sumpter. I've never laid a hand on anyone other than men who needed straightening out 'cause they were liquored up."

"Do you like whiskey?" The words rang more like an accusation than a question.

"On occasion, I've had a drink or two, never to the point I didn't know what I was doing." He grinned. "Not every man turns mean with liquor. I don't."

"I still don't like you touchin' Ma." The boy's stance wasn't as rigid, but he remained defensive.

"How about we let her decide if she wants me to touch her?"

Colin shook his head.

"She's a smart woman. One of the smartest I've come across. I think she can make the decision." He stood. "Let's get that deer and get back to see if Shayla's awake."

He snuck over the ridge with a quieter, stealthier young man following him.

Aileen's thoughts bubbled like the pot of water

she'd put on the fire. They bounced between fear for her lassie and the emotions Ethan Halsey had unburied. She sat in a chair pulled up to the small, rumpled bed where Shayla lay as still as death. She checked the fluttering rise and fall of her child's chest, the shallow wisps of breath that touched the back of her hand. The only signs that showed her darlin' still lived.

After Ethan and Colin left, she'd shed tears and asked God not to take her angel just yet. She needed her daughter to keep her days bright.

Memories of the heat of Ethan's hand on her cheek, warmed her body clear to her toes. When Patrick died, she believed no man could move her as he. Ethan's touch had proved her wrong and relit a fire she'd thought Mr. Miller had snuffed out forever. Did she dare let the man close? The monster she'd married hoping for a better life in America had been nice at first, but after he realized she still loved a dead man, he'd gone deeper into the bottle. He'd been a mean, vulgar drunk. She'd preferred the beatings to the taking of her body. Aileen shuddered.

The door opened. Colin walked in holding a piece of fresh venison the size of his head. The grin on his face melted her heart. He hadn't smiled like that in years. The accomplishment in his eyes and the turned up corners of his mouth made her heart sing with joy.

"Looks like my man brought us some dinner," she said, standing and peering past him to the one she owed more than she'd ever be able to repay. Ethan stood at the door, hat in hand, a shy smile tweaking his lips.

"She awake?" he asked in a hopeful whisper. Aileen shook her head.

Colin started to put the meat down on the uncovered wood table. Aileen hurried to stop him.

"Nae. If ye plan to bring home meat ye need to know better than to put it on the table," she scolded, grabbing an old plank she used as a cutting board. Scanning the small crock that held her cooking utensils, she couldn't find her knife.

Ethan nudged her aside. "We'll take care of this. You tend Shayla." He produced a long-bladed knife and deftly cut the meat into bite size chunks before sliding them into the boiling pot.

"Ah dinnae know what to do with the two o' ye waitin' on me." She sat in the chair beside the bed and stared at Shayla. She spoke the truth. Never in her adult life had someone taken the time to see she did nothing. Her marriage to Patrick had been full of love, but he worked long hours and fought to keep their land. It had fallen on her to keep the household going and take care of Colin. Then with Mr. Miller, she and Colin worked the mine as well as took care of the house and cooking. After his death, there was even more work.

Nae, she'd not had a soul care whether she had a moment's rest in fourteen years. She glanced over her shoulder at the man giving her this luxury. He winked and went about adding things to the pot and wood to the fire.

The heat from the cooking made the stench stronger. Though she lived in it for six years, she still couldn't stomach it.

"Open the window," she said to Colin, hoping fresh air would fill the room.

"What is that smell?" Ethan asked, opening the door as well.

The resentment she harbored for Mr. Miller emerged at the thought of their battles over his use of the corner.

"When Mr. Miller was drunk and rebellious, he would pee in that corner." She pointed to the empty corner to the left of the fireplace. "Ah've tried everything ah know to take away the smell, but ah can't."

"Colin, bring me buckets and a shovel." Ethan moved furniture to one side of the room to make a narrow path from the corner to the door. He'd dig all night if it would get the stench out of the shack. Scent played a large part in memories. Whenever he caught a whiff of cinnamon, memories of happy Christmases with his parents and brothers blanketed him. No doubt the vile smell of Mr. Miller's urine held bad memories for the mother and son.

Colin returned with two buckets and a shovel. Ethan went to work digging an area nearly three feet from both walls. The boy dumped one bucket while he filled the other. By the time the stew was ready to eat, he'd made a hole three feet deep.

"Does it smell any better to you?" he asked Aileen.

She nodded. "Ye dinnae have to do this." Her objection was flimsy and he smiled. He did have to do this. Any time he could help this family his chest expanded with pride.

"Do you have any ashes?" he asked, stepping out of the hole.

"Laddie, fetch Mr. Halsey the bucket o' ashes ah was savin' to make soap." When the boy headed out the door, she stood, stepping next to him.

"Mr—"

"Ethan. Call me Ethan when it's just the two of us." He wanted to push back the hair sliding onto her cheek, but refrained. He'd been fortunate to touch her once already.

"Ethan. Ye really dinnae have to do this, but we appreciate yer hard work." Her gaze skimmed over his face as if she searched for something.

"I know the power of bad memories," he whispered as Colin banged through the door.

The shock on her face before she stepped out of the way, proved his point. The smell was a constant reminder of the pain the man inflicted on her.

Ethan took the bucket and poured the ashes in the hole. "I'll fill that with clean dirt tomorrow." He glanced at the bubbling stew. "I'll clean up, and we can eat."

Aileen nodded. He gathered the buckets and shovel, leaving the small confines. The cool evening air swirled around his sticky body. He inhaled deep, filling his lungs. How could they have lived in that stench? He dropped all but one bucket and headed to the creek to wash off the dirt, the sweat, and hopefully some of the smell.

Now he knew why they ate outside the first day he arrived. But what had they done in the winter?

He stripped off his shirt and scrubbed the sweat from his body and the dirt from his arms. With the bucket, he poured icy water over his head and growled at the prickling of his skin. He grew up bathing in the snow-melt creeks. The cold invigorated even as his skin numbed from the exposure.

This was the same body-numbing water the Miller's took baths in. The thought of Aileen walking into the pool around the bend, brought his body to life. He doused his head with another bucket of icy water and stood, shaking like a dog. That kind of thought would get him nowhere. He had to remain neutral if he wanted to further his family's future.

He grabbed his shirt and spun to head back to the shack. One arm raised as he slipped it into his shirt. Aileen stood not four steps from him watching. Her eyes widened, no doubt, due to his bare chest. In the summer he didn't wear the long underdrawers. They were too hot.

Aileen had come out to thank Ethan and as-sure him that once he ate, there was no reason for him to stay. At the sight of his wide, muscular chest covered in brown, curly hair that v'ed into a line down his rippled stomach and disappeared into the waistband of his trousers, she couldn't find her voice. It took all her concentration to keep from reaching out and testing the hardness of his muscles.

"Did you need to talk to me?" He slid his other arm in the sleeve and started buttoning his shirt.

She shook her head to clear the improper thoughts.

"You didn't want to say anything?"

"Nae, ah mean aye, ah wanted to say some-thing." She wrung her hands. She was a grown woman who'd had two husbands. Why did this man reduce her into a young, tongue-tied girl?

"After ye eat, it would be best if ye traveled on home." She raised a hand when he started to protest. "There's nothin' ye can do. The lassie will wake when she wakes and ye bein' here won't make it happen any sooner."

"I'm not just staying for the child." He took a step.

Her actions earlier in the day had been wrong. She'd thought it over. She'd given him the impression he interested her. He didn't. Or rather shouldn't. But her legs wouldn't move, wouldn't carry her away from him.

"Ma! She's awake!" Colin's happy voice jerked her from her trance. She spun around and ran to the house. She gripped the doorway and peered at the small bed. Shayla's big, beautiful eyes stared at her. They weren't bright, but a wisp of a smile curved her small mouth. Aileen's heart raced in her chest. A sigh of relief whispered through her lips.

"Lassie, tis good to see yer sweet eyes!" She crossed the room, sinking to her knees beside the bed. She captured her daughter's hand and kissed the small fingers.

"My head hurts, Momma," Shayla whispered.

"Ah know darlin'. Ye were hit on the head by a board. Just rest, we'll no' leave ye." Aileen glanced up as Ethan entered the shack.

"How is she?" He stood behind her. The heat from his legs seared her back.

"She says her head be hurtin'."

"That's normal. You'll need to watch her for vomiting." He reached over her. His shirt grazed her head as he smoothed a curl off Shayla's forehead. "You rest sweetheart, and do what your ma tells you."

He straightened and dropped a hand on her shoulder. "I'm going to head home now that I know she's come around."

The comforting pressure of his hand and the soft words melted her resolve to stay aloof to the man.

"Ye can't head for home without somethin' in yer belly." She stood. He was so close, she noticed the small specks of gold in his brown eyes.

"I should head home..." his gaze drifted to her mouth and back up to her eyes.

"Ye can't leave without tastin' yer own stew." She brushed past him and filled a tin plate with the wonderful smelling food in the pot.

The chair creaked as he settled his body onto it. She turned from the fireplace, set the plate in front of him, and handed him a fork.

Their fingers touched. The connection ricocheted heat up her arm and straight to her center. She jumped back, clutching her hand tight against her body. The distress in Ethan's eyes didn't smother the fire his touch ignited.

Colin squeezed around her to fill his own plate. He plopped the plate on the table and his backside in the chair opposite Ethan. As the laddie fell upon his food with gusto, she dished her own plate. She took a seat in the chair to the right of the man who had, in one day, started crumbling all her objections to having a man around.

Ethan shoved his finished plate to the middle of the table and leaned back in his chair. His knee bumped hers. Startled by the contact when her nerves hadn't settled from the previous touch, she almost shot to her feet.

"Ma, what's wrong?" Colin watched her warily before he glanced at Ethan.

"Nothin'." She couldn't look at the man beside her, unsure if he'd touched her on purpose or by accident.

"Thank you for the meal, but I'd best head for home. I'm sure Hank and Clay are wondering how Shayla is doing." Ethan slid his chair back and stood. He towered over the table. His size didn't induce the terror that had surrounded Mr. Miller.

"We're the ones should be thankin' ye. For carrying Shayla home, bringing us meat, and," she darted a glance at the hole in the corner, "for cleanin' our home."

He walked to the door, plucked his hat from the peg, and turned back to scan first Shayla resting in the bed, and Colin, before his gaze rested on her face. "All any of you has to do is ask, and I'll help you all I can."

"Why?" Her question came out on a whoosh of air, more breathy than she'd planned. The spark of desire in his eyes sent her heart racing, conjuring up thoughts better left alone.

"Because, no matter what other people say, you're good people."

Chapter 11

Ethan arrived at his cabin near midnight. He entered, hoping Hank and Clay were sound asleep. The low flame of the kerosene lamp in the middle of the table barely cast a yellow glow beyond the flat surface. He hooked his hat on one of the empty pegs by the door and sat on his bed.

Before his first boot hit the floor, Hank sat up and swung his legs over the edge.

"Surprised to see you."

"You left the light on." Ethan dropped the other boot to the floor.

"That was Clay's idea. He figured you'd feel bad if you came home and found the lamp burned all night." Hank ran a hand through his already tousled hair.

"Doesn't bother me." Ethan stood to drop his britches to the floor.

"Did the little girl come around?"

"Yeah. She woke up just a little bit before I headed home. She's got a headache, and her eyes weren't too bright, but I think she'll come out okay." Knowing how much the mother loved her daughter, she had to come out fine.

"Did you find out why she was at the mill?" He didn't miss the accusation in his brother's voice.

"No, she was too weak to ask any questions."

"You could have asked the mother." Hank rose off the bed and headed to the stove in his long-johns. His bare feet scuffed across the smooth, wood floor.

"I didn't have a chance to bring it up." He shrugged his tired shoulders. He'd dug a fair-sized hole in the dirt floor of that pitiful place they called home.

"You were there all afternoon and evening. How could you not find time to ask?" Clay rolled to his side, resting his head on his bent arm.

"I was busy. That place is falling down around them. I can't believe they haven't taken sick during the winter." He moved to the stove and poured a cup a coffee.

"They're none of our business other than what you agreed to in the contract." Clay sat up and stalked to the table. Annoyance aged his face, making it more callous in the faint light of the kerosene lamp.

Ethan stared at one brother and then the other. "Do you think Ma and Pa would have turned their backs on a family in need?" When they both averted their faces, he raised the cup, "I didn't think so." He sipped the bitter brew. "Sheesh! How long has this been cooking?"

"Since this morning." Clay shook his head.

"We can't take on their problems. Getting this mill running and still working the mine is going to take all our efforts." He stared directly at Ethan. "We can't have one of us running off whenever the mood strikes."

Ethan surged out of the chair and paced the room. "If that girl had died, what do you think would have happened to all the money we've sunk into that mill so far?" He stopped, placed his hands on the table, and leaned down to peer into his brothers' faces. "Well, what do you think would happen?" When they didn't answer he continued. "I know. Aileen would have blamed us for the death and most likely have found a way to remove us from her property."

He slid back into the chair. "And I wouldn't have blamed her a bit. I made deals with her no sane businessman would make to get what we want. A stamp mill. Helping this family helps us. The more she gets from us the happier she will be." He leaned forward. "And we'll get the stamp mill and the profits to provide for our family."

"So you aren't doing all these favors for the Widow Miller because you're getting attached?" Clay stared into the coffee cup he casually spun on the table in front of him.

"I'd be lying if I said all three of them haven't affected me in some way. The boy because he needs guidance to become a good man and not a menace, the little girl because she is innocent and loving, and the mother—" He didn't have words to describe the feelings Aileen had lit in him. "Because she's had a rotten past and thinks poorly of all men."

"Even you?" Hank's intent gaze didn't bother him.

"She's slowly believing I don't plan to harm her. Once she and the boy fully believe it, I won't have to spend so much time with them." Ethan glanced into the cup of bitter coffee. The thought of staying away from the family tweaked at his conscience. They needed him— more than his own family.

"Right," Clay scoffed and headed back to his bed.

"What's that mean?" Ethan spun on the chair to face his brother.

"That you're smitten with that husband killer. Ethan, it isn't good for you to be spending so much time with her and them kids."

"She isn't a husband killer, and I can spend my time wherever I want." Ethan surged out of his chair and stepped in front of Clay. "You'd best get used to the idea of me taking care of that family. And to stop calling Aileen a husband killer."

He turned to Hank. "Is there talk going on among the workers?"

"Only when that fool Miles shows up." Hank shot a glance to Clay.

"And you're egging him on aren't you?" Ethan turned to Clay. "I don't want gossip giving any of the workers cause to go visiting the Millers. If I find out you and Miles started anything, you'll both answer to me."

Clay flung his body onto his bed, Hank blew out the lamp, and Ethan stalked to his bed. How was he to help Aileen and the children when his own flesh and blood were so prejudiced against them? He knew one thing for certain. He needed a plan to get them into a new cabin. With her pride and that boy's resentment, it was going to have to be a doozy of a plan.

Aileen patted her hair and glanced at Shayla before answering the door.

"How is she?" Ethan asked, holding his hat in his hand and scanning her face.

"Awake, but her words are slow." When her darlin' woke that morning, she asked for the happy man. But the way the words slurred out of her mouth made it hard for Aileen to smile and say she was sure he'd show up some time today. She now wondered if they should send for a doctor even though he wouldn't get here till the wee hours of the night.

Ethan nodded his head. "That can happen sometimes when a person receives a hit to the head." He smiled and entered the cabin, closing the door behind him. He glanced about the room, then reached out to her face. "You didn't sleep well." He gently traced the hollow under her eye with his thumb. The tenderness brought tears.

"Shhh... Don't cry." He stepped forward, drawing her into his strong arms.

How wonderful to be wrapped in his strength and warmth. His firm, broad chest was solid under her hands. She tried to stop the tears, but the ordeal of the day before and the long night watching her daughter toss and turn had taken a toll.

"She'll be fine. She's young. Her speech will come back, and she'll be her old self." His voice rumbled in the chest vibrating under her ear. The sound reminded her of listening to her father talk with his brothers when she was child tucked away warm in her bed in Scotland.

With her arms folded in between their bodies, she didn't have to fear they would wind around his solid form and give him cause to think she wanted his advances.

The rattle of the door latch brought her to her senses, and she pushed away. Colin couldn't find her in this man's arms. No telling how the boy would react.

"Thank ye for yer concern." She dried her face and turned to the table, straightening the bowl of porridge and spoon set out for Colin's breakfast.

"Any time you need to talk. I'm here." Ethan's softly spoken offer made her insides flutter. He walked to the bed and sat in the chair she'd occupied all night.

"How's my girl?" he asked, ruffling the hair above the white bandage wrapped around the child's head.

Colin stood in the doorway, a bucket of dirt in each hand. "What are you doing here?" he accused, moving to the hole in the corner of the shack and dumping the buckets.

"I came to check on your sister and help fill in that hole. I can miss work, you can't." Ethan stood, took the buckets from the boy, and nodded to the table. "Eat your food so you can give me a decent day's work."

Aileen started to rebuke the man for his harsh words, but when Colin sat in the chair and started wolfing down the porridge, she held her tongue.

As a man with four brothers, maybe he knew how to handle the boy.

Ethan winked at Aileen and headed out the door. She shook her head and smiled. She could get used to having him around. The thought stopped her cold. No man would come into this family. What made her emotions overrule her good sense? He was a man and sooner or later he would prove no different than Mr. Miller.

Sure he touched her with tenderness now, but that would soon end. Every man had a temper. Even her Patrick. He just took it out on his enemies. Never his wife and son. Where did Ethan Halsey take out his frustrations?

The man in her thoughts entered with two more buckets of dirt. He dumped the contents and tramped around in the hole, packing the dirt.

Colin pushed away from the table. "I'm headed to work, Ma." He plucked his hat from the corner of the table and stood. "Are you coming?" he asked Ethan.

"I'll be along as soon as I get this hole filled. Don't want your ma accidentally stepping in here and hurting herself."

Colin nodded and headed toward the door. He stopped and turned to Ethan. "'Member what we talked about yesterday?" he asked, his brows pulled into a scowl.

Aileen fisted her hands on her hips. "What did ye talk about yesterday?" What had the two of them cooked up?

"He knows." Colin didn't take his gaze from the man standing by her stove, his arms crossed in front of him, staring back at her son.

"I remember. Do you remember my answer?"

"What are ye two talkin' about?" Aileen stepped between the locked gazes. She stared at her stubborn laddie. His gaze dropped to the ground. She glanced over her shoulder at the man taking up the whole corner of her home. He shrugged.

"It's up to the boy to tell you if he wants." Ethan unfolded his arms and started toward her. She stepped to the side. His body grazed hers as he sidled around her and out the door.

She thought her body was beyond being awakened by a man. She was wrong. Her nipples tingled, and her heart thrummed against her ribs. She cleared her throat and glanced at her son.

"I'm going to work. Don't let him get so close to you," he admonished and darted out the door.

What had the boy and Ethan discussed about her yesterday? She picked up the cooled bowl of porridge for Shayla and sat on the chair next to her bed.

"M-m-momma. W-w-why ar-r-e y-you f-f-frowning?" Shayla asked as she held a spoon of food to her daughter's lips.

"It seems yer brother and Mr. Halsey have been talkin' about me."

"Only good things." Ethan's voice made her nearly jam the spoon into Shayla's nose.

"How dare ye sneak up on me?" She cleaned the porridge from her child's face not daring to turn and see his expression.

"I wasn't sneaking. You know I'm filling in this hole." He crossed the room and dumped the buckets.

"What was me laddie referring to earlier?" Aileen watched him turn from his task. His dark eyes sought hers. The connection took her breath away.

"Do you really want to know?" His deep voice sent tremors through her body. What would she do if that same voice whispered sweetness as they— She shook her head. Her thoughts wouldn't go there. Not with this man or any man.

"Aye, ah would prefer ye and my laddie dinnae talk about me."

"Your son told me to keep my hands off of you." He strode over to stand beside the chair. She had to crane her neck to gaze up his long length and see the heat in his eyes. "Do you want me to keep my hands off?" The words floated from his lips like a caress. Her skin tingled.

"Aye," she said even as her head shook the opposite. Buggar. Her traitorous body was going to get her in trouble.

The sly smile on his full lips sent tendrils of heat coursing through her at the same time it lit her temper.

"The laddie speaks true. Ye'll be keepin' yer hands to yerself." She shot to her feet. The minute she stopped, she realized the disaster of the situation. His taunting lips and soul-seeking eyes were much closer.

She stepped to the side, knocking her leg into the bed and toppling toward Shayla. Strong hands grasped her waist, turned her, and pulled her away from the bed, settling her body firmly against his.

His leg nestled between hers. The pulsing at the juncture of her legs had her biting her lip. She was too old to feel—this.

She pushed against him. He let go and backed away, ducking his head, hiding his face. Before she could think straight, he grabbed the buckets and disappeared out the door.

"M-momma?" Shayla's weak voice called from the bed.

"Ah'm here darlin'." Aileen melted onto the chair and turned her attention to her daughter. She had to stop touching Ethan. Each time his fingers touched or his voice caressed, her commitment to keep her distance from men wavered.

Ethan dipped his hat in the creek and dumped the contents on his head. What was he thinking grabbing Aileen's ripe body every time he had the chance? Not only did it make her uncomfortable, it made him randy as a jackrabbit.

He'd best get that hole filled and get back to the mill. The longer he hung out here the more chance there was he'd end up touching her again. Not that he didn't want to. Her lush body and rounded curves welcomed a man. Not to mention her seductive voice.

Damn! He jammed the shovel into the dirt and filled the buckets. Bent over to pick up the full pails, he caught sight of someone rounding the bend from the mill. He stopped, set the buckets down, and waited for Hank to come to him.

"When are you going to come to the mill?" His gaze wandered to the shack behind Ethan.

"As soon as I get a hole in there filled," He nodded to the house.

"You should have let the boy stay home and do

that. You're needed at the site."

"The boy needs to be around grown men who treat him decent." He tipped his head and studied his brother. "You are treating him decent?"

"Hell, yes. You know I wouldn't take nothin' out on a kid!" Hank pointed a finger at Ethan's chest. "Stop making Clay and I out to be the bad guys. We feel for this family, but that don't mean we intend to see you forget your priorities."

"I'm not forgetting my priorities. I've only missed being over there yesterday afternoon and this morning." Ethan picked up the buckets. "I should only be a half hour more. Go back and make sure everyone is doing their job." He headed to the shack.

When he reached the door, he looked back and found Hank in the same spot, watching him. He shook his head and bumped the flimsy wood with his bucket before pushing the door open and entering. This time he wouldn't barge on through like earlier and startle Aileen. He'd witnessed what she did to poor Shayla's face.

The child sat up in her bed. Her color looked better. "That's the way I like to see you. Sitting up and smiling." He sent the girl a warm smile and hurried to the corner to dump the dirt.

"Ah saw yer brother out there. If yer needed at the mill, go. Ah can finish." Aileen didn't look at him. She remained bent over the table cutting more bandages from the same pair of drawers she'd used the day before.

"I'm just about finished." He wanted to go to her and tell her it was okay to let him touch her, but he also knew the more he touched the more he'd want. She'd made it clear, she wasn't giving any man what he would eventually want from her, and he'd not take it unless she gave her consent.

Without another glance her way, he exited and filled the buckets. He worked steady, filling buckets, carrying them in and dumping them until he'd tamped the hole solid and level.

"I'm done," he stated when she didn't look up after his last trip into the shack.

She nodded her head. "Let the boy come home for his noon meal."

"I will." He stood in the middle of the room, unsure how to proceed. He wanted to tell her he'd be by that evening, but wondered if just stopping by might be the better action to take.

"Bye, Shayla." Ethan crossed the room, avoiding any contact with the woman and squeezed the child's hand. "I'll come by and check on you this evening."

Her eyes lit up and she smiled. "T-t-thank you."

The fragile child pulled at his heart. He sank down on his knees beside the bed and hugged her small body. "I've done nothing. Get well, I have a book I want to read to you." Her young eyes sparkled with interest.

"W-w-what is it?"

"It's a surprise. Now rest so you get well." He kissed the top of her head and stood. Turning from the bed, he caught a glimpse of the tears trickling down Aileen's face before she swung away from him.

Without thinking, he pulled her into his arms. "What's wrong?" he crooned, rubbing a hand up and down her back as he held her head against his shoulder. Consoling his brothers over the years had been automatic. Holding and consoling this woman brought his body to life and made his existence more valid.

"Ye dinnae have to promise the lassie anything." She raised her head and looked him in the eyes.

"No, I didn't. But I wanted to. I have a book I enjoyed as a child. I thought I'd bring it over on Sunday and read it to Shayla."

Her body stiffened, and her eyes became wary as she pushed to escape his embrace.

He let her go. She wouldn't come to his arms willingly if he didn't let her escape on her terms. And he wanted her in his arms. He was determined to prove to her not all men beat on women like her late husband.

"How would that look, yer comin' to our house on a Sunday and spending time?" She backed away, her posture lengthening, her jaw set in a hard line.

A smiled tugged at his lips. Her indignation at the prospect of gossip about them tickled. "What do you think they're saying at the site, knowing I was here yesterday and now this morning?"

The horror on her face was more than he could stand. He crossed the dirt floor to capture her hands. "This is actually to your benefit. If they think we're—no one will want to anger the boss by stepping on my territory."

She yanked her hands from his. "Ah'm no' territory or property. We are no' married and ye do no' own me! Nae one will ever own me again!"

Her voice shook with anger. Did he hear a hint of disappointment too?

"What are you disappointed about? Me, or the fact you won't let someone into your life?"

She glared at him and took a deep breath. "Ah'm disappointed in ye thinkin' ah would go along with this tale. Or anyone else. Take a look around. At me. Everyone would be laughin' thinkin' ye would want to be bundled with the likes o' us. Tis ye who are foolin' yerself."

He brushed a knuckle down her angel-kissed cheek. "Aileen, you are still a beautiful woman. Don't think so lightly of yourself." The surprise and desire that flashed briefly in her eyes told him more than her words.

Ethan stepped away before he did something they would both regret.

Chapter 12

Hunched over plans on the table, Ethan thought of the Millers. He'd stayed away from their shack the last few days. He still hadn't found out why Shayla had been at the site. On Sunday when he went over to read to her, he'd get the answer.

His plan was to get not only the girl hooked on reading, but also teach the boy. Colin would need more schooling if he were to become more than a laborer. With the intelligence Ethan had witnessed in the mother, the boy had to have a good head on his shoulders. He'd need to learn how to use it to make a living for his mother and sister.

Hank and Clay had gone to bed an hour earlier. He scanned the plan in front of him and penciled in a lean-to on the back. With the mill running it would be next to impossible to talk business. Another building to make the business transactions was necessary. The office would have living quarters. If he couldn't get Aileen to move in, Clay or Hank could use the house when they married.

He smiled.

The hard part would be convincing Aileen to move. She'd shown she had a head for business. He planned to make her in charge of the office. At first there would be little to do, and he could slowly train her.

Her stubborn pride would keep her in that filthy, falling down shack through the winter if he didn't hurry and get this built. He'd go to town tomorrow and talk with Fellowes about starting on the project.

Ethan ran a hand over the copy of Moby Dick sitting on the table. Memories of his mother reading to him plunged him into fond recollections. This story had sparked his interest in the power of words. He'd read every one of his mother's beloved books in the chest by his bed. He hoped to inspire Shayla and Colin with this story on Sunday and every Sunday after until he finished.

Once they became interested in the story, he'd teach the family to read. His chest warmed at the thought of bringing them the gift of letters and numbers.

"You still up?" Clay stood beside him. "What's that?" He grabbed the drawing before Ethan had a chance to stop him.

"Why are you drawing a house with one, two, three bedrooms?" Clay peered at him through narrowed eyes.

"We need an office for the mill. This will be the office." He pulled the paper from his nosey brother's grasp.

"That's not an office. That's a house. An office is one maybe two rooms." He plopped onto the chair next to Ethan. "You building a house for the Millers?"

"I'm building an office they can live in until they move on. I'll teach Aileen to do the figures. That way we can work in the mill and not have to pay for labor. She can run the office and live in the building as her wages." He'd thought this through. If he could convince her it was strictly business, she was bound to jump at the offer.

"What happens when they move on? That's what you said she'd do." Clay's scrutiny didn't surprise him.

"I'll move in or one of you if you've married by then." Ethan didn't like to think about the Miller's leaving. It was Aileen's plan. When she had enough money, she'd leave. He'd have to start asking more questions. Find out why she needed a large sum of money.

"So me and Hank got no say in this?" Clay leaned back in his chair. The hurt in his eyes and sullen expression were hard to ignore.

"I'm building it with my money."

"But it will draw you away from the mill." The accusation stung.

"Not like you think. I plan to put it across the creek on that flat expanse before the trees start."

"Where you can see the mill and the Millers' mine. I'd say this is being built for them and not you or any of us." Clay leaned forward, his forearms resting on the table. "Ethan quit kidding us and yourself. You're building this house for the Millers. Plain and simple."

Ethan shoved out of the chair and stood in front of the window. The moon carved a sliver of light in the dark sky. He was building it for the Millers. For Aileen. She deserved better than that shack. Deserved a life better than digging in an unventilated mine. He wanted to be the person who gave that to her. He wanted to see her laugh more and hurt less.

"Go to bed, Clay," he said, not turning from the window. His new-found attraction to the Widow Miller had him losing sleep and his brother's approval.

Saturday, he found John Fellowes shoving down an ample breakfast at Myrle's.

"Morning, Ethan," Myrle greeted him, smiling and pouring him a cup of coffee when he sat at the table with Fellowes.

"Morning, Myrle. I'll have what he's having." Ethan held out his hand across the table. "Morning, Fellowes. How's business?"

The man a few years older than Ethan wiped at his mustache then extended his hand. "A little slow. This time of year more people are pulling out than settlin' down."

"I've got a job for you. But I want it done by the end of October."

The man's eyes lit. "What's the job?"

"You heard I'm building a stamp mill?"

"Yeah, I figure you don't need me or you would have asked already." The man forked a large portion of fried potatoes into his mouth.

"I also need an office." When the man started

to say something Ethan raised his hand. "I could build a shack if I wanted that. I want this." He spread the drawings out on the table between them.

Fellowes whistled. "That's more than an office." He studied Ethan. "Looks to me like you're planning to get married."

"Married? Ethan why didn't you tell me?" Myrle placed his plate of food on the table in front of him and hugged his shoulders.

"I'm not getting married. I figure down the road when one of my brothers get married they can move in and run the office. I might as well have it built right the first time." He didn't miss the wisp of a smile and nod Myrle gave him. She knew. How?

"I'll take this and order up the lumber." Fellowes rolled up the drawing. "I take it you're building it near the stamp mill?"

"Yes. Come by this afternoon, and I'll show you where."

Fellowes wiped his mouth with his sleeve and pushed back from the table. "Delicious as always Myrle." He nodded to Ethan and left the establishment. The man hadn't cleared the chair before Myrle slipped onto it.

"Tell me the truth. Who you building that house for?" Her faded blue eyes danced with excitement.

"For my brothers. And until they get hitched, for the Millers. You happy you got that out of me?" He huffed and dived into the food getting cold in front of him.

She patted his arm. "It's the right thing. You'll

see." She left him to his food and his clenching gut. What would happen when people began to put two and two together? Especially when he moved the Millers into the house? He hoped like hell Hank and Clay changed their attitude by then. He'd need their support in this.

Aileen fidgeted worse than the lassie as they waited for Ethan to show up. He said Sunday, but hadn't specified morning or afternoon. Surely, he wouldn't think they'd go to church? The people of Sumpter would have a fit if they stepped into the house of the Lord. Not that they didn't do their own praying and acquainting with the Lord on this day. But she knew many still believed she killed Mr. Miller.

Instead of helping Colin in the mine, she'd put on a dress and brushed Shayla's and her hair until they both shimmered in the sunlight. The shortening days of summer still warmed enough to be comfortable outside without a shawl. Shayla sat in the warm light of the mid-morning sun in front of the shack. Her speech improved every day, and she didn't wobble as much when she walked.

Ethan had been right, her darlin' was gradually coming back to her old self.

"Happy Man!" Shayla shouted. Aileen looked up and watched Ethan ride his horse to the usual tree and tie it. He swung down out of the saddle and dug in his saddlebag before he turned and waved to Shayla. His gaze met hers as he walked toward them. The spark of approval in his dark eyes made her stomach flutter.

"Morning, Shayla, Aileen." He stopped at the chair, ruffling her daughter's dark curls, but his eyes remained focused on her face. His intense gaze and nearness made her insides quiver and heated her face.

"I'm ready, Mr. Halsey," Shayla said, grasping his hand and tugging.

He glanced down. "You hold the book while I gather chairs." He headed to the chairs under the porch roof. "Where's Colin. I'd like him to hear this story."

Aileen motioned toward the mine. "He's been in the mine all mornin'."

Ethan stood up straight. A frown marred his strong, good looks. "Have you checked on him?"

"Nae, he comes out when his belly calls to him." The concern on Ethan's face stilled her heart. "Do ye think somethin' is wron'?"

"You don't have proper ventilation in that mine." Ethan handed a chair to her. "You set up the chairs. I'll go check on him."

"He's my laddie. Ah'll go." She started toward the mine. A hand clasped her arm. Memories flashed. She wouldn't be a victim again. Swinging around, she fisted her hand and punched.

Her blow bounced off Ethan's chest. The puzzled expression on his face defused her anger.

"Don't go rounding on me. I'm not going to hurt you. You can't carry Colin if he's passed out. It makes more sense for me to go in." His hand released her arm and gently cupped her cheek. "Set up the chairs. Please."

He didn't wait for her answer before jogging toward the mine. The air she'd held after she threw her punch and waited to be hit back, whooshed out of her. If she'd taken a swing at Mr. Miller, she wouldn't have been able to crawl into the shack.

She stared at the wide shoulders, slim hips, and long legs that disappeared into the mine opening. Ethan Halsey might be a man who could change her way of thinking.

Ethan didn't see a lantern at the entrance. He stared into the black hole. The shaft ran straight back into the mountain. With one hand on the wall, he made his way through the darkness as quick as he could without ramming his head into the low ceiling. The musty scent of dirt and stale air assailed his senses as the darkness surrounded him. The scrape of his hands skimming the dirt walls and the shuffling of his feet through the debris on the floor mingled with his shallow breaths. He banged his shoulder into a protruding rock and cursed.

Where was the glow from the lantern Colin used? He strained in the dark to see any glimmer of light. His foot connected with something soft, and he tumbled forward. Instinctively, he shot his arms out before he struck the dirt floor. A mound under his lower legs wasn't hard like dirt or rock. He pushed his body back into a crouch and felt in front of him with his hands.

Something tickled his fingers. He moved his hand. Hair, head, neck. He'd found Colin. His gut tightened. What happened?

He stepped over the body and turned to the open end of the shaft. Crouching, he scooped the limp boy into his arms and stood. He placed his back along one side of the shaft and walked sideways to keep Colin's head aimed down the tunnel. In the dark, he didn't want to strike it on a rock sticking out from the sides.

It seemed like an eternity before the light at the entrance grew brighter. His first step into the sunshine brought Aileen to his side.

"What happened?" she asked, touching her son's hair as tears glistened in her eyes.

"I don't know. I tripped over him in the dark." Ethan covered the distance between the mine and the shack in short time. He placed Colin on the closest bed and sat next to him. His hands skimmed over the boy's limbs and body checking for injuries. Nothing appeared injured. Colin's chest expanded, drawing in great gulps of air.

"Black damp!" Ethan swore under his breath and walked toward the table.

Aileen sat on the edge of the bed, brushing Colin's hair away from his still face. "W-what is Black damp?"

"It's what miner's get when there's poor ventilation." He pulled a chair up alongside the bed. Shayla crawled onto his lap and curled up, watching her brother.

"Ye mentioned the ventilation the other day. What does it mean?" Aileen didn't take her eyes from her son.

"It means you've dug far enough into the earth there is more bad gas than good. You need to dig a hole that goes from the mine up to the ground level of the mountain to let the bad gas out and the good gas in. Otherwise," he grasped the hand resting in her lap, "you both are going to end up like this with no one around to pull you out."

She inhaled and turned frightened eyes to him. "What about Shayla?"

"She'd be without a mother or a brother. Aileen, you can't do any more mining until you get ventilation. Look at Colin. He won't be able to work for a couple days. Not till his headache goes away. He'll lose time working for me and won't be able to help you dig."

She shook her head as she stared at her boy. "Will ye show us what we must do?"

"Yes. But not until Colin is well. I don't want you messing around by yourself."

She jerked her head up and studied his face. "Why are ye so good to us?"

The softly spoken question and the wonder in her eyes made him swallow the lump in his throat. "Because I like you." He ruffled Shayla's hair. "All of you."

"There be no one else around who cares spit about us. Why do ye?" She raised a hand. "And dinnae say because ye like us. No one does what ye have done for strangers."

"I'd like to think if my ma and pa were still alive they would have helped you out a long time ago. They wouldn't have just heard the rumors and ignored you because of what others said."

She ducked her head. Ethan tipped her chin up, making her look into his eyes. "I would hope they would have taken the time to get to know you and helped. That is why I'm here. To help, be a good neighbor, and hopefully a friend." As he talk-ed, her light green eyes surveyed his face, watched his mouth, and a puff of air touched his face as a sigh escaped her slightly parted lips. He was close enough, he could just lean in—

"When are you going to read?" Shayla asked, putting her small hands on either side of his face. Aileen straightened. It gave him satisfaction to know she'd been leaning toward him as well.

"Right now. Run and get me the book." He slid the child off his lap and followed her outside to bring in another chair for Aileen to sit on if she wished, rather than the bed. It also gave him a chance to work out the stiffness created by being near the woman.

Halfway through the first chapter, Colin's eyes fluttered and everyone forgot about the book.

"Laddie, are ye wakin'?" Aileen asked as her heart thudded against her ribs. Both children stricken in a week. She'd go crazy if she lost either of them.

Colin's eyes opened, and he grasped his head. "Ma, my head hurts."

She pulled his hands down at the same moment Ethan placed a wet rag on the boy's forehead. The man knew Colin's problem. She glanced at the side of his face as he leaned over her laddie. The faint scent of shave soap flared her nostrils. It had been years since she'd caught the scent of a clean man. One who cared about his appearance.

"Colin, you breathed in bad air. It takes out all the good air in your lungs and gives you one heck of a headache." Ethan's deep voice consoled.

Colin glanced up at him. "H-how'd I get here. The last thing I remember was putting down the pick. I felt tired and figured I'd been in the mine a long time. Just as I thought it was funny I hadn't felt hungry everything went dark."

"The bad air makes you sleepy. Rest and don't get up too much until your head stops hurting. There isn't anything else you can do." Ethan sat back in his chair. Shayla leaned her elbows on his lap, holding the book.

Aileen patted her son's cheek and glanced at Ethan. He studied the boy. What did he expect to see?

"Do ye have time to stay for soup?" she asked, rising off the bed and straightening her skirt.

"He can't leave until he finishes." Shayla opened the book on the man's lap.

'Darlin' he cannae read the whole thing today. Look at how thick it is." Aileen laughed at her child's exuberance and walked to the fireplace where a pot of soup simmered. It appeared Shayla enjoyed listening to the deep timbre of his voice as well.

"I have the rest of the day, but your mother's right. I can't read this whole book today. How about I come every Sunday and read you a chapter?" He didn't watch her daughter, his eyes questioned her.

Aileen grabbed a spoon and stirred the soup as her heart skipped at the thought of having him in their home every Sunday. His presence filled the small room, and warmed it. She shook her head. Those were bad thoughts. She shouldn't relax around the man, and he shouldn't be hanging around so much.

"Mr. Halsey, 'tis more than ye should be givin' us. This one day is more'n enough." She finished stirring the soup and moved to grab bowls to fill.

He stood beside her and took the bowls, holding one out for her to fill.

"I want to show your children reading is good entertainment and teach them letters and numbers," he said in a low voice that fluttered her errant wisps of hair at the back of her neck.

She nodded her head as she handed him a full bowl and took another one to fill.

"Ah think we should discuss this outside, later," she whispered back, trying to ignore the warmth of his body so close to hers.

He put the two full bowls on the table and handed her another empty bowl. "I can't wait." His comment whipped her head. A mischievous smile tugged at the corners of his mesmerizing mouth.

She twisted back to the task of filling one more bowl. "Shayla, join Mr. Halsey at the table. Ah'll feed yer brother." She moved around the man, barely skimming her arm across his chest. The action sparked like striking flint. She darted a glance at his face. His eyes widened.

Aileen hurried to the side of the bed. The surprise in his dark eyes confirmed he'd registered the spark.

Ethan shook off the jolt he'd received when Aileen brushed against him. Her furtive glance and shaking hands meant the touch had sparked her, too. He'd have to speculate on his reaction. Never before had a woman's touch made his body combustible.

He glanced over at the child sipping her soup next to him. "Shayla, I never had a chance to ask you why you were at the mill the day the board hit you."

She darted a peek at her mother then peered up at him with glistening eyes.

"It's okay. Your ma isn't going to be mad." He looked over at the bed where Aileen sat feeding Colin. "You aren't going to be mad if she tells me?"

The woman shook her head. "Aye, lassie, ah'll no' be mad. Tell Mr. Halsey why ye were at the mill."

Shayla put her spoon down and leaned close. "Ma was busy. I didn't want to ask her to come and ask you, so I went myself." She peeked at her ma, who nodded for her to continue.

"What did you want to ask me?" Ethan set his spoon down and waited. The child swallowed twice.

"I wanted to know your birthday." She stared at her finger making circles on the table.

"My birthday? That could have waited until the next time you saw me." He couldn't believe she'd almost been killed because she wanted to know something so trivial.

She shook her head. "You could have had it before I saw you again, and then I couldn't have given you a present." Her big innocent eyes started to fill with tears.

He growled and pulled her onto his lap. "Shayla, you don't have to give me a present. I don't want anything from you or your family except friendship."

"Some friend." The accusation from the boy on the bed shot an icicle through his chest.

"Colin! Mr. Halsey saved ye today. That's no way to talk." His mother scolded before she raised her eyebrow in Ethan's direction.

"What makes you say I'm not a friend?" Ethan set Shayla back on her chair and took two steps to the side of the bed.

"I saw you and a man walking over the land across the creek. You pointed toward our house and the man laughed."

Before Ethan could say anything Aileen raised off the bed. She poked a finger in his chest and glared.

"Ye said no men would be comin' around the bend and botherin' us, yet ye brin' a man to point and laugh!"

"Don't use Colin's rudeness to start a fight that's not deserved!" Ethan grasped the hand poking him in the chest and held it—firmly but gently. "Maybe now's the time for our little chat—outside." He slid his hand to mate their palms and twined his fingers with hers, tugging her toward the door.

"Ma!" Colin sat up in bed and groaned, holding his head.

Chapter 13

Ethan stopped when Aileen pulled back, but he didn't let go. "Colin, I give you my promise, I'm not going to hurt your ma. We're just going to do some adult talking." He turned to Aileen. She shook her head and still resisted. He raised her hand to his lips and kissed the back. "I promise, I am not going to hurt you. I just want to talk."

The confusion in her eyes gave him enough of an advantage to lead her out of the house and over to the trees where they'd made several bargains.

Ethan kept her hand in his as he nudged her to sit on an upturned piece of firewood. He sat on the ground next to her, to appear less threatening.

"First, I plan to come here every Sunday and read to your family." When she stared at him, he continued. "I want Colin to grow up to be more than a laborer. He's going to need to take care of you and Shayla. I'll teach him to read and do numbers."

Her angel-kissed brow furrowed. "Why?"

"Why, what?" He could gaze at her all day.

"Why would ye help us?"

"I told you earlier. I think it's something my parents would have done."

She shook her head. "Nae. 'Tis more than behavin' as ye think yer parents would." She looked down at their clasped hands. His thumb slid back and forth over her knuckle.

He pulled his hand from hers and stood. How did he explain something he didn't understand himself? He peered down at Aileen. Her slender face, beautiful eyes, and rose colored lips made his groin ache. He wanted her in a way he'd never wanted anything or anyone.

He rubbed his palms on his thighs and slowly knelt on the ground in front of her. What should he say? He wasn't looking for a family. But his gut hurt thinking of not helping them.

"I've hired a man to build an office across the creek." She opened her mouth, but he placed a finger on her soft lips. He gulped. What would those lips taste like?

When he didn't remove his finger, she pulled his hand down, holding it in her lap. "Why do ye need an office? There where all those who come can stare at us?"

He ignored the heat coursing through him from the hand resting in her lap. "With the machinery running in the mill it will be hard to be heard while making business transactions. I wanted the office a bit away from the mill. It will have living quarters."

Her eyebrow shot up. "Ye'll be livin' in the office?" Her question came out in a whisper of wistfulness.

"No, not me—"

"Ah'll no' have anyone else starin' at us." She flung his hand from her lap and started to stand.

"You'll be living in it." He grasped her hands pulling her back down onto the log. Her eyes rounded, and her mouth formed a perfect rosebud.

"Nae! Why would we be livin' in yer office?"

"You can live there and be the office attendant. I'll show you what needs to be done when someone brings in ore."

"Nae, ye'll have no business with me in the office." The hostility in her voice and eyes surprised him.

"Why not?"

"Ye've heard the people talk. They all believe ah'm a husband killer. They shun my bairn. Ah'll no' bring that on yer family."

He rubbed his thumb across the backs of her hands. "Aileen, did you kill Mr. Miller?" She turned her head. He studied her profile and firm set to her mouth. "My way of thinking the bastard deserved it."

Her head jerked around, her eyes glistened with unshed tears. "Yer the first to say as much."

"Myrle feels the same."

"She's a fine woman."

"She thinks highly of you." Ethan smiled when she shook her head in disbelief.

"Nae, no one thinks highly o' me." She attempted to pull her hands from his.

"You're wrong. The more people get to know you, they'll forget about the past. What do you say? Will you be my office assistant?" He held his breath. If she accepted, it would be a huge step toward her trusting him.

"Can ah think about it?" She glanced over his shoulder to the shack.

"Yes, you can think about it. John Fellowes is the man building the office. Do you know him?" She shook her head. "Do you want me to bring him over for you to meet?" Fear flashed in her eyes. "You don't have to meet him. I just thought it might make you more comfortable."

"Ah know. Ah just…" She smiled weakly. " 'Tis best maybe for me to stay away. Until ah decide."

"Okay. I'll let you know if he plans to bring any other men with him." He cupped her pointed chin in the palm of his hand. "And we weren't laughing at you. Shayla happened to be doing some kind of a dance. Fellowes noticed and re-marked his daughter was just as energetic."

It took all his control to not lean over and touch her lips with his.

"Momma!" Shayla's curly head peeked out the shack door. "Can we finish the story?"

Aileen stood, "We're comin' in." She had to put space between her and this man. He made her want closeness, intimacy. His offer—she wanted to say aye and not think there were any strings attached, but the way he always touched her and leaned in. He wanted her. And the surprising thing—she wanted him.

She walked toward the shack. The decrepit building seemed to list more and more to the left. It would be wonderful to spend a winter—would the office be done by winter? She wanted to ask, but didn't want to appear anxious to move in. Hmmph.

She still hadn't decided they would move in.

Shayla darted out the door and grabbed Ethan's hand. Aileen smiled as he allowed himself to be pulled around her and into the shack. Stepping through the door, Colin sent her a scathing glower. He would not be happy to move or have her spend more time with the man.

She dropped her gaze and settled on the chair adjacent to Ethan and Shayla. He began to read, and she let her thoughts drift back to their conversations. Why did he feel compelled to help them? She studied him as Shayla nestled against the expanse of his chest. The deep timbre of his voice soothed more than just her daughter.

She glanced at Colin and smiled. He rested on the pillow, his eyes closed, listening to the story. The slight lift at the corners of his lips proved he enjoyed the story as much as the rest of them.

Ethan's lulling voice echoed to silence.

Shayla shifted to her knees. "Don't stop!"

"I said one chapter every Sunday. That's all you get." He smiled and touched a finger to her darlin's nose. Gentle. The word popped into her head. He was the most gentle man and yet the largest man she'd ever met.

"We cannae be takin' up all Mr. Halsey's Sunday." She stood and moved toward the door. "Thank ye for comin' by. Ah'll give some thought to what ye said afore." She opened the door and waited for him to leave.

He smiled and ruffled Shayla's hair before placing her on the chair Aileen had vacated. Then he bent forward and patted Colin's shoulder. "Don't get up until that head stops throbbing. It only makes it hang on longer. And don't come to work until you don't have any pain. Bending and such will only make it come back worse." Colin gave a slight nod, but said nothing.

Ethan rose and strolled to the door like she didn't stand with it open. He stopped beside her. She swallowed and tried to calm the quivers in her belly.

"I'm going to bring Fellowes over tomorrow to meet you. I want you to see he's a good man. A hard worker and has a family to support." His words didn't leave room for her to object.

She nodded her head, once.

"Good." He glanced back into the room, winked at Shayla, and snatched his hat from the peg by the door. "Tomorrow."

His long legs took him through the door and down the path to his horse. The way he carried himself, she bet he was a fine dancer. Where had that come from? She slammed the door shut and stalked to the fireplace to stir the soup.

"Ma, what did you two talk about outside?" Colin's probing took her by surprise. She should have known he wouldn't let her comment go.

"Mr. Halsey offered me a job." It wasn't only her pride she had to muddle through but that of her son as well.

"A job? Doing what?" He started to sit up. She hurried to the bed side.

"Stay put like Mr. Halsey said. He knows what he's talkin' about." She held his shoulders, keeping his head pressed into the pillow.

His young eyes narrowed. "What job?"

"He asked me to work in the mill office. Said

he'd teach me what ah'd need to know." Let that sink in. Later she'd mention they could live in the building.

"You? How does he know you could handle it?" The accusing tone riled her.

"Ah'm no' daft! Ah wrangled more out o' him over that mill on our property than a man would o'." She leaned over her child. "Ah'm no' daft to yer anger either." Pushing the hair off his forehead, she calmed and added. "Ah told him ah'd think about it."

"But the men—"

"Mr. Halsey would no' do business with men that would treat me wrong." She thought of the times he'd brushed his knuckles against her cheek. And his calloused finger upon her lips.

"He's in this for money, just like us." His scornful words shook Aileen from her warm thoughts.

"Aye, but he isn't a man that would do harm to get what he wants." She caught her son's hands and held them, rubbing her thumbs against his scarred knuckles. "It would do ye good to watch him with others. Ah'd wager he gets what he wants without poundin' on a man."

Colin pulled his hands from hers and turned to his side. She patted his shoulder and motioned for Shayla to follow her outside. Would be best to give the laddie some time to think about her words.

Ethan glanced at the Miller shack. He wanted to check on Colin, but Fellowes would show up any minute. He could use introducing the man to

Aileen as a way to see how the boy survived the night. It was useless to think she'd have an answer for him today. She'd probably wait until the office was done and she inspected it before she said yes or no.

The woman would keep him wondering until she'd checked out the building. Either that or haggle over the wages or hours. She would definitely be an asset to the company with that quick business mind of hers.

A horse splashed across the creek, drawing Ethan from his reverie. Fellowes dismounted and pulled tools out of his saddlebag.

The ringing of hammers, the clang of metal on metal, and men shouting orders drifted across the creek. "I can see where you want to place the office away from the mill."

"So how many people have you told about Ethan Halsey's office?" The man was discreet but when someone like himself did something totally out of character the locals picked up on it.

"The only person I've discussed the layout with is my wife. She had some ideas I think you might want to consider." Fellowes pulled the drawing out of his saddlebag. "I just told the lumber outfit it was for an office. If they wonder at the amount that's their business."

Ethan slapped the man on the back. "Thanks. People already think I'm crazy for building on the Widow Miller's land, if they get word of this, they'll be thinking I shouldn't be starting up a business." He laughed and so did Fellowes.

"Speaking of the widow. I don't know if you know much about her, but she's touchy when it comes to strangers wandering around." He looked across the creek and spotted Shayla playing under the pine trees. "She's been tough to deal with getting this mill going, but I promised her no one who works for me would disturb her or her children."

Fellowes turned his attention to the rickety shack. If he hadn't figured out the office was being built for the Miller's, Ethan was sure he'd figure it out soon. He was a smart man.

"I told the widow, I'd bring you by to meet her. That way she wouldn't worry about the kind of men working over here. She likes her privacy and as you can see, this building will butt into her seclusion."

Fellowes nodded his head. "Let's go meet this woman. Kate said she stays to herself."

"Um, something I might mention. I don't want you to think she and I are too familiar, but she refuses to be called Mrs. Miller. So when I introduce her as Aileen, I don't want you lifting a brow or wondering. That kind of stuff bothers her, too." Telling made him look like a whipped pup as well as gave away information Aileen liked to keep.

"I heard you've been jumping hoops to get this mill going. I won't say nothing to get it pulled out from under you." Fellowes clamped a hand on his shoulder.

"Thanks." Ethan waved toward the creek. "This is the best spot to cross."

"I'd say the first thing we need to do is build a bridge across this. Most of the miners are going to come from the other side and even if they approach from this side, they still need to cross to the mill."

"I agree. If you could do that, I'd be grateful. I'm going to have my hands full the next couple of months getting the mill finished and ready to run."

They crossed the creek and headed to the shack. Shayla jumped up from her playing and ran toward them.

"Happy Man!" She leaped at him, secure in the knowledge he would catch her. And he did, carrying her in his arms.

"Mr. Fellowes, this is Shayla. Shayla, Mr. Fellowes and some other men are going to be constructing an office across the creek." He tugged on one of her curls. "And you must stay away."

Her plump cheeks flushed crimson. "I won't go lookin' for you anymore. Momma said, what I did was wrong."

"She's right. You have to stay away from the mill site and the office Mr. Fellowes will build."

The door opened and Aileen stepped out, closing the door behind her. "Mr. Halsey." She acknowledged and took Shayla from his arms.

"Aileen, this is Mr. Fellowes. He'll be building the office across the creek." Her gaze settled on the man beside him. She held her breath.

"Aileen," Fellowes nodded his head, "I'll keep my men under control, and no one will cross the creek and bother you."

Her gaze flicked to Ethan. He was pretty sure he'd get a tongue lashing for having told the man she liked her privacy. How else was he to keep others away if he didn't set boundaries? To do that he needed this man's help.

"Ah appreciate yer concern." She glanced past both of them to the site. "When do ye plan to start and when will ye be finished?"

"I'll have men out here first thing tomorrow. Ethan wants this done by the end of October."

Her gaze shot back to his face. "That soon? Will the mill be workin' by then?"

He wasn't sure if her concern was for the mill running or her having to make a decision about moving in. "If all goes well, we should have the mill running by then."

"Ah see."

"How's Colin this morning?" It was a personal question. Before Fellowes finished the office, he'd figure out theirs wasn't a normal business relationship.

"He's better. Says his head dinnae hurt near as bad, but ah've made him promise to stay in bed today."

"Good. If his head isn't hurting tomorrow, let him up. A boy his age can't be contained for long." He caught a wisp of a smile before she nodded curtly.

"Come on, Fellowes, we still need to go over those drawings." He touched his hat. "Aileen, Shayla."

"It was a pleasure to meet you," Fellowes said, nodding his head and following Ethan.

Half way back to the creek, Fellowes cleared his throat. "Interesting woman."

"How so?" Ethan could use an unbiased opinion. Especially since his brothers had a hard time thinking of Aileen as anything other than the crazy woman.

"She puts on a hard face, but you can tell when she talks about her kids she'd do anything for them."

It pleased him this man saw the woman he did. "Might let others know she didn't take a club to you when we talked to her," he joked, watching the other man's reaction.

Fellowes smiled. "I've heard the rumors. Also know Miller had a temper." He shrugged. "Not my business what happened. Besides, I'm working for you not her."

"I just want you to squelch any comments that might pop up if you have men helping you." Ethan slogged through the creek and stopped. He crossed his arms and turned to look back at the shack. He didn't see movement. Would Aileen feel she had to stay hidden in the building while the workers built the office? He hoped not.

"I don't take kindly to men talking and not working." Fellowes pulled the drawing out of the saddlebag. "Here's what the missus suggested..."

Aileen watched through the window until the men left. She wrung her hands and stared at Colin sleeping in the bed. Could she go about her usual day with men working across the creek?

She bit her bottom lip and thought it through. Mr. Fellowes appeared to be a nice person. Ethan believed in the man. It would be nice to walk down the street and not have people glare or point. Could this sawmill actually make them respectable in the eyes of others?

"Momma?"

"Yes, Lassie?"

Shayla held the book Ethan read in her lap,

running her small hand back and forth over the cover. "When is Happy Man coming back?"

"He has lots of work. Ah doubt we'll see him until Sunday when he comes to read." Sadness squeezed her chest.

Shayla's bottom lip protruded. She raised her small face. "Why can't he come every day?"

"Because he has to get the mill runnin' and now this office built. And 'tis no' proper for him to spend so much time with us."

"Why?" Shayla put the book reverently on the table and came to stand beside her.

" 'Tis wrong for a man to be alone with a woman no' his wife." She thought of his touch and the warmth she'd seen in his eyes. Her belly quivered. What would it be like to be his wife? Safety. As quickly as the word swept through her head she banished it. No man was safe.

"He isn't alone with you. Colin and I are here." Shayla grasped her hand and kissed it. "We'll always be with you momma."

"Aye, darlin' ye will always be in my heart." The knowledge that her children loved her filled her heart. But a part of her had been empty for some time now.

Had she been a spinster and never known the love of a man, she wouldn't even know it was missing. But she'd known the love between a man and a woman.

And too many nights lately, she'd lain awake thinking what it would be like to be wrapped in Ethan's arms.

Chapter 14

Ethan rode his horse down the mountainside toward the Miller shack. He'd spent the last five Sundays reading and teaching numbers to the whole Miller family. They were quick, enthusiastic learners. He hadn't brought up his job proposal, waiting for Aileen to make the choice. But he knew from her lessons, she would be an asset.

This Sunday he had a special surprise. He dismounted his horse and walked toward the shack. The cooler weather made him itch to get the stamp mill operating. October had come in mild. As the month stretched toward November, the air grew crisper. Heavy frost covered the ground in the morning. Snow would be falling soon.

He rubbed his gloved hands together. Should he spring the surprise on them now or wait?

The door flew open, and Shayla hugged his legs. "Hello, to you too," he said, swinging her up into his arms. He loved her scent, molasses and something he couldn't describe— perhaps the scent of all little girls. Her small arms hugging him gave Ethan a sense of worth. He carried her though the door and kicked it shut with his foot.

Aileen turned from the fire, her face flushed from the heat. Or from the sight of him? The thought made him want to cross the floor and pull her into his arms.

The last month-and-a-half tested his patience. He kept his distance. Well, as much as he could with them both leaning over a slate working numbers. Many times, he could have tilted his head and kissed her. His face and lower body warmed.

She'd kept her distance, yet, at times she couldn't hide the desire in her eyes. It was damn hard to not take her in his arms and kiss her. Many nights he lay awake thinking he'd like to have her beside him.

"You're going to finish the book today," Colin said, drawing his attention from the woman. "Do you have something else to read?"

They'd all pleaded for more than one chapter a Sunday, and truth be told, he enjoyed staying longer as he read extra chapters.

"I plan to bring several books next week. You can each pick one to read yourself." Excitement lit the children's eyes, but Aileen dropped her lashes, hiding her thoughts.

"I have another surprise today." He rubbed his hands together. "Everyone bundle up, we're going for a walk."

The kids scurried to gather their coats and hats. Aileen took her time crossing the room and snatching a shawl from the hook by the door.

"Don't you have anything warmer?" he asked.

The wind on the way over had penetrated his oil-skin.

"Only the coat ah use when workin' the mine." She sounded offended.

"Put that on. No one will see you."

She questioned him with her eyes, but grabbed the heavy wool coat hanging on the peg below. She slid her arms in the sleeves of the coat and wrapped the shawl over her head.

He smiled and waved his hand toward the door for the kids to exit. Ethan put a hand on Aileen's back as she walked out the door ahead of him. Her head swiveled, her light green eyes flashed with desire as she stared back at him. He swallowed and drew his hand from her person. Even with the wool coat and her clothing, he'd felt connected to her.

"Head to the mill," he called to Colin. The mill was done. They'd placed the final stamp in place last night. Monday, each miner would start on the tracks to haul their diggings to the mill.

He wanted to show his accomplishment to Aileen. He'd thought about it all night. His brothers and the workers had patted him on the back congratulating him on completing the project in record time. But he wanted only one person's approval. Ethan captured her hand, tucking it in the crook of his arm.

Her steps faltered as she peered into his face. He grinned and patted her hand.

"Are ye sure ye want to be seen escortin' me?" Her warm voice low enough only he could hear.

"Aileen, I'd escort you anywhere you want to go." When she scowled, he couldn't help but laugh.

Her worries wouldn't make the day any less bright.

They rounded the bend. Her intake of breath told him she hadn't once ventured around the mountain arm to see the progress at the site.

"It holds four stamps. They're twelve hundred pounds each."

Aileen turned to Ethan. The pride in his voice echoed in his stance and the glint in his eyes. She glanced down at how his hand rested on hers. He wanted to show her this. Her knees weakened at the implication.

"Why?" she asked on a whoosh of air that constricted her chest.

"Why what?" His dark eyes studied her face. She tried not to show her emotions, but it was hard when her heart banged against her ribs.

"Why did ye brin' me here to see this?" Even as she asked, she half-feared the answer.

"Because I want you to see what leasing your land will do for your family." He grasped her hand and pulled her forward. Shayla stood at the door. "Go on in," he waved. Her lassie didn't need a second invite. She darted through the door her brother had already opened.

"'Tis safe?" Aileen scanned the interior. The outside of the building loomed tall and impressive. The inside, filled with machinery and open to the ceiling, appeared monstrous. The four massive contraptions on the second level had rods pointing to the level above it.

"There is nothing loose or working at the moment. It's safe for Shayla to look around." Ethan climbed the stairs along the side of the building, pulling her behind him. "I'll show you how this works."

His enthusiasm and her curiosity won over her objections. They climbed to the third level.

"This," he pointed to what looked like the end of a set of tracks, "is where the ore carts dump the rock. It falls down here," he moved his hand over a grill. "Here the smaller rocks fall on through the grizzly to the bin above the stamps and the bigger rocks go through this crusher and fall down into the bin." He grasped her hand, leading her back down to the second level. "These are the stamps. Those heavy steel weights at the bottom of the shafts crush the rock. See the pistons?" He pointed to the metal shafts protruding from the machine. "They move separate from one another, pushing the rock back and forth, like you chew food. They crush every bit separating the gold from the rock. Then," he led her down to the bottom. "The rock is like sand when it gets here. We'll coat these copper plates with mercury, and it will pick up the small pieces of gold. Then the rest washes through this." He pointed to a large flat surface with riffles like a sluice box. "This will catch the larger pieces of gold and silver, if there is any."

The satisfaction on his face made her smile. "Ye've done it. Built a stamp mill before the snow falls."

He put an arm around her shoulders. "It feels good to know how many people are going to profit from this."

Colin jumped down the short flight of steps and stopped in front of them. He glared at Ethan. "Get your arm off my ma."

She started to slip out of Ethan's grasp, but he

merely shifted his hand lower on her arm, tucking her body next to his. His move didn't threaten—it protected. Her mind buzzed. He protected her from her own flesh and blood.

Before she could think about the reasons, Ethan peered down at her. "Do you want me to take my arm from you?" His eyes didn't spark with indignation. He asked her permission to hold her. His question also pushed her to make a decision between him and her son.

Aileen took a breath and studied her son. His stance reflected a body ready to spring into action. "Laddie, Mr. Halsey isn't hurtin' me."

"Give him time." The coldness of the words chilled her heart. How did a mother teach her son not all men meant harm?

"Colin, I would never do anything intentional to harm anyone." He stepped toward the boy, leaving her behind. "Have you seen me raise a hand to anyone while you've worked here? Since I've met your family have I done anything to hurt any of you?"

She watched Colin. His gaze darted between her and Ethan. If only she knew what went on inside his head. He'd watched Mr. Miller beat her senseless too many times and was too small to know his father never laid a hand on her. Heaven help her, she didn't want him to grow up to hurt women. She'd witnessed his violent streak. She shivered, remembering.

"No. But that doesn't mean you won't."

To her surprise, Ethan shook his head sadly, and turned from the boy.

"Let's go see how much they have done on

the office." He took her hand and led her out of the mill. She liked the warmth and strength of his hand wrapped around hers. Colin glanced at their joined hands and rushed out the door. Instead of heading over the bridge to the office, he ran to the shack. The door thwacked behind him as he slammed it shut.

Shayla took hold of Ethan's other hand, and the three of them crossed the bridge.

Ethan squeezed her hand. "He'll come around. He's got some demons to conquer before he'll see I'm not going to harm you."

"Ah hope yer right." She shook off the doldrums Colin had instilled and stepped through the opening to the office. The room was the width of the building with a long, tall counter. Behind the counter another tall counter ran along the back wall. To the right of that stood a doorway.

"This will be the office." He walked to a small swinging door at the end of the counter. "As you can see, customers will stay on that side. This back here will hold the scales and receipt books for each miner who brings in rock." He pointed under the counter to a gaping hole. "I think I'll put a safe in there to store our share of the gold or if a miner wants to wait to pick their portion up until their carts are empty."

"Sounds like a grand idea." Learning how the whole business would run interested her.

"And this…" he led her through the door behind the counter, "is the living quarters."

The room was spacious. "Where's the fireplace?" She scanned the room for a hearth.

"I'm putting in a wood stove. Less mess and

more smoke goes up the chimney instead of into the room."

"But what about cooking?" She'd seen a wood stove at the mercantile. The surface could only hold a pot of coffee.

"It's out here." He walked through a door to the left and into a smaller room. "This is the kitchen. Where you cook and eat."

The smile on his face made her smile. It was a wonderful room with a waist-high drain board on one wall. A hand pump stood at one end of the counter.

"Is that..." she pumped it up and down and water came out the spout. "'Tis wonderful!"

"Fellowes' wife suggested this room and the water pump. Have to give her credit, it was a good idea." Ethan stood in the middle of the room a wide grin warmed his face and lit his eyes. "You like this?"

Did he bring her here to help sway her? The anticipation etched on his face gave him away.

"Ah've been teeterin' toward sayin' aye," she raised her hand when he started to talk, "but ah'm still makin' up ma mind."

"Fair enough." He took hold of her hand and drew her back through the main room. "Down here are three bedrooms and a water closet."

She'd never heard of a water closet. Following him down a hallway, two doors stood on each side of the hall. He swung open a door. A bathtub took up most of the space in the small room. Not just any tub. She knew that dent and scratch. He'd put her bathtub in this room with a pump handle poised at one end.

"What am ah supposed to use for a bath if ah don't move in here?" His presumptiveness raised her hackles and at the same time sent a rush of warmth through her. His actions proved how much he wanted her in this home.

"I'm hoping with one of your possessions already moved in, it won't take you long to decide to move them all in." He didn't even blush. The man stared her straight in the eyes. She gazed deep, drinking in the honesty and hope looming in the dark orbs.

"You can fill the tub with cold water and only have to haul in the hot water."

Aileen walked over to the tub and gave the handle a couple of pumps. Water squirted out, splashing against the bottom of the bathtub and running out a hole at the foot.

Taking the job would not only give her mind a good work, it would also provide her family with a wonderful place to live. She glanced over her shoulder at the man responsible for all this. He grinned and nodded as if he understood her thoughts.

Shayla tugged on her coat. "Momma, can I get Colin? I want to show him the water."

Aileen nodded never taking her eyes from the man standing like a statue by the door. Shayla darted out the door, and Aileen walked across the small room.

"'Tis more than I ever dreamed o' livin' in."

Ethan raised a hand and brushed his knuckles across her angel-kissed cheek. "Say you'll take the job and move in here." He moved his hand around behind her head and drew her face up to his.

"Please." Before good sense could tangle with his foolishness, he touched his lips to hers. Just a soft brush, a tantalizing tease to his senses. A barely audible sigh escaped her lips. It warmed his cheek and set his groin on fire. He didn't want to scare her, but he needed a more satisfying taste. His other hand settled on her arm. He urged her body one step closer and tilted his head to place his lips against her sweet mouth.

He moaned as her body pressed against his. Her mouth opened slightly, and her lips moved like the wings of a butterfly over his closed ones.

The tip of her tongue traced the seam of his lips. His body snapped to attention. He wanted her more than anything he'd ever come across in his life. Her arms wrapped around his neck. Even through the wool coat, he felt her breasts meld against his chest. He never thought he'd care for a woman this way. Wanting her so badly he ached. He'd never kissed or made love to a woman—only used a prostitute now and then when the urge had consumed him.

Ethan pulled back from her demanding lips. Damn! He didn't know the first thing about seducing a woman. And she was a practiced woman.

She looked up at him, the desire in her eyes quickly flashed to pain. Her arms unwrapped from his neck, and she took several steps back. "Ah'm sorry." She blushed and turned from him.

"No. It wasn't you." He didn't know what to say. His male pride couldn't tell her he didn't know how to proceed. She was interested, her kisses proved that.

"Ye dinnae have to explain, ah understand. Ah

have a less than reputable past, and ah'm a mother o' two." She hurried out the door.

"Aileen. No. That's— You don't—" Damn! What did he say? By the time he came to his senses, she'd crossed the bridge and headed to the shack.

Colin hurried out to her. He glared at Ethan and entered the rickety building with his mother.

Should he go over and act like nothing happened? He licked his lips. There was no way he could pretend she hadn't kissed him and tapped a passion he'd yet to experience. He couldn't let her think she was undesirable, not when his body yearned to hold her.

Damn! How could kissing a woman open up so many problems?

He stared at the shack. His nose stung, and his eyes watered from the cold air blowing. He swiped the sleeve of his coat across his face. His horse stomped and blew air.

How pathetic he'd become to allow a kiss to make him timid. It was a damn good kiss. One he wouldn't mind repeating.

He stalked toward the shack. He wouldn't let something that should have made them closer stand in the way of reading to the family. He had a book to finish.

Ethan raised his hand to knock on the door. It pulled open, and Colin glared at him.

"We've decided not to have you read." His adolescent voice cracked as he tried to sound like the man of the house.

"I want to finish the book. I'm not going to let a small indiscretion on my part ruin the day for everyone." There he said it. Made the whole incident his fault—he'd initiated the kiss. And after he finished the book, he'd ask Aileen to come outside where he could explain that ending the kiss had nothing to do with her and everything to do with him. He cringed. He'd never told anyone he was inept. He'd never been before.

He stepped forward, opening the door farther and stepping in the house. The boy bristled. Colin's hostility invaded the small room.

"I told you not to come in." Colin pushed the words out between clenched teeth.

"No, you said you didn't want me to read. Fine, I don't have to read."

"Yes! Read!" Shayla shot forward, throwing her arms around his legs. "Yes! Read!"

He smiled down at the upturned face grinning at him and invading his heart even more. Ethan glanced to the far side of the room. Aileen had her back to him as she stirred a pot emitting a heady aroma in the room.

"I'd like to talk to you a minute." He pried Shyala's arms from around him and took a step toward Aileen. She jerked at his words, but didn't turn to look at him.

"We've nothin' to discuss." She kept her gaze averted. That rankled.

Covering the three steps it took to put him directly behind her, he raised a hand to touch her cheek.

Colin sprang on Ethan's back, his thin arm around his neck in a choke hold. "Don't hurt her!"

"Damn it, boy!" The gangly child couldn't hurt him, not bare-handed anyway, but it was frustrating. Ethan wrapped an arm behind him and scooped the boy from his back. He held Colin under his arm as the long legs kicked out in front of Ethan and small fists beat on his back.

"Would you knock it off?" Ethan stood the boy on his feet. "I'm not going to hurt you, your ma, or Shayla. When are you going to get that through that dense head of yours?" Colin took another swing. Ethan sidestepped, and the boy landed on the floor on his hands and knees.

Shayla giggled. Colin sent her a glare and fisted his hand, rounding on her. Ethan caught the boy's hand as it rose.

"If I ever catch you or hear of you hurting any female whether they are your family or some other, you will answer to me." Ethan spun the boy around and looked him dead in the eyes. "Men don't hit women. Cowards hit women." When the boy's gaze finally lowered, Ethan dropped his fist.

Colin grabbed his coat off the back of the chair and flung the door open. He'd disappeared by the time Ethan crossed the floor to close the door.

"That boy is holding in a lot of anger." Ethan turned to Aileen. Her pale face and sad eyes tugged at his conscience. "Did his pa beat you?"

Her eyes snapped with anger. "Nae! But the boy was too small to remember his da." Her eyes softened. "His da was a strong man, no one dared to cross him. But with me and the boy, he was like a gentle lamb. Never a raised hand. An occasional raised voice, but only when speaking about his enemies." She dropped her gaze to the floor. "He was a lot like ye."

The thought she compared him to her first husband, a man she loved, warmed him nearly as much as her kisses. Which brought him back to something that should be said. But damn, he wasn't ready to tell her he knew next to nothing about the coming together of a man and a woman. As he thought of mating with Aileen, the body part involved flared. That part wasn't the problem, it was the courting steps he'd never done.

His face heated at the images his mind concocted.

"Ah didn't mean to say…" Aileen's color deepened, making her freckles less noticeable.

"Colin's pa was a good man. I try to be a good man." He had to get this conversation on to firmer ground. Maybe he wouldn't have to tell her the truth. He could skirt around the subject until he'd had a chance to talk with— Who?

Shayla tugged on his hand. "Are you goin' to read?"

Yeah, read. Finish the book and leave. Then he could get away from the woman and think about how a man his age found out how to react to a woman whose presence turned him into a randy school boy.

"Of course. Looks like your brother will have to read the ending himself." Ethan picked up Shayla and sat on a chair. The child spread the book open in front of them on the table. Aileen picked up something she was sewing and sat in another chair. He flipped to the chapter, ignored the woman not five feet from him, making his body hum, and began to read.

Chapter 15

Ethan swung the fifteen pound hammer, pounding the spikes into the track as Clay and Hank laid them out. The physical activity the last few days had dropped him into bed every night too exhausted to think about the mess he'd made. He'd spent part of the night before haggling with Clay over the schedule for the miners to use the mill. It really didn't matter, but he wasn't going to give in. Not when he could be in control. The mill, his brothers, these things he had control over.

Kissing Aileen—he'd lost control. And he needed some guidance. He wanted to make things right for her. She knew a whole lot more about intimacy between a man and woman than he did. He found himself thinking about her at inopportune times. And about the affection growing between them. He just didn't want to disappoint her with his ignorance.

The ringing of metal echoed in his ears as sparks flew from the contact of the hammer and the spike. A few more feet and they'd head down the side of the mountain toward the mill. Two days earlier they cleared trees and underbrush making way for the path of the tracks.

Miles sauntered up the cleared area toward them. "Mr. Tulley sent a piece of mail for ya," he said, handing the envelope to Clay.

"It's from Zeke." Clay opened the envelope and started reading. "Him and Maeve are headed this way after someone." He held the letter out.

Ethan wiped at the sweat on his forehead and took the paper. He scanned the writing. "Don't know when they'll get to stop by, but will keep us posted." He took the canteen Hank offered and gulped down the cool liquid.

"Didn't give much detail about what they're doing," Clay reached for the letter.

Ethan handed it to him. "Probably not for general knowledge."

Clay only scowled and stared at the letter.

"You seen much of the widow woman?" Miles asked Clay.

Ethan glared at the man. Why did he want to know something like that?

Clay shot a glance at Ethan. "Why?"

"Just wondered if she still has her claws out and scratchin'?" Miles' derisive tone simmered Ethan's blood.

"You keep away from her," he growled.

Miles backed away, his eyes growing in size. "I wasn't meanin' nothin'"

"Just stay away from her. I think you've caused that woman enough grief spouting your bitter lies."

"I never—"

Ethan stepped forward. "You've been lying to the whole community about that woman just because she wouldn't have you sniffing at her skirts." Miles' face blazed crimson under his scraggly whiskers. He'd hit the truth. Ethan rounded on Clay. "Tell your friend how Mrs. Miller has treated you."

Clay crossed his arms in front of his chest. "Miles, Ethan is right. I don't know where you come off saying the things you have about her." Clay flicked a glance at Ethan then looked his friend in the eyes. "She's a good woman. A bit high and mighty when it comes to business, but she ain't what you've been saying she is."

His brother's praise for the woman eased Ethan's heart. He'd hoped one day they would all see her as the woman he saw.

Miles' chin dropped to his chest as he stared open-mouthed at the three of them. "What? You're going to believe a woman who murdered her husband over someone you growed up with?" He spat on the ground. "You're all as crazy as she is!" He threw his hands in the air and headed back down the cleared area.

"I think it's going to take more than you two talking good about the widow to make him change his mind." Hank picked up a rail and set it in place.

Clay tucked the letter in his pocket and put a spike in the rail hole.

Ethan picked up the hammer. "I agree." He brought the hammer down hard on the spike, nearly setting it with one swing. If only it was so easy to make people's distrust disappear.

Aileen stretched, rubbing her aching back. She peered up through the ventilation hole. The faded light and dim shadows of limbs told her it was late afternoon. There was enough rubble around her feet to keep her busy for two days hauling it out of the mine.

She propped the pick against the side of the mine and grabbed the lantern handle. Colin didn't need to know how hard she'd been working to make up for the days he'd been unable. With the mill done and the men setting out track to get the diggings to the mill, Colin had switched to working with Mr. Fellowes on the office.

The man had been as good to Colin as Ethan. Training him on the finer points of carpentry. Also teaching him anger got you nowhere. Mr. Fellowes, according to Colin, didn't even curse when a heavy board landed on his foot. He'd told that story over and over again, letting her know it had completely amazed him.

She walked back through the mine and thought of the man who helped dig the ventilation holes. The one kiss, well, you couldn't call it one kiss—She smiled. She bet he'd never kissed a woman before. His lips, though soft to the touch, had remained firm under hers. No, that man had never seduced a woman. She could be his teacher for a change. The thought made her heart hammer in her chest and the juncture of her legs throb.

It had been a long time since her body came alive under the hands of a lover. Not since her first husband. Could she make Ethan her lover and not have him think he had to marry her? Colin wouldn't take well to another man in their lives. Even Ethan.

She stepped into the late afternoon sunshine and found Shayla talking to the bajin Miles. The little man offended her in more ways than his leering gaze. She knew he was the root of the rumors about her.

"Shayla, go to the house." Aileen stopped better than two arm's lengths from the man. Her body shivered in disgust.

It still made her seethe to think he tried to court her right after Mr. Miller died. He treated her like some simple woman who would take up with anything just to have a man. She'd shown him the door, and he'd spouted lies about her ever since. What brought him here now?

"What kind of lies you been tellin' my friends?" He took a step toward her. Instinct from years of dodging drunken assaults took over. Her nerves quivered, readying her body to shift quickly and be on the defensive.

"Ah dinnae tell lies." She narrowed her gaze at him. "Might be ye need to look at yerself."

"Listen, bitch. I growed up here. I've got more respect than you'll ever get." He lunged forward, grabbing her arm, and twisting it behind her back. Though smaller, he compensated by using quick, restrictive moves.

Pain shot up her arm, but fear of being seen caused her to glance about frantically. They stood out in the open and in clear view of the office. The hatred in his eyes and leering smirk on his face proved he didn't care and didn't believe anyone would help her. She closed her eyes and thought. If she screamed Colin would hear. No! She couldn't have him come to her aid. Not again.

"Leave me be," she said through clenched teeth.

"I've got plans. Plans I've been thinkin' about for some time." He shoved her toward the shack.

Shayla. So far her darlin' hadn't seen the violence in men. She had to do something. Shayla couldn't know this side of men. Not now. Not while she was still so innocent.

She dragged her feet to slow their momentum and give herself time to think. He twisted her arm and shoved. She wouldn't be a victim again. With a spurt of strength and dignity, she came around with her other arm and jabbed her elbow into the man's chest. He wheezed and let go, giving her enough time to dash to the shack, slam the door, and throw the board across.

She braced her back against the door to tell Shayla to hide. Her gaze darted around the small room. The lassie was nowhere to be seen.

"Darlin'? Are ye hidin'" she cooed, wanting her to stay hid, but wondering where she could be.

The door popped behind her and forced her forward, throwing her into the table. She turned as the vile man stepped through the doorway and walked across the door.

"You're going to pay for that." Miles came at her, his eyes wild and his mouth drooling. She backed into the table and froze. All those horrible years came back to her. It wasn't Miles—it was her dead husband— drunk and raging, headed for her.

Ethan looked up at the sound of a strangled cry. Shayla raced through the clearing toward him.

"Momma! He'p!" she shouted as Ethan dropped the hammer and ran to her.

"What's wrong with your momma?" He knelt in front of the child as she clung to him. Her small body heaved as she gasped for breath.

"Man." She panted. "Mean. Got her."

Ethan picked her up and turned to Hank and Clay. "Keep her here." He gave Shayla a brief hug and handed her to Hank. Then set off down the clearing at a run. He heard footsteps behind him and knew it was Clay.

He cut to the right through the trees—a more direct route to the shack. He broke out of the trees. Fear tightened his chest at the sight of the busted down door. He growled and quickened his pace. If anyone hurt Aileen—

He burst through the open doorway. Aileen was sprawled on the table with Miles standing between her trouser-clad legs. Ethan grabbed the man by the back of his collar, picked him up, and threw him against the shack wall. The whole building shuddered and creaked.

Ethan looked down at Aileen's stricken expression. Her torn blouse splayed open, revealing her chemise and heaving breasts. It appeared the man hadn't had time to...

"Don't let him leave," Ethan said over his shoulder to Clay as he leaned down to help Aileen.

"Nae! Dinnae touch me!" she screeched, pushing away from him.

"Shhh, Aileen. It's me." He moved to the side of the table and sat in the chair to make himself less threatening. He touched her cheek with the back of his hand. "I won't hurt you." She gazed into his eyes and slowly the fear faded.

He pulled her shirt together and placed a hand behind her back, helping her to a sitting position on the table. He stood, moving around the table to nudge her legs together with the side of his thigh. Thank God she wore men's britches when working. Otherwise it would have been much too easy for the little weasel to have… He seethed at the thought of what the man had planned to do. His hands clenched in fists, his muscles bunched. He wanted to rip the vile man to pieces.

Aileen's shattered composure made him gulp down the rage. "Are you all right?" Her brief nod did little to squelch his anger.

Miles came to and tried to talk his way out of the incident with Clay.

"Can I leave you for a moment?" Ethan asked, touching Aileen's pale cheek. She stared at him, eyes wide, but nodded. He gave her a smile and crossed to the man still sitting on the floor.

"Get up!" Ethan grabbed him by the shirt front hauling him to his feet. "Outside."

"Ethan." Clay shook his head.

"I'm just going to talk to him. Keep Aileen company until I get back."

Clay shrugged and moved toward Aileen.

"Be slow and quiet." Ethan added and pulled the whining man out the opening.

Not wanting Colin to happen along and witness what he was about to do, he pulled Miles a good distance into the trees.

"Now, why were you stupid enough to go bother a woman we'd just finished telling you to leave alone?" He held Miles up by the shirt front.

"She's nothin' but a bitch."

Ethan's fist connected before he could constrain his anger. The smaller man's head snapped back. Blood spurted out his crooked nose.

"Owww! Why'd ya go and do that?" Miles held his nose with one hand making his words sound hollow and muffled.

"Because that woman you just referred to as a bitch has more brains and courtesy than you've ever or will ever possess." He stood the man in front of him. "If I ever see you along Cracker Creek or anywhere near her when she's in town, I'll make sure you haven't any teeth to go with that broken nose." He shoved Miles. The man staggered backward and fell to the ground. "If you had done more than ripped her clothes, you wouldn't be walking away from here." He strode over to the man and knelt down. "You harm a hair on her or those kids and you won't see your next birthday."

"You can't—"

Ethan glared at him. "I've got more people behind me than you do. I won't be charged for killing you if I'm protecting a woman or child. Think about it."

He stood and hurried away from the disgusting man before he broke more than his nose.

Hank and Shayla walked hand in hand across the clearing toward the house. Hank raised a brow but kept on walking when they met him coming out of the trees. He scanned the doorway and walked through with Shayla dragging him.

Ethan crossed the threshold as Shayla crawled on her mother's lap. Aileen sat on the bed. She'd pulled a large man's shirt on over her torn shirt. Clay poured tea into cups. He looked up.

"Miles?"

"He won't be back." Ethan knelt beside Aileen. "Are you okay? Did he hurt you?"

"Ah'll have some bruises and my arm hurts the way he twisted it, but ah'm fine." She glanced up from where she'd been studying Shalya's face. "Thank ye," she whispered as tears started to glisten in her eyes. She kissed the top of Shayla's head, hiding the tears.

He turned his attention to the girl. "You were smart to come find me." He took her small hand in his and smiled into her wide, concerned eyes.

She patted her mother's arm. "Momma's gonna be fine."

"Aye, lassie, ah'll be fine." Aileen brushed at the tears sprung from a mixture of aftershock, relief, and gratitude. After Ethan pulled Miles away, she hadn't pulled out of the nightmare that clenched her. His size and looming body had kept her locked in terror. Until he'd made himself vulnerable. His loving gestures broke through her fear. With each gesture the man chipped away at her resolve not to let another man into her life. Colin would—Cach!

"We cannae tell Colin about this!" She grasped Ethan's arm. "The laddie cannae find out." If he thought a man had hurt her—She looked at Ethan's brothers and then down at Shayla.

"Please, dinnae tell Colin about this. He—he wouldn't understand." She held Shayla's chin. The child had to understand. "Darlin' 'tis a secret we must no' tell yer brother." Shayla's small face scrunched in thought. "Please, lassie?"

"Why can't Colin know?" Ethan leaned forward, watching her.

"Ye've seen his temper. Tis best he dinnae find out." She hoped that offered a good enough answer. She couldn't, wouldn't tell him the truth.

Hank lifted the door. The middle boards had splintered from the force Miles had used to enter. "How are you going to explain this?"

Her head began to ache. And her arm throbbed. "Ah..."

Ethan stood. "I'll go see if the office is ready to move into. We can have your stuff moved in within the hour."

She captured his hand. "Ah dinnae say ah'd take the job."

"It looks to me like you don't have any other choice. For one, the office will have a good lock on it and secondly, if the broken door doesn't bother you, I've noticed the list to this building is worse since I threw Miles against the wall. It could fall down around you during the night." He gave her hand a squeeze. "Start packing. We'll move you as soon as I get the all clear from Fellowes."

She stared at his broad back as he left the shack. Turning her attention to the two men sipping tea at her table, she gave them a weak smile. "Does the man always get his way?"

"No. You seem to have gotten your way on several things over this mill," Hank said, watching her.

"Ah suppose. But what if ah dinnae want to live in that place?" She didn't want the two studying her to think she had coerced the man into building the house for her. Even though he had built the 'office' to house her family.

Chapter 16

Aileen and her family moved into the new building by early evening. Ethan couldn't help but smile. Miles' stupidity actually helped him. He'd informed Colin they couldn't live in the shack any more because it was about to fall down. The boy had been apprehensive and said they'd only stay in the office until he could get their home repaired.

Ethan approved of the boy learning new things and using them. He doubted once Aileen got used to the comforts of the office she'd want to move back to the shack, but the woman had surprised him more than once.

He and Hank carried the last cot into the building and placed it in the room that would be Aileen's.

"Will be hard for the bairn to sleep in their own rooms." Her eyes sparkled as she scanned the room.

"They'll get used to it." He turned to her as Hank left the room. "I'm sorry it took something so drastic to get you moved in." He placed a hand on her cheek and smoothed the worry lines beside her eye with his thumb. "But I'm glad you're here. I'll feel better."

She turned and kissed his palm. "Thank ye for comin' to my rescue." The warmth in her eyes and the moist spot where she kissed his palm sent need coursing through his body. He slid his hand to the back of her head and drew her up on her toes. The inviting smile on her pink lips aroused him even more.

He lowered his head and touched her petal soft mouth. Her lips parted and the tip of her tongue traced the seam of his mouth. He wasn't sure what she asked, but he opened. The sensation of her soft, sweet tongue touching his nearly buckled his knees. He sagged against her, clutching her body against him, using her as a prop to hold him up. So there was more to kissing than just touching lips.

She rubbed against him, hardening his shaft even more and eliciting a moan. He pulled back unsure how far this would or should go. Cripes—there were children and his brothers lurking about somewhere.

The sultry look in her eyes and the smile curving her lips were his undoing. Ethan pulled her back into his arms, kissing her as she'd just kissed him. To taste a woman—this woman—was heady. If he'd known how kissing could jolt the body and how good a woman felt in his arms, he'd have courted a long time ago.

"Ahem!"

Aileen jerked out of his arms. He stepped back feeling like he'd been caught stealing. Damn!

Hank walked into the room, placing a pair of worn out boots on the floor. "Colin said these belonged to you."

Ethan watched Aileen nod slightly. Her eyes had cleared, and she held her head high.

"He's right." She retrieved the boots, setting them at the end of the cot. Then turned and gave him a smile before brushing past both he and Hank to disappear out the door.

"So, big brother, looks to me like you have taken this relationship a little farther than you've been letting on." Hank crossed his arms, barring the door.

"Not sure what you're talking about?" Ethan crossed his arms and returned the amicable gaze.

"Something short of a bonfire happened in here". Hank darted a glance downward and then back to his face.

Ethan's ears burned. His hardened member still strained at his britches. And damn Hank's hide for noticing.

"It's only the second time we've kissed, and I'd thank you to not be jawing about this to anyone."

"As familiar as you two were getting, I don't think that was a second kiss."

"Are you calling me a liar?" Ethan took a step toward his brother. He'd swipe that smirk off his face.

Hank raised his hands in surrender. "Hell, if that was only your second kiss, I hope you know what you're getting yourself into."

His ire faded as his brother's words sunk in. "What do you mean?"

"You two were all but devouring each other.

I'd say it's been a while since either of you had a good roll in the hay." Hank cocked his head to one side as Ethan's cheeks flamed. "Damn! Ethan, don't tell me you never…"

"I've been with a couple, you know…" he ran a hand over his face. This wasn't something he wanted his brother to find out, but then again, where was he to get instruction on how to court Aileen if he didn't ask someone.

Hank slapped him on the shoulder. "We've all been with those kind, but have you been with someone who doesn't do that for a living?"

Ethan stiffened his shoulders and threw them back, straightening his body to his full height. There was only one person he knew who wouldn't laugh at his ignorance. He'd wait to ask his questions then.

"I haven't been a hermit."

"At least you know where to start then!" Hank laughed and spun to leave the room.

"You mention any of this to anyone and you'll be pulling extra shifts when the mine is up and running."

Hank waved his hand and continued through the short hall.

Ethan leaned against the doorjamb. Now what should he do? Ask Aileen to forgive him for being so forward? He didn't know what came over him. He thought of her ardent kiss. She'd put just as much into the kiss as he had. And from the passion in her eyes, she'd enjoyed it as well.

The memory of her hot tongue enticing his lips to open and her sweet taste shot heat to his loins.

"Happy Man!" Shayla rushed down the hallway and grasped his hand. "Come see my room!" She tugged him to the door across the hallway.

"This is very nice." Ethan stepped inside the small space with a cot along the wall. "Is this where you're going to sleep?"

"It's all mine! Momma said so." Shayla smoothed the faded blanket on the bed and scanned the bare walls. He, too, studied the room. Two small dresses hung from pegs on the wall. A worm leather satchel sat on the floor beneath the garments. He knew the bag held two petticoats, drawers and one pair of stockings for the child.

"Shayla, when is your birthday?" He wanted to find out the birthdays of each family member and give them a new outfit for their special day.

"When the flowers are pretty." She smiled, "And Momma's and Colin's birfday is when I go to bed during the day."

Ethan watched the child. What did she mean? Her birthday would be spring or early summer for the flowers to be blooming, but going to sleep during the day?

"What else can you tell me about your mother and Colin's birthdays?"

"It's hot and we swim instead of baths."

"Summer." Ethan grinned. Well, it looked like he'd have to purchase them Christmas presents.

"Shayla, dinna be pesterin' Mr. Halsey." Aileen stood in the doorway, her proud gaze resting on her child.

"She isn't pestering me. In fact, I enjoy our conversations." His words made Aileen's brow furrow in a worried crease. Now what would she be worried the child would say?

"For all ye've done for us, we'd be pleased if ye and yer brothers joined us for dinner tomorrow night." She finally looked him in the face. He couldn't tell if she wanted him to accept alone or if she wanted Clay and Hank there as chaperones.

"We'd be honored, but let me give you some money to purchase what you need." He slid a hand into his pocket.

"Nae! How can ah be repayin' ye if ye buy the food!" Her eyes lit with indignation.

"Having someone other than us cook is worth buying the supplies. Of the three of us left, none of us are very good cooks."

Her soft laughter floated through the room, caressing his ears and warming his heart. "Ah've all ah need if one o' ye could bring some venison. Colin's learnin' so much from Mr. Fellowes ah hate to ask him to take off a day to hunt."

"Clay's been itching to go hunting. I'll have him bring the kill to you." Ethan took a step toward her. He wanted to feel her in his arms again. Learn all her curves and taste her lips. But she backed into the hall and headed to the common room.

He entered and found Hank and Clay listening to Colin explain how he'd helped Fellowes with the building. The smile and pride on Aileen's face as she watched her son filled Ethan with contentment. He'd help put the pride in the young man's voice and the pride on the woman's face. His belief in both of them had made a difference in their lives.

"Hank, Clay, I hate to pull you away, but we have to finish up the track and check on the others before dark."

"Don't go!" Shayla grabbed his leg, clutching it in her small arms.

"We have work to do. And we'll see you tomorrow night." He ruffled Shayla's hair and looked over at his brothers. "Aileen offered to cook dinner for us for helping her move in."

"Thank you!" Clay said, striding across the room and taking Aileen's hand. "If I have to eat another burnt biscuit I think I'm going to hurt my brother." The woman giggled and shot a wary glance toward her son. Colin didn't play into the humor. He watched the man closely.

"Burnt biscuits can happen to anyone," Hank said, pushing Clay aside. "If you can brew a pot of coffee that doesn't taste like kerosene, I'd be forever grateful."

Aileen's mirth-filled gaze connected with Ethan. "See, I told you they would jump at the chance to eat someone else's cooking."

"So ah see." She turned to Clay. "Ethan said ye'd be able to brin' me venison for the meal?"

"If he's willing to let me out of working a few hours in the morning." Clay turned his attention to Ethan.

"I offered your assistance, didn't I?" Ethan took the opportunity to step up to Aileen. He wanted to hold her one more time before he left, but wasn't sure how to go about it with so many people watching.

Hank turned to Colin, "How about you show me and Clay that wood box you were talking about on our way out?"

Colin nodded enthusiastically and they all left

the room, with Shayla trotting after them.

"How'd you do that?" the accusing tone in Aileen's voice dropped his gaze to her face. Her eyes danced with humor. She'd been hoping for a moment alone as well.

"Not sure. I think Hank's had more experience with women than I have." There. He did it, told her he was inept.

She slid her arms around his neck and pressed her body against him. "That's okay. Ye taught me numbers, ah'll teach ye what a woman wants." Her lips brushed his lightly, back and forth, teasing, tingling. Her wet, warm mouth opened, and he surrendered to her instruction.

Aileen owed the man kissing her back passionately, yet, she wasn't sure how much she was willing to give. She wanted him. Her body wanted him. He'd demonstrated his gentleness and now revealed his desire. He drew her hips tight against his, pressing his hardened length against her belly. His hands made an unhurried path up her sides and around just brushing the swells of her breasts. The feel of his strong, yet, gentle hands brought back faded memories of being loved. A feeling she'd given up hope of reveling in again.

She placed her hands on either side of his rugged face and pulled back enough to keep their lips separated as she looked into his eyes. "Ah've a hunger for ye. But ah've bairn to think about." The desire in his eyes didn't lessen as his lips curved into a smile that dazzled her senses.

"I'll keep my hands to myself when the children and others are present as long as you promise to slip into my arms when we're alone."

She studied his face. Was he willing to not bed her? Even though he was rock hard and must be hurting.

"Will ye be all right with that?" She placed a hand on his hardness and he groaned. She nearly moaned as well at the heat and strength. Mr. Miller hadn't been a lover. He'd been a taker, making her fear and abhor his boaby. But the man whose boaby she now held in her hand would never take her. He'd be gentle.

He pushed away from her and stood with his back to her as he pulled deep breaths of air in and out. "Aileen, don't do that again, please."

"'Tis what ah mean. Ye can't be feelin' me up and kissin' without lettin' yer male urges free. It'll hurt ye." She put her hands on his shoulders. "But ah'm not ready to go that far. As much as ah feel safe with ye..."

Her breath hitched when he turned around. The passion glazing his brown eyes weakened her resolve. It took all her control to not drag him into her room.

"Aileen, to know you feel safe with me and are willing to share kisses," his finger skimmed her cheek with the faintest of touches, "is all I need."

The scurry of small feet grew louder. Reality crashed around her, and she stepped away from his caress.

"For now."

She sought his gaze, but he ducked his head and moved through the door.

"Night," he called as Shayla burst into the room. Her lassie danced around the room as large as the whole shack they lived in until a few hours earlier.

"My tummy is talkin'." Shayla grasped her hand and tugged her toward the kitchen.

"Then we'll have to find it something to eat." Aileen followed her daughter into the room. To cook with such grand things like running water and a cookstove elated her as much as the safety she felt in the arms of a man again.

Ethan's parting words bounced around in her head. Their meaning sizzled her blood and her skin tingled with anticipation.

When and how would they be able to quench the desire they both felt?

And would one tussle sate their thirsts or only fuel their need?

Chapter 17

Ethan used the excuse of needing more spikes to take a trip to Sumpter and visit Myrle. They would have a fine meal tonight at Aileen's, and he hated to have two good meals in one day when he'd rather stretch them out, but he wanted, no, needed answers. And Myrle was the only person with whom he felt comfortable discussing the situation. Asking his brothers how to seduce a woman didn't set well. As the oldest he should know these things, not have to ask his younger siblings.

Myrle was like a mother or beloved aunt, and his stomach didn't knot near as bad thinking about talking to her as it did his brothers.

He pushed through the door to her establishment and glanced around. A few of the customers he knew by sight. The Widow James glared at him before hightailing it through the kitchen door.

Before he could decide the best spot to sit, Myrle slipped through that same door, drying her hands on her apron. "What brings you here today?

I heard you've been working everyone till they dropped putting that mill of yours to rights."

He gave the small woman a hug and looked down into her concerned face. "I need advice." He glanced around at all the faces watching them. "But it's private."

Her eyes twinkled, and a smile split her face. "One minute." She hurried across the room and stuck her head in the kitchen. "Ethel, Sadie, take care of things for a while. I've got some business to tend." Her short legs worked double time crossing back to him as she untied her apron and flung it over a chair. "Let's go into the parlor. It's more private."

He followed her tiny frame through another door off the dining area and into a small feminine room. All the furniture, kerosene lamps included, resembled the mossy trees high on the mountain sides. The fringe hanging from everything was downright unsettling. The bright, cheery colors and flowers appeared almost as garish as the brothel he'd stepped into a couple of times. If there'd been the same cloying scent of perfume, tobacco smoke, and liquor he'd have found the first door out. The scent of beeswax and kerosene tickled his nose. Myrle sat on a cushioned settee and patted the seat next to her.

"What is so important that we have to talk in private and on a day when you could be getting lots of work done on that mill of yours?"

Ethan turned his hat over and over in his hands. Now that he was here, he wasn't sure the words would come out. "I—well you see—" He took a swipe at the sweat beading his forehead, opened the top button of his flannel shirt, and pushed his sleeves to his elbow, trying to release the heat of embarrassment burning him up.

"It's a woman isn't it?"

He started to shake his head in denial, but the gleam in her eyes said she already knew. So he nodded quick and brief.

"I've been a married woman and had a wonderful, loving husband." She placed a wrinkled hand on his arm. He stared at the hand, unable to look the woman in the eyes and tell her he hadn't a clue how to be romantic.

"Just follow Aileen's lead. She also had a wonderful, loving husband. She'll show you what she wants."

He jolted at the mention of Aileen. He narrowed his eyes, searching the woman's face. "What did my brothers tell you?"

"Nothing. Is there something to tell?" The play at innocence didn't escape his ears.

"No, there's nothing to tell." He stood, slapped his hat on and headed for the door. He should have known better than to come here. Hank and his loose lips had to have said something to her. But when? He'd kept both Clay and Hank so busy the last couple of months neither one of them would have had time to slip to town and discuss his infatuation with the Widow Miller.

He stopped at the door, glancing over his shoulder. Myrle remained on the settee, grinning. "Not sure how you knew, but keep it to yourself. She's a might touchy about this."

Myrle nodded, and he opened the door, walking into the eating area. He tipped his hat to the

Widow James and acknowledged the men he knew, before he left the building and hurried back to work. Hard work would help ease the need boiling inside him for a woman he had no business thinking about.

Aileen pushed the dishrag across the last breakfast dish. She shook her head, ridding it of thoughts of Ethan. Instead, she turned to thoughts of making their new living quarters a home. She'd kept treasures of her past hidden in the trunk that traveled with her from Ireland. It was one of her few possessions Mr. Miller had left unscathed in his rages. Now she had a house worth showing them off.

A loud banging on the kitchen door sent her hurrying across the room. Clay stood outside, a fresh roast in his hands.

"Will this do for dinner tonight?" he asked, crossing the threshold to place the meat on the drain board.

She snatched the cast iron pot and held it under the roast. He dropped the sizable chunk of meat in the pot.

"Aye, should feed yer brothers and us fine." She placed the lid on top and set the whole thing on the drain board.

"I hung the rest of the meat in the lean-to. The weather's cool enough it should be fine till you use it all." He pumped water and washed his hands as if he was in his own home.

Aileen took a step back. For all her plans and making the building her home, she had to remem-

ber it wasn't. The office and living quarters belonged to the Halsey brothers, even if her bed and
belongings were in it and it sat on her land. The
realization sat in her stomach like a sour apple.

"See you tonight." Clay wiped his hands on his
pants and headed back out the door. She followed,
closing it and leaning against the wood.

This roof wouldn't fall down around her, and
the winds wouldn't howl through the boards this
winter, but she still felt trapped. Living in a house
that wasn't hers. That never would be if the Halseys had anything to say. Ethan had put the clause
in the contract that he would get first crack at their
land when they sold. And they would. Just as soon
as they had enough money to travel to Ireland and
reclaim Colin's land.

Remembering the true reason she'd allowed
the Halseys run of her land helped her to swallow
the bitter taste of defeat. She pushed away from
the door and returned to the stove.

"Ma!" Colin burst through the door and skidded to a stop inches from toppling her over.

"Aye, laddie, ah'm right here. There's no need
to holler." She poured water into the cast iron pot
with the roast and turned her attention to the
young man flushed with excitement.

"They're dropping off the rails for our track.
Mr. Halsey says I can help him start laying it
tomorrow." Colin grabbed a slice of bread left over
from the meal and chomped on it like he hadn't
eaten less than an hour earlier.

"Ah see. And this has ye all excited, to be layin' track." She smiled when he frowned and scuffed
his shoe across the wood floor.

"It's not just the track. It means we'll be able to move all those trailings we've been piling. And…" He glanced at her before directing his gaze to the toe still polishing the floor. "I'll be pulling in a wage again cuz Mr. Halsey offered me a job at the mill."

Was that pride lighting his eyes? She stared at his face and ran her gaze the length of him. His shoulders had squared, his arms folded across his chest, and his legs spread in a solid stance to give him the appearance of someone not to be messed with.

"Braw! Ye've become a man afore my eyes." She pulled him into a hug even though he tried to step out of her embrace. She clung to him, remembering the day he'd arrived a squalling bundle of joy. The day he took his first steps, and his da was so proud of his stout wee legs. And how he kept her from diving into despair when Patrick was taken from them both.

She stepped back, swiped at the tears tickling her cheek and smiled. "Ye should be watchin' that they put the tracks in the right spot."

His smile was worth more than any gold they ever dug out of the mine. "See you tonight." He headed toward the door.

"What about the noon meal?"

"I'll be fine till dinner. There's lots of work to do." He disappeared out the door, and her heart pounded with pride. A couple of years under Ethan's teaching and he'd be a fine man.

Which brought her back to Ethan Halsey. She could find nothing at fault with the man. He'd been aggressive to use their land, but had also given them more than any other person would have. He was attentive to both children and set her blood heating.

Just thinking of the kiss they'd shared sent her heart fluttering in her chest. Emotions she'd long thought would never touch her again, were stealing into her heart. But she couldn't let herself get attached. It was too late for Shayla, but her lassie was young and would soon forget. As soon as they had the funds, they would head to claim Colin's property. If that greedy Englishman still held the O'Lear land, she'd offer him more than he could refuse.

A polite knock on the kitchen door shook her from her reveries. Who would come calling—here? She crossed to the door and opened it with hesitance.

A woman with faded blonde hair tucked under a bonnet smiled up at her.

"I'm Mrs. Fellowes. My husband, John, built this for Mr. Halsey." Her gaze showed admiration as it flit around the room.

"Aye, yer husband did a fine job." Aileen didn't know what to do. The woman appeared sincere in her greeting and hadn't shown any animosity.

"Would ye like to come in for a cup o' tea?" She stepped back to allow the woman entrance, still reeling from the sight of a woman in her presence neither glaring nor looking haughty.

"I'd be delighted." Mrs. Fellowes crossed the threshold and held out a basket. "John came home last night and said you and the children had moved in. I figured you wouldn't have time to venture to town for yardage for curtains." The woman stopped awkwardly.

"Aye, to be sure, ah've a job on my hands to get this place livable afore the mill opens and ah'm workin'." She took the offered basket, placing it on the table. Her hands shook as she gathered her two least-chipped cups and saucers and placed them on the table.

"Ye be havin' a seat, Mrs. Fellowes."

"Martha, please call me Martha."

"Aye, Martha, ah'm pleased ye came by today." She almost hummed as she poured boiling water into her teapot and added tea. She set the pot on the table and took a seat across from the woman.

"John had to come finish some business with Ethan and I asked to come along." She smiled and untied her bonnet. "I'm glad you aren't upset with my unannounced visit."

"Nae, just surprised."

The woman frowned. "I know there have been some in town who've not been friendly. And I'll admit, I've not taken the time to get to know you. But John would come home every night after working with your boy all day and go on and on about how intelligent and what a quick learner he was. I thought to myself, it takes an intelligent woman to raise a boy like that, and I want to meet her." The sincerity in the woman's eyes and the kind words her man said about her laddie, brought tears to Aileen's eyes.

"Oh, I'm sorry!" Martha started to stand.

Aileen put out her hand, stopping the woman and dabbed at her eyes with her apron. "Nae, 'tis tears o' happiness ye be seein'" She cleared her throat and smiled at the woman. "Ah've no' had many in some time no' think o' me and my bairn as monsters. It makes my heart happy to have someone say otherwise."

"Momma! Momm-" Shayla burst into the room from the living quarters. She smacked into Aileen's side and grinned at Martha.

"My, you are a pretty child!" Martha exclaimed.

"'Tis my gem, Shayla." Aileen rubbed her daughter's back. "Shayla, darlin' say hello to Mrs. Fellowes."

"Hello." She slipped around the side of the table and stood before the woman, grinning and shining like a gold nugget. Aileen's heart swelled for the second time today.

"How old are you, Shayla?" Mrs. Fellowes asked.

"I'm four. I'm gonna be five when the flowers come out again."

Martha glanced over Shayla's head to catch Aileen's gaze. "You have two very intelligent children."

"That she does." Ethan's deep, strong voice startled Aileen. She stared at the door from which Shayla had just burst and found Ethan and Mr. Fellowes standing in the kitchen.

"Ah've never had so many people visit at one time." Flustered at so much attention, she sprang out of the chair and headed to get two more cups from the cupboard. If anyone else showed up they'd have to go without as she only had the four unpacked.

"We're not staying long," Mr. Fellowes said, moving to stand behind his wife. "Martha, I've finished my business with Ethan are you ready to go?"

"There's no need to rush off, John," Ethan took a seat at the table as if he lived there. The move warmed and frustrated Aileen. It was comforting he felt so at home, but she didn't need more talk about she and Ethan circulating around the community.

She placed the cups on the table and poured tea, ignoring him as best she could with her body humming at his nearness when she pushed a cup and saucer across the table to John.

"What were you two ladies talking about before we interrupted?" Ethan asked, pulling Shayla up onto his lap out of habit. He didn't miss Mrs. Fellowes raised eyebrow or Aileen choking on the tea she'd just sipped.

He smiled at the women and took a sip of his tea.

Aileen's eyes sparkled with pride. "We were discussin' the children."

"Colin is busy laying out the track from your mine to the mill. Should be ready for you to transport trailings by next weekend." Her lips formed a surprised 'o' and he wanted badly to lean over and taste them. He pulled his attention from her to the child squirming on his lap.

"When you gonna read to us some more?" Shayla asked, taking his face in her hands to make him look at her. She was so much like her mother. Wanting his full attention when she asked a question and wanting to see the answer not only in words but actions.

"What's today?" he asked, making her think.

"Two days after Sunday." Her small brow furrowed and her lips pursed.

"What happens on Sunday?"

"We read the Bible and you read to us." Her eyes lit with understanding.

"So I read to you two days ago which means I won't read again until this coming Sunday." He laughed at the lower lip protruding from her small mouth. A perfect replica of her mother's.

"Lassie, 'tisn't becomin' to be stickin' that lip out. Scoot on out o' here. Mr. Halsey is a busy man." The child slid from his lap and looked across the table at the other guests.

"Bye Mr. and Mrs. Fellowes." She waved and vanished through the door into the living quarters.

"She is a delight!" Mrs. Fellowes exclaimed.

"Yeah, she gets under your skin right quick." Ethan smiled. As well as the mother.

They fell into small talk, with Mrs. Fellowes doing most of the talking. Ethan watched Aileen. Having people drop by on a social call hadn't happened to her in a long time. Yet, she was a wonderful hostess and didn't once let on her discomfort. But he sensed it. Her eyes watched everything never once softening. She sat rigid in the chair, her hands clasped a little too tightly about her cup. Her fingers turning red under her nails gave her away.

Finally, Mrs. Fellowes stood. Her husband and Ethan stood as well. "It was wonderful to spend some time with you Mrs—"

"Call me Aileen, please." Aileen's curt response drew Ethan's gaze back to her.

"Aileen. I hope you stop by our place on one of your trips to town. I'd love to visit with you some more." Mrs. Fellowes tied her bonnet under her chin and nodded at her husband.

"Ah'll see." She followed the husband and wife to the door and as soon as it shut behind them, she turned to him.

"Did ye put her up to visitin' the poor lonely widow?"

Chapter 18

"No! I didn't put her up to anything. I was as stunned as you when John showed up with her sitting beside him on the wagon." Aileen's features relaxed, and her shoulders slumped. So that was it. She thought he was forcing people into her life. Not that she couldn't use a female friend.

"Ah've never had a visitor since leavin' Ireland." She stacked the cups and saucers. Picking them up, she looked at him. "What made her come today?"

Ethan sat back down. "I don't know. John said when he mentioned coming out, she offered to ride along."

"Ah've never met her. Is she one to gossip?" She crossed to the sink, lowering the dishes into the wash basin.

"I don't believe so. I don't think John would be married to a woman like that."

She turned to him. "And what kind o' woman would ye marry?"

Her question and guarded eyes struck him just as forcefully as if she'd slammed the spike hammer into his chest.

Truth? That's what he'd always favored. "I've never thought about it."

"Why?" She sat in the chair across from him. Wisps of dark curly hair framed her face and accentuated her pale green eyes.

"Because I've never thought of marrying." Was that surprise and... no it couldn't be?

"So ye dinnae believe ye are the marryin' kind?" She'd said it playfully, but her eyes watched him closely.

"I've raised my brothers. From an early age, my pa told me if anything happened to him it was my place to keep the family together and provide."

"Surely, he dinnae mean even as they became adults."

"Maybe not. But I don't know any different. And this mill will make them all financially secure." He reached across the table palm up, hoping she'd place her hand in his.

Hesitantly, she set her hand palm down on his. He wrapped his fingers around her hand. "This mill will also help make your family's dreams come true." He probed for more details about her past, the one she wanted to return to. "I haven't forgotten your comment the money would get you home. Where exactly is home? And why are you so desperate to return?"

Aileen gasped and tried to pull her hand free, but he held it firmly. "Ah've my reasons for no sayin' much about Ireland."

"What are you scared of?" His thumb rubbed

slowly back and forth across her hand. How could such a small gesture turn her insides to mush?

"Ah'm no' scared o' anythin'." She straightened her back and glared at him. How dare he mess with her senses and hound her about things best left alone.

"Then tell me what happened to Colin's father."

"'Tis nothin' to tell." She tried to pull her hand away, but this time he twined their fingers together. Binding them even closer.

"I say there is. Something happened to your husband that made you leave a land you're desperate to get back to."

She ducked her head. There were things she couldn't tell. She'd not bring harm to her laddie.

He cupped her chin, forcing her to look in his eyes. "You should have pulled enough gold out of that mine in the last four years to have passage back to Ireland. What is it you really need the money for?"

She swallowed. How did one hide from such concern? And patience.

"Ah cannae tell ye. Ye could say something to harm us." She pulled her chin from his grasp and jerked her hand from his, fleeing to stand at the drain board. The loss of contact left her feeling vulnerable and lost, but she couldn't depend on him. There hadn't been a man yet she could depend on.

"Aileen, I don't understand how telling me about your first husband can hurt you, but I'll not ask again."

She heard the chair slide back and waited for the closing of the door. Instead, warm air floated across the back of her neck. She held her breath as strong arms encircled her shoulders, drawing her back against his strong body.

"I would never do anything to intentionally hurt you or your children. If you feel it is best, I don't know everything about you that's fine. But know I would never tell anyone." He placed his chin on the top of her head.

His solidness wrapped around her like a comforting blanket. She felt safe when he was near. Oh, to be able to say something, but she couldn't. She couldn't risk him slipping to his brothers or anyone.

"Ah know ye'd no' harm us intentionally. Ah just cannae tell ye."

"That's fine." He gently spun her in his arms. "I just don't like us fighting. I prefer the opposite."

His dark eyes simmered with desire. His head tipped forward, his lips covered hers. He was a quick learner. The kiss deepened, sending tremors of delight through her body. She wound her arms around his neck, pulling her body tight against his.

Knowing he didn't care to marry allowed her to be more wanton. He didn't wish to be tied down any more than she wished to be a wife.

Aileen pulled her lips from his and caught her breath. She stared into Hank's eyes. "Ah've an itch that needs scratched." The words were out. Would he take the hint?

"Oh, lady, I'd love to scratch your itch." His hands moved down her back, pulling her hips against his. His need was hard.

"No' now!" she laughed, pushing against his chest.

"When?"

"Stick around after dinner, and we'll figure it out." She sidestepped away from him. If she didn't put space between them, she'd forget it was the middle of the day and pull him into her room. "Ye best leave now. Wouldn't want someone to come lookin' for ye."

"They know I brought John over to retrieve his wife."

"And they left a long time ago." She shook her head. How could a smart man miss the little things that caused gossip?

As if he just realized the situation, the jovial expression on his face fell. "I'm sorry. I should have left right away, huh?"

"Nothin' to do about it now." She motioned to the door. "Be gone. Ah dinnae want to see ye until dinner."

He smiled and headed for the back door, scooping his hat off the table on his way. The door closed behind him, and she slumped into the chair. What was she going to do? She'd all but served herself up to him tonight. Her stomach fluttered with anticipation as her mind cautioned the arrangement. She did crave to be loved by a man. To feel strong, safe arms around her as she floated on the ecstasy only the union of a man and woman would bring. But what happened after the one night?

Ethan whistled as he dismounted in front of the Sumpter telegraph office. He pulled the paper with his advertisement out of his pocket and pushed open the door. At the rate they laid the track, their first ore cart would dump next week. He'd hoped to have the miners work, but they all wanted to keep on digging in their mines. If he could find a handful of competent men, they could still pull a good profit and pay the help.

He handed his advertisement for the Bedrock-Democrat, the Baker City newspaper, to the telegraph agent.

"This is kind of long," the man said as he tapped the pencil to count each word. He looked up. "This would cost you less to ride to Baker City and hand it over to the newspaper office."

"I don't have time to ride to Baker City." Ethan waved his hand. "Just send the message and tell me what I owe."

The staccato taps of the telegram being sent lifted one more burden from his life. The extra dollar was worth knowing the advertisement would be in print in the morning and hopefully men would apply for jobs either by the end of tomorrow or the following day.

That meant he'd have to hang around the office in the afternoon and the following day to interview, or have Clay or Hank—no, he would.

His body heated thinking of what Aileen had promised tonight, and what they could explore tomorrow if he hung around the office.

"Ahem."

Ethan shook off the thoughts and focused on the man holding out his hand.

"I said, that'll be a dollar twenty-five."

He dug into his pocket and pulled out the appropriate coins. "Will they acknowledge they received the message?"

"You didn't ask me to ask for a reply." The man huffed back to his chair and tapped out a brief message. "There. Should hear back from them in a minute or two."

Ethan nodded his head. "I've got a couple things to pick up at the mercantile. I'll swing back by before I head out." The man nodded and went back to writing in a journal.

Tucking the advertisement back in his pocket, Ethan headed to the mercantile. He should take favors to their dinner hostess and her children. He'd thought on it all the way into town. Yep. It was the thing to do.

The bell over the mercantile door jangled as he pushed the door open and wandered inside. He knew exactly what he would get Shayla and Colin. A doll and a knife. But their mother... he wasn't sure.

The last time he'd strolled at his leisure up and down between the tables gawking at the wares had been years ago as a child. These days, he hurried to the counter, handed the clerk his list, and went about other errands while they filled his order. Scanning the dolls and carved wooden horses, memories of a simpler time washed over him. A time when he'd only thought about the moment and how he could torment his brothers or cajole another piece of pie out of his mother. He'd entered this store a hundred times with his parents and wished for things he knew he'd never have but enjoyed the dreaming.

He shook his head. The day his parents died all the fun had been stripped from his life. The only dream he wished to fulfill had been his father's. Make the Halsey name something to be proud of.

He'd become a parent at too young an age. Granted his brothers were grown and didn't require his fatherly care. But once he started looking out for them— he couldn't stop.

"What brought you to town?"

The familiar voice yanked him back to the present. He smiled and then remembered their last parting. His face heated with embarrassment.

"I sent a telegraph to the Bedrock-Democrat advertising for workers at the mill." He tipped his hat to Myrle and made his decision. He plucked a pretty, blonde-haired doll from the table and a set of wooden dominoes. It would be better to work Colin's mind than to give him a weapon.

"You've made that much progress?" Myrle asked, her gaze resting on the toys in his hands.

She wasn't talking about the mill. Not giving her the satisfaction of seeing him flustered again, he took her by the elbow, escorting her down the aisle toward the women's fripperies.

Loudly he said, "Yes, the mill will be ready to start running the end of the week." In a lower voice he added. "Help me pick out something that would be good as a thank you gift to Aileen."

Myrle tittered and pointed to a pretty set of handkerchiefs. "I assume this is a thank you gift and not a 'hoping this will lure you into my bed' gift."

Ethan stared down at the pint-sized woman. He wanted to—Who was he fooling. The thought had crossed his mind. He lowered his chin, hiding his face in the shadow of his hat brim. Was he just buying gifts to bribe Aileen? He probed into his actions.

He stared Myrle in the eye. "Aileen is making dinner tonight for Clay, Hank, and myself. I figure it's the least I could do." He held up the box of wooden tiles. "And Colin has been doing the work of a man, so I figured I'd give him something fun." He shook the box. "After dinner, we can all play the game." He raised the doll up, glanced at the happy face and smiled. "And Shayla, well, she just deserves a doll."

Myrle patted his arm. "I apologize for the way my thoughts were running." She picked up the fancy handkerchiefs and placed them in his hand. "When you do decide to follow your feelings—be careful neither one of you gets hurt." She tucked her basket of goods in the crook of her arm and marched out the door.

Her words sunk into his belly like a large fist. Who could get hurt and why? He started toward the door.

"You going to pay for that or just waltz right out of here?"

Ethan glared at the clerk and stomped to the counter. It didn't help his mood any to have the man's eyebrows raise at the sight of his purchases.

"You aren't getting none to friendly with that husband killer are ya? " The clerk pushed the items together and held his hand out. "That'll be three seventy-five."

Holding the money back just far enough so the man had to lean over the counter, Ethan said, "Aileen Miller isn't a husband killer and her children shouldn't be treated poorly because you all have nothing better to do than listen to false rumors."

The clerk snatched the money and handed him back his change.

Ethan dropped the change in his pocket and remembered the advertisement. "Hang this up where people can see it." He handed the paper to the clerk and left the establishment with his gifts tucked under his arm.

It appeared the women of the town weren't threatened by Aileen, but the male population was running scared. He snickered. That was fine with him. They'd keep their distance. And with luck, the women in the community would welcome Aileen into their circles. For all her claims to like being alone, she'd hung on every word Mrs. Fellowes said.

Shoving the gifts into his saddlebag, he mounted and headed home. He planned to shave and look sharp for dinner. Thinking of what might happen after the meal, he nudged his horse into a canter.

Chapter 19

Aileen stood in her bedroom, dressed only in her shift, using cold water to sponge off the day's sweat and dirt. The roast was in the oven. The mouth-watering aroma filtered through the rooms mixing with the scents of soda bread and pastries stuffed with wild berry preserves.

She brushed her hair until it crackled with life. A small hand mirror propped on the wash stand allowed her to see her reflection. She dug into her jar of pomade, rubbed it between her hands, then smoothed down the wayward strands, taming her curls. Twisting the hair at the sides of her head, she drew them back into a bun at the nape of her neck. She peered into the small mirror one more time.

Presentable. That's what she was and all she'd be. The lovely, young Highlander who captured the heart of an Irish lad had disappeared. In her place stood a woman who'd been through more than any one person should in a life time. Sighing, she pulled on her best cotton blouse and stepped into the only skirt she owned that didn't have a stained hem.

"Momma! Momma!" Shayla burst into the room.

"What darlin'?" Aileen hastily buttoned her top and glanced down at the glowing face of her daughter.

"When are they gonna get here?" Shayla skipped around the room, dragging her hand across the worn blanket and ruffling the trousers and dress hanging from pegs on the wall.

Aileen stopped her daughter just as she started to smack a hand into the bowl of water on the washstand. "They'll be here sooner, if ye find somethin' to occupy yerself."

"I've done everythin'." She bowed her head, and her small lips formed a pout.

"Darlin' have ye drawn a picture for Mr. Halsey?" She laughed at the surprised expression on her child's face.

"No! He'p me get some paper." Shayla captured her hand, dragging her out into the living quarters. She found the sheets of paper Ethan gave them to work numbers on and practice writing. She gave Shayla one without any marks and a pencil.

"Think careful afore ye start. Ye'll no' get another piece." She laughed at the small furrowed brow and moved into the kitchen to check on things one last time. Truth be told, she was anxious for their visitors to arrive as well.

This would be the first time she hosted a meal since leaving Ireland. Patrick had invited many of their friends over several times a week before—she shook her head. Tonight was not a night to dwell on the past. Tonight—she placed a hand on her fluttering heart—could give her something she hadn't realized she craved. The closeness of a man and woman.

The outside door opened. Colin entered, from the top of his knit cap right down to his boots, he was covered in dirt.

"Take off yer bits and use the water in my room to wash."

"I liked the shack better. You weren't so bossy about being clean." Scowling, Colin sat down to unlace his boots.

"The only reason ah allowed ye to behave like a heathen was ah dinnae give a care about the place. This isn't ours. We're usin' it and therefore need to take care o' it." She waved the spoon in her hand toward the door. "Put yer bits aside the door and go wash up."

His muffled stomp brought a smile. When would the boy learn a man doesn't always have to huff around?

She scanned the set table. She'd dug to the bottom of her trunk to find the matching plates that traveled over the ocean with her. Patrick's mother had given her the dishes on their wedding day. She swiped at the tear tickling the corner of her eye.

Her life had changed drastically after his death. She finally believed she might have some control. That is if she could figure out what to do about the man who crept into her thoughts at all hours of the day and night.

The sound of voices in the other room sent her thoughts flying and her hands to smooth out the apron covering her thread-bare clothing. She'd used the material Mrs. Fellowes brought for curtains to make the garment. She'd had to hurry through the chores, but the result was worth it. The cheerful yellow gingham brightened her whole outlook.

The door from the main room opened, and Ethan's head peaked through. "Smells delicious in here." His gaze roamed from her feet up to her hair. "And looks even better."

She couldn't squelch the grin tugging at her lips. "Ye dinnae look half bad yerself." He'd cleaned up. His face looked smooth and inviting. She took a couple steps closer and breathed in the scent of fresh-shaven man. Shave soap with a hint of bay rum.

He took a couple steps toward her. Desire smoldered in his eyes. Would he take her in his arms? She held her breath. Even as she willed him to, she hoped he didn't.

"Momma! Look what Mr. Halsey brought me!" Shayla burst into the room with an expensive, fragile doll. "She's beautiful!" Shayla hugged the toy to her and whirled around the room.

"Ye shouldn't have given the lassie such an expensive gift." When Aileen was pregnant with the child, she'd imagined all the fine things she'd give her. The enthralled face and bright eyes on her daughter brought tears to her eyes. If only she could have brought that joy to her.

"Shhh... There's no need to cry. I brought you a gift as well." The joking tone jerked her attention to the man who'd skillfully placed his arm around her shoulders. She spun from the embrace and glared at him.

"Gifts will no' bring ye in favor with me." She pushed the words out between her clenched teeth.

Ethan raised his hands, holding the boxed handkerchiefs in the air. "I didn't bring gifts to put me in favor. Honest." Lowering his arms, he watched Aileen breath in and out, expanding her chest and bringing her attributes to the forefront of his thoughts, when he was trying his hardest not to think of the invitation she'd given earlier.

"Then what do ye call the doll for the lassie and..." she pointed to the box in his hand.

"These are gifts from Hank, Clay, and me to you, Shayla, and we gave Colin dominoes." He offered the box of frippery to her, hiding a grin as she eyed the offering, then him, then the gift. She wanted to take it. Her eyes had lit up at the sight of the feminine scraps of cloth.

"There are no strings attached to this gift. It is a thank you for making us dinner."

"Nae, ah be makin' dinner for all yer help with movin' and offerin' a place for us to live." She touched the lace edge of the handkerchief.

"Don't they have customs in Ireland or Scotland where guests invited to dinner bring gifts?"

"Aye."

If she was going to be ornery, he could too. "Then take the box and get back to cooking, my stomach is grumbling."

Hank walked through the open door followed by Colin and Clay.

"Are you all eating while we're in the other room explaining how to play dominoes?" Hank nodded to Aileen and watched Ethan.

"We're just discussing etiquette of dinner

guests." Ethan took the doll Shayla handed him and scrutinized the porcelain face, but kept an eye on Aileen.

She shot him a scowl that should have landed him on the ground, before she turned a sweet smile on his brothers. "Have a seat. 'Tis nearly ready." She set the box high on a shelf where it would be out of the way and opened the oven door.

He hurried to her side to help lift the heavy pot with the roast. "Let me get that."

She swatted at his hands, set her mouth in a determined line, and reached for the pot with towels in her hands. "Sit down like a gentleman and let me do my job."

Defeated and feeling foolish, he sat in a chair and tried to ignore the smirks and raised eyebrows of his brothers. What was it about this woman that made him do things he wouldn't normally do? Like offer to help in the kitchen. This was her kitchen, and she obviously had everything under control.

He snorted. She'd proved stronger than him. Hank and Clay had nearly busted their jaws when their mouths fell open at the gifts he told them were from all three of them. After the initial shock, they badgered him all the way here.

Now, they each watched him as he worked to keep his gaze from straying to Aileen bent over, reaching into the oven. He turned his attention to Colin.

"How many more cross members will it take to get your track finished?" He received a nod of approval from Hank and an enthusiastic squaring of shoulders by Colin.

"By my figures we've got two hundred feet

left to go and setting a cross member every three feet…" Colin drew the numbers on the table cloth with his finger, then raised his head. "I figure it would be best to have about seventy more. That's a couple extra for spots that need more stabilizing."

"You're a quick learner," Clay said as Aileen placed the sliced meat on the table along with soda bread, preserves, and boiled potatoes.

Ethan stood, starting a chain reaction as his brothers rose and then Colin while they waited for Aileen to take off her apron and slide into the vacant chair beside him.

When they were seated, Ethan waited to see if Aileen expected a blessing. She pushed the plate of meat towards him without glancing his way.

They all started filling plates and then their bellies. After the plates held only crumbs, Clay groaned. "That was the best meal I've had in a long while.

Aileen smiled and stood. Ethan bolted out of his chair, but the other three males just groaned and leaned against their chair backs.

As long as he was standing, he grasped empty dishes and headed to the drain board.

"There's no need to help," Aileen said, brushing past him.

"I'm up and could use the movement after all the food I ate." He returned to the table for another load.

"Ah baked these today as well." Aileen sat a heaping plate of baked goods on the table.

Clay groaned again and slowly leaned forward to take one. "I'm stuffed, but these look too good not to at least try."

Hank took one as well.

"Tea?" Aileen asked.

Ethan settled back in his chair and plucked a pastry oozing with preserves. "I'll take some."

"Me too," Hank added.

Clay just shook his head.

Ethan watched her move about the kitchen. He liked how she took charge. The fact she didn't appear to be thinking at all about her comment that morning bothered him. He hadn't stopped thinking about it. In fact, his body heated at the memory of the kiss.

She carried two cups and saucers to the table. She placed one in front of Hank and as she leaned over to place one in front of him, their gazes locked. She was thinking about it!

The desire burning in her eyes was hard to ignore. But he had to with her children and his brothers sitting at the table.

The cup and saucer rattled when she finally set them on the table. She grabbed her apron, dipping her head elegantly through the loop, and tied it behind her. When she started pumping water, Ethan stood again.

"Hank, Clay why don't you go in and play a couple games of dominoes with these two while I help Aileen with the dishes." Luckily, Colin and Shayla thought it was a great idea and hurried to the door calling the men to join them.

Hank passed him on his way to the door. "Make sure all you do is dishes," he said in a low voice.

Ethan stared at his brother. How did he know the thoughts running in his head?

Clay lumbered to the door. Just before he stepped through, he winked and then said loudly, "Bet it takes all night before any of you can beat me."

Ethan groaned at his brother's innuendo. Aileen had finished pumping water into the basin and was now adding hot water from the reservoir on the cook stove.

"There's no need to help me." She dumped the boiling water into the dish pan.

"The faster you get the dishes done, the faster we can," he cleared his throat, "get to know one another better."

She rounded on him, her fists perched on her hips. "Ah dinnae know what came over me earlier. But thinkin' the thoughts ye are—" She shook her head. "'Tis a bad idea."

"How can wanting to hold you in my arms and not worry about someone barging in be a bad idea?" He wasn't going to let her off that easy. Her statement conjured up images of her naked, and he planned to hold her to it.

"Because...well just because." She turned to the dish pan, scrubbing the dishes with vigor.

He placed his hands on her shoulders. She flinched but didn't move out from under his lightly resting hands. He felt the warmth of her skin through her blouse. She wasn't a woman carrying too much meat. She wasn't too skinny either. Doing a man's work had given her hard muscles.

Gently, he pulled her back against him and slid one arm around her. He sniffed her hair. She smelled of baked goods, soap, and woman. He preferred this to the sickly sweet scent of the prostitutes he'd visited.

Her pulled up hair revealed her long neck. The smooth skin beckoned. He placed a light kiss below her jaw. Her chest expanded as she sighed. He smiled. She could put her claws out all she wanted, but she was attracted to him.

"Aileen, I don't want to fight with you. I only want to hold you and spend time with you." He spun her slowly. Her eyelids veiled her thoughts, and her lips trembled.

He placed a hand on either side of her head and tipped her face up. "I promise to never hurt you. It's not in me to harm a woman or a child." Lowering his head, he captured her mouth and savored the softness, warmth, and taste of her.

Her arms circled his neck, and her body molded to his. He moved his hands down her back and over her backside, cupping the firm mounds in his hands. Desire knifed through him. He ran his hands up, kneading her back and capturing her head once more.

With effort, he pulled out of the kiss and leaned his forehead on hers. "Let's finish these dishes and go for a walk."

Her dazed eyes cleared and she nodded. Together they finished the dishes in record time. Her cloak was by the back door, but his coat was in the room where the others played dominoes. Not wanting to disturb them or let on they were headed outside, Ethan left his coat and pulled Aileen out the door like a smitten youth.

Once outside, he captured her into his arms again. He'd never get enough of her sweetness. They were both panting when he pulled away and grasped her hand, leading her over the bridge and toward the stamp mill.

"Why are ye takin' me to the mill?" she asked but followed obediently.

"Because it's a little warmer in there and better than standing out here in the open. And if Clay or Hank decide to check on us, and find us gone, they'll come looking. At least in here, we'll have some notice when they show up."

She started to protest, but he captured her lips once more and danced her over to a corner where he'd spread a blanket earlier.

Chapter 20

Aileen whirled out of his strong arms. It was one thing to carry on with heated kisses and quite another for him to be so sure he'd already spread a blanket.

"Ah'm no' some loose woman ye can just spread a blanket and have me spread my legs." She fisted her hands on her hips and stared at him. Mon! But he was a handsome man. And his touch turned her body into a pool of hot puddin'.

"I didn't plan to seduce you here." His lips curved into a mischievous smirk. "I didn't plan it, but if it happens, I'm not complaining."

She burst out laughing. "Mon, but ye are too truthful for yer own good."

He pulled her into his arms. "I love to hear you laugh. It's a sound I could listen to every day and never tire." The sincerity glistening in his dark eyes formed a lump in her throat.

The man knew what to say, she'd give him that. "'Tis been a while since ah've felt like laughin' much."

She craved the arms that held her tight. He pressed her head to his chest. His heart beat steady and strong under her ear. Her arms circled his waist. She closed her eyes and reveled in the masculine scent, the strong body, and the tender hold.

"Aileen, all I want from you is your trust and some time alone with you." His voice rumbled under her ear. "If we—you know get to the point where you want to do more than hold each other and kiss, well—I'm willing."

She couldn't hold the snort that escaped as she backed out of his embrace. "Ah swear 'tis all ye men think about. Yer boaby."

In the faint moonlight filtering through the windows, his face contorted in confusion.

"What's a boaby?" he finally asked.

"Yer—man thing." She pointed to his crotch and burst out laughing as his face deepened in color.

"You're a wicked woman to talk so brash," he said, pulling her back in his arms and kissing her till her knees gave way.

With gentleness, he lowered her to the blanket. The minute her back hit the cold material, she reared up. He steadied her with his hands, caressing the back of her neck, down her aching shoulder muscles, and lower, cupping a breast and fondling it. His touch was soft, tentative, and captivating.

She moved into his hand, allowing him to feel and elicit shimmers of warmth through her body. This was a man she could trust not only with her body, but with her life. She had known it the first day he set foot on her land, and tonight she knew it with her heart.

She wound her arms around his neck, rubbing her body against his, kissing his neck and cheek. She snuggled her face against his freshly shaven cheek. He moaned and pulled her tighter, moving his hips against hers. She knew he had to be about to explode, but she wasn't giving in. Not this first time. If she finally gave herself to a man after the horrors she faced with Mr. Miller—She shivered at the thought of that man's handling of her.

"Are you cold?" Ethan pulled the blanket up from the side, covering her.

"Nae. Ah had a flash o'—" How could she tell this man, who was nothing like Mr. Miller, that she thought of that monster when he kissed her.

"I will never hurt you." His warm lips traveled down her neck, leaving a wet trail. He nuzzled the opening of her blouse, popping open the top button and exposing her to his hungry lips. The softness of his kisses and the reverence in which he held her, took her breath away. She buried his head between her breasts, giving him what he sought and knew the next time they were alone, she would not deny him.

"Ethan! We're heading home!" Hank called from outside.

"Damn!" Ethan sat up, helping Aileen to sit beside him. He wasn't going to have either one of his brothers find him or Aileen in any state of undress. He buttoned her blouse and pulled her to her feet. She smiled up at him, wrapping her arms around his neck and enticing him with her sweet lips.

He pulled her into his arms, drinking in what she offered. Footsteps crunched on the river rock they put in front of the mill to allow drainage of excess water.

"We better continue this another time. I think we have company coming." He kissed her quickly and kicked the blanket into a heap in the corner. He'd get here early in the morning and hide it before anyone showed up to work.

Capturing her hand in his, he opened the door and caught Hank in the act of reaching for the latch.

"You giving Aileen a tour in the dark?" The sarcasm in his brother's voice didn't bother Ethan. He'd learned tonight Aileen was having the same feelings toward him that he had for her. Just knowing his feelings were reciprocated elated him as much as if they had done more than kiss.

"We just wanted some time alone. Thanks for entertaining the kids." Ethan smiled at the expression of surprise on Hank's face. His brother thought he'd deny what they'd been up to. Well, he'd soon learn his older brother was courting the woman.

Aileen tugged at the hand he still held. "I'll walk Aileen back to the house. How about you and Clay round up the horses?"

He stepped past Hank, leading Aileen to her kitchen door. "I hope you don't mind, but it's about time my brothers and anyone else knows how I feel about you." Before she could make a comment he kissed her quick and walked away. He didn't want to ruin a perfect night with her rounding on him.

And she would. He smiled at the thought of sparring with her tomorrow. Because he knew they would when he came to wait for men to interview for work at the mill.

Hank held out his horse's reins. "So you're not going to hide anymore?"

Ethan swung up onto his horse. "No, I'm not."

"Not what?" Clay asked, riding up beside them.

"Not hiding the way Aileen and I feel about each other." Ethan nudged his horse up the clearing alongside the track to their mine.

Clay trotted up beside him. "You're what?" He grabbed Ethan's reins, stopping the horse. "You know what people are going to say?"

"That it's about time a woman took my fancy?"

"No, that you're just as crazy as she is. You think that's going to be any good for business?"

"It's nobody's business but mine who I court. And it shouldn't have anything to do with business." Ethan nudged his horse forward. If people were so narrow-minded they didn't do business with them because he was courting Aileen, then they didn't need their business.

"I think you're looking for trouble with this. Can't you just take care of your randiness in Baker City and keep Aileen strictly business?"

"I'm not randy!" Turning in the saddle, he peered at Clay. "I enjoy Aileen's company and find her fetching. If you have a problem with that, then maybe you need to find other means of work than the mill."

Clay raised his hands. "I'm just telling you what people will say."

"Only people like Miles would think that way."

Ethan started his horse toward home once more. They'd just have to hope people like Myrle and Mrs. Fellowes would spread good words about them and with time the naysayers would come around. He'd like Aileen to feel a part of the community before she left.

The thought of her leaving set like a sledge hammer in the pit of his stomach.

When they arrived at the cabin, Ethan noticed a telegram stuck in their door. He dismounted and pulled the sealed note out of the crack. Stuffing the missive in his shirt pocket, he helped tend to the animals. In the cabin, Hank lit the lantern and they all sat at the table to see what the note said.

Ethan read it out loud. "We should be in Sumpter on Friday. Stop. Zeke and Maeve. Stop." He looked at his brothers then around the cabin. "What's today? Tuesday?"

Hank nodded.

"Someone needs to go to town tomorrow and get a regular bed."

Clay looked at him like he'd caught a fever. "Where do you plan to put it?" He swung his arms, emphasizing the already filled space.

"At Aileen's. We'll move her cot in with Shayla and put the bed in her room for Zeke and Maeve while they're here." The more Ethan played the idea over in his head, the more he liked it. Yes, a nice bed for Aileen. One that two people could fit comfortable in. He unbuttoned his shirt.

"You doing this for Zeke and Maeve or you and Aileen?" The accusing tone from Hank was uncharacteristic.

He narrowed his eyes. "What if I said both?" He looked from one brother to the other. "What do you two have against Aileen?"

"She's got a bold mouth. And you can't see she's making a fool out of you." Hank stood up and slapped his hands down on the table as he leaned toward Ethan. "Can't you see she's just using you to get what she wants?"

Ethan shook his head slowly. His brother didn't have a clue. If anything he was using her. "She's not using me. I gave in to all her requests because I want that mill for this family."

"You know good and well there could have been another way."

Ethan glanced at Clay. He nodded his head.

"Neither one of you see. I helped this family, yes. But they are not using me." He stood, turned out the lantern, and dropped his trousers. "Let's get to sleep. I have interviews to conduct tomorrow. Clay, you go to town and get the bed." He flopped onto his cot.

Ethan lay on his back, staring up at the black space above him. What was it going to take for his family to see Aileen wasn't manipulating him? Anyway, not more than he was willing to allow.

The memories of their shared kisses warmed his chest and didn't harden him. Contentment eased his worries. It was satisfying to know he could think of her and feel more than a need to release his desire. What did it mean?

Aileen placed the last breakfast dish on the

drain board when the office banged shut. Expecting to see Ethan, she hurried through the living quarters and pushed the door to the office open. A man of average build and height stood at the counter. He pulled a dusty derby off his head as she entered.

"Would yer husband be around?" he asked in an Irish lilt.

"Ah've no husband." She eyed him warily. What would an Irishman be doing here asking about her husband?

The perplexed expression on the man's face almost made her drop her guard and soothe him, but she was more concerned over why he was in the office.

"I'm lookin' for a Mr. Halsey. I assumed he lived here." The man smiled. A tooth on the right side of his mouth was black.

"He should be here shortly. Ye can wait for him outside." Aileen turned to head back into the living quarters.

"I'm Orin Healy."

She spun around at the name, but kept her expression neutral.

He smiled, his eyes narrowing. "And who might you be?"

"My clerk," Ethan walked through the office door. Relief ebbed through her. She could leave now.

"What can we do for you Mr.—" Ethan held his hand out to the man.

Mr. Healy shook hands and sized up Ethan. Aileen hid a smile as the man tipped his head back to look into Ethan's face.

"Healy. Orin Healy. I heard in town you be

lookin' for workers."

His statement twisted her gut. She didn't want him around. He had the same name as Patrick's cousin. If he was the same man, it wouldn't be long before Roderick found them.

"I didn't expect anyone to show up for interviews until this afternoon." Ethan moved the half door and took a position at the counter, placing himself between her and the man.

"I happened to be at the telegraph office and the agent asked me to deliver the message to the newspaper." The man raised his hand when Ethan glowered at him. "I wasn't readin' anythin' I shouldn't have been. The man just handed me an open piece o' paper with the advertisement."

She'd heard enough. He sounded like the conniving man she remembered. She turned to go through the door.

"Aileen, would you hand me a piece of paper and a pencil, please?" Ethan sent her a confident smile.

She wasn't sure what he was up to, but she did as he asked, staying as far away from the man as she could and not look ridiculous handing Ethan the supplies.

"Mr. Healy, write down your name, past work experience, and where I can contact you if I decide to hire you." He slid the paper and pencil toward the man and turned back to her. "I could use a cup of coffee." He grasped her elbow and escorted her into the next room.

"Why are ye even givin' him the time o' day?" She spun blocking his entrance to the kitchen.

"Every man who comes in asking about working here will have the chance to apply." He peered into her face. "What's wrong with him? Was he inappropriate before I arrived?" She saw the anger start to build in his eyes.

"Nae, but ah dinnae like his attitude."

"He sounds Irish to me. I'd have thought you'd like to talk with someone from Ireland."

She ducked her head. She wasn't ready to tell Ethan everything about her past. Or the fact she feared running into anyone who knew her and Patrick.

Ethan took a step toward Aileen, she backed away. Something about the man in the office disturbed her. Was she worried he'd be jealous if Healy had talked sweet to her? He was jealous the man affected her. Wanting to lay claim, he pulled her into his arms and kissed her. When she didn't fight, he deepened the kiss, wandering his hands down her back and drawing her hips tight against his own.

"Momma?" Shayla's hesitant voice doused his desire like a bucket of cold water.

Aileen started to bolt from his arms. He didn't relinquish his hold. He wanted Shayla to get used to him holding her mother.

"Act normal. She hasn't seen you kiss a man and needs to know I'm not hurting you," he whispered.

Aileen nodded her head, relaxing against him and smiling at her child. "Darlin' what is it ye need?"

Ethan circled an arm around Aileen's shoulders. Her head came to the bottom of his chin. He looked over it and winked at Shayla. The child giggled and ran over, throwing her arms around both their legs.

The emotions that overcame him nearly made his chest burst. Pride, protectiveness, and—love. He choked on the thought. Gasping for air, he let go of Aileen and took a step backward. He couldn't love them. He didn't want a family.

Aileen and Shayla became a blur as his world spun out of control.

"Ethan." Aileen's voice sounded shrill and distant. "Ethan!"

He shook himself and pushed through the kitchen door to sit on a chair. Shayla climbed onto his lap and stared into his face. Out of the corner of his eye he watched Aileen bustling about the room.

She shoved a cup in his hand. It was warm and the steam wafting up, tickling his nose, smelled sweet. "Drink. It will set ye to rights."

He raised the cup to his lips and looked into her concerned eyes. What was he to do? He'd told his brothers he was courting the woman. And he wanted to, but he'd planned to do it until she left and then continue on with his single life.

Studying the angel-kissed face watching him with concern, he knew there was no way he'd be able to let this woman walk out of his life. He loved her and her children. He gulped the hot liquid, hoping it would do more than set things right, but also help him find a way to prove his love and hopefully keep her from going back to Ireland.

Chapter 21

Aileen handed out papers to six men throughout the day as they came to interview for a job at the mill. A couple of the men she knew from town or through Mr. Miller.

She put check marks on the information of the men who treated her poorly. If Ethan still hired them after she told him her feelings, she would pack up and head back to the shack. Nothing would make her be subjected to that kind of treatment again. She'd learned to stand up for herself, and she wasn't about to let the likes of those men change her newfound courage.

The door opened as she shuffled the papers into a pile. Clay entered the office. The glower on his face would have made Shayla run for cover. His stilted movements showed his agitation.

"I'm bringing a bed in for your room. I'm going to bring it through the kitchen. Move the table to the side so we can carry it in." His words were sharp.

"Ah don't understand? Ah dinnae order a bed?" His agitation was rubbing off on her.

"Ethan ordered me to get it this morning and bring it here to go in your room."

Anger bubbled fast and hot. "Ah dinna ask for it, and ah'm no' takin' it!" She stomped past Clay and into the cold, fall air. "Where's the eejit?" She scoured the area around the mill looking for Ethan. The gall of the man to order up a bed thinking she would fall into it with him.

She found him striding toward the office with Colin on his heels. Confronting him with the laddie nearby wasn't the best of plans, but her reputation was at stake.

Crossing her arms and taking a stance in their path, she waited for Ethan to get close enough she didn't have to raise her voice.

"What is the meanin' of puttin' a bed in my room?"

Colin stepped to her side and squared up his young shoulders.

"It isn't what you obviously think." Ethan started to pass her. She reached out, stopping him with a firm grasp of his coat. "Ah told ye, ah'm no loose woman, and ye'll no' wiggle into my bed."

Colin took a step toward Ethan. At his angry snarl, she turned her attention to her son. The fury in his young eyes scared her more than any beating she took from Mr. Miller. Fearing for Ethan, she stepped in front of him, forgetting her anger.

She put her hands out. "Colin, go on. 'Tis a riff 'tween Mr. Halsey and myself. Ye dinnae need to worry." To emphasize she wasn't scared of Ethan, she grasped his arm, pulling it around her mid-section. It was a forward move on her part in the broad daylight with so many men milling about, but she couldn't have her son thinking the man had or would do her any harm.

"Do as your ma says. You know she's got a temper to go with her fiery hair." A large hand smoothed her wayward strands. "Besides when she gets all riled up, I find it invigorating battling her with words not fists." His comments warmed her more than his caress the night before. She never thought she'd find another man who enjoyed bantering with her.

Colin moved away with halting steps and as he did, Clay came striding up to them. "Kind of making a spectacle of yourselves, aren't you?" He didn't wave his hands, but his eyes rolled, emphasizing the fact the workers laying the last of the tracks were close enough to witness the exchange.

If Ethan's arm hadn't felt so secure and his warm, unyielding front hadn't been pressed against her, she would have fled in mortification. But standing in his arms and facing his brother's accusation, the rightness of the moment kept her from fleeing.

"We're not making a spectacle, you are." The first thing Ethan noticed when Aileen came charging toward him was the fact she didn't wear a shawl. The wind had a bite to it today. When she'd stepped in front of him, he'd thought she was using him to brace against the wind, until he'd seen the rage in her son's eyes. She'd stepped in front of him to protect him. He would have laughed if her fear hadn't rippled in the air, and the boy's stance and expression hadn't seethed with fury.

Clay swung around, heading toward the wagon backed up to the kitchen door.

Aileen stiffened under his arm as he escorted her toward the wagon. To laugh would make her even more furious, but he found her anger over receiving a bed endearing and ridiculous.

"We received a telegram from my brother Zeke and his wife Maeve. They're going to be here on Friday." He stopped at the wagon and inspected the bed. Even though Clay didn't approve of the office or Zeke and Maeve staying with Aileen, he'd purchased a well-stuffed mattress.

Aileen glanced at the bed and entered the house. He followed her. She spun in her tracks as soon as he'd cleared the threshold.

"Why are ye tellin' me about yer kin when ah want to wrin' yer bloody neck." She threw her hands in the air and as he opened his mouth to comment, she started in again. "Ah see what yer up to and it won't work on me. Ye can put that bag o' stuffin' in my house but ye cannae make me sleep on it."

He couldn't keep a laugh from bursting forth. Anger didn't hamper her looks, it enriched them. He found her sainted words and wanton actions comical. He'd never come across such a contrary woman, and he'd never been so intrigued either.

"Hold on. Before you have me hogtied and strung up, can I tell you what's happening?"

She crossed her arms under her ample breasts. Her light green eyes narrowed and her soft, rosy lips locked in a disapproving line.

"The bed will go in your room. We'll move your cot in the room with Shayla. When Zeke and

Maeve are here, I'd like them to stay here in your room on the big bed." When she started to protest, he held up a hand. "It wouldn't be proper for them to stay at the cabin with Hank, Clay, and I. We just have a one-room place with single cots. I figure they won't stay more than a day or two and then you can have the bed, no strings or bodies attached."

"So ye want me to cook for yer family? And act as their servant while they be here?" She uncrossed her arms and stalked toward him.

"No. I don't want you to be their servant. I'm sure Maeve will pitch in and help with the cooking. I just want them to get to know you and you to know them. That's all. And it would help me out to have them stay here."

Clay pushed the door open with the mattress. "You two gonna talk all day or help me get this in the house."

Ethan moved to help him, and Aileen shoved the table to the side of the room. He and Clay pulled in all the pieces to the bed while Aileen moved her cot into Shayla's room.

"Ah've no bedding for a bed that size."

He didn't miss the wistful look in her eyes. She would enjoy sleeping on the mattress and stretching out across the expanse.

"Clay did you think to buy any?" Ethan turned to his brother who stood in the doorway watching them.

"No, didn't think about it. Just got the best bed they had, like you said."

Ethan dug into his pocket. "Take this and purchase whatever you need for the bed." He held out several gold coins toward her.

"Nae! What would people think?" Her eyes widened in horror.

"They'd think you had a need for new bedding."

"After yer brother bought a bed this morning. No one in Sumpter is that daft."

"What did you say when you bought the bed?" he asked Clay.

"Said Zeke and Maeve were coming for a visit, and you sent me to buy a bed."

Ethan nodded. "See, everyone will know the bed is for company."

"And they'll all know it was brought here. For me."

"Not for you. For company. I can't help the fact you'll be able to use it when Zeke and Maeve aren't here." He had to make her see reason. They needed bedding, and he wanted her to purchase it. To get what she liked.

"Take the money and go to Myrle. She can go to the mercantile with you if it makes you feel better." Ethan turned. He was through wasting time over a simple thing. "Come on. We need to check out the tracks and decide who to hire."

"Ah made marks on some o' the papers." The warning in her voice stopped him.

"Clay, I'll meet you at Wilken's tracks." Clay frowned but he left.

"What do the marks mean?"

She moved past him, down the hall, and into the main room. Her hands twined round and round each other. Why was she so nervous?

"Aileen, what's wrong?" He moved to draw

her into his arms. She sidestepped him.

"Ethan, ah know ye grew up with most of these men, but they..." She turned, wringing her hands and avoiding eye contact.

He grasped her shoulder, making her look at him. "What do the marks mean?"

"The men with marks spoke to me like ah was a whore." She glared at him. Her pale eyes sparked with indignation, and her spine snapped straight. "Ah'll no' be workin' with men that dinnae treat me respectable."

"I am running a business—" Her face reddened and her eyes narrowed. "If a man you've marked has worked in a stamp mill before, I need his knowledge, however—" He held up a hand as she started to speak. "I will let him know his job depends on showing you respect." She opened her mouth to speak, again. "And if you tell me he isn't, I'll fire him."

She studied him. Her silence squeezed his chest. Surely, she understood good business.

"Ah'll accept this deal, but if one o' yer workers lays a hand on me or speaks bad, ah'll tell ye and if ye do nothin', ah'll no' work nor live here."

Ethan wasn't surprised by her answer. She was a woman who wanted respect and deserved it.

"I agree." He held out his hand to shake. When she tentatively placed her hand in his, he pulled her against him, wrapping his arms around her. "I think a kiss would seal this agreement." He lowered his head, capturing her sputtering lips.

This woman was influencing him in so many ways. And all good. Her hands clutched the front of his coat. If the darn thing wasn't on, he'd feel her body mold to his… and there was a bed just down the hall…

As if she read his mind, her fingers uncurled, and she pushed gently against him, putting space between them.

"Mr. Halsey, ye have work to do." She touched her fingers to her lips and looked up at him.

"I do. And you have a trip to make to town." He placed a gold eagle coin in her hand and curled her fingers around it. "Go to Myrle, tell her I asked you to purchase bedding for when Zeke and Maeve visit. She'll go to the store with you and make certain no one gossips."

Her eyes shimmered with uncertainty. "I'll keep Colin busy. You and Shayla can have a nice afternoon in town." He headed for the door to the office and stopped. "How much bedding do you need?"

The coin warmed Aileen's palm. She didn't want to do this, but knew by Ethan's question he had no idea what was needed.

"Sheets, a blanket or two, cover, and pillows."

"That's too much for the two of you to carry." The concern in his eyes would always please her. She'd spent too many years wondering if anyone would ever care about her well-being to not be affected.

"Do you know how to drive a wagon?"

"Aye."

"Then take the wagon Clay used this morning." He put up his hand as she started to object. "You are doing an errand for Cracker Creek Stamp Mill, there is no reason you shouldn't use the equipment."

"'Tis no' necessary." She took a step toward him. How was she to make him see, his generosity wouldn't help her in the eyes of the community.

"I'll not have you and Shayla packing all that. The wagon will be in front of the building when you get Shayla rounded up." He left without giving her a chance to argue.

There were times when she wished she were a man so she could knock some sense into Ethan Halsey.

Chapter 22

A wagon stood in front of the building when Aileen and Shayla stepped out the door. One of the horses was tethered to the hitching post and not another person appeared in sight. She lifted Shayla onto the seat and untied the horse, wrapping the rope through a loop on the harness.

Lifting her skirt out of the way, she placed a foot on the tire spoke. She grasped the side of the wagon and bench to climb onto the seat. As she shoved off with the foot on the ground, hands circled her waist helping her upward momentum. They weren't Ethan's large hands.

She spun around as soon as her feet hit the solid footing of the wagon. Mr. Healy stood beside the vehicle, grinning his black-toothed smirk.

"Ah dinnae ask to be helped, and ah dinnae care to have yer hands on me." She twisted the reins off the brake handle and held them ready to lash out at the man should he try to climb aboard the wagon.

"I heard you be headin' to town and would like to offer my services as I'm headin' that way as well." He put his hand up as if to lever himself aboard.

She slapped his hand hard with the reins. "Ye can walk. Ah'll drive myself." Her backside barely brushed the seat before she smacked the leather straps on the rumps of the team, causing the wagon to lurch forward. He should not have touched her nor presumed she wanted him to drive. She'd have a word with Ethan about this man. He was trouble. She knew it the minute she laid eyes on him.

They passed the stamp mill. She kept her eyes forward though she badly wanted to seek out Ethan and tell him about the Irishman's behavior. Shayla, however, gawked and waved.

"Who are ye wavin' at?" Aileen asked, wanting to know just who watched them drive to town in Ethan's wagon.

"Colin and Happy Man." The child spun to sit on her knees and watched over the back of the seat as they moved on down the road.

"What are they doin'?" No sense in letting her aggravation fall upon her daughter.

"Colin's puttin' long sticks on the ground, and Happy Man is hitting them with a big hammer."

Aileen wanted to turn and watch Ethan swing a hammer, but to stop in the road and turn and stare at the man would be worse than driving into town in his wagon and buying bedding for a bed he purchased.

A heavy sigh slipped between her lips. How had she managed to get caught up in such a mess?

Not that long ago she was content with only her children and the pittance of gold they dug out of the ground. Greed had bound her to a man who didn't want a family and for the first time in a long time made her believe there were good men.

That greed would also get them back to Colin's rightful place—the O'Lear land.

"Momma, why're you frownin'?" Shayla's innocent question startled her.

"Ah'm thinkin', darlin'." Her goal since leaving Ireland was to reclaim Colin's heritage. It would mean traveling back to Ireland and finding someone to bargain with the Englishman. Colin had the lawful claim to the land by birth, but she knew the man who stole the land would never willingly give it back. They would have to purchase it through another. He would never sell it back to an Irishman.

"What about?" The child's question again pulled her out of her musings.

"Our future darlin'." Today was a beautiful day if a bit cold. She pulled a wool blanket from under the seat and wrapped it around their legs. She'd dwell on their future another time. Right now she had to face the present and anyone who questioned her riding into town in a Halsey wagon.

Ethan stretched his back. It felt like he'd been pounding rail stakes his whole life. First he'd hammered in the spikes for the mile of track from their mine to the stamp mill, then he'd helped a couple other miners, and now he and Colin were finishing the quarter mile track from the Miller mine to the stamp mill.

Colin looked up from where he knelt placing another spike in a hole. "If you're too tired I could take a swing or two at this spike."

The boy'd been hankering to drive a spike since they started on this line. Shrugging, he tipped the handle of the sledge hammer toward Colin. "I could use a break, just be careful you don't hit your leg. You break your leg and your ma will break my head."

The spindly lad grasped the handle in both hands and gave a yank. His far foot came up off the ground as he grunted. The heavy head of the hammer rose about as high as the boy's ankles and fell back to the trampled grass.

Ethan kept his lips in a firm, straight line even though the corners ached to curve into a smile. The boy ignored him and picked up the mallet one more time. He managed to clear his ankles and make it about half way to his knees before the heavy tool fell back to the ground, narrowly missing his foot.

When Colin looked up at him, his gaze softened. Instead of the wariness and anger that made his eyes appear cold, they gleamed with admiration. "You've been swinging this hammer for almost two weeks solid." The statement came out on a breathy sigh of reverence.

"Just because a man has strength doesn't mean he has to use it in everything he does." He uncorked the canteen and took a drink. "But every now and then, I like to put my body to the test. Makes it feel good." And worn out. He wasn't about to tell this upstart he went to bed tired so he wouldn't think about his mother.

Mr. Healy and Clay walked toward them from the stamp mill. Ethan took the hammer from Colin and put the spike in with two swings. He didn't like the way the Irishman riled Aileen that morning, and he didn't like the fact that the man hung around after applying for a job. Especially, since he seemed to be poking around and not helping in any way.

"Ethan, Mr. Healy here was just explaining the newest processing method for skimming the gold." Clay stopped far enough back to stay clear of the swinging hammer.

Colin propped another spike in a hole and sat back to allow Ethan a swing. It would be hard to turn this man away when he had the knowledge they needed. He slammed the next spike in the ground with one swing and continued to pound in spikes, talking while Colin set them. "Is that so?" The metal of hammer hitting spike rang out. Once, twice, three times. "And where did you learn this, Mr. Healy?"

The sound of metal on metal chimed again.

"In South Dakota. I be workin' in the mines nearly four years before my feet began a itchin' and I set me sights farther west." Mr. Healy's eyes followed each stroke of the hammer.

One, two. The spike speared the metal to the cross board "So you have itchy feet. Where all have you been?" Ethan didn't miss the way the man's gaze darted between him and the boy.

"I've hung me hat from the East coast to the West coast and a few spots north and south."

He avoided any specific places. A sure sign he

was hiding something. Ethan planted the last spike and leaned on the hammer handle. "When did you come over here from Ireland?" He saw Colin take an interest in the conversation at that point.

The man continued his inspection of Colin. Ethan stepped between the two. "Mr. Healy, thank you for all your information, we'll let you know by tomorrow if we'll hire you."

"What do you mean if?" Clay crossed his arms in defense of the man.

"Clay, stay here and help Colin and I finish the last bit of track." He turned from the Irishman, hoping he'd take the hint to leave. To help sway the man, he added, "Good day, Mr. Healy." The man slowly turned and walked back the way he came.

"What do you mean you'll think about hiring him?" his brother said before the man moved completely out of hearing.

Ethan shook his head and pointed to the next hole in the track. Colin placed a spike in it, and he swung the hammer. When the man neared the front of the stamp mill, Ethan leaned on the hammer handle.

"That man may have the knowledge we need, but I'm positive he's up to no good."

Clay shook his head. "You're just saying that because he offered to drive Aileen and Shayla into town."

Ethan pushed the hammer handle away from him and marched up to his brother. "What are you talking about?"

"Mr. Healy offered to drive Aileen into town for a ride and she refused." Clay stared at him, defiantly. "You just don't like the man helping her."

"I didn't know a thing about that." He wasn't going to add that the man made Aileen uneasy, her reason for declining his offer.

"Face it, some man comes here with an accent like hers—"

"He's Irish, she's Scottish. They aren't a thing alike." He turned to Colin who stood to the side listening. "Are they?"

"Ma speaks mostly Scots but a little Irish," Colin said. "That's from living in Ireland for a while and listening to my da."

"See, that man and Aileen have nothing in common. He'd better stay away from her." Ethan handed the hammer to his brother. "You two finish this. I'm going to read the applications from today."

He hadn't looked the papers over and wondered if Aileen had added one of her marks to the Irishman's application. If so, it would give him even more reason to talk Clay out of hiring the man.

Aileen drove the wagon straight to Myrle's. She'd leave it tied up here and walk to the mercantile. People might think one of the Halsey brothers was taking a meal and not connect her with the vehicle if she and Shayla could get in the building fast enough.

She climbed over the side and lifted Shayla down. Grasping her daughter's hand, she hurried up the steps of the house and inside. It was mid-afternoon and the place appeared empty.

She wasn't sure what to do to find Myrle. The few times she'd had tea with the woman, she'd noticed the door to the left led to the kitchen, the logical place to find the proprietress. She walked to the door, stilled her racing heart, and put her hand up, giving the door a push. Myrle sat at a small table with two other women. The one facing the door scowled.

"Excuse me?" She wasn't going to let the woman's glare keep her from speaking to Myrle. Ethan depended on her to do a job.

Myrle and the other woman turned at the sound of her voice.

"Aileen! What a surprise," Myrle waved to an empty chair. "Won't you join us?"

"Ah— Nae, Myrle could ah speak with ye?" She motioned her head toward the door behind her.

Shayla tugged on her hand to join the women, but she wasn't going to let her daughter alone with the woman staring daggers at her.

"Certainly." Myrle pushed out of her chair and crossed the room. "It's been a while since we visited." She ushered them out the door and back into the eating area. "Let's sit here." The small woman led them to a table in the corner farthest away from the kitchen.

"Thank ye." Aileen pulled out a chair for Shayla to crawl on and took a seat, untying her bonnet and placing it in her lap.

Myrle took a seat across from her, twined her hands together, and placed them on the table in front of her.

Aileen opened her mouth to speak, but the woman shook her head and smiled to someone behind her.

"Edith, would you bring us each a cup of coffee and cookies and milk for the child?" Myrle smiled, however her eyes held a warning to the woman.

Someone humphed, and the kitchen door smacked shut.

"You have to forgive Edith. She's had her sights set on Ethan for a long time. She still can't get over he's taken a shine to you."

Aileen sucked in air and stared at the woman. "He's no' shinin' me. Ah'm workin' for the stamp mill. That's why ah came to ye. He said to ask for yer help to purchase beddin' so the people wouldn't talk."

Myrle shook her head again as Edith brought a tray with coffee, milk, and cookies.

"Thank you!" Shayla exclaimed, taking a cookie and nibbling.

Aileen studied the other woman as she took her time leaving the room. "Ah've no intentions on Mr. Halsey." She looked back at the older woman watching her daughter with a tender gaze.

"That may be, but I do believe he has intentions for you."

"Nae. We have a business agreement." She didn't want to think of the times they'd kissed, and the pleasure she received from being held in his arms.

The woman chuckled. "You can both call it business all you want, but I've talked to the man and he has it bad for you, and I see a new woman emerging in you."

Aileen started to protest.

"No, don't you dare tell me any different. I've watched you both for many years. I'm like a second ma to those Halsey boys. I can tell you, Ethan hasn't cottoned to any woman, but he lights up when he talks about you and your children."

The woman's words fluttered her insides and lightened her heart. Did he really care for her? Could it be he wasn't just randy? She'd felt that from him, but he denied wanting a family. That left her believing he was only out for one thing.

"If ye know him so well, ye know ah must do the favor he asked." Aileen took a sip of coffee and watched Shayla gulp the milk and eat another cookie.

"I just don't understand why I have to go with you to buy bedding. How could that start gossip?" Myrle sipped her coffee. Her faded blue eyes studied her over the rim of the cup.

"Clay purchased a bed this morning from the mercantile. He brought it to the office, where me bairn and ah live, but it isn't for me, 'tis for his brother and wife who are coming to visit." She took a breath. "Ah know someone has figured out the bed is at my home. They will be sayin' things that aren't true if ah buy the beddin'."

"That's because too many people around here have nothing better to do than spread gossip." She stood. "Finish your coffee while I get a shawl and let Edith and Sadie know I'll be gone for a while."

For the first time since Ethan asked her to purchase the bedding, she found herself excited to help him. He'd done so much for her family she wanted to do things for him. And if purchasing the bedding for his brother and wife helped, she had to do it. Having Myrle along would give her support.

The woman bustled back into the room.

"Come on, we need to hurry so you two get back to Cracker Creek before dark." Myrle stretched out her hand to Shayla. When her lassie's tiny fingers curled around Myrle's small hand, the woman beamed with delight.

Aileen made a note to bring Shayla to visit with Myrle. It appeared the woman had been cheated out of motherhood. She took Shayla's other hand and the three walked down the street to the mercantile.

Myrle nodded and smiled at the people they passed. Aileen tried to do the same, but the glares and outright snubs she received began to slow her steps.

"Chin up. You have as much right to walk this street as the likes of them," Myrle said loud enough for many along the way to hear. At the mercantile, Aileen held the door for the older woman and Shayla to enter.

"Afternoon, Myrle," called the store owner.

"Afternoon, Mr. Kepler. Aileen and I are looking for bedding." Myrle motioned for Aileen to follow. The woman's small boots tapped a fast cadence as she walked the length of the wood floor to the back of the store.

Aileen captured Shayla's exploring hands and followed the woman. Stacks of bedding on a table in the back caught her eye. Some day she would own bedding like this. Many a night she shivered through till dawn under the thin wool blankets Mr. Miller had provided for bedding. Either that or she slept in a chair next to the fire to keep it going so the bairn wouldn't get cold. She'd long since given most of the blankets to Shayla and Colin.

"Did he have anything for the bed?" Myrle asked.

"Nae, 'tis just a frame and mattress." She ran her hand over a finely stitched coverlet.

Myrle picked up the coverlet, placing it in her arms. "Then we'll need everything." Before Aileen could protest, she added two sheets, two pillows, three blankets, and handed Shayla two pillow slips to carry. "That should take care of things."

She followed the smaller woman to the counter. Myrle turned to her, "Is this being charged to the Halsey's?"

Aileen wanted to melt into the floor at the narrowed gaze she received from the man behind the counter. "Nae, they gave me this." She set the items on the counter and dug the coin out of her skirt pocket.

"Why are you buying personal items for Ethan?" the merchant asked, ignoring the coin she'd extended.

"Because I asked her to." Ethan's strong voice jolted her so, she dropped the coin on the counter. His presence elated and dismayed her. Would he make this more intimate than she cared?

He strolled up to the counter, nodded to Myrle and smiled at Shayla. "And they aren't personal items for me. Zeke and his wife are coming to visit. I want them to have a place to stay." He picked up the coin, grasped the merchant's hand and placed the money in his palm. "As an employee of the Cracker Creek Stamp Mill, Aileen will be asked to come in and make purchases. It would be in your best interest to help her with these purchases or I can take my business to Baker City."

Aileen bit her lip to keep from smiling as the merchant's mouth dropped open.

"Close your mouth, Earl, or you'll catch flies," Myrle said, taking hold of Shayla's hand and heading to the door. Ethan placed the pillows in Aileen's arms and gathered the rest of the bedding in his.

There wasn't anything she could do but follow Myrle out the door and down the street to the wagon. A horse was tied to the back of the vehicle. Ethan moved the animal aside and placed all the items into the wagon box.

Aileen turned to him. "Why did ye come to town?" She glanced over her shoulder at the people starting to filter into Myrle's for dinner.

"I realized how late it was getting and didn't like the idea of you two traveling after dark." He picked up Shayla. "But since it's nearly dinner time, how about I buy two pretty girls a meal?"

"What about Colin?" She offered as an excuse not to be seen in public with him, even though she'd never had a man buy her a meal.

"He's fine. Hank is hanging out at the office to keep an eye on him." He started toward the front of the building.

She couldn't get her feet to move. Not only would word be around that she and Ethan were together at the store buying bedding, but if they were seen together eating at Myrle's.

"'Tis no' right." Her words sounded weak even to her own ears.

He strode back to her. "What isn't right?"

"To have ye buy my dinner. Will give people an idea we're—" She couldn't finish the thought.

The suggestion in the man's eyes made her mouth go dry.

"We're what Aileen?" The deep timbre ignited her insides as the twinkle of mirth in his eyes sparked her ire.

"Ye know! Ah'll no' be despised any more than ah am."

"If anyone so much as makes a comment, I'll put them in their place. Come on. There's no sense riding home on empty stomachs when Myrle is a fine cook." He grasped her elbow escorting her up the steps and into the building.

Chapter 23

Heads turned, but Ethan smiled politely and escorted her to the same table where she'd sat with Myrle earlier. He placed Shayla on a chair and held out one for her. Her face heated at his attention. A quick glance around the room confirmed her concerns. The other patrons tilted their heads together, talking about them. About her.

"Ah cannae do this." She stood, holding her hand out to Shayla.

"Don't." His one word resonated through her as a plea, a warning, and a dare all rolled into one.

She wanted to have it out with the man. However, his hand extended toward her, a warm smile lit his imploring eyes, and the apologetic lift of his shoulders weakened her knees, and she sat back down.

"That's the feisty woman I'm growing fond of."

Before she could retort, the woman who'd glared at her earlier in the day arrived with coffee. After singeing her with a hostile glance, the woman turned all her attention to Ethan and her back to Aileen.

"Mrs. James, have you met Aileen and her daughter Shayla?" Ethan grinned at the appalled expression on the woman's face. He wouldn't let this old biddy snub Aileen. He hated the way the merchant treated her and now the Widow James. He'd not stand for it. Aileen had done nothing other than survive a living hell with her last husband.

"I know who she is," the woman answered.

"Well turn around and greet her proper." Ethan motioned with a finger for the woman to turn and face Aileen. She hesitated, so he took the matter of politeness out of her hands and gave it to Aileen.

"Aileen, this is the Widow James." He glanced at Aileen and witnessed a flicker of determination in her eyes. When the woman turned, he winked at Aileen. "The widow here thinks I'd make a good catch as a husband."

The widow gasped and raced to the kitchen, her apron ties fluttering behind her.

"That wasn't very nice o' ye," Aileen said with a twinkle in her eye.

"I know. And Myrle will give me an earful about it, but she had no right treating you the way she did. All because I choose to spend time with you over her." The sparkle remained in her eyes as they gazed at one another across the table.

He could get used to making her smile. Each time those eyes lit up and her rosy lips curved at the corners, he warmed all over.

"Ahem." Myrle stood beside the table, holding three plates of food. "Not sure what you said to Edith, but she refused to bring your food."

"Just the truth, Myrle." Ethan winked at Aileen.

"May be, but she's riled now more than when you were after her tub."

"Aileen, would Shayla like some milk?" He had to stop Myrle from revealing the whole tub incident. He'd tried to wipe it from his mind.

"Ah'd rather hear about the tub." She smiled at Myrle as she waited expectantly.

Myrle pulled out the vacant chair and sat, placing her body to give Aileen her full attention.

"Don't you have something you need to do in the kitchen?" He tapped Myrle on the shoulder, hoping she'd take the hint.

"When you told Ethan he had to bring you a bathtub—"

"Myrle, this isn't anything she's interested in."

"Aye, ah'm very interested." Aileen blinded him with a seductive smile and gave her attention to the infuriating woman leaning toward her.

"The mercantile was out and you said he had to have it to you the next day. He came here because they told him Edith had been the last person to purchase a sitting tub..."

Ethan groaned and started eating his meal. There was no sense letting the food get cold, especially when his protests went unheeded.

"I wasn't here at the time, and Edith was thinking he was going to propose to her when all he wanted was her tub." Myrle laughed. He glared at her back. He didn't find the story even a little bit amusing. Aileen on the other hand tittered behind her hand. Her gaze lit on him. The merriment lighting her eyes was a spectacle. Maybe Myrle telling the story wasn't so bad.

"Anyway, when I came through the door, she was huffing through into the kitchen, and Ethan looked lower than a boy who'd lost his puppy."

"Where did ye get my tub?" Aileen's question surprised him.

"From Myrle. She had one and I ordered her up a new one." Now he had to fess up about the tub not being new. "I know I promised you a new tub—"

"Nae, ye promised a bathtub, new was never discussed." She patted his hand. The action spoke more than the words. She understood he'd been uncomfortable asking for the tub, but he'd done it for her.

"I'll let you two finish your meal so you can get back before it's too late." Myrle left and a few minutes later Edith brought a glass of milk to Shayla. She set the cup on the table and left without a look or a word.

Ethan wanted to say something, but Aileen kept her eyes downcast and ate her food. He'd wait until the drive back to the stamp mill. They would have plenty of time to talk.

After the meal, he picked up a sleepy Shayla and grasped Aileen's elbow. She didn't move away from his touch or peer about the room to see who watched. These small concessions meant she was warming to his attentions.

At the wagon, he helped Aileen up then handed her Shayla. The child was sound asleep and limp as a new blade of grass. He climbed up beside the two and headed the horses out of town.

Aileen positioned Shayla's lower body across

his lap with her upper body and head in her lap. He pulled her legs up close to his body. The child's stockings were thin, her legs cold to the touch.

"It's cold out tonight. Toss this blanket over her and the other around your shoulders." He handed her the two old blankets stored under the seat.

She tucked the blanket around her daughter with gentleness. To his surprise, she spread the other blanket across his shoulders and hers, bringing them even closer together. He leaned down, kissing the top of her head.

"I'm glad I came after you." The horses knew the way home, allowing him to peer down at the lovely woman seated by his side. The sliver of a crescent moon made the night an inky black. He could only catch a faint glimmer of the moon in her eyes.

"Ah hadn't realized how late we'd set out for town." Her hand rested on his arm and she squeezed. "Ah'm glad ye came, too." He heard the smile in her words. The child on his lap, Aileen's closeness, and friendliness all crept into his heart and gave him a sensation of belonging.

He wrapped an arm around her shoulders, drawing her tighter to him. Before meeting this woman, he'd not realized a person could crave the nearness of another.

Her arm draped over her child, and she rested her hand on his leg above his knee. The heat of her palm on his thigh ignited a fire that blazed a path to his loins.

"Ye have done more for me and my family than any person has ever done." Her low, seductive voice alone would have stiffened him, but that—combined with her hand—he was ready to pull the wagon over and toss her in the back.

He swallowed several times. The child stirred on his lap and set his thoughts to other things. "What about your first husband?"

"Ah loved him with the fierceness o' first love. And he loved me, but no' as much as makin' the Sassenach pay for takin' his family's land." She leaned her shoulder into his side and tucked her head against his chest. "My Patrick worked enough to keep us fed and clothed. His passion wasn't makin' money but savin' the Irish way o'life."

"Who are the Sassenach?" He liked the feel of her curled under his arm.

"The English. They take the land from the Irish along their borders, using any means possible. The land is ideal for their sheep."

"A person can't take another's land."

"Aye, on the borders they can and do." She sighed heavily. "When my father came to the house, ah knew Patrick had gone too far." She rubbed her face against his chest. He felt the warmth of tears. Ethan rubbed his hand up and down her arm.

"He accused the Sassenach of takin' his family's land illegally. He'd told me the night before he had proof." She snorted. "The eejit went to the man and told him he had papers showin' they stole it."

They sat in silence a moment as she steadied her breathing. "He was dead the next day. Run over in the street." Her back straightened. "Ah asked to see him. My father tried to keep me away, but ah snuck in. My Patrick had been beaten no' run over. A wagon wouldn't have battered his face so."

"That very day my father forced Colin and ah onto a ship headed for America. He said we couldn't stay in Ireland with the Sassenach thinking we had papers to prove his wickedness."

"Ye know the truth of Mr. Miller. Ye are the first man to treat my family so well." She turned her head and kissed his hand. "And ah fear ye are startin' to make me feel things ah've no' felt in a very long time."

Her confession on the tail end of her story raised his heart into his throat. He'd known her life with Miller wasn't a life at all, but she'd just confessed though her first husband didn't assault her, she'd not been treated with the respect she deserved. At least not in his opinion.

He pulled her closer, tipped her face up to his, and found her lips with his. They were salty from her tears and sweet when he delved deep.

The horses snorted. He held her against him and peered into the darkness ahead. Before the heavy wagons brought all the supplies to the stamp mill it would have been insane to travel this path in the dark. But the wagons had made ruts and there wasn't any way to get off the track unless the horses bolted and dragged the wheels out of the furrows.

A flash of moonlight off something ahead in the road caught his attention. He stared into the darkness.

"What is it?" Aileen asked in a hushed voice.

"It looks like a rider." She started to pull away.

"Don't." He slid his hand down, sliding her hip against his. "I don't care who sees us together. And I'd think after our conversation you wouldn't either."

"Ah dinna want to cause ye trouble." The conviction in her voice surprised him.

"You could never cause me trouble."

"Ye've seen how people treat me. Ah dinnae want that to happen to ye and yer family."

He hugged her close. "If we can't handle a little gossip we don't deserve to run a business."

Ethan scanned the area as they neared where he glimpsed the wisp of light. He made out a horse and rider hiding in the trees along the road as they passed. The person made no move to acknowledge his presence. That was fine by him. He didn't want to unnerve Aileen by bringing the man to her attention. He'd question the individual the next time they met.

They rounded the last corner before the mill. As they passed the building, he scanned the area. Everything appeared in place. Hank's horse was tied to the hitching post in front of the office.

He pulled the wagon up to the kitchen door. Hank came out followed by Colin. Ethan handed Shayla down to Hank and helped Aileen down. She followed his brother and her daughter into the house.

"Help me with these things," he said to Colin. The boy followed him to the back of the wagon and held out his arms. He loaded his arms and then took the rest of the bedding in his own.

"I know you bought this bed for my ma." Animosity didn't coat the boy's words.

"I bought it for my brother and his wife when they arrive. But your ma can use it once they've left."

"She's a prideful woman," Colin said, standing by the wagon staring at the horses.

Ethan watched the boy in the fringes of lamp light escaping the door. "She is. That's why I have to find ways to give her the things she deserves."

"She deserves a lot. Mr. Miller was a bastard to her." The venom in his words as he said the man's name put Ethan on alert.

"She's told me that. And if the man were alive, I'd make sure he never touched her again."

The boy jerked his head around and stared at him. "I'd do the same to you if I thought you hurt her."

"I know. But you don't have to worry. I care about your ma, and I'll do everything I can to make her life easier."

The boy nodded and headed to the house. He didn't know what to make of the exchange. The boy was warning him and at the same time letting him know he approved of the help he gave his mother.

Ethan entered the door and spotted dominoes spread on the table. Hank and the boy must have been talking as well as playing the game. He smiled. He'd made the right decision in asking Hank to stay rather than Clay.

He followed the boy through the kitchen. Hank stood in the main room, warming by the stove.

"Thanks for staying. You can leave if you want, I'll be along shortly." Ethan kept his voice casual. He really hoped to spend more time with Aileen. Alone.

"I can wait." Hank pulled a chair up to the stove.

"It really isn't necessary. I can find my way home."

"You sure?" The censure in his brother's voice raised his hackles.

"Yes. I am."

Hank shrugged and stood. "I'll wait to say good-night to Colin then."

Ethan nodded and headed down the hall to the bedrooms. Colin had placed his arm load on the bed. Ethan placed his beside the others. "Hank wants to say good-night," he told the boy.

Colin tipped his head. "You aren't leaving with him?"

"I want to ask your mom some things." He took his hat off his head and tossed it onto the chair in the corner.

"You had a long trip from town with her. You could have asked her then." Colin's gaze rested on the hat.

"Your ma did all the talking on the way home."

The boy nodded, but seemed reluctant to leave him alone in the room.

"I'm only going to help your ma make the bed and discuss the men she thinks will make good employees." He put his hand on the boy's shoulder. "Go say good night to Hank. If you want, you can look back in here and see I'm not doing anything untoward."

Appeased, the boy spun on his heel and nearly ran into his mother as she entered the room.

"I'm glad you bought this. It's pretty." Ethan picked up the flowered cover for the bed.

"Ah dinna. Myrle saw me admirin' it and put it in my arms. Tis too beautiful for the likes o' me." Aileen hurried around him, taking the cover and the blankets. The cover was the prettiest thing she'd ever seen. And to know it would be on the bed she slept in almost made her giddy. She turned to place it on the chair. Ethan's hat claimed the seat.

"And what would yer hat be doin' on the chair?" Seeing it there in her room made their relationship more intimate.

"I tossed it there when I was talking to Colin." He picked his hat up. "Would you rather I hang it from the bedpost?" The mischievous grin lessened the meaning as he did just that.

"Ah'd prefer ye dinnae set foot in my room." She said it teasingly. His eyebrow arched. He took it in the tone she intended.

"Then I guess you'd rather make this bed by yourself." He picked up a sheet and unfolded it, waving the cloth over the pillows and other sheet still sitting on the bed.

She dumped the items in her arms on the chair and scooped the others out of his way. Watching him try to center the sheet on the bed was painful. She placed the pillows on the other bedding and moved to the other side of the bed.

"Ye have no' made enough beds," she said,

grasping the other side of the sheet and helping him settle it over the mattress. With deft moves, she folded the corners and tucked the edges under the mattress. She glanced across the mattress and found Ethan watching her. "Ye are no' tuckin' the sheets."

"I prefer watching you." The deep timbres of his voice sent shivers up her arms.

She moved slowly around the end of the bed to fold and tuck in his side. When his arms encircled her, pulling her against him, she didn't resist. She'd been hoping for a moment alone with him ever since he came to her rescue in the store.

His breath was warm on her face as he kissed her ear and whispered, "I've wanted to kiss you all day." His large hands grasped her hips and turned her to face him.

She slid her hands up his hard chest, snuggling inside his coat. His warmth enveloped her. The security of his arms stunned her. She never thought she'd have that emotion in a man's arms again.

His fingers cradled her head as he brushed his lips across hers. He deepened the kiss, nibbling her lips and skimming her tongue with his. Mon! He was making her knees weak and her center throb.

She wrapped her arms around his neck, pulling her body closer. He held her away from him. "Aileen, I don't think I can leave here tonight with only a kiss."

She kissed his cheek, savoring his manly stubble and the plane of his jaw.

"Ah dinnae want ye to leave with only a kiss."

Chapter 24

Ethan couldn't believe what he'd heard. He leaned back and peered into her smiling face. "You mean? We can?" When she nodded, he could have whooped, but remembered the children.

"What about Shayla and Colin?"

"Shayla is asleep for the night. Colin will just have to get used to the idea o' his ma wantin' a man." She stepped out of his arms. "Take yer coat off while ah finish the bed."

He pulled the garment down his arms and hung it on the back of the chair. All the time he kept his eyes on the woman bending, pulling, and transforming the bare mattress into a comfortable, floral oasis.

When she finished the task, he wedged the chair under the door knob. He may have told Colin he could look in, but he wasn't going to take the chance the boy would.

He turned from his task and found Aileen standing beside the turned down bed in her shift.

"Do ye need help with yer clothes?" Her sultry voice, the one he fell for the first day they met, melted him again.

He shook his head as his hands fumbled with the buttons on his shirt. Swallowing the lump in his throat, he watched her blow out the lamp sitting on the stand by the bed. The room was cloaked in darkness. He willed his eyes to focus in the dark. Her hands pushed his aside and finished unbuttoning his shirt. Her scent—soap, earth, and faint floral tickled his nose and tightened his gut.

This was different than the times he'd gone to the brothel. Tonight, he wanted to bring the woman undressing him tenderness. He wasn't sure how since his other experiences had only been like a rutting buck, but he would restrain himself. He had to prove to this woman he could be gentle.

She slid her hand down the front of his britches, and he couldn't suppress a moan as his cock surged at her touch.

"Aye, ah know ye'd be a brawny one in bed." Her voice was no louder than a whisper, yet her words rang strong and bold.

Placing his hands on her arms, he moved up her smooth skin to her round shoulders and slender neck. He had to kiss her. He wanted to give her something.

Their mouths melded and their tongues caressed. He lost himself in the kiss until her hands splayed across his bare chest, sliding down the ripples on his stomach and once again—He sucked in a breath as she skimmed the top of him. The wisp of flesh against flesh had his body humming clear to his toes.

She pushed both hands down his hips, shedding his long johns and britches, pushing them to his boot tops.

"Sit," she ordered and gave him a slight push. He fell back in the chair. Her hands skated down his leg and one by one his boots and socks were removed and his clothing disappeared.

"Now ye can come to bed," she whispered, capturing his hand and pulling him across the room.

Before she slipped into bed, he grasped the bottom of her shift, pulling it up over her body and off. In the dark he couldn't see her. Starting at her slender neck, he ran his hands down, over firm round shoulders, to the front, cupping breasts that filled his hands with weight. Satisfied with the feel, his hands glided down over a soft stomach and out to the curve of her waist and over wide hips.

Splaying his hands across her firm round bottom, he pulled her against him and kissed her hungrily. She had the full, ripe body of a woman.

She sagged in his arms. Catching her under the knees, he laid her upon the bed and settled his body over the top, resting on his forearms so as not to hurt her. Her soft breasts against his chest and his shaft resting between their lower bodies nearly sent him over the edge. He bit his lip in an effort not to attack her like a starved animal.

"Ah know ye want to have at me." Her hand brushed the hair from his forehead. "Ah dinnae mind. Once ye take care o' that matter, ah can teach ye how to make love."

His heart thrummed in his chest. "I want to

make this special—for you."

"Ah'll get special when ye aren't holdin' back." She spread her legs under him and wrapped her arms around his neck as she writhed against him and kissed him with abandon.

He growled and sunk into her with one slow move. She gasped and thrust her hips against him, drawing him in deep and tight. He wrapped his arms around her and matched his thrusts to hers, gasping as his seed burst into her, bringing him completion.

His body felt weak and invigorated.

"Nae, ye can't sleep. Now ye have work to do." The teasing voice pulled him from his euphoria. He started to pull out, but she grasped his backside, holding him in.

"Nae, leave it in." She grasped his head and nudged a nipple to his lips. "Ye may feast upon these with yer mouth and hands."

He didn't need to be asked twice. Taking the breast in his hand, he marveled at the silkiness of the skin. He massaged the mound and sucked on the nipple. Her body moved under his and small mewing sounds filled his ears as he continued to experiment with his tongue and teeth on the nipple as it hardened.

Aileen clutched the bedding under her. She knew he'd take his time learning her body, sending small ripples of delight through her. It was what she wanted. To be treasured. He moved to the other breast, tasting, nipping, and jolting her. His hand slid down her side, over her hip and back up to her breast. His hot hand sliding across her skin was as exhilarating as his administrations to her breasts.

He grew, filling her. Her body was strung tight and humming for release. Not since her Patrick died had she felt the vibrations warming her body and clouding her senses.

"Now. As ye did before, only kiss me, so ah dinnae cry out." She clutched his arms and tilted her pelvis toward him as he began thrusting. His mouth descended on hers as the first volley of sensations wracked her body.

She hummed into his mouth and raised her body to take him deeper. Sensing her needs, he pushed a hand beneath her bottom, holding her up to take his thrust more fully.

He was panting, but she had to have him kiss her. She wanted all of him when it hit. Her hands fisted in his hair, dragging his mouth to hers. Caught in the heightened arousal of his hand splayed across her backside, his boaby taking her with authority, and his mouth sucking the air from her lungs, her body exploded in a rain of sparks, jolts, and an exaltation muffled by his kiss.

His body shuddered, and he moaned against her shoulder. She felt the surge of him as he spilled, again.

She took the weight of him and sank into the mattress as her spent body reveled in the aftershocks.

"Ye did well for yer first time," she whispered, kissing his cheek and rubbing his wide, solid back. If only he could spend the night, she could discover all the muscles on his great body.

"It wasn't my first time with a woman, but it was my first time with a woman I cared about." His words warmed and sent off warnings as he gathered her close and turned to his side.

"'Tis only fun we are havin'. Do no' think because o' this we are gettin' married." She tried to pull out of his embrace, but he held on, fondling her breast and kissing her neck.

"I have no plans to marry. I've told you that. But I don't see why I can't have some feelings for the woman I seduce."

She turned to peer at his face in the darkness. It was dark, but she had to try and see if he told the truth. "'Tis the truth ye are sayin'?" She felt his face with her hands, trying to decipher if he only spoke the words she wanted to hear.

"I have a large family to care for. You plan to leave when you've accumulated enough money. For us to think this could go anywhere other than what we just enjoyed is foolish." His words sounded genuine, yet they settled in her stomach like week old haggis.

"Ah hope ye are sure about this. Ah'd hate to see ye suffer from layin' with me." She touched his lips with her thumbs as her fingers smoothed the wrinkles at the edges of his eyes.

"If you're willing to agree to this kind of an arrangement, I don't see how I could suffer." His lips touched hers as he kissed her long and lingering. He raised his head.

"As much as I'd like to taste and explore more of you. I'd better get home. I told Colin I was only staying to talk with you. I don't think he believed me, but I don't want to get him against me."

Aileen stiffened in his arms at the mention of her son. She held something back about the boy. And it had to do with his temper.

Ethan eased off the bed. He'd made light of the time they'd just spent together, even though he didn't want to leave—ever.

Aileen started to follow. "Stay tucked in warm. I'll stoke the stove on my way out." As he groped around on the floor for his clothes, a spark snapped and the lantern soon burned low.

Aileen stood beside the bed, in nothing but the angel-kissed skin she wore into the world. The next time they made love, he wanted to do it with the light on. He wanted to watch the emotions play on her face.

Gathering her in his arms, he marveled at the ecstasy of flesh meeting flesh. Her skin ignited his in a way he'd not known till now. He bent and was rewarded with her up-turned face and lips he'd tasted thoroughly earlier.

He couldn't get enough of her. His body responded like a randy school boy—awkward and needy. One hand cupped her bottom, pulling her tighter as his leg slid between hers. She rubbed her center against him. He raised his head and looked into her love-hazed eyes.

One for the road. He laid her back across the bed and entered as she rested her legs on his shoulders. Their fingers entwined as he watched a smile curve her lips and her eyes flutter closed. He thrust and she took all of him. Her ample breasts bobbed with each entry. Her head thrashed back and forth and her hands clutched his. She quivered and hissed a satisfied, "Aye."

Her body went lax, and her eyes slowly opened. She licked her lips, and he thrust one last time, growling her name and collapsing across her on the bed.

"Ye have done well for no' using that thin' much." She laughed her entrancing laugh and hugged his face to her breasts.

"I didn't know I could perform that well, myself."

Her chest vibrated under him. She slapped his backside. "Be off with ye or ye'll never get gone."

His muscles were loose. He'd not experienced this relaxed state before. Using the light of the lantern, he retrieved all his clothes and dressed under her watchful eye. Hat in hand, he leaned down and kissed her.

"Let's make this a habit," he said, drawing back and standing before her.

"Let's no' and it will be all the better when we do." Her coy answer wasn't what he'd hoped for, but she wasn't saying it would never happen again.

She sat straight up in bed, not bothering to cover her breasts. He stared at the large, dark circles that encompassed her tantalizing nipples. Nipples he couldn't wait to sample again.

"Ye cannae be grabbin' at me durin' the day with people around." Her stern tone drew his thoughts from her provocative position to her face.

"I'll not act like a liquored up cowboy if that's what you're getting at." He grinned. "However, if I can corner you by yourself, I don't see any reason I can't steal a kiss."

"We'll see about that." So she was back to spar-ring was she?

"I'll be here first thing in the morning. We need to go over the applications." He smiled when she sent him a questioning look.

"We? Ah thought it was to be ye and yer brothers who made the decision?" She picked at the flowered cover.

"I want your thoughts first, then I'll go defend our choices with them."

Her eyes sparkled, and her plump, rosy lips opened to reveal even teeth as the significance of the smile staggered him.

"Thank ye."

"For what?"

"For takin' my thoughts." She slipped out of bed and crossed the room. Standing on her tiptoes, stretching her body, she placed a chaste kiss on his lips. "It means a lot."

He wanted to drag her into his arms and curl up in the bed with her, but instead he spun her around and smacked her backside. "Hop into bed. I'll see you in the morning."

He pulled the chair from the door, slid his arms in the sleeves of his coat and left. Walking softly past the bedrooms, he looked toward Colin's door before entering the main room.

The stove door squeaked when he opened it. He glanced over his shoulder. When no one came to see about the noise, he shoved in wood until the door barely shut. It would be cold in the morning, and he wanted enough coals to make starting the fire easier.

Outside, he climbed onto the wagon and headed the team home with his horse still tied to the back. He pulled gloves out of his coat pocket and hunkered down into his jacket, hiding from the cold night air. Before long snow would be falling if he judged the weather right.

They'd been lucky to get the stamp mill finished and nearly all the tracks from the surrounding mines operational. He'd kept his promise and finished the project before winter. Hank and Clay worked just as hard as him and deserved a break. When they made their first week's profit he'd split it between the two of them and send them off to have some fun.

He'd also have to thank Hank for staying with Colin while he collected Aileen and Shayla from town. If he was lucky, Hank probably gave up on him showing. But he'd no doubt drill him with questions in the morning—a morning that would come within hours from the position of the moon.

His sated body slumped with fatigue. But it was a welcome exhaustion, one he'd been working himself to the bone to achieve. Reliving the intimacies he'd just experienced with Aileen, his chest ached with contentment.

The two times he'd lain with a prostitute he'd never thought of her or the event afterwards. Every detail of his coupling with Aileen was etched in his mind.

He'd experienced more than lust. He'd become a part of her and wanted to continue that intimacy—that bond. Even though he made light of what they did and told her he didn't want to marry, if he were to marry—it could be to no one but her.

The thought of her leaving dampened his spirits as he pulled in front of the barn and climbed out of the wagon. Before he could sink into his bed the horses had to be unhitched, put in the corral, and fed.

When the animals were cared for, he wandered to the cabin and found the lantern sitting on the table turned low. He hung up his hat and coat. As he lower his tired body to the cot, Hank sat up.

"Good thing I didn't wait for you." The sarcasm in his voice didn't escape Ethan.

"Can we talk about this in the morning?" He sat on the cot and wished he were sliding into bed with Aileen and not sharing a cabin with his brothers.

Chapter 25

"It is morning." Hank reclined back on the bed.

"Not morning enough." Ethan unlaced his boots, pulling them and his socks off. Undressing himself was disappointing after Aileen disrobed him.

"You should have thought about that before you spent half the night in that woman's bed."

"She's not that woman. Her name is Aileen, and she deserves just as much respect as any other woman in these parts." Ethan stood to step out of his pants and turned to his brother. "And if she's so bad you didn't have to hang out with her son as long as you did."

"She makes good cookies and there's something eating that boy." Hank sat up. "Something, I'm not sure anyone is going to be able to corral."

"Yeah, I've noticed. That's why I had you stay with him." Ethan thought about the man he'd seen on horseback not far from the stamp mill. He tossed his pants and shirt to the end of his bed.

"Let's talk in the daylight. I need sleep." He crawled into bed and barely registered his brother's voice as he drifted off to sleep.

Aileen hummed as she made the morning meal. She'd known Ethan would be giving in his love making. For as pig-headed as he was in other areas, he'd been willing to listen to her and to take initiative when he wanted something. Aye, she'd not go without her needs being fulfilled as long as she remained here.

That thought sobered her. He loved Shayla, worked at healing her laddie, and had an appetite for her. How was she to leave him when they were ready to head back to Ireland? It would be hard to find another who fit their family so well.

"Ethan stayed a long time last night," Colin said, entering the kitchen.

She'd feared this moment since waking. Yet, she still wasn't prepared for the anger in his young eyes.

"That he did. We were enjoyin' each other's company and lost track o' the time." She wouldn't deny Ethan stayed. Her boy was too smart.

"Did he do anything to hurt you?" His eyes glinted like steel. Yet the wistfulness in his voice gave her hope he wanted her to find happiness.

"Nae, he dinnae harm me. He only made me feel bonnie." She smiled, thinking of the strength and gentleness the man conveyed.

"Are you going to marry him?" The undertone of suspicion didn't surprise her.

"Nae, Ethan and ah are friends. He's no' lookin' for a wife and ah'm no' lookin' for a husband." She ruffled his hair. "We both know how my last marriage went. Ah'll no' be tied to a man and no' be able to get away."

Colin nodded his head. "Good." He picked up his spoon and dug into the bowl of porridge in front of him.

Shayla skipped into the kitchen. "Momma, my tummy is talkin'."

"And what is yer tummy sayin'?"

"It wants ta eat." Shayla giggled and sat at the table.

"Then ah best get yer tummy some porridge." She turned to the stove and dished up a bowl.

A rap on the back door echoed across the room as she set the bowl in front of Shayla. Her lassie slid off her chair and skipped to the door.

"Happy Man!" she exclaimed and tugged the door wide open.

Aileen turned from the man holding her daughter and smiling at her with satisfaction warming his eyes. She placed a hand on her fluttering stomach. After the night they spent, she believed he'd make a late appearance this morning, yet here he was with the sun barely peeking over the treetops.

"Morning, Shayla. Colin." His deep voice warmed the room.

"Coffee?" She looked into his eyes and saw his nerves crackled as well.

"Please." He placed Shayla in her chair and crossed the room. His fingers skimmed hers when she handed him the cup.

The charge from the touch drew her gaze to his. His eyes masked nothing. The dark windows to his emotions revealed he'd lied to her about his intentions. His eyes weren't filled with desire this morning, they were filled with contentment and—She looked away. Nae, he couldn't do that to her.

"Hank and Clay will be here in an hour to look over the applications. We need to talk about them." Ethan had wanted to get her alone, now it was to question her on more than the applications. Fear had flashed in Aileen's eyes before she turned her head. When he'd first arrived, her face had lit up. What scared her? Something he did last night? But why would she greet him with warmth then show fear?

She nodded and untied her apron, leaving the kitchen by the door leading into the main room. He followed her, uncertain what to do or say.

He stepped in front of her before she entered the office. Her eyes flickered with irritation before she lowered her lashes, concealing her emotions. Cupping her chin, he raised her face and placed a kissed on her set lips.

"I don't know what I did to scare you this morning, but you should know by now, I'll never hurt you."

Her eyelids opened. Desire darkened her eyes. "Ah know ye would no' hurt me person."

"But?" Her words were confusing.

"In here," she touched her chest, "Ah fear for us both."

"I don't—"

"Ethan, you here?" Clay called from the office.

"You're early. Hold on." He wasn't ready to confront his brothers with the applications until he and Aileen had gone over her concerns. Her comment hit him like an unexpected blow to the head.

"We need to discuss the applications now, and this," he motioned between them, "later." He grasped her elbow and opened the door into the office. Hank and Clay were shuffling through the papers on the counter.

"Why's there a little mark on the corner of some of these?" Clay held up three papers.

"Those men aren't to be considered." Ethan took the pages from his brother without looking at the names. Aileen stepped closer to him. Her way of showing her gratitude with people present.

"What do you mean? Harley is a hard worker." Clay stared at him like he'd just spouted a profanity.

"They aren't to be considered. Who's left?" Ethan took the papers and noted the Irishman's application had a corner torn. When he lifted it out of the pile, Aileen stiffened beside him.

"I'd say with tossing half the applications out without our consent we're down to what you have in your hand." Hank leaned over the counter to read the names.

Clay poked a finger at the Irishman's application. "That one for sure. He knows a lot about the recovery process and can teach us."

Ethan had to agree, but he could tell Aileen wanted to say something.

"Ah dinnae want that man around." She stared

at his brothers, then turned her angry eyes on him.

"Lady, this is one time you aren't going to use your wiles on my brother." Clay slapped his hands on the counter and stared back at her.

"She hasn't used her wiles on me for anything." Ethan put his arm around Aileen's shoulders as she started to lean over the counter toward Clay.

He turned her to face him. "I know this man is no good. I've felt it. Seen it. But he does have knowledge we need." She started to pull out of his grasp. "No, don't run or get all riled up." He tucked her against his side so she couldn't run away. "We'll hire him for two weeks. That's it. While he's here, you," he pointed to Clay, "are to keep him in your sights and learn everything you can about the recovery process from him." He squeezed Aileen's side. "And he's not to come near this building or Aileen or the children." He glared at his brother. "Is that clear?"

Clay's eyes blazed with anger. His jaw clenched and his hands fisted on the counter. "I don't understand why you let this woman dictate how we run our business."

"She isn't dictating anything. I am." Ethan withdrew his arm from around Aileen, pushed her behind him, and leaned over the counter. "My responsibility is to my family and to the people who have made this business a reality. Aileen and her children have as much at stake here as we do." He glanced at Hank, who had his gaze on the woman behind him.

"Learn what you can from Healy then cut him

loose. He lies and he sneaks around. I'll not have him here any longer than we need him." Ethan handed the remaining applications to Hank. "Hire these men."

Without another glance at his brothers, Ethan took Aileen by the elbow, escorting her back into the living quarters.

She rounded on him as soon as the door shut behind them.

"Ah dinnae want that man here."

"I know, but he does have knowledge we need to make this business work. He'll only be here two weeks. And if he so much as looks this direction, I'll take care of him." He cupped her cheek and smoothed his thumb across the worry lines beside her eye. "I won't let anything happen to you or the children."

Desire lit her pale eyes before she shielded them with her eyelashes.

"Ye won't always be around to keep us safe." The sorrow in her voice tugged at his heart.

"I'll always be here for you."

"Aye, here."

She could have slugged him in the gut her words hit so hard. "We'll deal with that when it comes." Even as he said it, he didn't believe he would be able to let her go. Not now that she'd shown him contentment in a woman's arms.

Shayla wandered out of the kitchen. "Momma, I'm lonely."

"Where's yer brother?" Aileen used the diversion to put distance between she and Ethan. The man had a way of crumbling her defenses by a touch and even a look.

"He left to work." Her darlin' skipped over to Ethan.

"Can I go with you?" Shayla asked and smiled.

"No, I have a lot to do and some of it is dangerous for a little girl." He patted her head. "But I'll come by this evening and read to you. How about that?"

"Yipee!" Shayla clapped her hands.

Aileen's heart banged against the inside of her ribs as his gaze sought her approval.

"That is if your ma doesn't mind." His eyes begged her to say yes. Her chest squeezed so hard she couldn't speak, so she nodded her head.

"See you after dinner." He patted Shayla one more time and disappeared out the office door.

She had a lot to mull over after their conversation this morning. And she'd have to keep an eye out for the bajin Irishman. He snuck up on her once, but he'd not do it again. At least and live to tell.

Chapter 26

Ethan kept an eye on Healy and Clay, making sure his brother kept the man busy and away from the office. He didn't like the way the man snuck around. Something about the Irishman and Aileen didn't make sense. Tonight, after he read to Shayla, he'd question her about the man and the things she'd said this morning.

He entered the stamp mill. The first loads of rock ran through the large stamps. The pounding, crunching, grating and loud din of steel striking rock made it hard to talk with anyone, so he wandered through the building checking on the stages and the men overseeing each phase.

Pride swelled his chest and balled in his throat. Over a year ago this was all a dream and now the twelve-hundred pound presses squeezed gold from rock that would have been tossed aside. Their oldest neighbor and long time friend of the family was given the honor of being the first miner to put his diggings through. The old man stood at the bottom of the mill watching the gold pieces accumulate in the riffles.

Ethan put a hand on the man's shoulder.

"This is the easiest I ever acquired gold," the man shouted, slapping Ethan on the back. "Your pa would be mighty proud of you boys."

"Thanks, Joseph, that means a lot."

"Ethan! Ethan!" Hank hollered from the door and waved him over.

He left the man staring at his collecting riches and hurried to his brother.

"What?"

"We've got company."

He looked beyond Hank and spotted Zeke and Maeve sitting in a buggy. "They're early."

"Yeah, you going to tell Aileen her house guests are a day early?" A mischievous smile lit Hank's face.

"What's them coming early got to do with anything?" Ethan headed past Hank.

"She might want to wash the bedding before they crawl in."

His brother's insinuation hit him like dropping a spike hammer on his foot. Would the bed have the scent of their coupling?

"You give them a tour. I'll go tell Aileen." They approached the buggy together.

He hadn't seen the two since their hasty wedding at the train depot. His brother looked almost civilized in a dapper suit and Stetson. If he had to pick, he'd say Zeke was the best looking of the brothers. Not so much because of his dark good looks, but more he carried himself with confidence and the love for the woman at his side glistened in his eyes. Maeve was a contrary woman. Tall, thin, almost fragile in appearance, yet she was tougher than half the men he'd come across in his lifetime. Her black hair and creamy white complexion resembled a china doll, but her piercing blue eyes showed her strength.

"Zeke, Maeve. Looks like your new jobs are agreeing with you." Ethan slapped his brother on the back and nodded to his sister-in-law. He knew she wouldn't favor a hug. The two of them were still working out their relationship.

"Hank, give them a tour of the place. I'll be right back." He didn't miss Zeke's raised eyebrow or Maeve's curious expression. He hoped Hank didn't fill them in on everything going on around the place.

He entered the office and hurried behind the counter to the door of the living quarters. He opened the door without knocking. Shayla sat on the floor playing with the doll he'd given her.

"Happy man!" She jumped up to hug his legs.

"Where's your ma?"

"Kitchen."

He pried her small arms from his legs and followed the spicy aroma filling the room. Pushing open the door, he inhaled the scent of apple pie and reveled in the sight of Aileen. Wisps of hair had fallen from her bun and curled around her perspiring face. She turned from placing the pies on the drain board and smiled.

"Did ye smell them clear outside?"

He crossed the room and swept her into his

arms, lowering his mouth to her tempting lips. She was all he would ever need. As the thought ricocheted through his head, he deepened the kiss. Slowly, with much regret, he pulled back and stared into her hazy eyes.

"Woman, you make me do things I've never even thought of before."

She shook her head and smiled. "What?"

"I never thought I'd look at a woman and want to kiss her so bad it made me ache."

"Sweet talkin' me will no' get ye pie any sooner." She pushed against his chest and stepped out of his embrace.

"Momma! Momma!" Shayla rushed in the room. "A lady and man are talkin' to Hank."

"Oh, yeah." Ethan ran a hand over his face. "Seems Zeke and Maeve arrived a day early."

Aileen stared at him. The guests she was preparing for had arrived early. The bed.

"Ah have to wash the bedding." She couldn't look at him. The things they did would surely be noticed by their guests.

"I'll bring around the tub, you start some water boiling." Ethan headed out the kitchen door.

"Shayla, darlin' those people will be stayin' with us. Go to my room and put all my clothes in yer room. Ah'll be sleepin' with ye."

The child screeched with delight and ran out of the room. Aileen filled all the pots with water and placed them on the stove. At least she had baked goods to go with dinner tonight.

Ethan came back in. "What else can I help you with?"

"Go to the lean-to and brin' in a roast." She hesitated. It was only fitting the whole family eat here tonight. "Make it a large one as ye and yer brothers are welcome to eat here tonight with yer family."

"I hate that this is making more work for you." Ethan started across the floor. She raised her hand.

"Keep yer distance until yer family leaves. Ah'll no' have any more Halseys thinkin' bad o' me."

His eyes flashed with irritation, but he headed back out the door.

The closeness they'd enjoyed last night would have to wait until the house was empty of visitors. She'd not be caught in a compromising position and have Ethan's family force them to marry.

She hurried into the bedroom and stripped the bed of the sheets and hung the blankets around in an attempt to air them out. Shayla had moved her few belongings and was gleefully hanging them on the pegs in her room. She had to smile at her lassie's delight in sharing the room.

Ethan picked up a pot of boiling water as she entered the kitchen. He nodded and hurried out the door with it. She followed, dumping the bedding in the tub. She shaved soap into the water as Ethan dumped the rest of the hot water. There was a bite to the air. On his last trip, Ethan brought her coat. She slid her arms into the sleeves and began stirring the contents of the tub with a stick polished from all the years she'd used it to stir the laundry.

"There you are." Hank came around the side

of the building followed by a man dressed in a wool suit and warm coat wearing a Stetson and a woman dressed in a stylish gown of blue wool and a dark, long, wool coat. The woman was tall and elegant. What she could see of her hair under the stylish bonnet was shiny black, a stark contrast to her translucent skin. She wasn't pretty, she was breathtaking.

For the first time in a very long while Aileen was conscious of the state of her dress and plainness. She wanted to make a good impression for Ethan's sake.

Ethan stepped beside her. "Maeve, Zeke, this is Aileen—" he glanced down at her and she nodded, "Miller. She lives in the back of the office and is our office assistant."

Zeke extended his hand. "Mrs—"

"Nae, just call me Aileen." She extended her hand to the man who looked so much like the other brothers there was no denying he was a Halsey. He had an air about him she'd noticed in Ethan. This was another man who liked to take charge of situations.

Zeke's brow furrowed, and he scanned the area. His gaze rested on the shack across the creek. "Isn't this where Miller was found—"

"We'll explain all the particulars later," Ethan pulled his brother's hand from her grasp and his attention back to the group.

"Aileen, I'm pleased to meet you, and sorry we're causing you any inconvenience." Maeve stepped forward, putting an arm around her shoulders. "Let me go in and change, then I'll help you with the laundry."

"Ye must be tired from travelin'. Ah can manage."

"No, I insist. Zeke, would you get my bags from the buggy?" She turned to her husband. Aileen noticed the quick look that passed between the two, but had no notion what it was about.

"Hank, Ethan, help me gather my wife's belongings. It will take more than one man, I'm afraid." Zeke laughed jovially and headed around the side of the house. Hank fell in step behind him. Ethan hung back, watching her.

"Go." Aileen waved in the direction his brothers disappeared.

Maeve smiled and crossed her arms. "I never thought I'd see the day Ethan was waiting on a woman."

Aileen jerked her gaze from the man's retreating back. "What is that to mean?"

"I'm impressed with any woman who can get that man to fetch and carry."

She narrowed her eyes and studied the woman. Was Maeve afraid of Ethan? What could he have done to make his sister-in-law fear him?

"He dinna fetch and carry for me." She stirred the contents of the tub. "Now, my darlin' Shayla— she's got him fetchin' and carryin'."

Maeve laughed. "Your daughter? That I believe. The only time I've seen a gentle side to that man was with a newborn foal." She pulled her gloves off her hands. "Lift out one of those sheets, and I'll hang it on that tree limb."

People didn't help her willingly. Aileen

watched the woman warily as she raised the heavy, wet bedding out of the tub. Together they wrung out the excess water and carried it to a tree not far from the building.

"Your bags are—" Zeke and the other men came out the kitchen door as she and Maeve hung the pillow cases over some low hanging limbs.

"Guess you don't need to change after all." Zeke grabbed his wife around the waist, snugging her body up next to his.

Envy whistled through Aileen. She cast a quick glance at Ethan. He watched her intently. It wouldn't do to have him think she wanted more than what they had right now.

"Ah'll put the roast in the oven." She hurried past the men and into the kitchen, creating distance between herself and Ethan.

She no sooner had the door shut than it opened.

"Do you need help?" Maeve unbuttoned her coat and hung it on the peg by the door.

"Ye must be tired. Go clean up and settle in." She plopped the roast in the pot and began slicing an onion over it.

"I'm fine. In our line of work we don't get a lot of sleep at times and have to be ready to work at a moment's notice." The woman moved across the kitchen like a cat on the prowl.

"What kind o' work are ye in?" She didn't remember Ethan ever saying what his brother and sister-in-law did.

Maeve watched her. "Ethan hasn't told you? I thought—" Aileen scowled. "Well, you two seemed—" She picked up the coffee pot. "Ummm, I guess I got the wrong impression."

"And just what was yer impression?" Aileen finished slicing the onion and picked up some carrots she dug out of the ground the day before from her small vegetable plot by the shack.

"As soon as we arrived Ethan hurried to you, I assumed warning you we were early. Which, he wouldn't have done unless he wanted to stay on your good side."

Aileen nodded then stopped her motion and stroked the knife harder on the carrot to strip away the tough skin.

"And when we came upon you at the wash tub, he looked at you for approval before he introduced you. Again, trying to make you happy." Maeve filled a cup with coffee.

"And ye noticed all this because..."

"It's my job. To notice how people act and memorize their faces." Maeve leaned down and sniffed the pies. "Yum. Are these for tonight?"

"Aye." What kind of job did she have? She wanted to find Ethan and ask him, but didn't want the woman to come up with any more ideas than she already had.

"Momma?" Shayla came through the door from the living quarters.

"Aye, darlin'?" She turned to her daughter, glad for the change of thought.

"Hi!" Shayla smiled at Maeve with her hands behind her back, her small body twisting.

"Shayla, this is Mrs. Halsey, Ethan's sister-in-law." Aileen put her hand on her lassie's shoulder.

"Mrs. Halsey, this is my gem, Shayla."

"Please, call me Maeve. And I can see why Ethan is fetching and carrying for this beauty." Maeve leaned down and held out her hand. "I'm pleased to meet you, Shayla."

The child took her hand and pumped it like the water spout at the drain board. "My momma's gonna sleep with me cuz you're here."

"I see that makes you very happy." Maeve captured her hand and Shayla's pumping arm in her other hand, stopping the motion.

She's good with children. Aileen couldn't help but like the woman after the way Shayla cottoned to her.

"Shayla, be a darlin' and show Maeve the living quarters." She motioned to the kitchen door and wasn't surprised when the woman continued to hold her daughter's hand and they both practically skipped out the door.

It was easier to work on the meal without the woman watching her every move. Her stomach clenched. She had to find a way to tell Ethan not to do anything untoward during the meal.

Ethan turned to Zeke when they finished visiting the mill. "What brings you here?"

His brother leaned against the rock outcropping. "We're following a man who killed a Pinkerton client's son."

"You think there's a killer here? In Sumpter?" He didn't like the idea of a cold blooded killer in their community.

"We know he headed this way." Zeke pushed away from the rocks and lowered his voice. "He killed a boy. A twelve-year-old boy, Ethan." Zeke paced back and forth. "I'd be after this scum even if I wasn't being paid."

"How do you know he's here?" Ethan thought of Colin and every other boy that age in the area.

"He doesn't know he's being followed and doesn't seem to care if he leaves a trail." Zeke stopped. His jaw twitched as he stared him in the eye. "We believe this isn't the first time the man killed a boy. Since taking on this job, William Pinkerton discovered other instances in the last five years. Each year the boy is a year older."

"Tell me about your client's son." There had to be a reason the man came to Sumpter.

"The father is a big holder in a mine in South Dakota. He's got a nice wife, three daughters, and he had a son. The first born. Just about broke their hearts when they found the boy." Zeke narrowed his eyes. "I'm going to find the killer, and so help me—"

"You can't take the law into your own hands." Ethan put a hand on his brother's shoulder. He knew Zeke had a passion for bringing murderers to justice. After their parents and youngest brother were killed, Zeke talked nonstop about ridding the world of murderers. His decision to join the Pinkertons hadn't surprised him as much as Zeke's choice of the prickly woman he married.

"I won't. But it doesn't mean I can't make the man's life hell until I get him to a lawman." The smirk on his brother's face told Ethan the man would make it to a jail barely alive.

"Do you have a name for this person?" Having been involved in the stamp mill he may have missed some newcomers that arrived in the area the last several months. When he and Aileen ate at Myrle's he'd noticed a couple new faces. The one stranger he did know about was the conniving Irishman. Just thinking of the man put a foul taste in his mouth.

"Don't have a name. But he talks with a fake Irish accent."

"We just hired an Irishman. Orin Healy. I knew there was something about the man…" Ethan wanted to find the man and beat him to a pulp.

"He's not an Irishman. Least ways that's what our client's wife said. She's Irish and said the man wasn't a true Irishman." Zeke scanned the area. "But it wouldn't hurt for you to point him out to me."

"He's easy to find. I have Clay dogging him, learning about the gold recovery process and keeping him away from Aileen."

Zeke grinned. "I thought there was more going on than her being an office assistant." He sobered. "But didn't she kill her husband?"

He shook his head. "No. She didn't do it. Though if she did, no one should fault her for it. The man was a beast to her."

Zeke's eyebrow lifted a fraction.

"Her son can vouch for the beatings. He takes protecting his mother from men very serious. A word of warning, you don't want to rile that boy. He's got something simmering underneath I haven't figured out."

"How old's the boy?"

"Twelve."

Zeke whipped his gaze around to stare him in the face. "Aileen isn't Irish. What is she?"

"Scots." Ethan scanned his brother's blank face. "Why?"

"Nothing. Just keep the boy close. Don't let him go off anywhere alone."

"You think…" Ethan couldn't say it. If something happened to the boy, Aileen would be devastated. The bond between mother and son was strong.

"I don't know. He's the right age. We know the man is in the area. Could be your Healy fellow." Zeke stared at the stamp mill. "Think I'll go find Clay and get a look at this fellow."

"Should I warn Aileen?" Knowing her temper he wasn't sure giving her all the information was a good thing.

"No. Let Maeve deal with her. I'll fill her in tonight, and she'll keep an eye on Aileen." Zeke headed toward the stamp mill.

Ethan stood by the rock outcropping staring at the office. He wanted to go to Aileen and—what? Comfort her? She would only ask why. He had an urge to see her and Shayla. Without a good reason, he headed to the house and hoped inspiration hit him on the way.

Chapter 27

Aileen fussed with her hair and smoothed out the best dress she owned. Dinner was in the oven, the biscuits ready to pop in when she pulled the roast out. Maeve had been a big help even though she informed her she wasn't a cook.

Inhaling, she let her breath out slowly and dipped her head into the apron. She grasped the ties, wrapping them to the back and tied them.

"Momma, you look bonnie," Shayla said, smiling and clapping her hands.

"Thank ye, darlin'. Ye look bonnie yerself." They both had cleaned up with a pitcher of water and dressed in their best clothes. She'd brushed and braided Shayla's dark hair until the copper hues shone in the lantern light.

"'Tis time to get the food on the table." She took her daughter's hand and headed down the hall. It surprised her to find the Halsey brothers all sitting in the living area, talking and laughing.

They all rose to their feet as she and Shayla

entered.

"Mon, ye dinna have to rise for the likes o' us." Even though she admonished them, the act filled her with warmth.

"Need help in the kitchen?" The imploring in Ethan's voice made her chuckle.

"We're doing just fine. Go on back to yer visitin'." She started to hustle Shayla into the kitchen, but the little scamp pulled from her grasp and flew onto his knee.

"Guess she's going to stay with us," Ethan said apologetically.

"Aye, Ah believe so." Warmth blossomed in her chest as she entered the kitchen. What would it be like to have these people around all the time and to feel a part of a family again? She shook her head. Now was not a time for dreaming. There was a meal to put on the table. Her plans for the future had nothing to do with this family. Her stomach roiled at the thought of moving on. They would move back to Ireland for her laddie. He deserved more than breaking his back in a mine.

"Need help?" Maeve entered the kitchen in the same stylish dress she'd arrived in, but the hem was void of the dust and her hair re-pinned.

She wanted to say no and get her kitchen back to herself, but she couldn't be rude to Ethan's visitors. After all, they were his family and she only an occupant of his building. Which sat on her property. Pride swelled her chest. She wouldn't be beholden to any man again. Between the gold they'd pull from the mine and her job here, her family would not have to rely on anyone.

She pulled the roast out of the oven and slid the pan of biscuits in.

"Keep an eye on these." She pulled her shawl from the peg by the door.

Maeve was beside her in two strides. "Where are you going?"

"To get preserves from the lean-to."

"I'll get them. I might burn the biscuits." Maeve took the shawl from around her shoulders and wrapped herself in the old wool garment and disappeared out the door.

Something was going on. The woman had flown across the room like her skirt was on fire. Had the family all convened to see if the husband-killer was going to do in their beloved Ethan? She laughed at the idea. The expression on the woman's face had been concern for her, not fear.

She lifted the roast out of the pan and placed it on the platter. Dipping out the carrots, she placed them around the roast. The scent of the baking bannock filled the air. She checked the biscuits to make sure they weren't browning too quickly.

Zeke entered the room. "Where's Maeve?"

"She went out to the lean-to for preserves." Before she could tell him his wife should return any moment, he crossed the room and exited through the door.

Those two moved faster and smoother than a mountain lion. What did they do?

Ethan came through the door holding Shayla's hand and the rest of his brothers and Colin trailed behind.

"Smells good in here." He released Shayla's

hand and crossed the room toward her. The men watching knew he'd spent considerable time with her the night before, but she still didn't want him making any demonstrations toward her. She needed to find something to keep him busy.

She held a knife out to him. "Ah'd like ye to cut the roast." She smiled at the men slowly taking seats at the table.

"Where's Zeke and Maeve?" Clay asked, helping Shayla onto a chair.

"Maeve went out to get preserves and her man went after her." Aileen glanced at the back door. "But they should o' been back by now."

"I'll go see what's keeping them." Hank headed across the room as the two hurried through the door. Their faces were flushed. By the twinkle in their eyes, they'd been doing more than looking for preserves in the lean-to.

"Here's the preserves." Maeve set the jar on the drain board and hung the shawl on the peg. Zeke took a seat, but his gaze never left his bright-cheeked wife.

Again, wistfulness overcame her. She'd spent a lot of years believing she'd never be wanted by a man or experience the love and strong arms of a man who cared for her. She glanced sideways at Ethan. He earnestly carved at the roast. His brow wrinkled and the tip of his tongue peeked between his full lips.

She turned to the oven and pulled the biscuits out. To have such thoughts was wrong. In a couple of years they would leave here and never return.

"I think this is ready." Ethan presented the

platter with every speck of the meat carved.

"Aye." She motioned for him to put it on the table and placed the biscuits beside the platter. She turned to retrieve the preserves while Maeve poured coffee for the adults and water for her bairn.

Placing the preserves on the table, she reached behind her and loosened the apron strings. She slipped the garment over her head, and her gaze locked with Ethan's. The heat in his eyes caused her breath to catch. Her heart hammered against her ribs, she couldn't draw her gaze from his. The full force of his devotion glittered in the brown depths.

"If you sit down we can eat." Colin's voice broke into her trance.

Her face heated. She ducked her head and slipped into her seat. Beside the man causing her heart to patter. He took a portion of the meat, offered the platter to her, and then passed it on.

She stayed out of the conversation, choosing to listen and learn more about the Halsey family. There appeared to be one more married brother who had a child. And would be visiting, knowing Maeve and Zeke had arrived.

Maeve turned to her. "I know your accent isn't Irish. Where is it you're from?"

Aileen glanced at Ethan. She didn't like to talk about herself. She'd only told Ethan what she believed wouldn't jeopardize her family. And this woman who told her earlier her job was to watch people wanted to know about her.

"Ah'm Scots." She bit a carrot, hoping to stop

any more questions.

"What brought you over here from Scotland?" The woman's blue eyes scanned her face as she waited. She could wait all day. The answer wasn't coming from her.

"We came from Ireland," Colin said. Aileen slanted him a glare, hoping to keep him from saying any more. He ducked his head, but not before his light green eyes defied her.

Zeke's head snapped up, and he watched her. "You came here from Ireland? When? Why?"

She turned to Ethan, beseeching him with her eyes to keep quiet. He placed his large, warm hand over hers—fisted around her skirt.

"Aileen, I didn't want to say anything until Zeke was sure—" Ethan cleared his throat and looked across the table at her laddie. "We'll all talk after dinner." He squeezed her hand, glanced pointedly at his brother and fell back to eating.

What was going on? Why couldn't they say why they were here? And what did Colin have to do with it? She could barely swallow the bite of food she put in her mouth. She watched each of the adults at the table. No one was talking any more. Each concentrated on their food.

"Happy Man is going to read to me after dinner," Shayla announced brightly into the tension-filled silence.

"He mayn't want to with his family here—"

"I promised Shayla I'd read to her tonight." Ethan stared into her eyes, "And I never break a promise."

His words warmed her like the sun's summer

rays. He'd not tell his brother her business unless she allowed it.

"Ready for pie?" she stood, picking up dishes as she rounded the table.

Maeve jumped up, clearing the other side of the table.

Zeke patted his belly. "I can always find room for pie."

"We know!" all the brothers said in unison causing everyone in the room to laugh and ease the gloom that had hovered over the last half of the meal.

After the pie was eaten, Ethan picked up Shayla and motioned with his head toward the other room. "Come on, Colin, I think you'll like the story I'm going to read."

Colin glanced toward Aileen, she nodded. Hank and Clay also stood to go into the other room. Apparently, she would be alone in the kitchen with Zeke and Maeve.

Ethan leaned down and kissed her head before whispering, "Only tell them what you're com-fortable with, but do answer their questions. It's important."

She stared at his back until he and Shayla dis-appeared through the door. Rubbing her palms on her skirt, she moved to the sink to start the dishes.

"Let us help." Maeve pumped water into the basin, and Zeke moved to the stove, draining the reservoir of hot water and adding it to the basin.

She wasn't sure what to do. Ethan had men-tioned they would question her. But what about? And why? Grabbing a dish cloth, she waited for

Maeve to set a clean dish on the drain board.

"You seem to have made an impression on my big brother." Zeke's comment made her jump.

"More like a thorn in his side." She dried the dishes, placing them on the shelf where they belonged.

"No, I don't think he'd kiss a thorn." The chuckle that followed his statement had her peering at the man.

"Ye know my last husband was found dead by the mine." When his eyes lit with interest she smiled. "Ah'm no' a good one for yer brother to be sniffin' after."

"But he seems to find you of interest. Something he hasn't done before." The man leaned against the counter, crossing his ankles and arms. Beside him his wife cleaned the dishes.

"It is only cuz I dinnae let him have his way. He'll soon tire o' the bickerin', and ah'll be out a place to live and go on back to diggin' for bing."

Maeve glanced at her and grinned. "I think there's more than bickering going on between you two. You look to him when situations get uncomfortable, and he guides and sustains you when he thinks you're getting unsettled." She went back to washing the dishes. "That's more than bickering." The mirth in the woman's voice jabbed a nerve. Her hands fisted even as her head reminded her these people would never see her as anything other than the crazy widow.

"Is this why ye came? To see if ye can badger the poor woman yer brother took pity on?" She couldn't stop the tears that burned at the back of her eyes. She wanted to run from the room and hide until the lot of them left.

"No." Maeve turned, putting her arms around her. "He doesn't pity you. You're much too strong for anyone to pity. He loves you."

She jerked out of the woman's embrace. "Nae! He cannae." Aileen bolted out the door and into the cold winter air.

Ethan loved her. She'd feared that was what she saw in his eyes. If he loved her, his next step would be to ask to marry her. She glanced at the shack that reminded her of the years of living hell she'd spent in a marriage full of abuse.

She'd never consent to that again. Not even for the man she loved.

Chapter 28

Ethan closed the book he read and glanced over Shayla's head as Zeke entered the living quarters with a sheepish expression on his face.

"You might want to take a coat out to Aileen."

"Why?" Ethan set the book on the floor next to his chair.

"She took offense and ran out the back door."

Colin surged to his feet. His fisted hands raised, ready to take a swing. "What did you do to my ma?"

"We didn't do anything except tell her the truth." Zeke didn't back away from the boy.

"What you told me earlier?" Ethan set Shayla on the chair when he stood.

"No. We didn't get that far."

"What did you say then?" He put a hand on Colin's shoulder, showing solidarity toward someone hurting his ma.

"We..." Zeke ran a hand over his face. "Well, we just told her you loved her."

Colin spun, ramming an elbow into his gut. The air whooshed out of Ethan.

"She doesn't want to marry. Never. You can't love her. She doesn't want a husband." Fear dilated the boy's eyes.

"It's okay. She and I already talked about this. I don't know why she took off." Ethan stared over the boy's head at his brothers all watching the exchange with perplexed expressions.

"Watch these two, I'll go look for Aileen." He snatched his coat from the back of a chair and went through the kitchen to grab a wrap for Aileen. Maeve stood at the sink finishing the dishes.

She glanced up. "She loves you, but for the life of me I don't know why she fears you loving her."

"It's a long story." Ethan plucked Aileen's shawl off the peg and rolled it up, tucking it inside his coat.

He stepped out into the dark, fall evening. The brisk air made him shiver. Only a month until Christmas and the world would soon be white.

Where could she have gone? Without a coat, she'd need shelter. He doubted she'd run to the shack. The building listed to one side, about to fall down. And she'd stay away from the stamp mill. A small crew worked there through the night. That left the mine.

He crossed the bridge and headed around the rock outcropping. A faint light shone from the end of the mine. At least she found shelter out of the biting wind.

Entering the tunnel, he followed the growing lantern glow. He rounded a corner and found her huddled over the lantern for warmth.

"I brought your shawl."

She jerked and stared at him. Her eyes reminded him of a trapped animal. He held the shawl out.

"Maeve told me why you ran." He approached her crouching figure and dropped the shawl over her. Then lowered his body to the dirt floor and opened his arms to her.

She sniffed, pulled the covering around her shoulders, and fell into his arms. "Ye cannae love me."

"Why?" he stroked her soft hair and breathed in the scent of apple pie, roast, and Aileen.

"If ye love me, ye'll want to marry me—ah—ah cannae do that again. Ah'll fear ye every day." Her body shuddered in his arms. He drew her closer, warding off the cold and the fear.

"Why would I treat you any different if we're married than I do now?" Her logic was misguided, but he knew what put it there. The fists of a man she'd been legally bound to.

"Ah know it makes no sense." She snuggled deeper into his arms. He closed his eyes and reveled in the feel of her. If she didn't leave, he'd live with her without a proper marriage if it quieted her fears. Even though it would mark them both sinners in the eyes of the community. They'd have one another and that's all he needed. His brothers wouldn't shun them. His family and Aileen. A man couldn't want anything more.

"We'll discuss our future later." He tucked a finger under her chin tilting her face up toward his. "Right now we need to talk about your past." She started to pull away, but he kept his arm securely around her.

"Zeke and Maeve are following a killer." She sucked in her breath. "He's killed young boys. The last one was the son of an important man. He called in the Pinkertons to find the man." Aileen stared at him.

"Yer brother and his wife work for the Pinkertons?" The relief in her voice had more questions buzzing in his head.

"Yes. They've followed this man to Sumpter. And believe he plans to kill another boy."

Her eyes widened with fear. "My laddie?"

"Why would you think Colin?" She knew something. Fear and anger lit her eyes.

"Ah dinnae tell ye everything about his da to keep him safe. But if this man is lookin' for him. 'Tis safer to tell ye the truth." She sat up in his lap and grasped the front of his coat.

"Patrick's ma came from England. Just before he died, he'd discovered his grandfather on his ma's side had left him his estate. Patrick was still decidin' what to do when he was killed. Everyone said he died because o' the Irish land act and how Patrick was always stickin' up for the tenants and tryin' to help them keep their land. But ah seen him." She nodded her head once. "Patrick's English cousin, Roderick. He was in our village the day my Patrick died." She peered into his face. "He had the look of Patrick but the blonde hair of his mother's side." Flames of indignation lapped from their pale depths. "That land belongs to Colin. It was to go to Patrick and his heirs. My father told me was best to leave and return when Colin was old enough to stand up to the cousin. That's why we are savin' and no' spendin'. To get back and get Colin's inheritance."

"You think this Roderick would come all this way to keep the estate?" That's why she guarded her past and the gold they took from the earth so closely. She planned to establish Colin on his family's land.

"From what Patrick said it was a grand place. He'd visited it once as a laddie. A place a greedy man would want to keep."

No wonder she worked so hard to get back to a life where she could be a woman of leisure. "Do you think it's this cousin killing Irish boys thinking he's getting rid of Patrick's heir?"

She shook her head. "Nae. He wouldn't dirty his hands. 'Tis someone he pays." She captured his hands in hers. "We cannae let anyone know Colin is o' Irish blood. Or his da's name."

"I'll talk to Zeke and see what he thinks. He's got more experience with this. In the mean time, we'll all keep a close watch on Colin. Don't tell him. I don't want him causing a fight with some man who doesn't have a clue what is going on."

"Ah agree."

He pulled her down against him and sought her soft lips. He'd held her long enough without tasting. She flowed over him and in him as the kiss deepened. Her insecurity and need for comforting made his chest ache. He wanted to be everything she needed, yet, wasn't sure how.

He pulled out of the kiss. "Let's go back to the

warm house. This ground is cold."

She hugged him one more time and then rose. He stood, bent to pick up the lantern, and drew her protectively under his arm.

"I'll see if Clay and Hank can keep Colin interested in a game of dominoes while we talk with Zeke and Maeve." She stiffened but nodded.

"Do they know who this man be?" She asked as he blew out the lantern and left it at the mine entrance.

His gaze drifted to the stamp mill. "Not exactly."

She peered up at him. "But ye have an idea?"

He shrugged. She would be as volatile as her son if she knew who he suspected. They couldn't divulge too much information. He hated keeping things from Aileen, but it was for the best. Too keep her safe.

"I'm not voicing my thoughts to anyone. No sense in causing trouble if there is none." Her steps faltered. She didn't like his answer.

They arrived at the kitchen door. Ethan folded both arms around her. In the darkness, her features were hard to distinguish. But he knew where to find her mouth. He leaned down, placing his lips against hers. When her body relaxed in his arms, he raised his head.

"Don't run away." He kissed her before she could say anything.

"Don't fear my love." He kissed her again. A sound beyond the door made her stiffen.

"And don't be afraid for people to see us together." He captured her lips once more, reveling in their softness and sweetness. She sagged in his arms, and he smiled against her lips.

The door opened. He glanced sideways and found Colin in the doorway, his arm in the air about to put his coat on.

"You looking for us?" Ethan asked calmly and pushed past the boy into the kitchen.

"Guess I don't need to ask what you've been doing." The boy's voice dripped with anger.

Aileen started to pull away. Ethan drew her back against his side. Why did she fear her son seeing her with a man? He was tired of pussyfooting around the boy.

"No, you don't have to ask." He glanced at Aileen. The multitude of emotions contorting her face made him angry. "And you better get used to it."

Colin rose to his full height, stretched his neck like a rooster charging into a fight, and glared at him. "You aren't going to hurt my ma."

Ethan slid Aileen behind him. "I won't hurt your ma. But if you don't back off and let her have a little happiness, I'm gonna put you over my knee and paddle you."

"There's no need to be goin' at one another." Aileen stepped from behind Ethan. She didn't know whether to laugh, cry, or be frightened the way the two of them battled over her.

She stood in front of Ethan, crossed her arms, and faced her son. "Ah enjoy my time with Ethan. And ah'll no' have ye spoilin' it by actin' like an eejit every time ye see us together." Colin ducked his head. She smiled, pressed her lips together and swung around to the man standing so close behind her she could feel his heat. A reminder of the kisses they'd shared moments before made it hard for her to remain stern. She wanted to melt into his arms and revel in his love.

"And ah'll no' have ye puttin' yer hands all over me when ye have the notion just to pique my laddie."

"I've never—" She held up her palm toward him.

"Ye dinnae do it on purpose, but ye need to think o' his feelings as well." She glanced over her shoulder at her son. "He and ah have been through a lot. 'Tis hard for him to no' be the man."

She reached back, and Colin slid his hand in hers. Pulling him forward, she made him look up at the man standing in front of them. "Ethan cares for me, for Shayla, and for ye." When he tried to turn, she held his head. "Nae. Ye know he will no' let anything happen to us. To me."

Aileen gazed up into the dark, caring eyes of the man looming over them. He nodded and ruffled Colin's hair.

"Go in the other room. Tell Zeke we're back and see if you can beat Hank at dominoes." Ethan's deep voice was barely above a whisper as he instructed Colin. It wasn't in him to hurt a child or a woman. The realization had been long coming, but it was the truth. She knew it now.

The boy shuffled out of the room. He would be harder to convince.

"Thank you." Ethan put his hands out, grasping hers.

"For what?"

"For not tossing me aside like your son wanted."

"He may be my first bairn, but he cannae dictate how ah feel." She placed her hand on his cheek. He'd shaved for dinner. By this time of night he usually carried a stubble of whiskers. She ached to find security in his arms again tonight.

The door from the main room to the kitchen opened, but she didn't step back. She curled next to Ethan and watched Zeke and Maeve enter.

"Looks like you found her." Zeke's gaze raked over the two of them.

"And you talked things out." Maeve smiled and moved to the stove. Aileen remained wrapped in Ethan's warm embrace while the woman poured four cups of coffee and placed them on the table.

"Sit. We have several things to discuss." Maeve had positioned the cups two on one side, two on the other.

Ethan nudged her toward the chairs closest to them. She sat and wasn't surprised when he claimed her hand in his. His fingers wrapped around, blanketing her with security.

The other couple sat across from them. Maeve smiled, but it didn't light her eyes. Her face had become expressionless. Zeke, too, had taken on a less than comforting pose.

She glanced at the man beside her. He winked and gave her a reassuring smile that lit his eyes. Whatever the other two had to say, he was on her side.

"I'm assuming Ethan told you why we're here?" Zeke glanced from her to his brother and back to her.

"Aye. Ye are after a man who killed a boy." She wasn't going to divulge anything else. She only trusted Ethan. He knew the truth. That was all that mattered.

"One the age of Colin."

"Aye."

Zeke studied her. "You wouldn't happen to know why this man is killing Irish boys?"

<h1 style="text-align:center">Chapter 29</h1>

"If ah dinna know the man, how could ah know why he is killing boys?" Aileen glanced at Ethan. Had he told Zeke Colin was Irish?

"But your son is Irish. And this man seems to be after boys of your son's age." Zeke leaned forward. His intensity drove her back against the chair and her hand to clutch Ethan's.

"How did ye know my son is Irish?" She didn't like the man knowing so much about her family.

Maeve smoothed the front of her dress. "I asked him. He has an Irish name and with you being Scots I would have figured him to have a Scots name like Shayla." Maeve leaned forward. "If he's told me, who else do you think he's told?"

Aileen turned to Ethan. "This is why we kept to ourselves. That and Mr. Miller's death." She grasped both his hands with hers. "He cannae go around tellin' people about his da. Ah've told him that before." She started to stand, to go in the other room and give her laddie a talking to.

"Sit." Ethan pulled her back into the chair and smoothed the lines beside her eyes. "Zeke, we believe the man is looking for Colin. He's an heir to an English estate. It seems Aileen's first husband had just inherited before he died—"

"Was killed!" Aileen interrupted. He patted her hand.

"Was killed. Aileen believes by a cousin who took over the estate and is now trying to kill off the rightful heir. Colin." Aileen stiffened as he told her tale.

"Okay, so we know he has finally found his target. All those other boys must have had a similar situation. Come to America with their Irish mother. The one thing our man didn't know was that the real boy's mother wasn't Irish." Zeke glanced at her.

"My name is common among Irish and Scots. That side o' the family dinnae care for the likes o' the O'Lears. Ah doubt any o' them even know ah was Scots." Aileen's heart ached for the parent's of the boys the man had killed.

Zeke stared at Ethan. "Now that we know he's after Colin we sit back and wait for him to attempt something."

"Nae!" Aileen shot to her feet. "My laddie will no' be used for bait!"

"Shh." Ethan stood, drawing Aileen against his chest. Her body trembled as she clung to him. He wanted to stave her fears and be her strength.

"Ah'll no' lose my laddie. Ah cannae."

"You're not going to lose him. There will be one of us with him at all times." Ethan kissed the top of her head. He would do anything for this woman and her family. "I promise."

She stared at him through tear-filled eyes. "It's a promise ye better keep."

Keeping her son alive could mean the difference between him holding her in his arms for the rest of their lives or losing the only woman he'd ever love.

"I will."

She turned to Zeke and Maeve. "Don't be tellin' my laddie what ye know. He's got a hot head and could harm himself." She pushed out of his arms. "Ah'm goin' to tuck Shayla in and talk with Colin about keepin' his past quiet."

Without so much as a good night, she slipped through the doorway. Ethan stared at the closed door. She was too strong for her own good. Would she remain here in the protection they could provide for her son, or would she try to slip away?

"We need to keep an eye on both Colin and Aileen." He sat back down and stared across the table at his brother.

"You think she's going to bolt?" Zeke took a sip of coffee.

"I'm not sure. She's a strong woman who fights for what she believes in. And she believes her son deserves his estate in England. If she thinks there's a possibility he'll be killed or lose it, I'm sure she'll take off." He glanced at his sister-in-law. "What do you think?"

"You want my opinion?" Her stunned response made him chuckle.

"Yes. You're a woman. Maybe not a mother

yet, but if you were in her shoes, what would you do?" With his question, he had finally drawn his sister-in-law to his side. He saw it in the softening of her face and the slight curve to her lips.

"She loves you. She also believes in you. Your truth. I'd say, she'll stick around. Unless something does happen to the boy. Then you better be prepared." The sympathy in her eyes expressed what he already knew. If the boy was killed, he wouldn't have a chance with Aileen.

"So we keep the boy safe." Zeke stood, took his wife's hand and helped her stand. "It's been a long day."

"I have something else I need to tell you." Ethan motioned for them to sit back down. "The other night when I brought Shayla and Aileen home from town after dark, there was a man on horseback watching us. I could have called him out, but I didn't want him to know I saw him. It might be your killer, but there was something familiar about his shape..." He shook his head. He'd been trying to place the person ever since he saw him. "Anyway, just keep an eye on the whole family."

Zeke nodded.

Clay poked his head through the doorway. "Hey, are you ready to head home? I'm tired of being beat by Hank."

"I just want to make sure Aileen is fine, and I'll be ready to go." Ethan turned to Zeke. "I'm glad you and Maeve are staying here."

Zeke slapped him on the back. "Big brother, I won't let anything happen to your woman." He gathered Maeve against him and the two left the room.

Ethan picked up the cups and carried them to the drain board. He pulled the coffee pot from the stove, added some wood, turned the damper down, and blew out the lantern.

He entered the living quarters and found Aileen standing by the wood stove. Moving quietly, he caught her around the waist and drew her body against his, kissing her neck.

"Where'd everyone go?" Her scent and lush body drove him crazy. He wanted to gather her in his arms and find a place to show her how much he cared for her.

"Hank and Clay went to check on the stamp mill and get the horses ready. Zeke and Maeve and the bairn are in bed." She rested her head against his chest.

He spun her to face him. "Everything will be all right. Zeke and Maeve know what they're doing, and I'm not going to let anything happen to you or the children."

"Ah know. Ah told Colin to no' be tellin' anythin' about him to anyone." She shook her head. "By his reaction, he's said somethin' to someone, but ah didn't want to pry and get him worried."

"I'll check around tomorrow. Maybe I can figure out who he's been spending time with lately." He bent his head. "In the mean time, how about a good night kiss?" Their lips met. It wasn't a hot passionate mating. He wanted to show her she meant more to him than the heated coupling of the night before.

He slid his lips across hers, opening slightly and tasting her. She sighed, melting against him, and he deepened the kiss. The thought of never having her to hold or indulge slammed into his ribs like a hammer. He would do everything possible to make sure nothing happened to her son.

Booted feet thumped across the office floor.

"It's time for me to go." He kissed her once more and gently turned her toward the bedrooms.

She motioned with a hand toward the wood stove. "The fire..."

"I'll get it. Good night." Ethan opened the stove door as Clay entered the room.

"Ready?"

"Just let me fill the stove." He shoved the firebox full and closed the door. "Ready." He glanced at the hallway even though he knew she wouldn't be standing there.

Zeke sleeping in the building made it easier for him to leave. There was trouble afoot, and he didn't like being over the ridge when he should be here, protecting the people that had found a place in his heart.

The next day, Aileen couldn't shake the feeling of someone watching her. Which was ridiculous, she hadn't left the building all morning. Ethan had appeared while she prepared the morning meal. He ate along with the bairn and his brother and sister-in-law.

When Zeke and Colin left for the stamp mill, he'd stayed behind to show her more about her job in the office. With the mill running, she was now in charge of logging in the information Hank brought her about each miner and the gold removed from their rubble.

Working with the numbers was exciting. When she did a figure right she was not only proud of herself, but of Ethan for giving her the chance to prove she could be more.

There it was again. A prickling along the back of her neck. She glanced up from the entry book and stared out the office window. Several men mulled around in front of the mill. None stood still and watched her. The hair on her arm bristled. She walked around the counter and over to the window.

The Irishman and Clay stood at the corner of the stamp mill. Clay had his back to the office—and the Irishman. Yes, his gaze darted in her direction while he conversed with Clay.

She hurried into the living quarters. She'd get the rest of the material Mrs. Fellowes gave her for curtains and make a pair for the office window.

Colin came through the kitchen door. "Ma, I'm going to start filling ore carts. It's our day at the stamp mill on Sunday, and I want to keep the mill running all day with our diggings."

"That's an ambitious thought," she said, turning and smiling. He grew taller every day, becoming a man.

"Ah haven't been in the mill for a while. How about ah come and help ye?" She turned to go change into her work clothes.

"You stay here. I like you doing woman's work

instead of men's." His changing voice stayed deep and the conviction in his words stopped her.

"Ye sound so much like a man and act so much like a man—" She crossed the room and embraced him. "Ah'll miss my laddie, but ah know ye are goin' to be a fine man."

He pulled out of her arms. "Ma, why are you so mushy lately? If falling in love makes you that way, I'm staying away from girls."

Aileen burst out laughing. "Ah laddie, ye'll find ye cannae stay away from them any more than ah can tell my heart no' to love again.

"Wait for me. Ah'd like to help with the first cart of our ore that is put through the stamp mill."

He nodded, understanding her need to have a hand in something so momentous. "Eat some cookies while ye wait for me to change."

"Where's Shayla?"

"She and Maeve are out lookin' for something to use as a table center piece." She shrugged. With winter sneaking closer every day, she knew the woman had taken up the task as a means to spend time with the child. Why, she wasn't sure, but at least she knew someone watched over her daughter.

Colin shook his head in disbelief and reentered the kitchen. Aileen hurried to the room she shared with Shayla and quickly donned her trousers and work shirt. She rarely thought of the clothes in terms of Mr. Miller's any more. Over the years, they had become hers. Putting them on, once again, brought back insecurities she thought she'd shed. She shook her head to expel the unwanted thoughts and hurried to the kitchen for her coat and Colin.

Together they walked to the mine. Knowing the amounts of gold the other miners had crushed from their rubble, made her anxious to see what they could press from their rock.

At the mine, she lit the lantern and walked behind Colin as he pushed an ore cart inside. The track stopped before they reached the pile of rubble they'd been accumulating.

"We still have to pack it by buckets to the cart, but at least we don't have to pack it all the way out to the sluice," Colin said, handing her two buckets and picking up two for himself.

"Aye." She bent to the task of filling buckets while Colin carried them to the cart.

When the cart was full, she turned a bucket over and sat down. "Tis still a job for two people." She commented when Colin did the same with a bucket.

He smiled at her. "I'm glad. I like working with you, Ma."

"Aye, laddie. Ah enjoy my time with ye as well."

A sound echoed through the tunnel. "Did ye hear that?" She craned her neck and listened.

"Just a rock falling off the wall." Colin stood. "I'll push this out and bring in another one."

"Ah'll help." Aileen stood. The hair on the back of her neck prickled. She didn't want to leave him alone.

"I can do it." He placed his hands on the end of the cart and pushed. Grunting, he gave it another hard push. The metal wheels squeaked under the weight of the load.

She placed her hands on the cart and pushed. After a couple more shoves the cart moved at a slow rate down the tracks.

"I-I'm-glad-the-tracks-are-down-hill-from-the-mine," Colin said between breaths.

"Aye." Each push of the cart set her legs on fire. She'd have to ask Ethan about an easier way to move the carts once they were full.

Sunlight glowed ahead at the entrance. They steadily moved toward the light. Once the cart was in the open, she stood, wiped the sweat from her brow, and found a place to sit and rest her rubbery legs.

"There's got to be a better way." She shielded her eyes with her hand and peered at the office, hoping to see Ethan and wave him over. There wasn't a body moving around the building. Gazing up at the sky, she figured it neared the noon hour.

"Let's go home, eat a meal, and come back to load another cart?" She suggested standing.

"I want to push this empty cart in. Besides we left the lantern in there, and we'll waste fuel if we leave it burning." Colin grabbed a cart waiting on a side rail and started into the mine.

Knowing the laddie, he'd start loading the cart and forget about the noon meal. She followed behind, holding onto his shirt as the tunnel became darker.

The rumble of the wheels grew louder the darker the tunnel became. Following along, she stumbled.

Colin stopped. "Ma, here, take this side." He grasped her hand, placing it on the edge of the cart.

The cart moved forward. The tug on her arm kept her moving through the shaft. Colin's shirt sleeve rubbed hers. A faint light from the lantern glimmered ahead. They both moved forward faster. The light grew, and they soon came to the end of the track. The lantern sat on the rock where they'd left it.

She picked up the lantern and turned to head back. The rumble of rolling rocks echoed in the tunnel behind her. Colin cried out. Fear coiled in her gut. She spun around and found him pinned to the ground with a large boulder on his leg.

"Laddie, hold on, ah'll help ye." She set the lantern down and pushed on the rock. How had such a large boulder rolled from the side? The shaft walls had never appeared weak before.

Her feet slid out from underneath her. Colin moaned. His head lolled to the side. "Laddie! Laddie!" She leaned down, placing her cheek in front of his mouth. His breath came in pants. Pain whitened his face and squeezed his eyes shut. She had to get help.

She started to grab the lantern. She could move faster with the light. But what if he came to? He'd be in the dark and know she left him. She chewed on the inside of her mouth. But she had to hurry.

She bent to snatch the lantern. Someone grabbed her about the waist.

"No one here to stop us this time."

The voice sent shivers up her spine.

Miles.

He ripped her shirt open. Fear and anger battled within her. Her laddie needed her and this beast kept her from getting help. The man's boney fingers dug into her flesh. He squeezed her breasts as his disgusting breath puffed against her cheek.

Colin needed her.

She stomped on Mile's feet and threw her body backwards knocking him off balance. His arms flew out to stop his fall, and she surged forward. Scrambling deeper into the tunnel, she sought a dark place to hide.

She had to get back to Colin. Would Ethan come looking for them or would history repeat itself?

Chapter 30

Ethan wandered through the quiet house. Where was everyone? Time spent alone with Aileen had been his goal, but she wasn't around. Opening the office door, he stepped inside and scanned the small room for any sign of her.

He navigated through the office and flung the outside door open. He didn't see a sign of her around the shack or the mine. A full ore cart sat in front of the mine and one cart was missing. Surely, she wasn't filling the carts by herself?

He hurried across the bridge, jogging to the mine. At the entrance, he hunted for a lantern. Behind a box, he found one with dents and a tilting chimney. He shook it, a small amount of fuel sloshed inside. It had to do. Wasting time to go back to the stamp mill for another one wasn't an option. His gut told him something was wrong.

Pulling out his match safe, he lit the lamp and headed down the tunnel using the weak light to guide him. He kept his pace to a brisk walk to avoid stumbling even though his heart raced and he wanted to rush.

The faint light ahead loosened the knot in his gut. His strides lengthened, carrying him toward the beacon.

The lantern sat on the ground precariously. But a rock, half the size of the ore cart, wedged between the cart and the mine wall blocked his way. Peering over the rock his heart stopped then beat frantically. Colin lie sprawled on the ground. His face was a ghastly white and—the way his leg twisted under the rock—he looked dead.

Ethan hurtled his body around the other side of the cart and felt the boy's neck for a pulse. The slow throb against his fingertips slowed his own heart. He was alive. Relief reduced the pounding in his head.

Why in blazes did he come in here by himself? Where the hell was Hank or Zeke? They were supposed to stick to him while Clay stayed with the Irishman.

He unclenched his fists and shoved them under the rock. His muscles bulged and his head pulsed as he tried to raise the boulder off the boy's leg. It was wedged too tight. He scanned the area. There had to be something to get the rock off the boy. He needed a lever. His hands clenched into fists, again. He wanted to break something.

Reeling in his frustration, he focused on helping Colin. To fail would be to fail Aileen. His gaze locked on the pick leaning against the wall. He grasped the handle and swung the tool, lodging the pick under the rock. Leaning back, using his weight as well as the strength in his arms, he pried at the wedged rock. Sweat popped out on his forehead and his arms ached from using every muscle to pull on the handle. The ore cart creaked and the rock scraped the wall.

The small movement gave him renewed encouragement. His stomach unclenched when the rock dislodged and rolled backward.

Ethan knelt beside the boy. He refrained from pulling the child into his arms, to comfort and appease his own need to be comforted. He focused on the injured leg. The bone protruding from the boy's trouser's made his stomach lurch. The pool of blood steadily growing made it hard to stop the dread and urgency swimming in his head.

Colin moaned and his eyes opened. Pain shrouded eyes stared at him.

"Ma—"

"I'll take you to her as soon as I get that leg splinted."

The boy raised up and fell back against the dirt wall. "No. He's after her."

Intense rage ripped through him. "Healy!"

Colin fell back into unconsciousness.

"Damn!" Ethan scanned the area. Could Healy and Aileen have exited the mine before he arrived? The ground around the boy was disturbed from dislodging the rock. He grasped the lantern and held it low to the dirt. The faint light wavered from his shaking hand. She needs you. They both need you. Containing the emotions threatening to thwart his attempt to find Aileen, he peered at the ground. The scuffed prints of someone running headed deeper into the mine. These were followed by the imprint of a boot heel. Aileen was fleeing deeper into the mine. Into the dark and away from help.

He glanced back at Colin. The pool of blood grew around his shattered leg. The boy had to be tended.

Aileen would fight like a she bear knowing her son was wounded. He'd get the boy's bleeding stopped and the leg splinted. Then he'd go after the woman. Tending the boy would be a hard task. His mind cried out to race after Aileen. His heart ached with the knowledge she was no match against a man who had killed before.

Aileen ran deeper into the darkness. Her ragged breaths echoed in her ears. She couldn't hide from him if she kept running and gasping for air. She'd have to confront him and hope she could get around him and back to Colin. A vision of her son with his leg under that huge rock gave her a burst of resolve.

She frantically felt along the wall for a hollow they'd dug while chasing a vein. She fell forward when her hands found the sunken area.

She flipped, smashing her back into the cold wall and dug her fingers into the side, filling her hands with dirt. She held her breath, but her lungs ached with the need for air. Gasping, she inhaled and heard him.

His breathing came in great gulps and puffs. His footsteps not as agile. He wasn't used to moving about in a mine. His feet scattered rocks as he shuffled them. The breathing came closer. She held her breath and pressed tighter against the wall. Her heart beat like a racing horse and thundered in her head.

The warmth and stench of his breath flickered across her face and was gone. She waited until his shuffling steps grew faint.

With one hand on the wall, she stepped into the shaft and headed back the way she'd come. She hurried along, picking up her feet to avoid making noise. She had to get back to Colin, he needed her.

Ethan pulled off his coat and shirt. As he shredded his shirt, each rip represented what he'd do to Healy when he got his hands on the man. He folded the largest piece of cloth into a neat square, wishing he could control his emotions as easily. He placed the square and other strips within arm's reach.

"Colin?" He gently patted the boy's face. "Colin, I need you to wake up." His stomach churned at the thought of what he had to do next. The bone had to be put back in place. The jagged end that protruded through a hole in his britches had ripped open his leg, causing all the blood.

When Colin didn't respond, Ethan carefully stretched the boy out on the ground. Gulping back the bile rising in his throat, he positioned Colin's injured leg between his own. The bone had to be pulled and slipped into place. Cold sweat beaded his forehead. Fear and lack of confidence had never swamped him as it did now. He'd always had control of situations. Always dealt with them head on.

He stared at the growing pool of blood. The boy would bleed to death if he didn't get on with it. Shaking off his doubts and fears, he pressed his feet against the boy's upper leg and then grasped the ankle and began to pull.

Colin cried out, then went limp. He glanced at the boy's face. He'd fainted. He'd not feel the worst of it.

He returned his attention to the injured limb. Ethan grimaced. The sight sickened him, but to save the boy he had to do this. His hands shook as he continued the steady pull and watched the bone disappear into the flesh. He turned the foot, aligning it with the boy's knee.

Exhaling, and holding the foot in place with one hand, he swiped a long john-covered arm across the sweat dripping in his eyes. The hard part was over. Picking up the folded piece of flannel, he pressed it against the open wound. Careful not to bend the leg and pop the bone out of place, he wound a strip of fabric around the square, tying it tight to stop the blood loss.

Standing, he scanned the area for something to use as a splint. The only pieces of wood other than the pick handle were the cross ties on the track. He pried the pick under the steel track and popped up the spikes in the last two cross ties. The pieces of wood were thick and long, but he had no other choice of material for a splint.

He leaned the pick against the wall of the tunnel and knelt down to get the cross ties. A shadow loomed over him. The upper body of a person with a pick poised to strike.

Adrenaline kicked in. He sprang from his crouched position and rolled to the side.

Aileen—wild hair, torn shirt, and a haunted look in her eyes, swung the pick and let it fly. Relief rushed through him in a wave of warmth at the sight of her. Then he saw the rage contorting and darkening her face. The ugliness slammed into him like a loaded ore cart. The fury behind the explosion of power that sent the heavy tool flying through the air knotted his stomach. He'd never seen such violence in anyone.

A thud and moan resounded beyond the empty ore cart.

Disregarding her victim, Aileen fell to her knees beside Colin.

Ethan remained on the ground watching the woman. Who had she flung the pick at with such vengeance? Could she have killed Miller? His head throbbed. There had been no one else around when Miller was killed. It had to be her. Self-defense he could stomach, but she'd just shown cold-blooded rage.

Colin moaned.

He couldn't neglect the boy, no matter what the mother had done. But he'd keep his distance from Aileen until he had time to think things through. He picked up the cross ties and knelt at Colin's foot.

"How did this happen?" he asked when Aileen turned to him.

Her eyes shimmered with unshed tears.

"Thank ye," whispered across trembling lips. His heart nearly shattered. He almost forgot she'd just hurled a pick at someone.

"Who did this?" he asked, turning back to Colin.

"Miles. He pushed the rock on Colin then attacked me. Ah got away, drawin' him into the mine, then ah hid in a vein hollow. When he went by, ah hurried back here." She held the boards as he wrapped the strips of cloth around the splints and the boy's leg.

Ethan worked, avoiding eye contact with the woman. Why was Miles after Aileen? And why injure the boy? To get to the woman? The boy would fight like a man to save his mother. He'd proven it time and again. But that didn't answer who was moaning behind the ore cart.

He tipped his head toward the ore cart. "Who'd you try to kill?" He tried to keep his voice neutral, but he noticed her flinch at the accusation in his voice.

"The Irishman."

Healy? "Was he with Miles?" Now he knew why Miles was watching Aileen. Healy must have pulled him into the scheme.

"Nae."

He gawked at her with disbelief "Then why did you throw the pick at him?" If the man hadn't harmed her, how could she show such violence?

"He had ye in a vulnerable spot, and ah dinnae like the man."

Ethan stared into her eyes. She talked about it as though swinging a pick at someone was an everyday occurrence. He'd been a fool. Believing an angel resided in that angel-kissed complexion. Or been played for a fool.

He scowled. How could he have fallen in love with such a callous woman? He thought of her soft touch and the love he'd witnessed when she looked at her children—he moaned inwardly—and him. She'd shown him a side of himself he'd never believed in. Yet, he couldn't deny the moans growing louder behind the ore cart.

"Yer lookin' at me funny."

He ducked his head and continued to wrap the boy's leg. Confusion swirled. How could she be so loving and caring? She took in his family, made them all feel special and welcome. And then maneuvered him into paying for the track, ore carts, bathtub, and an agreement of no payments for stamp mill services. He shook his head, not wanting to listen to the click of doubts rattling his brain. He finished wrapping the leg.

"I'll check Healy." Before he could rise to check the man someone landed on his back. Roaring to his feet, he ripped the arms from around his neck and turned.

Miles jumped up and lunged for Aileen. He pulled her against him, one arm wrapped around her long, white neck. The other hand held the tip of a knife at her side. Her face paled, and her eyes widened in fear. All doubts dissolved.

The woman who captured his heart was in danger.

"Let her go, Miles." He kept his voice even, unflustered despite the knot that twisted his gut and his heart pounding against his ribs so hard he was sure a rib would crack.

"She's mine. What I did for her—" The wild-eyed man rubbed his face in her hair. Aileen kicked out with her legs.

She stopped and her eyes widened with fear. The side of her shirt sliced opened and a small bead of blood darkened the material.

"What did you do for her?" Ethan moved to his right, forcing the man to step to his right. If he could get the man backed into the ore cart, he might be able to do something. He needed action.

Miles laughed. "Only took care of her troubles." He raised the knife up to her face, stroking her cheek with the shiny blade.

Ethan started forward. The way the man caressed her face sent shivers down his spine. Jealousy ripped his gut.

"What troubles?" he said as his jaw clenched.

"I seen Miller drag her out of this mine by the hair that day. And that boy—" he pointed to Colin still unconscious on the floor, "whacked him a good one with a board. Miller went down, and the boy managed to get his ma out of there." He sniffed her hair. Ethan moved to his right some more.

"What happened after the boy and the woman got away?" Ethan watched the man, but he glanced at Aileen to see how she was doing. Miles' story had caught her attention.

"Why, I finished the bastard off with the same board!" Miles glared at Aileen. "Then when I come around to collect for my good deed, she laughed at me." He slid the knife down to her throat. "You laughed at me!" His face twisted in disbelief.

"Ah-ah didn't know." Aileen squeaked.

"And when I came to collect again, you beat me up." He glared at Ethan then looked down at the boy. "If that pipsqueak wasn't around protecting her, it was you." He pointed the knife at Ethan and shoved Aileen forward. "You're all going to die." Miles bolted down the mine cackling.

Ethan started to follow, but Aileen crumpled to the ground. He caught her before her head hit the track.

"Aileen. Come on, sweetheart, wake up." Ethan kissed her brow. "Don't go getting all female on me now." Cradling her in his arms, he slid down the wall to sit next to Colin.

She hadn't killed Miller. The announcement had erased all his doubts about the woman. She was the woman he fell in love with. But why had she looked relieved when Miles confessed to killing him? It's no wonder she would want to blot out that day. Colin hit the man first. Had she believed all this time Colin had killed the man? How her heart must have been torn between doing right and protecting her son. He embraced her to his heart. As long as he was alive, she would never suffer.

"Aileen, sweetheart." He placed a kiss on her cheek. Her eyes fluttered open. A smile quivered on her tempting lips before he caught a flash of disillusion in her eyes. She lowered her lashes, pushing out of his arms.

"Hey, don't. Hold still. You had a bad time of it. Take it easy." She didn't look at him, just stood. Something happened. But what?

"Let me check Healy, then we need to get Colin and get out of here." Ethan watched her turn to the boy, ignoring him.

Something was up. What could it be? He started toward the ore cart. Healy slowly rose from behind it. A bump on the side of his head dripped with blood.

"Here, let me help you." Ethan grabbed the man's arm, flinging it across his shoulders and carried him near the lantern light. He didn't miss the flash of anger in Aileen's eyes as he helped the man sit against the wall a fair distance from the boy. Miles wasn't the man Zeke and Maeve were after, and he still had reservations about the man nursing his head.

Healy pointed his finger at Aileen. "She be an ill-tempered woman. I never was seein' what Patrick saw in her."

Ethan sat back on his haunches and studied the man. "What are you talking about?"

"She hasn't told you anythin'?" Healy narrowed his eyes and peered at Aileen as she busied herself with the boy.

"No. Aileen, what's this man talking about?" Ethan turned his attention to the woman who had become as frosty as the first time he met her.

"Orin Healy is Patrick's cousin on his da's side." Aileen didn't want to look at Ethan. He'd shattered her heart when he thought her capable of killing her husband. She'd witnessed the horror on his face after she'd clouted Orin.

And Orin—the man had a knack for always showing up at the wrong time. Where was he when that beast Miles attacked her? Why couldn't he have been around then? No, he had to show up when Ethan was tending to Colin. So, to keep him from doing exactly what he was doing now, she'd beaned him.

"Why didn't you say so when he applied for a job instead of insisting I not hire him?" Ethan glanced from her to Patrick's disgusting cousin. "Do you think he's the man trying to kill Colin?" Her heart lurched when Ethan took a position between she and Colin and Orin.

"Nae, he's never liked the English side o' the family." She shot the man a glare. "Nor the Scots side."

Ethan turned to her. "Then why did you bash him on the head if you don't think he's going to hurt Colin?"

She turned from him. How did she explain her hatred of the man, and her fear he would bring trouble to them.

"Because she's believing if I found her and the boy, the English will be findin' him, too." Orin's tired voice struck a nerve.

"What do ye know?" She popped to her feet and crossed to the man.

"I was asked by Patrick's da to come lookin' for you and the boy when he heard Roderick had a man after you. I don't know who he be, but I'm always one step behind him. Until now. I been thinkin' I'd just hang around and keep an eye on the two of you and take care of the devil before he did you any harm."

"Why did you come in the mine?" Ethan edged

his way closer to her. Her body reacted when her head knew it was for naught. He believed her a killer.

"I slipped your brother. Yeah, I knew you had him watchin' me every move. The boy told me he planned to fill the ore carts. I figured I'd be comin' to help him and tell him more about his da."

"Ye've been talkin' to him!" Aileen hurtled herself at the man. "Ye have marked him good as dead!"

Ethan's strong arms held her against his body. "Colin isn't going to get better by us standing in here talking. Let's get out of here." He set her on her feet. "Don't lay into him until we're out of this tunnel."

He let go and spun her to face him. "Promise you won't hit him over the head until we get out in the sunshine?" The joking tone did nothing to dispel her anger.

"Ah'll no' kill anyone—including ye."

He frowned and handed her the lantern. "Lead the way."

She stared into his eyes. He was hurt and thinking. His usually dark eyes were clouded with his thoughts.

She turned on her heel and stepped around the ore cart. She glanced over her shoulder as Ethan bent to pick up Colin.

Kaboom! The tunnel quaked under her feet. A wall of dust plummeted toward them, knocking her backwards. She dropped the lantern and covered her face as a shower of dirt and rock rained around her.

Chapter 31

The boy squirmed under Ethan. The tunnel was pitch dark and filled with dust. He tried not to gulp in the grit sifting through the air. Panic squeezed his chest at the silence. Where was Aileen?

"Aileen! Aileen!" he scrambled off Colin and crawled on his hands and knees bumping into rocks as he felt along the floor. "Say something. Aileen!"

A moan to his right stopped his forward motion. "Aileen?" He reached out willing his hand to touch her soft body. Rough cloth met his finger tips. Grasping the limb under the cloth, he clenched a male arm strewn with muscle. Healy. A lump the size of a fist slid down his throat and landed in his stomach. Where was she? He couldn't lose her now, not after realizing how much she meant to him.

"Are you alive?" Ethan asked, running his hands the length of the man to see if rocks pinned him to the ground.

"Aye. Just be feelin' a bit dizzy. Two whacks to the head in one day is a mite hard on the noggin."

"Where was Aileen before the mine collapsed?" Ethan sat up calculating where he'd left Colin.

"She be standin' near the ore cart when the tunnel blew." The man's voice sounded about chest level. He was sitting.

"And where do you think we are from there?" The boy was behind him, deeper into the mine.

"I'd say if you were to go about twenty feet..." a rough hand hit his chest and moved up his arm. Healy directed his arm. "That direction you should come to the ore cart."

"Colin is directly behind me." He took the hand holding his arm and set the arm to his side. "Go sit by him. When I find Aileen, I'll let you know and you start talking so we can all gather in one place and make a plan."

"Why would someone blow up this mine?" Healy's voice moved away from Ethan.

"It was Miles. He caused the rock to fall on Colin and attacked Aileen. And he confessed to killing Miller four years ago." He set off in the direction Healy indicated. Crawling on his hands and knees, he felt the area on both sides of him as well as in front before he moved forward. In the darkness, he didn't want to miss Aileen.

He pushed the panic squeezing his chest aside just like the debris under his hands. Becoming weak wouldn't help the situation. He had to be strong for Aileen's sake when he found her and for Colin's if—He didn't want to think about what would happen should he find Aileen in any condition but alive.

"Miles? Isn't that the small fellow who hangs around Clay?" A grunt followed the question. "Found Colin. He be breathin' kind o' soft."

"Just make sure nothing reinjured his left leg." Ethan's heart hammered in his chest when his hand skimmed something other than rocks. He shuffled his knees over small rocks and ground his teeth as the gravel dug through his britches into his skin. He'd found cloth. With buttons. It had to be Aileen's blouse. He moved his hand along the garment and discovered her chemise-covered side. Her body moved slightly away from his hand and back in an even rhythm. She was alive. His heart rammed into his ribs. If she was alive there was hope for a future with her.

"Aileen? Sweetheart can you hear me?" He pushed his knees next to her side and ran his hands up her body. Shoving rocks and dirt, he found the swells of her breast. Her neck was covered with dirt but no large stones. Her face felt gritty. He gulped back the lump of dread as he placed his hands under her head and probed for cuts and bumps. Something warm and sticky spread over his fingers.

"She hit her head," he called out to Healy. "I'm going to check her lower half and then try and make my way over to you."

Ethan wiped the blood on his pant leg and ran his hands over her stomach, down her hips, and each leg; feeling for any other injuries and clearing the debris from her person.

"Appears to be just the head injury." He gathered her in his arms and stood, hoping the ceiling of the tunnel hadn't collapsed. He didn't need to hit his head and become unconscious as well.

"Okay, I've got her. Start talking." He shuffled his feet, turning to face the opposite direction and began a slow foot-dragging gait through the rubble on the floor of the mine.

"Now, I'd say this reminds me of the time me and Patrick—em you aren't mindin' if I tell stories o' Patrick?"

"You can talk about your mother dancing naked in the street for all I care, just keep talking so I can find you." He was actually fascinated by the man who first won Aileen's heart. Patrick sounded like a man he would have called a friend had they met.

"Well there, and if Patrick and I didn't have some fun in our day. That was before he caught sight of that wench in your arms. Once she came into his life. I was having to find myself another partner to go scheming with."

The man's voice was the only beacon Ethan had to guide him toward the boy. Concentrating on the voice and not so much the words, he followed the lilting tone until it sounded right below him, and his boots bumped into something softer than the rocks he'd been kicking.

"I do believe your standin' on my pant leg." Relief resonated in the man's voice.

"Where is the boy from your legs?"

"On the side away from you."

"Are you in any shape to carry him? We'll go deeper in the mine. There's a ventilation hole you should fit through." He felt the man stand beside him.

"I've got the boy. Which way do we wander?"

"The way my feet were pointed. To keep from jostling the boy's leg on the side of the tunnel or hitting his head, walk with your back against the wall." Ethan backed up to what he hoped was the opposite side of the tunnel wall. "I'll go first."

He heard the man shuffling and grunting along behind him. Counting his steps, Ethan tried to remember how far from the end of the track the hole had been dug. The damp scent of earth permeated the blackness around him. He slid his feet along the ground, stopping when he bumped something to check it out with a foot and see if he could scoot the rock out of the way or if he had to go around it.

A cold gust of air brought the scent of pine swirling around his head. "We're getting close. How are you doing?" he called back to Healy.

"We're coming." The man's voice was only a few steps behind him.

The air grew fresher and colder. Faint rays of sunshine filtered through the trees and down through the hole, giving him a guiding light.

Aileen moaned and wiggled in his arms. He bent, pressing his lips to her forehead. "We're almost there. Hold on."

He stood under the hole judging the distance. "Let's put these two down." They placed their burdens side by side at the edge of the dim light from the hole.

"I'll lift you up to the hole. You're going to have to dig in with your feet and hands to work your way through the narrow part."

Ethan put a hand on the man's shoulder. "You'll have to go to the stamp mill and get help to dig the hole larger and get us out." He glanced at the woman and boy. "Aileen hasn't been any too friendly to you, but I hope you can find it in you to help us."

"Sure and she's got a fiery temper. But I've always liked her." Healy slapped him on the back. "She's a fine catch, and Patrick would be proud to know she's found happiness again."

Ethan studied the man's face. Not a hint of resentment lingered in his gaze. His solid smile and honest stare brought a beam of happiness to Ethan. The man meant what he said.

"Let's get you out of here so we can get proper doctoring for the boy." He made a stirrup of his hands and bent so Healy could step into it. Ethan lifted the man, pushing him toward the hole. Glancing up, the sunlight disappeared and Healy's weight disappeared from his hands. He stepped back as dirt and pebbles rained down around him.

The hole was a good twenty feet deep. He remembered thinking they weren't above the mine when they kept digging the hole and didn't find the shaft.

Grunts and strange curse words came from the hole along with scraping noises. More dirt and rock fell around him and light appeared. Ethan hurried under the hole and looked up. The shape of a head peered down.

"I'll be headin' down to the mill now," Healy called down.

"Hurry!" he called back as Aileen moaned and rolled her head back and forth. The boy remained unmoving and quiet.

He knelt beside her. "Aileen. Sweetheart. Wake up." He patted her cheeks. She rolled her head back and forth. Slowly, as though they were heavy, her eyelids raised. The dazed appearance and the slight tremor in her body worried him.

"Sweetheart, it's me, Ethan." He picked up her hand and kissed the knuckles. Her other hand raised, and she touched his cheek.

"W-what happened?"

"I believe Miles dynamited the mine entrance. We're under the ventilation hole. I lifted Healy through. He's gone for help." He kissed her hand again. "Stay put and try to stay awake. You took a nasty hit to your head."

Aileen squinted in the faint light. He'd just shown her tenderness, yet she couldn't shake the way he'd looked at her before the explosion. How could he believe her a killer and tend to her so lovingly? Her head throbbed from the strain of thinking.

"Colin!" She tried to stand, but slipped back against the side of the tunnel.

Ethan placed a gentle hand on her shoulder and slid down onto the floor beside her. "He's right beside you."

Ethan would take excellent care of her son, but she still wanted to touch him. To let him know she was with him. "Ah'd like to scoot closer to my laddie."

He stood, picked her up in his arms and placed her next to Colin. Then he sat down on the other side of her. "Healy should be back with help in an hour. But I'm not sure how long it will take them to make the hole larger." He placed an arm around her shoulders. She drew away even as her body wanted to sag against his strength and warmth. But she couldn't—not after seeing his reaction to her wielding the pick and hurling it at Orin.

She had to rethink her feelings toward Orin. He hadn't shown the anger she'd expected from her hitting him with the pick. And here he was helping get them out of the mine.

Ethan placed a finger alongside her chin, turning her to face him. She didn't want to look into his eyes. If she did, she'd fall apart. But his presence wouldn't give her a chance to sort out her feelings.

Staring up into his eyes, her chest squeezed at the tenderness staring back. How could he look at her that way when...

She clutched his arm. "Don't look at me like that."

He smiled. "Like what?" His large hand cupped her cheek.

The love shining in his eyes and the huskiness of his voice conflicted with the questioning gaze that had stared at her earlier when she'd thrown the pick.

When she'd seen him gently tending Colin, her feelings had hit her full force. She loved the man. She didn't want to leave him. He was good for her and her family. But the look of disbelief and confusion in his eyes had hurt as violently as any blow Mr. Miller had inflicted on her. To have him believe she was capable of killing—

"Like you love me. I saw it in your eyes. You thought I had killed Mr. Miller." She used his shoulder to lever herself to her feet. Her head whooshed, and her vision blurred. This was no good. Standing wouldn't make her appear any stronger if she fainted. She slid back down to sit beside him. The heat and virility of him zinged heat through her.

"I've never believed you killed Miller." His caressing voice tugged at her body and her heart. She slumped against him, soaking in his strength and comfort.

"Aye. Ah saw the look in yer eye when ah threw the pick at Orin. Ye thought me capable of taking a life." She pushed away from him, reaching over to smooth her son's hair. Miles' confession had lifted her heart. All these years, she'd thought her son had killed Mr. Miller. It had weighed heavy on both their minds. She could hardly wait for the boy to wake and she could tell him he hadn't killed anyone.

Ethan captured her hand, drawing her attention to him. "I've felt you would do anything to protect your children. You've proved that over and over again." He put his hands on either side of her head and used his thumbs to tip her head up, making her look him in the eye. "You've been protecting Colin, believing he killed Miller."

She started to shake her head, but his eyes

narrowed, waiting for her to tell the truth.

"That day," she paused and exhaled, forcing all the bad memories to come forward. "The laddie and ah were workin' in the mine. Mr. Miller came home drunk and wantin' his meal. Ah'd lost track o' time in the mine and dinnae have it ready." She took a deep breath and clutched her shaking hands in her lap. "He dragged me from the mine, and when ah lost ma footin' and fell, he kicked me in the stomach." She looked up at him clutching her belly. "Ah screamed at him no' to hurt the baby. He laughed and kicked me again. Ah fainted from the pain and when ah came to, Colin stood over Mr. Miller holding a board. Ah started havin' pains. The baby was comin'." She expected to see fury in the man's eyes, but he took her hand and held it between his.

"How did you manage the baby coming?" The reverence in his voice nearly brought her to tears.

"Colin helped me to the shack." She looked over at her son. "He was so brave, so grownup that day. Helpin' his sister into the world." Ethan squeezed her hand, and she saw the pride in his face as he too studied the boy.

"When Mr. Miller dinnae come stormin' into the shack after the baby was born, Colin left me alone. He came back sayin' the man was dead. We packed food for several days and hid in the old shack up the creek."

She placed a hand on Colin's chest, measuring his breathing. "Aye. We've both thought he caused the man's death. But ah would never give him up. He is my soul." Tears burned her eyes. "Ah can only hope this news will lift the devil that's been fightin' in him."

"With your love and my guidance, he'll be a fine man." Ethan lowered his lips to hers, brushing them softly, tempting her. She moaned, pressed her body to his, and wound her arms around his neck.

He drew his head back. "Does this mean yes?"

"To what?" The throb in her head was replaced with a nice hum of pleasant feelings.

"That you'll marry me?"

The question shocked and brought back the throbbing as well as panic constricting her chest.

"Ah cannae." When she tried to pull out of his embrace, his arms locked around her.

"Why can't you? You love me. I love you. I care deeply for your children and their well-being." His warm breath danced across her face, reminding her of his sweet kisses. Her heart fluttered.

"'Tis no' a time to be talkin' rubbish." His arms remained around her. Rather than fight him, she leaned against his solidness. She could have this the rest of her lifetime.

"What about Colin's future? We'll be goin' to get his land back."

"I'm sure you could use my persuasive nature to help." The jesting in his voice sparked a nerve.

"Gettin' my laddie's inheritance back is no laughin' matter. It is his legacy. His da's gift." She spun out of his arms and moaned from the pain it caused in her head.

"I'm not saying it's a laughing matter. I'm saying, I'll go with you to get it back for Colin." He pulled her back into his arms. "I know how much this means to you and must mean to Patrick's family to send Healy here to look after you."

"But ye wouldn't be happy livin' in England." She could see him yearning for his mine and his family and slowly hating them. Possibly to the point of drinking and...

"Would you be happy living in England?" His question caught her by surprise.

"Ah, ah have no' really thought about it." She tried to recall if she'd set foot in the country before.

"Then let's worry about that day when it comes."

Colin moaned. Aileen knelt beside him as Ethan loomed over her.

"Laddie, how are ye holdin' up?" She pushed the hair from his forehead. His skin was clammy and cold. "He dinnae feel right." Fear shook her. She couldn't lose him. Not now, not when they knew the truth.

"Healy should be back with help soon." Ethan put a large hand on her son's forehead. She glanced up and saw the worry etched on his brow.

He caught her watching and smiled. "He's been through a lot. Soon as we get out of this shaft we'll get him to the doctor in Baker City." He placed his hands on her shoulders and squeezed. His strength always seemed to quiet her fears.

"Thank ye for doctorin' my laddie. Ye have a gentle touch."

He chuckled. "Tell my brothers that. They always screamed like little girls when I'd try to doctor them."

"We did not."

Ethan shot to his feet and peered up the ventilation hole.

Chapter 32

He'd never been so happy to hear Zeke's voice. "Colin's injured."

"I know. Healy told me. I've got six men to dig. The rest are working on the front of the mine to get Clay."

"Clay?" Ethan's gut twisted. "What's Clay doing in the mine? Is he hurt?"

"We don't have any answers yet." Zeke's frustrated answer did little to settle him.

A lantern lowered through the hole, narrowly missing his head. He grasped it, untied the rope it dangled from, and flipped up the mantle. Aileen stepped up beside him. He placed the lamp in her hands. He pulled out his match safe and lit the wick. Light filled the area, casting a ghastly white light on Colin's pale face.

"Send down another lantern," he shouted to the hole above him.

"You only need one lantern," Zeke called. "Step back we're going to start digging."

"Send another lantern down. I'm going to see if I can get to Clay from this side." Ethan raised a hand up to grasp a lantern.

Aileen grabbed his arm. "Ah dinnae want ye to leave us." The uncertainty in her eyes held him a moment.

"Clay could be hurt. I have to see if it's quicker to get to him from this side." He patted the hand on his arm.

The lantern appeared. He handed it to Aileen. "Follow me with the lanterns. You and Colin need to move away from the debris." Dirt poured down through the hole from the men above. He slid his arms under the boy, being careful of his splinted leg and carried him back down the shaft with his mother following.

With care he settled Colin on the ground and turned to the woman. She placed the lanterns on rocks and knelt beside her son. Her color was returning. The blood-crusted, disheveled hair sent fear spiraling in his gut. He'd come so close to losing both her and the boy. All because of some lunatic's misplaced devotion.

He pulled her into his arms and covered her lips with his own. There was no way he'd let her out of his life. Not after he'd found the love he was sure his parents experienced. They'd find a way to make things work.

When she sagged against him, he gently sat her on the ground beside her son. "I'll see if I can find Clay. When Zeke gets down here, if I'm not back, get out of here and take Colin to the doctor."

She shook her head, clearing her eyes. "Nae.

When Zeke gets here, we'll come find ye."

"Take care of Colin." He kissed her forehead, glanced at the boy, and picked up the second lantern. He headed toward the entrance of the mine.

With the path lit, he moved quickly. They weren't that far from the end of the tracks and the ore cart.

He skirted the cart and stepped over piles of rock. The air still held dirt particles. He covered his nose and squeezed through fallen sections of the tunnel, all the time searching each inch with lantern light for signs of Clay.

Why had his brother come into the mine? Had he seen Healy enter and followed? If so, it was his fault for ordering Clay to keep an eye on the man. Fury at himself for bossing his brothers around and not giving them credit for being responsible men ate at him as he shuffled through the debris and called out to Clay.

"Over here!" Clay's voice sounded strong, but disoriented. Ethan shoved aside rocks.

"Call again!" He stopped to listen.

"Over here!"

Ethan turned to his right and spotted Clay staring at the wall of rock in front of him. His brother didn't turn toward the light as he approached. Ethan placed a hand on his shoulder and he jumped.

"How'd you find me so fast? It's pitch dark in here." Clay moved his hands in front of him as though searching.

"This lantern makes it pretty easy to see you." Ethan took hold of his brother's arm.

Clay jerked out of his hold. "That's not funny. There's no lantern in this mine."

Ethan grasped Clay's hand, placing it close enough to the lantern to feel the heat.

"Damn!" Clay rubbed at his eyes with the heels of his hands. "I'll kill that bastard!"

"Who?" Ethan set the lantern down and pulled Clay's hands from his scratched face.

"Miles! He was messing around in here. When I hollered at him, he threw a stick of dynamite at me. The end was burning, and I batted it away. I didn't get down before it blew and knocked me backwards." Clay spread his hands and shoved against Ethan's chest. "I'll kill him!"

Ethan took hold of his arm. "You can do that after we get out of here. Zeke's got men digging the ventilation hole bigger so we can climb out through there."

Clay stumbled on the rocks. "Just leave me here. Tell everyone you couldn't find me." Clay pulled out of his grasp.

"What? You think I'm going to leave you here? To die?" He grabbed the back of Clay's coat and shoved him along in front. "You don't know the blindness is permanent. I'll not let you rot here feeling sorry for yourself."

Clay swung his arms and stiffened his legs like two logs.

Growling, Ethan put his shoulder into his brother's back. "You want a broken leg by being a jackass that's up to you, but I'm going to get you out of here."

Clay's legs began to wobble, and his body

shook.

"Come on, stop fighting me, you're in no shape." Ethan draped his brother's arm over his shoulders and half carried-half dragged him back to Aileen and Colin.

Aileen hurried over to them. "What happened?" She grasped Clay's other arm and helped lower him to the ground.

"Miles threw dynamite at him. Says he can't see." He didn't miss the way Clay's head dropped closer to his chest at his words.

"Clay, you're sitting next to Colin. He's got a bad broken leg. Don't move around too much." He drew Aileen next to him and kissed her head. "Take it easy and talk to him while you see if he has any other injuries. I'm going to see how Zeke's doing." She nodded and slid out of his embrace.

He kept hold of his lantern and moved down the shaft toward the ventilation hole.

Dirt and pebbles rained down. The pile grew, making a nice ramp for them to walk up when the hole was large enough.

"Zeke, I've got Clay. How much longer till we're out of here?" Ethan shielded his eyes from the falling debris and stared up into the hole.

The clank of shovels stopped.

"I think we're about there."

"Step back and I'll take a look with the lantern." He held the lantern up to the hole. "About three more feet. I'm surprised someone hasn't fallen through."

The sound of the shovels resumed, and he backed up.

With Clay blind at the moment, he had to think of his responsibilities. He couldn't ask Hank or anyone else to put their lives on hold to help Clay until he got his sight back. How could he marry Aileen and saddle her with the burden of caring for his brother, too?

He was exhausted and didn't want to think about anything other than Aileen saying she loved him.

But he couldn't do that to her.

His eyes burned as he thought of what he had to do. He couldn't make Aileen his wife. Not until Clay was better. And he couldn't ask her to wait for him. That wouldn't be fair. She might find someone when she took Colin to claim his land.

The thought stuck in his throat like a fist full of dirt. He didn't want anyone else putting his hands on her. She was his.

He shook his head. She wasn't anyone's. She became free when Miles killed Miller. And she wanted to remain free. She'd understand his reasons for having to back out on his proposal. Heck, she never even said yes.

Thud. Zeke landed on the pile of dirt. "Hey, big brother, you got everything under control?" Zeke sobered. "Is everyone okay?"

Ethan snickered sarcastically. "Yeah, every thing's great. Colin has a severely broken leg, Aileen has a gash on her head, and Clay—"

"What happened to Clay?" Zeke grabbed his arm, hauling him to his feet. "It isn't—you know?"

"No, he isn't dead, but he wants to be." Ethan put a hand on Zeke's shoulder. "Miles—"

"What's Miles got to do with this?"

"Clay came upon Miles setting the dynamite and Miles threw some at Clay."

"Damn! How bad is he?"

"Just cuts and scrapes, but he can't see. And he's feeling sorry for himself." Ethan picked up the lantern. "Come on. There's no telling if this mine will hold together much longer."

They hurried down the shaft to where Aileen tended both Clay and Colin.

"Ye made it!" Aileen stood, willing her feet not to carry her into Ethan's arms. He looked drained and didn't need her hanging on him.

"Aileen, you and Zeke help Clay, I'll get Colin." She watched Ethan gingerly scoot his hands and arms under Colin and lift him like he weighed no more than Shayla. Mon! She'd forgot all about her little gem.

"Ah have to get out. Shayla!" She started to pull Clay, he stumbled and growled.

"She's fine. Maeve's been keeping her company while we worked." Zeke flashed her an encouraging smile.

"She'll be wonderin' where we are, if we're safe..."

"I've had a man letting them know everything we did. She's fine. Maeve loves children. She's taking good care of her." The man's tone revealed his love and reverence for his wife.

She glanced back at Ethan carrying Colin. Would he talk of her in the same light to others?

His gaze caught hers, and her heart stopped. Something was wrong. Shadows darkened his gaze.

Zeke crawled up the dirt pile first and grasped Clay's hands, directing him with his voice.

She stood beside her laddie and Ethan. "What's wrong?" She placed a hand on his arm.

"We'll talk after everyone's been seen by the doctor."

The resigned timbres of his voice clenched her insides. What he had to say wasn't going to set well. She knew it as much as she knew she loved him.

Chapter 33

Ethan stood in the doorway of Colin's room, watching Maeve and Shayla shoo Aileen into the bedroom with the new bed. Zeke had the foresight to send a man to fetch a doctor as soon as the mine blew. The doc rewrapped Colin's leg after giving the boy laudanum for the pain.

Aileen wouldn't leave the boy's side until the doctor pronounced him fine. His leg would heal in time.

Hank and Zeke set up cots in the living quarters for Healy and Clay. The doctor would see them next. Aileen insisted he check her last, since there was nothing wrong with her. Ethan snorted. One look at the woman and you could see she was worn out.

"The boy's going to be fine. You did an excellent job on that leg, Ethan." Doctor Spangle put a hand on his shoulder. "You keep this up and I'll be out of a job."

"I doubt that. I only did what was necessary to

keep the boy from bleeding to death." Ethan ran a hand over his face. Now he had to figure out how to stop the bleeding in his heart when he told Aileen he could no longer be a part of her life.

"Clay, sit down!" Zeke's command was followed by cursing from all his brothers. Ethan hurried down the hall and into the room housing the rest of the invalids.

Clay flailed his arms, keeping everyone at a distance as he moved toward the door.

"Sit down!" Ethan boomed and took hold of his moronic brother, shoving him back on the cot. "It's stupid to go wandering around when you can't see."

"Oh, now I'm stupid as well as blind." The bite to his words and the way his shoulders slumped disturbed Ethan more than the fact his brother couldn't see.

He motioned for Hank and Zeke to pull up a chair in front of the cot. He grabbed one, too. They made a barrier in front of the bed.

"If I thought you were stupid, I wouldn't have stuck you with Healy to learn how to slough the gold dust." He smiled when Clay turned his head toward him.

"A lot of good that's going to do you now." His dejected tone rankled Ethan. Halseys didn't give up.

Ethan nodded to Hank to say something.

"Why do you think that? This may only last a couple of days."

Clay turned to the sound. "Hank, you ever heard of anyone only being blind a couple of days?"

"Sure, I heard tell of a man who had a hit to the head. He cleared up in a few days." Zeke nodded to the others and smiled.

"Where'd you hear that?" Clay asked, shifting his face in the general area of Zeke.

"Right there shows you, you aren't as bad off as you think." Ethan waved his hand, and Clay leaned back as though avoiding a blow. "Did you feel that?"

"Yeah."

"You just figured out each one of us by our voices and what told you I waved my hand?" He held his breath hoping his little ploy would settle his brother down.

"I felt a breeze." Clay's brow furrowed in thought.

"You'll just have to rely on things other than sight until it comes back. Quit feeling sorry for yourself." Ethan stood, noticing the doctor had finished his examination of Healy.

"Doctor Spangle's going to take a look at you now." He pulled his chair away from the cot. "Hank, Zeke would you—"

The outer office door slammed, next the inside door burst open. Their youngest brother, Gil, followed closely behind by his wife, Darcy, strode across the room.

"Myrle told us what happened." He stopped in front of the cot and looked down at Clay.

"Gil?" Clay stood, reaching out with his hands.

"You sure you can't see?" Gil asked, stepping forward and giving Clay a hug.

"Hey, let me in here," Darcy, the small, dark-haired woman with the spirit of a whirlwind, held a baby in her arms as she pushed up beside her husband to put an arm around Clay. Her brother, Jeremy, followed close on her heels. He was nearly as tall as Gil and becoming a handsome young man.

"You even brought the baby?" Clay patted their child's round head.

"Why would we leave her home?" Darcy asked, stepping back and handing the wiggly bundle to Ethan. He looked down at his niece. Her round, pink face laughed back at him, and he fell in love. What would it be like to hold his own child? Holding this child and Shayla would be the closest he'd ever come to that experience. His stomach roiled and bile rose in his throat. He shoved the baby back to its mother and left the building.

He'd just about had everything a man could want and then—He'd been cheated more than if he'd lost his sight. After finally finding love, he had to ignore it and fulfill his family obligations. Why had he been the oldest? He wanted to be like Gil and ride off, striking out on his own. Or Zeke, carrying out justice. Where was the justice in being shackled to your responsibilities?

He wanted to shout his frustrations to the gloomy, November sky. He couldn't. He was the role model, the one his father depended on to keep the family together. Damn responsibility!

The rock outcropping dividing the Miller mine from the stamp mill loomed in front of him. He didn't know how he crossed the bridge and ended up here, staring blindly at the lights of the stamp mill. The sun had set long ago. The cold, dark night shrouded him, deepening his loneliness.

He leaned against the rocks and cloaked himself in despair as he hashed out ways to tell Aileen he couldn't marry her, and he couldn't see her any more. To see her would make him want her. He couldn't string her along with maybes when he had no idea of what the future would hold for Clay.

Aileen grew tired of being fussed over. First Maeve and her insistence she get cleaned up and wash her hair so the doctor could look at the gash on her head, and then some feisty little woman claiming to be the wife of another brother came in and started bossing her around. The only consolation was the woman thrust a beautiful, dark-haired, dimpled child into her arms as she and Maeve talked in the corner.

Would a child from Ethan's seed be this adorable? She glanced at the corner to make sure her thought hadn't been said aloud. After asking her to marry him, she'd expected him to at least come check on her when the doctor left, but she hadn't seen nor heard his wonderful voice in over an hour.

She didn't plan to say aye to his proposal, but she could use the strength of his arms about her. Darcy approached the bed, her arms outstretched in invitation to her child. The baby smiled, giggled, and lunged toward her mother. Fearing the lassie would fall, Aileen moved to steady her, but the smaller woman was strong and agile, catching the child and smiling at Aileen.

"She's a tough one like her ma." Darcy winked and sat on the edge of the bed. "I understand Ethan and you are getting pretty close."

Heat scalded her cheeks and the tips of her ears prickled. "That would be between the two o' us," she said, trying not to be drawn in by the woman's innocent looks.

"I'm sorry, but in this family, nothing like that is between just the two concerned." Darcy turned to the other woman in the room. "Right, Maeve?"

The tall, lithe woman Aileen had come to respect crossed the room, a wry smile on her lips. "I'm afraid once a Halsey sets his sights on a woman the whole clan rallies around and fights to help him keep her."

Aileen gasped and leaned deeper into the pillows. "Ah dinnae want to be kept by a man." She stared from one woman to the next, and they both burst out laughing.

"You don't know these Halsey men. You can't fight their allure." Maeve placed a hand on hers. "And believe me, if Ethan is anything like Zeke, you don't want to." She winked.

Aileen's breasts tingled thinking of the way her body responded to Ethan's touch. And how he made her feel safe.

"If he's so taken with me, where is he now?" There remained the problem. Though he'd said he didn't think her capable of killing anyone, he still had his doubts. That had to be the reason he stayed away.

"Zeke went out to see why he's staring at the stamp mill like a lost puppy," Darcy said. "And you want to look so ravishing, that when he returns, he'll crawl in this bed and take your mind off everything that's happened."

Aileen stared at the two women. She was at their mercy. But the thought of having Ethan slip into her bed and her arms—a tremor of anticipation crept through her. She gave in. She'd let them do what they wanted.

"How come you're not in checking on Aileen?" Zeke's voice jerked Ethan out of his depressing thoughts.

"I don't want to give her hope we have a future." There he said it out in the open. Now he'd have to act on it not sit here like a coward.

"What are you talking about? You love the woman don't you?" His brother leaned against the rock beside him.

"Yes." That was one thing he knew for certain—he would always love Aileen. And no one else.

"Then what's with no future? Seems to me you should be in there pressuring her for a date to get married."

He stared at his brother. "Why?"

"Umm, she has children, and I have it on good authority that you two—you know..."

"What's that got to do with getting married? I've known you to have lain with women before you married your wife. You didn't marry them."

Zeke coughed into his hand. "They were women who knew how to prevent getting with child."

The words hit him as hard as if his brother had backhanded him. With child. He hadn't even thought of the aftermath of making love to her. Could she be carrying his child? But how could he pull her into the mess he now had?

He hadn't thought about it. Figured she was old enough she couldn't get pregnant— after all she had two children and—Damn! Four years she'd been without a man. Could that make her more fertile? Less?

"What am I going to do? She doesn't want to marry and I can't. Not now." He pushed away from the rock and paced in front of Zeke.

"Why can't you marry her now?" Zeke crossed his ankles and his arms.

Ethan stopped and stared at him. "Are you that dimwitted? I have to take care of Clay. I can't ask her to take on my responsibilities."

"If she loves you, she'll want to help."

"I can't ask her to do that. She has plans, places she wants to go. I can't have her not go because we have to stay here with Clay." Ethan waved his arms in the air. And when she moved to England, he'd never see her again. The knowledge churned his gut like a pint of sour milk.

"Ethan, you don't have to shoulder all the responsibility. We can all take turns with Clay. And who knows? He may get his sight back and then you'll have lost out on the woman you love." Zeke pushed away from the rock and put a hand on his shoulder. "Forget about the rest of us."

Ethan glared at him. How could he forget? Every day since his parents' death he woke up knowing he was the oldest—the one to look after the family and each night when he went to bed, he was reminded again.

"I mean it. I want you to walk into that room, look the woman you love in the eye, and tell her you're going to marry her, and if she doesn't pick a date, you will."

Zeke's hand in the middle of his back pushed him toward the building.

"Besides, if you aren't happy, none of us will be happy. Think about that." Zeke pushed him through the outer door of the office and into a room full of people. He noted the smiles and nods of encouragement as Zeke maneuvered him down the hall, knocked on Aileen's bedroom door, pushed it open, and shoved him in.

Aileen roused out of the light sleep she'd fallen into when the two women finally left her alone. Exhaustion from all she'd been through had finally won.

Staring at Ethan, her heart lodged in her throat. His eyes glowed with desire, but his lips didn't curve into his devastating smile, and he leaned against the closed door. Tendrils of dread skittered up her back.

"Ye still believe ah'd kill someone."

His body jerked as if something slammed into his back. "No." His emphatic word and quick shake of his head chased away some of her apprehension.

"Then what has ye holdin' back?" She opened her arms, inviting him closer.

He took one step, then another, and sat on the bed, his calloused fingers gingerly touched her cheek.

"You. Me. My family." The words came out in a hoarse whisper.

"Ah need ye. My bairn need ye." She put a hand on his unshaven, dirty cheek. "And my heart needs ye."

His arms circled her. The smell of dirt, sweat, and all the things she'd come to know as his scent filled her senses and made her heart light.

"I can't have you any way but as my wife." He pulled away but held her shoulders in his firm hands as his gaze searched her face. She returned his gaze, seeking answers of her own. The misery in his eyes squeezed her chest. His gaze dropped to her mid-section. "Especially if you're with child."

She sucked in air. Where would he get a notion—"Ah'll no' marry ye just to make ye feel ye did the right thing by me." She pushed out of his arms.

"No." He ran a hand over his face. The scratching of his whiskers eased her fighting spirit. The man had been through the devil, he didn't deserve her spitting at him.

"I don't want to marry you because you might be with child. I want to marry you because I can't imagine a day without you in it." He grasped her hands.

"And what about this family thing, ye mentioned?" She squeezed his hands, forcing him to keep eye contact.

"I didn't want to make you my wife and then

say, 'here help me take care of my blind brother'." He smiled crookedly. "I didn't want to make more work for you."

"And now?"

He shook his head. "Zeke enlightened me. He says it's a poor excuse. He seems to think there's enough Halseys that one shouldn't have to take on all the burdens."

"He's right. Yer a large clan. Ye dinnae have to always be tellin' people what to do." She put her hands on her hips and glared at him.

His shoulders squared as though a weight had been lifted. He reached out, grasping her by the shoulders and pulling her toward him. His lips landed on hers with possessive firmness. She forgot all her worries. She never wanted to know what it would be like to go another day without his kisses.

Ethan's heart rammed against his ribs. He could let his family responsibilities go. He wanted this woman, her children and any they might make together. Let his grown brothers shoulder some of the tasks he'd been hogging.

He deepened the kiss. Aileen sagged against him, clutching his dirty clothing. "Is this a yes?" He drew his lips only inches away from hers, gazing into her dazed eyes and watched as his question took shape in her head.

She closed her eyes and gave a firm nod. "Aye. Yer brother's wives told me a little about ye Halsey boys."

"Lord, I can imagine they filled you full of all kinds of contrary ideas." His brothers had married well. Their choices the best fit for each of them, but they were two high-spirited and feisty woman.

He gazed down at his angel-kissed woman. She came from the same mold.

"Nae, no' contrary ideas, only when a Halsey man loves ye, ye cannae get away."

"There's truth to that." He slid his arms around her to prove he planned to keep her.

Chapter 34

Ethan stood in Myrle's dining room waiting for his bride to enter on the arm of Orin Healy. He still couldn't believe how fast his brothers' wives and Myrle had pulled the whole wedding together. It had only been a week since Miles blew up the mine.

No one had seen the man since. Most speculated he either became buried in his own mishap or he'd hightailed it, knowing no one in the area would hide him after what he'd done.

Colin was developing into a different young man than the one he'd first met. When Aileen told him Miles' confession about killing Miller, the boy had wept. Today, he sat in a chair beside Ethan, as his best man, waiting for his mother.

His brothers and their families all sat in the first row of chairs beaming as if they were the ones waiting for the bride. They'd given him their blessings, even Clay, who had taken the longest to realize Aileen wasn't a monster.

"She's comin' ain't she?" Colin's voice wavered with concern. The preacher also watched the parlor door intently.

Ethan peered down at the boy and smiled. "She's coming. Women just like to look their best on their wedding day." As he said it, he hoped that was the reason. And not that she'd changed her mind.

The door to the parlor burst open and a flustered Myrle ran straight to him. "He's got her and says he won't let her go until he sees the boy."

Ethan's gut twisted with dread. "Who has her?" Zeke and Maeve still hadn't found the man they followed to Sumpter.

"Some man. He knocked out Mr. Healy and grabbed Aileen. He's got a knife, and he's wild looking." Myrle rushed to him. "He's talking foolish. Something about Roderick and finally got the right one."

His brothers surged forward. "Gil come with me," Zeke started for the front door. "We'll try to get behind him. Ethan, you and Maeve go into the parlor and keep his attention."

Colin started to get out of the chair.

"Hank, keep him in here." Ethan put a hand on Colin's shoulder. "You coming in there is only going to make things worse for your ma. You know she'll do anything, and I mean anything, to keep you safe."

Colin nodded.

"Where's Shayla?" Ethan's heart stopped. The plan was for her to walk in ahead of her mother.

"She disappeared before the man showed up,"

Myrle said, wringing her hands.

"Darcy and Myrle go outside and see if you can find her. We don't want her walking into this mess."

Darcy wrapped Clay's arms around the baby and turned to her brother. "Jeremy, you come too." The two headed out the door with Myrle.

Ethan nodded to Hank, then he and Maeve strode to the parlor door. It wasn't latched. He pushed it open and stepped through the threshold. The tall, wild-eyed man clutching his soon-to-be bride swung his head their direction. One eye twitched.

"Who are you?" the man asked, tightening his grip on Aileen and poking her with the knife point.

"I'm her husband." Ethan noted Healy starting to move his head and drew his gaze quickly back to the disturbed man harming the woman he loved.

"Not yet." The man's laugh grated. His gaze darted around the room, his face held no remorse. "I finally found the righ' boy. Give 'im to me or you'll never marry 'is ma." The knife pricked Aileen's side. Drops of blood marred her wedding dress, but her eyes begged him not to say a word about Colin.

The abductor's wild gaze scanned the room. "'is mot'er getting married an all, I know 'e's 'ere. Bring 'im to me. I've been waiting a long time to collect."

Maeve stepped forward. "Surely you heard of the mine that was blown up. The boy was in the explosion."

The man gaped at Maeve and shook his head

slowly. "There wouldn't be a wedding if the boy died." He nodded to Aileen. "She wouldn't 'ave married bein' in mourning."

"Look at the way she has eyes for only this man. Look at this man. Do they look like they care about anything but each other?" Maeve moved forward as she talked.

Her words rattled the man, but he wasn't close enough for Ethan to make a move. As Maeve continued forward, the man backed up, the knife digging into Aileen. He wanted to shout for all of them to stop.

The window behind the man shattered and someone screamed as Zeke and Gil burst through the opening. Aileen catapulted into Maeve's arms. Within seconds, Gil and Zeke wrestled the man to the ground. Ethan barely opened his mouth before Maeve shoved Aileen at him.

Aileen wept in his arms. He smoothed her hair and hugged her tight. He'd come close to losing her, again.

He walked her into the other room. Darcy and Myrle had Shayla between them. She ran forward, clutching her mother's legs. Colin struggled under Hank's hand to get up. Ethan escorted Aileen to her son.

She wrapped her arms around him and rocked him back and forth murmuring words he didn't understand. Ethan picked Shayla up and crouched beside the mother and son. They both put an arm around him, pulling him into their world.

Maeve strolled forward. "Gil and Zeke have Roderick's man under control. Come on, we have to make a wedding happen."

Aileen stared up at the woman. "Ah'm to shook up. And look at Ethan; he's white as a ghost."

"All the more reason to get this over with. He can keep you where he can see you." Maeve helped her to her feet. "Myrle could you find some bandages? We need to wrap her wounds. Darcy, run up to my room and get my cinnamon colored gown."

Ethan watched as his sisters-in-law pulled a stunned Aileen into the parlor.

Orin stumbled out of the room and the men all surged forward, catching him before he fell to the floor.

"He's in no shape to give the bride away," Hank said, pressing a kerchief to the man's head.

Colin stood up, leaning on his crutch. "I'll give my ma to Ethan." His eyes pleaded forgiveness.

"I think that's a great idea." Ethan couldn't stop his chest from swelling. The boy shot him a bright smile and clunked down the aisle to the parlor.

Darcy stepped back. "Oh, you look lovely! Ethan's going to be speechless."

"I hope not!" Maeve laughed.

Aileen turned to look at herself in the mirror Myrle had brought down from her bedroom. She couldn't believe the woman looking back at her still existed. She hadn't dressed so fine or made her hair this fancy in years.

Colin hobbled through the door on crutches. "Ma! Ma!"

Her heart lurched, something else had gone wrong.

His feet slid to a stop, and Colin stared at her open mouthed.

"Shayla, has something happened to Shayla?" She started to move around him when he stuck out a hand.

"No. Mr. Healy isn't going to be able to give you away." He swallowed, "And... well... I'd like to give you to Ethan."

Tears stung her eyes. "Oh, laddie. That would make this a perfect day."

He turned beside her and extended his arm. She looped her arm in his and squeezed his elbow against her side.

Darcy crossed to the door. "Shayla!" she called.

When Shayla came through the door her mouth fell open, and she shrieked with glee. "Momma, yer bonnie!"

The smile spreading across Aileen's face hurt. There was nothing going to spoil this moment.

"Head on out, lassie. After that scream we dinnae want all the men folk hurryin' in here."

Shayla laughed and stepped out the door. Colin and Aileen followed. He looked up at her and smiled a true from his heart smile. She blinked back the tears forming and stared straight ahead at the man whose eyes widened with a feral gleam.

Straight backed and solemn, Colin escorted her down the aisle at a pace that nearly had her screaming as she continued to be devoured by

Ethan's gaze.

When they arrived in front of him, Colin took her hand and placed it in Ethan's. "I'm giving you my mom knowing you will always honor her."

"I promise." Ethan's deep voice rang through the room with clarity. Colin stepped to the side, and Ethan drew her up beside him.

"There will never be a day that I don't love you." His whispered declaration brought tears to her eyes.

The preacher read the vows and smiled as he said. "You may now kiss the bride."

She took a step toward Ethan. He folded her in his arms. The love shining in his eyes as his lips descended sent heat curling to her toes. There would never be a day she regretted loving this man.

About the Author

All my work whether it's my romance or my mysteries have Western or Native American elements in them along with hints of humor and engaging characters. My husband and I raise alfalfa hay in rural eastern Oregon. Riding horses and battling rattlesnakes, I not only write the western lifestyle, I live it.

I love to hear from fans. You can find or contact me at:
patyjag@gmail.com
or my website:
www.patyjager.net

Continue to the next page to find a listing of my historical western books or visit my website:
https://www.patyjager.net

Historical Western Romance
Gambling on an Angel
Improper Pinkerton
For a Sister's Love
Christmas Redemption

Halsey Brother Series
Marshal in Petticoats – Gil's story
Outlaw in Petticoats – Zeke's story
Miner in Petticoats – Ethan's story
Doctor in Petticoats – Clay's story
Logger in Petticoats – Hank's story

Halsey Homecoming Trilogy
Laying Claim – Jeremy's Story
Staking Claim – Colin's Story
Claiming a Heart – Donny's Story
A Husband for Christmas - Shayla's Story

Letters of Fate Trilogy
Davis
Brody
Isaac

Silver Dollar Saloon
Savannah
Lottie Mae
Freedom

Contemporary Western Romance
Perfectly Good Nanny
Bridled Heart

Historical Paranormal Romance
Spirit of the Mountain
Spirit of the Lake
Spirit of the Sky

Windtree
Press

Thank you for purchasing this Windtree Press publication. For other books of the heart, please visit our website at www.windtreepress.com.

For questions or more information contact us at info@windtreepress.com.

Windtree Press
Hillsboro, OR